Champion of Forno

Kevin Colbran

BALBOA.
PRESS
A DIVISION OF HAY HOUSE

Balboa Press books may be ordered through booksellers or by contacting:

Balboa Press
A Division of Hay House
1663 Liberty Drive
Bloomington, IN 47403
www.balboapress.com.au
1 (877) 407-4847

Because of the dynamic nature of the Internet, any web addresses or links contained in this book may have changed since publication and may no longer be valid. The views expressed in this work are solely those of the author and do not necessarily reflect the views of the publisher, and the publisher hereby disclaims any responsibility for them.

The author of this book does not dispense medical advice or prescribe the use of any technique as a form of treatment for physical, emotional, or medical problems without the advice of a physician, either directly or indirectly. The intent of the author is only to offer information of a general nature to help you in your quest for emotional and spiritual well-being. In the event you use any of the information in this book for yourself, which is your constitutional right, the author and the publisher assume no responsibility for your actions.

Any people depicted in stock imagery provided by Getty Images are models, and such images are being used for illustrative purposes only. Certain stock imagery © Getty Images.

Print information available on the last page.

ISBN: 978-1-5043-1647-7 (sc)
ISBN: 978-1-5043-1648-4 (e)

Balboa Press rev. date: 01/17/2019

Contents

Graduation

THERE WAS A HUSH IN THE STADIUM AS THE FORNO strode to the dais.

"Citizens of Forno, we are here to welcome our new officers to carry forward the Forno. These young graduates one day may be here delivering this speech. This honour is the quest of all citizens. After five years of effort, the first to graduate is Cadet Captain Ito Roos."

At the front of the parade, a tall, athletic woman in an immaculate uniform came to attention and briskly marched forward; Ito Roos marched to the podium to receive her commission. As she did, she remembered her journey here, her father Tedos, Colonel of Engineers and her mother Iso, Merchant Captain, all were in her thoughts. As the top student throughout her education, this background had prepared her for the Academy. At the steps, Ito surrendered the issued sword to the sentry, before completing the final distance to stand before the rostrum.

Ito halted before the dais and saluted. THE Forno returned the salute and declared, "Ensign Ito Roos congratulations, may you travel far on your quest."

Next, the Commandant stepped forward and presented the sword of honour, "Congratulations Ensign Roos, carry this sword with honour to mark the effort as Valedictorian of your intake. Return to your company Madam."

Ito clipped the sword and scabbard to her harness, saluted, about turned and marched back to the formation.

When she had returned to her mark the ceremony continued, the Cadet Lieutenants, serjeants and finally the other graduates. While she waited she thought back on the long road travelled to arrive here, the initial intake had started with over a thousand men and women. Over the years this had been reduced to the hundred graduating as fleet officers. There were a few retirements from accidents; some others diverted to lower grade positions as soldiers and mechanics when leadership hadn't been to the standard required. The board reassigned another group anonymously.

The Commandant called the parade to order then handed over to the parade commander; who dismissed the assembly; once released from the ranks, Ito joined her parents where they congratulated her.

"Hi Mother, Father," Ito said as she greeted them, "Seems like forever to get here."

"Now the rest of your life is ahead of you," Tedos said.

"Thanks, Dad," Ito said.

"Has the Admin told you of your first posting?"

"The *Forno Challenge* and Uncle Fedo is the captain."

"I have advised him to work you hard so that you don't get bored."

"I would hate for that to happen," Ito laughed, "I have a couple of days at home before I join the ship."

The Navy had assigned Ito Roos as a junior officer on the *Forno Challenge* Captained by Senior Captain Fedo Roos.

Apprentice Merchant

AFTER A SHORT LEAVE WITH HER FAMILY, ITO GATHERED her gear to join her new ship.

Roos hailed a Taxi to take her across town knowing that it would be a long time before she saw her home again. As her vehicle travelled along the beautiful avenues, the gardens reflected the concept of receiving points for diverse ways for growing their future.

Arriving at the Navy base, Ito found the *Forno Challenge* standing in all its glory on the pad as she strode towards the boarding ramp.

The *Challenge* was a Globular Spaceship designed to carry cargo on several decks with extensive accommodation for trainees in all functions from pilots, mechanics to soldiers.

"Hello, *Forno Challenge*, Ensign Roos reporting for duty," Ito said, saluting as she crossed the entry deck.

The Duty officer returned the salute, "Welcome aboard. Crewman Fotoos will assign you to a cabin, carry on."

"Ma'am," Ito acknowledged and followed the crewman.

Having stowed her gear, Roos reported to the bridge where she found Captain Fedo Roos.

"Ensign Ito Roos. Reporting for duty, sir," Ito saluted and stood at attention.

"Stand easy, welcome aboard, Ito," Fedo said, "You will be assigned to each section of the ship until you know all of them by heart. However, discipline requires that we observe protocol. Ensign Roos, Carry on."

"Aye, aye sir," Ito acknowledged as she marched out to find the First Lt and receive her first assignment.

"Welcome aboard Ensign Roos. Want to start at the dirty end?" Lt Stoos asked.

"Yes, sir, that would get it out of the way rather than work backwards," Ito accepted, "Besides they won't expect too much."

"Niece of the Captain? Then expect all the shitty jobs," Stoos said with a grin to indicate he was pulling her leg, "Another newbie is your friend Zento Hoos."

"That's nice," Ito said, meaning the opposite as he was her closest competitor at the Academy as Cadet Lt and a pain in the behind who was always looking for the easy pathway.

"You hide your glee well, just as long as you compete to do the best job and not against each other," Stoos said firmly, "Your file is extensive, and your intake was the highest achieving in recent times; I expect you to maintain this standard. Report to Engineering, Ensign."

"Aye Sir," Ito acknowledged and marched out to commence her duties.

Ito had studied the layout of the ship before marching in and serving as a cadet on a similar vessel; she knew where to go for her first assignment.

The ship was a training vessel for both Navy and Merchant Fleets, secondly Merchant Freighter and lastly a Warship to project Fornoon Hegemony.

To fulfil these roles it had an excessive complement of crew and trainees, ample cargo capacity and armed with weapons and shields.

The next mission was on a merchant run, display wares, research the local market with a sub-task of intelligence gathering. The program had the lift-off for 0700 the next morning.

Arriving at Engineering, Ito located the engineering chief and reported, "Ensign Roos reporting for duty in Engineering, sir."

"I am a chief mechanic, not a damn officer, address me as chief and jump when I say hop," Chief Ghos stated, "Stay up until I tell you to land, got it?"

"Yes chief, I am here to learn," Ito said.

"Keep that attitude, and we will get on just fine. I am assigning you to my slackest crew. I expect you to be part of the team and make the B team the best," Ghos said, "Make your way aft and find Leader Bosos. It shouldn't be hard as he will be yelling at his latest boy."

Roos followed the directions and as warned soon heard a man yelling at someone; zeroing in on the commotion she discovered the source of the argument, obviously Bosos and damn, Zento Hoos.

Waiting for a pause in the harangue, Roos asked, "Leader Bosos, I am Ito Roos, Chief Ghos said to join your team.'

Throwing his hands up in frustration, Bosos said, "What have I done to deserve this? Chief has it in for me. Yes, I am Leader Bosos, you will address me as Mister, or Leader Bosos until told otherwise. Know this Ensign Hoos?" Thumbing towards Zento.

"He thinks his shit don't stink. Is that what they teach you at the academy? The First lesson, you know nothing. The second lesson, you have a lot to learn about real life. The Third lesson is that you will be part of the team, and I am the leader. One of these days you will have to tell me what to do, I will then depend on you to protect my bum."

"Yes Leader," Ito said with a smile.

"You'll do, there is a spill in passageway Zebra 5," Bosos I ordered.

"Yes Mister," Ito acknowledged, grabbed the mop and a bucket and left to remedy the problem.

Behind her, Bosos started back onto Zento, "See that is teamwork, got it? Ensign?" Bosos asked making the title sound an insult.

There was a mumbled reply, which made Ito laugh.

It wasn't long before she located the offending spot, it only took a minute to remedy and return the gear to where she had found it. On the return, she touched up a couple of other spills.

"Done, Mister Bosos," Ito reported.

"I will check, Ensign Roos," Bosos said but didn't move. Zento seemed to have absorbed the hint and had left on the errand that had been the subject of the debate.

"Over here; this gauge monitors the fluctuations of the main reactor. Don't bother telling me that the computer does that. For the rest of the shift, you are making sure the computer is doing its job," Bosos ordered.

"Yes, leader Bosos." Ito acknowledged aware that this was a patience lesson.

As it had a chair and associated computer screen, she monitored the gauge with one eye while she called up the diagnostics and compared the input to the data.

After less than half an hour of comparing the two, she noticed that a variance had crept into the pair, aware that this was probably a test, Ito reported this to Bosos who came over with a slightly pleased look.

"Found a problem?" Bosos asked.

"Yes there seems to be a variance between the gauge and the record," Ito reported.

"Yes, there is, adjust the computer like so," Bosos said as he demonstrated the fix, then wandered back to his station.

After a couple of adjustments, Ito ran the diagnostics and spotted the cause. A small program was running which randomly fed an erroneous pulse into the computer. Investigating the programming further; there was another correcting the record of the gauge output. Now to tell Bosos or fix it, Ito thought, *'No, I will just inform him, I am not cleared to reprogram.'*

"Leader Bosos, would you like me to leave this subprogram alone or should I remove it?" she asked.

"Very quick, Hoos was on it all yesterday, and he didn't spot that. Leave it there; it only runs when there is a novice at the switch," Bosos laughed, "I suppose you guessed it was a test?"

"Naturally, otherwise I would have removed the error program," Ito admitted.

"I will set you a couple more demanding tasks before I let you loose on the working modules," Bosos said, "Now you can assist Mechanic Geos to align a mechanism."

"Was there any reason that Chief Ghos would suggest that you ran a less than optimal crew?" Ito asked.

"Not to me he doesn't, if you have a spare hour or two, you can check the stats," Bosos laughed, "That is a part of the routine of weeding out the high fliers who think life owes them something. You are the first in ages to ask that."

Ito nodded smiling inwardly and accompanied Geos to the new task, which they carried out without fuss. Job complete, the pair continued inspecting the equipment.

At the end of the watch, Ito was happy to have a meal and hit her bunk. In the next cabin, she could hear Zento grumbling about his treatment to his cabin mate.

'Well mate, you can do it the hard way or read between the lines to see what they do want,' Roos mentally advised as she settled down a good nights sleep.

Waking before the alarm, Ito went through the routine of starting the day before arriving at Leader Bosos' station five minutes early.

Bosos wasn't surprised by this or when Zento stumbled bleary-eyed with only seconds to spare.

"Ah, good to see two young workers bright eyed and bushy tailed, ready to start the day. We lift in an hour, Ensign Roos to assist Mech Geos, Ensign Hoos to Mech Jisos, carry on," Bosos ordered, receiving two 'Leader' acknowledgements.

The two left to join their guides.

"How come you are his favourite?" Zento asked sourly on the way.

"In individual categories, you either match or exceed my scores," Ito said, "The one that drops you is teamwork. You are an excellent solo performer, so if you work on your teamwork, you will go places."

"Thanks for the advice, why didn't you mention that before?" Grumbled Zento.

"I believe no more than a dozen times or so a year," Ito laughed, "It is hard catching you not talking about some injustice."

Zento just grunted as he spotted Mech Jisos. Geos waved her to a bench which was their station for takeoff; this wasn't a problem with most of the maneuvers used gravity drive until well clear of obstacles, before moving onto the in-system drive.

Once the bench displayed the ready lamp, Geos started the next inspection round which filled the rest of the shift.

The cruise out to the jump point was uneventful, and they went through the process before resuming the run through the grey Hyper. As expected of a massive freighter everything was smooth, and the restraints were superfluous.

The routine activity set in and nothing happened until they emerged into the Novi system.

The patrol challenged the ship, and a customs inspection team came aboard to search the compartments. The inspectors were arrogant in their approach, raising all the crews' hackles. The regular crew were too experienced to react, so Roos took her cue from them. Zento, of course, was fuming and started to curse which started to draw attention. Roos sidled over and elbowed him in the diaphragm winding him, "Perhaps you should see the Doctor about that asthma?" Ito then whispered, "Cool it. Staying calm is the behaviour we are here to learn."

"Oh, yeah, Why wasn't I told?" Zento asked.

"Perhaps you slept through the brief," Ito said.

Eventually, the Customs team left, and their ship resumed its station. The *Challenge* continued down to the port for unloading and negotiating the next load.

"Ensign Roos to the bridge," The intercom blared, Geos pointed the way.

Ito trotted up forward to find out why the bridge summoned her.

Captain Roos was waiting, "Good morning Ensign, would you like to observe a merchant at work?" Captain Roos asked.

"Since it is it part of my job description, Sir," Ito answered, "I would be delighted."

"Hum, neat trick with Hoos," Fedo said, "Is it part of the training package? If this regime weren't pushing for a reaction, Hoos could go this time."

"Aye sir, Lead on," Ito acknowledged, "I catch him out all the time; if he watched me instead of flapping his gums it wouldn't be needed."

The brief having settled the purpose for the summons, the trading party assembled and left the ship to commence the negotiations at the trade ministry.

They were escorted in with armed soldiers very evident. At last, the guard brought the trading team before an official.

"Good day sir, May I inquire as to the display of distrust?" Captain Roos asked, "If you don't wish to trade, you don't have to lay out the Welcome mat."

"It has come to our attention, that there is a move to undermine the government," The Novi official said.

"Not me, it is bad for business," Fedo said, "Anything I can do to assure you that it is not our intention?"

"Unlikely, but as we are still interested in the trade, please be aware that we will monitor all your movements," Official said, "You may continue."

"Thank you, Sir. May I suggest that you are wasting your resources?" Fedo asked.

"Ours to waste, Captain," Official said, "Good day."

The team then were escorted to their first client.

"Quaint reception, Ito?" Fedo asked, "So what did you learn?"

"Not to play cards with you," Ito said, "I suppose you have an idea what he was talking about?"

"Perhaps, do you remember the lecture I gave at the Academy?" Fedo asked rhetorically.

This hint settled the question as the lecture had centred on plausible deniability and best not to mention to the right hand what the left was doing. This explanation left most of the students baffled, the ones who understood and followed up, disappeared into the intelligence core. While Roos followed the drift, she was also wary of the seamy side of the military intelligence having lived in a military family and the advice only to volunteer unless you knew where the job was leading.

"Nice day here, perhaps a little dry," Ito commented, "How long will the talks take?"

"We should be wrapped up shortly, despite his objections the government is keen to promote trade as they want our equipment," Fedo advised.

"I look forward to seeing you in action, Captain," Ito said.

"Let us do it," Fedo said then as he walked up to the merchant that he had the appointment with, "Good day sir, I am sorry that I am tardy, an official decided to have a chat."

"Good day Captain, a little bird suggested that you had a little side trip. Shall we begin?" Kleinan asked waving them to the waiting seats.

The talks went on with neither side allowing the other to gain a significant advantage. At last, they struck a bargain which pleased them both.

"Well thank you, sir, That was most entertaining, even made me think I was getting the better deal," Kleinan said as he shook hands on the deal.

"But of course you did, I will be unable to pay my crew, you have pauperised me," Fedo said with a smile.

"There you go again, please go while I still have a shirt to wear," Kleinan said.

"As you wish, I will see you next time," Fedo said.

"But of course, it has been a pleasure," Kleinan ended, as he escorted out.

The guard reformed, as the trade team returned to the ship.

On the way, Ito said, "Was that part of the way to do business? Each claiming to be robbed by the other?"

"Keep an open ear, and you will learn all that I know," Fedo grinned.

The cargo arrived, and the ensigns were co-opted to aid as stevedores, Zento as usual, complained at the menial labour.

"You need the exercise, remember teamwork, and I will enjoy the extra points even if you don't," Ito laughed.

The teams got stuck into it, and the new cargo was secured. Once the team had completed the task, they returned to their duties.

Clearance received they lifted off and made their way to the jump point without further drama.

Curious Roos requested an interview with the Captain. The first Lt arranged a meeting, and she was soon talking with Fedo.

"Now let me guess you want to know all?" Fedo asked, "However I am turning this into a quiz, tell me what happened."

"Well the local bosses have a bee in their bonnet, perhaps the spooks are in action," Ito offered, "If they are, I would think that you have been briefed and may or may not approve."

"Mmm, close and I don't, we have a nice trade setup, the pot stirrers aren't doing me any favours," Fedo said, "Now why do you think such an expensive and over-manned ship is visiting?"

"If the spooks start something, we pull their chestnuts out of the fire?" Ito suggested.

"As long as you understand that such conjecture in the wrong ear may be unhelpful for your career," Fedo advised.

"Noted, so what is the next stop," Ito asked.

After being told, she returned to her cabin with something to think about besides sleep.

Zento knocked on the door, "Can I have a word?"

"If you are quick," Ito answered, not keen to spend too much time on him.

"You accompanied the Captain off-ship, why wasn't I invited?" Zento asked.

"Have you an hour? I don't. You will probably go the next time and no it wasn't nepotism," Ito answered, "I have the best rating for maintaining a poker face, and while the merchant wasn't a problem, the official reception would have had smoke emerging from your ears. The official was deliberately provocative and keeping a straight face was difficult, whereas I have no problem separating you from a credit."

"You are probably right. So anything you can tell me?" Zento asked.

"I had to guess, and the captain didn't confirm any of those, except to ask if I listened when he gave those lectures on trade negotiations."

"Oh, those, I thought he was rather obscure and lost me," Zento admitted.

"Do you remember Tyos and Geros?"

"They were reassigned if I remember?"

"After they asked questions?"

"Yes, and the last time I saw them, they were officers in Intelligence. Their memory wasn't as good, and they ignored me."

"Which is a hint to play safe and ignore them right back."

"Ah, thanks, I learnt a lot."

'As did I,' Roos said to herself, she hadn't known for sure where those two had ended up.

When they emerged into the next system, it was to a watery world dotted with large islands; the customs ship intercepted. The inspection this time was polite and efficient.

After they had landed, Captain Roos called for Zento to form part of the party leaving Ito to entertain herself with ship duties. The routine of off-loading and loading the cargo went smoothly, and they were soon on their way to the next.

As they entered the new system Ito was on watch on the bridge, Captain Roos announced, "Fvelsving, they like to tell everyone that they are an independent system beholden to no one. The actual situation is that the Imperials have a nearby mining planet which uses Fvelsving as a supply and recreation depot," Fedo said, "A small detail, it has trading connections to the Oxzens as well as us. Our spooks are ordered to avoid any activity. The Imperials would look upon that with displeasure."

Aside to Ito, Fedo asked, "Do you have a problem dealing with 'bluebags'?"

"I suppose I can hold my breath for a while and learn as much as I can," Ito said as the official propaganda was negative.

"I deal with a man called Roxz. I believe that you will find him amusing."

"As you wish, I know how to maintain a calm demeanour."

"That's my girl," Fedo said, then aloud, "Standby for the customs inspection." This check was quick and efficient. The officer was chatting with the captain like old town week.

After landing and the team walked over to the admin building Roos noticed an odd yellow saucer. At her query look, Fedo identified as, "A tramp freighter run by a Droman whatever that is and another who looks like a Corellian."

They arrived at a warehouse, and when they entered, a Blue Oxzen came and greeted Fedo enthusiastically, "Fedo my old friend, who is your delightful companion?"

"My niece, Ito, this old reprobate is El ali Roxz, merchant extraordinaire," Fedo said.

"Delighted to meet you, now Fedo, did you bring this jewel to distract me from a fair deal?" Roxz asked.

"As if I could put anything over you?" Fedo said, "For now, show us to comfortable seats, and we will try to arrange a deal that doesn't send me to the poorhouse."

They went into his office and started trading, after a while, Roos began to feel a little left out, noting this, Roxz suggested, "Why don't you inspect my warehouse, young lady, I am sure that would interest you?"

Surprised, she agreed and after a nod from Fedo started wandering around to survey the goods. Most were familiar with a few she couldn't identify. While she was doing this, a bearded Corellian wandered in with a large bird on his shoulder. Spotting her, this man came over and asked in a strange accent, "Good day; I am Mike Cox. How come I haven't seen you around before?"

"Ito Roos from the *Challenge*, first time I have visited, are you off the yellow saucer?"

"Yep the *Yella Terra*, this is Humph," He said thumbing at the Bird.

"I thought that your captain was a big bear also named Humph?"

"As I am usually," The Bird said in a five-year-old's voice.

"I learn something every day," Ito said, "I may see you around from time to time."

Then she returned to the office to find Fedo wrapping up the bargaining.

"Ready to return to the ship?" Fedo asked, "We have settled here."

"Yes, I ran into the pair from the *Yella Terra*, didn't find out where the bearded fellow is from and the captain was a large bird," Ito related.

Fedo just gave her a look and waved her back to the *Challenge*.

Once inside, Fedo asked, "Can you give me your ideas?"

"The entities from Droma are shapechangers, and the man named Mike Cox is from an unexplored planet."

"Yes I have heard the first, I would like to know more about the man," Fedo said, "I have given the crew leave, so if you happen to run across your bearded friend, perhaps a little more information would be helpful."

She took that as a hint and attended the leave briefing session.

After the usual dire warnings about health risks, the Chief gave earthy advice, "Stay clear of these guys," Throwing up holograms of several enormous and rough-looking aliens, "Garmaurgins, Slithers and Hortogs, these fellows are disappointed if they don't get at least one fight every hour. You should smell them before you see them. If you follow the recreation directives and stay away from restricted areas, you shouldn't run into them. All crew are to carry sidearms, please don't shoot too many customers, not wearing these will attract the wrong sort of attention. Have fun; I have a credit bet that less than six end up in sickbay. Carry on."

Ito considered staying onboard as she didn't like to waste her rest time, but the captain hinted intelligence was worth collecting.

So gathering a couple of sensible crewmates, she headed out. Ito had memorised a couple of innocuous watering holes and thought that her bearded friend might visit one of those.

Ito and her friends had a couple of light drinks from sealed bottles, selected from known and reliable sources. The principle of not knowing what is in it could kill you.

Ito guided her companions through several bars before seeing her man this time accompanied by a big jolly Teddy Bear.

Trying not to look too obvious, she drifted over casually and asked, "What is a nice boy like you doing on a rough planet like this?"

And received a big grin, "Hey that is my line, I was about to try on you," Mike returned, "I hang with strange people who love to watch the tipsy antics."

"Good morning Ito Roos," Humph said in the little voice, "Enjoying yourself?"

"Indeed, I like watching how the other half live," Ito said, "May I ask where is Droma?"

"Nearly right around the wheel," Humph said, "And yourself?"

"Goosos, about halfway antispin," Ito said only half fibbing, the named planet was a nearby client system.

"I am from Earth, nearly neighbours," Mike said.

"Watch this girl Mike; she will find out what colour undies you are wearing and what you had for breakfast," Humph laughed.

"I will promise to interrogate you softly with sponge rubber spikes. So, where did you get such an unusual ship?" Ito asked playfully.

"Built it myself, reminds me of my house on Droma, quite practical, you are most welcome to visit," Humph invited, "Don't worry I don't bite and I have almost housetrained Mike ."

"Ha. Can I have a return inspection?" Mike asked.

"I will have to clear it with my Captain," Ito said, "Those four stripes on your shoulder, what do they signify? My emblems indicate Ensign."

"Pilot in command, referred to as captain, as does Humph as he is the owner," Mike said, "Is that a military rank?"

"Sometimes, also means I am just out of school learning the ropes," Ito answered thinking he was finding out more than she was.

"Well since we have had enough fun for the day, would you like to have the tour?" Humph asked.

Observing her companions who were busy drinking, Ito thought, '*why not,*' Aloud, "Never stop learning my Dad says. Shall we go, on the way I can ask my captain."

"Sounds like an excellent finish to a pleasant day," Mike said as he stood and headed for the exit.

As they adjusted their eyes to the bright sun, they almost bumped into three drunken men. These demanded belligerently, "Watch where you are going." Then pushing for a fight, one reached for Ito, "Give us a kiss Darls."

Ito slapped his hand away and assumed a defensive position. This action triggered profanity, and the three started to swing fists, Mike floored one and tied the other in a neat knot while Ito demonstrated to the first drunk, that this was no way to treat a lady. Humph just stood there looking amused. One of the thugs went for his gun then thought better of it when he stared into two pistols trained on him. Stumbling off, the thugs pretended that they had better things to do.

"Handy moves," Mike noted as he holstered his weapon, "Ladies' finishing school I presume?"

"Of course, some of it did stick, yourself?" Ito replied.

"Mum wouldn't let me go to a ladies college said it would corrupt me, the Kindy playground was rough enough," Mike said.

"Have you had your playtime, children?" Humph asked, "If so, shall we enter my home?"

Ito and Mike grinned then shrugged, following their guide into the saucer.

Nothing stood out inside, with controls and fittings similar to the Corellian ships. As was the machinery in the engineering bay, the only odd thing was the extensive hydroponic gardens lining the passageways and the video screens showing rural scenes. Both of these would be redundant with only two in the crew, pleasant but not functional.

Ito asked, "Did you have a Corellian vessel to copy?"

"Very astute, you spotted it straight off. If it works why change," Humph said, "Would you like to call your captain?"

Humph indicated where the radio was situated.

"Yes Thank you," Ito said, then after selecting the ship frequency radioed, "*Challenge*, Ensign Roos calling, is the Captain available?"

"Yes Ensign Roos, Captain speaking," Fedo answered.

"Sir, I am visiting some friends you have heard me talk about, may I show them how to run a real ship?" Ito asked.

"Certainly, I would be delighted to meet them, *Challenge* out." Fedo ended the call.

"Well if you are ready, I should warn you the Captain may bite if you scuff his deck," Ito said.

"Perish the thought," Humph said, "After you."

So the trio made their way over to her ship chatting about what their home planet looked like and the differences from this one.

"It is strange that the few I have seen, the sameness outweighs the differences," Ito observed, "I suppose we all breath and eat nearly the same."

Reaching the *Challenge* ramp, Ito called, "Hello *Challenge*, Ensign Roos with two visitors." She was surprised when Captain Roos answered from the entrance.

"Welcome aboard, I am Captain Fedo Roos," Fedo said.

"I am Humph, and this is Mike Cox, it would be our pleasure," Humph said shaking hands.

Mike whispered a question, "Relation?"

"Uncle but you bet that doesn't get me any privileges," Ito whispered back.

As they walked through the ship, Humph asked, "Ito says she is from Goosos, the nameplate indicates Forno?"

"That is what we tell everyone, sometimes it saves arguments," Fedo said, "Droma? Beautiful place?"

"Very but is a little boring after four odd centuries, I needed to have a wander," Humph supplied.

"Many wandering around?" Fedo asked a little taken back at the age mentioned.

"As far as I know, including me, one," Humph laughed.

"You are from Earth, do they have many wandering?" Ito asked Mike.

"I would have to give the same answer. Humph enticed me from an exciting life on a small farm with a dazzling story of aliens and mysterious planets to be visited. As an innocent youth I was enthralled," Mike said, "Now I know the horrible truth that Humph is a slave driver and only wanted my sweat to water his garden."

Ito gave each a puzzled look as the easygoing relationship seemed to belie the statement.

"Oh, not your sparkling wit and raconteur?" Humph asked, confiding, "He does supply breath and fertiliser as well."

"Is there anything in particular that you would like to see?" Fedo asked not wanting this to turn into an all-day session.

"Just the Bridge and Engineering, if you would," Humph replied, "Nothing that Mike can break."

Mike whispered to Roos, "He crash-landed his ship behind my farm when his last crew pushed the wrong button."

"I heard that; he was a primate and became bored," Humph said, "At least Mike knows when to keep his hands in his pockets."

By now they had reached the bridge, and the chatter stopped, Humph asked a few pointed questions and received accurate answers, as the control layout were Corellian standard there wasn't much new. That planet's factories were famous as they construct reliable and robust vessels. Other similar races copied the best features.

Moving to the engineering, Roos introduced the guests to Chief Ghos who greeted them casually.

"Good day, make yourselves at home, meaning touch nothing if you want to keep your fingers," Ghos said.

"I can grow new ones, but I will abide by my host's request," Humph said, "Nice layout. If you need a new job, I can use another happy face."

"No poaching, this ship would fall apart without him," Fedo laughed.

"That won't get you any favours," Ghos grunted, "You will still have to join the line."

"Well, that is about all I can show you," Fedo said, "Would you like a brew in the galley?"

"No thank you, we have taken enough of your time, I have appreciated the tour," Humph said.

Ito showed them out and waved goodbye from the ramp.

Fedo was waiting when she passed the bridge, and he beckoned her over.

"Your opinion?" Fedo asked.

"Droma is around the rim opposite to here; Captain Cox is Rimward from Forno. I don't believe I should challenge either to a card game; Mike hides it under a veneer of cheerfulness and Humph didn't miss a thing," Ito considered, "I believe he could build the *Challenge* from a pile of junk."

"This has extended our knowledge of this pair by multiples, yet there is as much to learn," Fedo said, "Be very careful crossing paths with these races."

"My assessment as well," Ito agreed, "Everyday brings new knowledge."

"Tell them to throw the dirt into the hole when you admit there is nothing else to learn," Fedo said, "Carry on, I am sure you have something better to do."

"Aye sir," Ito said recognising a dismissal.

She returned to her cabin to resume the activity that she enjoyed. Reading the latest updates in technology and intelligence.

In the morning the *Challenge* was due to lift to its next port, arriving in Engineering as per usual Roos was early, and Zento struggled in looking a little worse for wear.

"Ghos is grumpy; he lost the bet because seven visited the sickbay, so best keep out his way if you have any sense left," Bosos said, looking with disfavour at Zento. Ito had heard that Zento had led his friends to the wrong hotel and the local customers had shown them the door, the windows and other openings.

That they survived was more luck than skill. Zento often returned after leave like this as in some areas he was a slow learner. If wasn't for Zento's skills and quick recovery he would be looking for another occupation.

The whole ship had heard the welcome aboard when he emerged

from the sickbay, even though it happened behind closed doors in the Captain's cabin.

His other accomplishment of rapid recovery saved his hide yet again, and he resumed his duties quickly.

The travel to the next system was unremarkable as was the following, by this time Ito had been moved to the kitchen as was Zento who thought this was even worse than Engineering. He let all and sundry except the Chef know what he thought of this. Ito, on the other hand, knew that likely she would be in a scout ship for her first command and would have to cook or starve. With a crew of three, one on duty and one sleeping meant the 'captain' had to carry a share of the load, or all would be miserable.

'Zento is going to have to learn this unless he intends to spend his career as a junior officer on a big ship,' Roos thought, *'He has been told often enough, surely he is not that thick?'*

As they approached the next system, there was a flurry of work happening on the bridge with the order to assume a high level of alert. As Ito's action station was the close laser weapons, these were set and hold fire unless shut down, just lifting her finger would allow the firing of the guns aimed with a computer radar link. These were a defence against fighters and missiles.

As they emerged from hyperspace, other pulses showed a significant number of Fornoon ships converging at a staging position and once the fleet had assembled orders were given to drive towards a planet.

"Action stations," Blared the Intercom.

That was the signal to man the weapons station and bring the weapons up to standby, the computer now actively tracked surrounding vessels and assigning them icons as friend or foe.

Orange meant the next level where approaching blips would be targetted ready for the final step of actual firing. The weapons controller could retag the target if the IFF were friendly.

Red when declared, meant finger off the button and the computer shot anything on an intercept course or hostile within range. Once this was triggered, it was extremely hazardous to approach the ship as it was on automatic and as likely to fire at friends as enemies.

As the fleet approached, Orange was declared, and Ito switched the console to live tracking with one finger on the hold button and another on the cancel switch to reset to safe. Watching the screen for enemy ID, Ito concentrated while the two groups approached each other. The oncoming fleet was assessed as hostile and of a lesser force than the Fornoon fleet. Command lifted the condition to Red, so Ito removed her finger from the pause button.

This lopsided tactical situation had occurred to the hostiles, who after unleashing a barrage of missiles; vectored to an escape course. As the wave of missiles entered the defensive zone, Roos' canons flared into life zapping one after another as it zeroed on each blip until the order to resume 'Orange state' before relaxing to 'action' when Roos hit the cancel switch reverting to watch and track.

The Fornoon fleet continued to the target planet and while half, including the *Challenge*, set themselves into a defensive cordon. The other half descended to occupy strategic points with the troopers dispersing to fortify buildings which cut off approaches to strategic sites.

After blockading the strategic points, the local supporters of the usurping faction did the final push to disarm the loyalist ground forces.

After a time at action stations, the duty crew gradually took over to relieve the tired personnel. This procedure allowed the troops to recover and be available in case of further assignment. After a couple of watches, each of the crew had recovered.

Signals from scouts reported that the system fleet had dispersed into for and against factions, which rendered the threat ineffectual.

Once the tactical command had settled the situation, the bridge announced the next phase over the intercom, "Supernumeraries to the Cargo hold." This order was to all trainees and the supernumerary crew; these were now to assemble equipped in ground battle gear.

Ensigns Roos and Hoos as military trained, now assumed their other role as a platoon commander. While this may seem a radical change; when the pair were cadets they performed as privates, junior NCO then Senior and the period before graduation held officer status and leading platoons in similar actions. This programme had happened during assignments to working troop ships as landing force officers. After graduation, the administration assigned half of the group as army and specialist officers.

During this assignment, Ito had assembled her platoon regularly; conducting tactical exercises with her serjeant and corporals on an available time basis.

In the cargo hold, Ito gathered her Platoon and awaited orders. While they waited, the NCOs thoroughly checked their section's gear. The most likely instruction would be to relieve the garrisons so these could rest and regroup to act as strike forces able to react to countermeasures attacks from the loyalists.

The shuttles started to arrive, and the troops boarded ready to be dropped to the surface.

Her platoon was assigned a position at the head of a cross-city road, covering approaches to government buildings.

Once landed Ito located the Lieutenant in charge to discover the tactical situation and weapons sites. Serjeant Gtoos recorded the information and once the briefing finished arranged the platoon for the best effect setting the corporals in a roster to cover relief for rest and recuperation to allow for twenty-four hours surveillance.

The strike troops withdrew to rest and regroup. This interval was the critical time; if the loyalists were aware that reinforcement troops were in the process of settling in this would be the opportune time to counterattack.

They had practised this scenario using computer games; the worst case was that the first evening after the strike group withdrew; the loyalists would be likely to challenge the garrison.

So at the critical time, Ito ordered all her platoon to 'stand to' quietly in preparation, minimising movement after sunset and the gathering twilight.

Gtoos and Ito had consulted and considered that the assault they would stage likely would be from cover in a park adjacent.

As they waited, a lookout signalled movement in the park; several people were assembling in the dark, only showing with infrared viewers.

Using her radio, Ito warned her troops to await orders, then contacted company HQ to report the activity. The Company would then independently assess the threat and deal with it, so Roos' B platoon didn't have to give away her heavy weapons too soon. A small attack was often used to locate heavy equipment which the insurgents would target the next wave. As they were already in the optimum position and moving them would be difficult.

The Company responded by ordering B platoon to stand to, while C platoon attacked the insurgents.

The wait wasn't long before a firefight erupted behind the shadowy group dispersing them. Lt Hoos commanded C platoon; once the area was clear, C platoon returned to Company HQ to standby for similar deployments.

While Ito stayed on alert as C platoon retired to their staging post, she warned the rearguard for attacks from the rear. Well that she did as laser fire started pinging their protective armour. A small number of insurgents intended a double feint.

"Heavy weapons hold fire, seconds to me," Ito ordered.

The second man at each position crept rearwards to the assembly point where Ito joined them ready to charge any insurgents who had evaded the guard line.

Spotting a party that had done just that, Ito called, "Foreward," and routed the insurgents before they could cause damage. Once the position was secured, the platoon restrained prisoners and treated wounded.

This situation of to and fro carried on for several days before C platoon was relieved by the original team; Shuttles then lifted Ito's platoon back to the *Challenge*.

After storing her gear, Ito reported to the bridge for debriefing.

All the officers had assembled and were giving their reports in turn.

Captain Roos addressed them. "Well done, mission completed,

we now hand over to the regular ships and return to the exciting merchant business," Fedo said, "Carry on, dismissed and have a good rest."

Seeing that Ito was hanging back, Fedo waved her over, "What do you think happened?"

Thinking '*I would prefer answers,*' she offered, "Our new friends wanted our help to assume their rightful position as the government. There were some who objected, so we stood in the way."

"Close enough, you performed to expectations officially," Fedo said, "Your parents will be proud as am I."

"Thanks, I had better hit the showers," Ito said.

"Do that, you have work to catch up on," Fedo said.

Later in the week, the ensigns were called forward for a ceremony, Fedo announced, "I have pleasure in awarding promotions to these fine officers, Lieutenant junior grade Ito Roos step forward."

She did so, aware that the order of the advancement and position meant a minor bragging right over her peers. Usually, these were handed out in alphabetical order. Saluting, Roos accepted the rank badge and the campaign token accompanying it.

"Lieutenant junior grade Zento Hoos step forward," He called, then by alphabet called the rest of the intake signifying equal standing on the official reports and recorded as having the same time of promotion.

Reporting back to the first Lieutenant, Roos was assigned a more permanent role as Assistant Engineering officer. This role was administrative, concerned with personnel and repair supplies.

When reporting to the Engineer Officer, her status had risen slightly; Chief Ghos now acknowledged 'Ma'am' as she walked up to him. "Good day Chief, I see the place hasn't fallen apart since I was here last?"

"By sheer chance and not the skills of the students, Lt j.g. Roos," Ghos replied both acknowledging and reminding her that her status had only changed slightly.

"I am sure we can still depend on your good luck, Chief," Ito said.

Her role continued with regular stints as a platoon leader, and she still had dirty hands as she brushed up her skills in Engineering.

As the wheel turns, the system sent new graduates to the *Challenge*, where the crew taught the same lessons she had learnt. This time she viewed the stumbling students with amusement with the hope that she hadn't been as naive.

As all good things come to an end, the time arrived to leave the comfort of the *Challenge*, actually to enter the real world.

When she marched to the Administration building, it was as Lt Roos senior grade. As still a relative junior, the clerk dispensed the news that she henceforth would join the fleet as captain of the scout *Rambling Gambler*.

First Command

THIS TIME ITO HAD TO WALK FURTHER TOWARDS THE smaller parking points where the Navy housed minor ships. Eventually, she found the designated park.

On the pad in all its glory was her ship, *Rambling Gambler*, a scout. Not new but heaps better than serving as a junior officer in a large vessel. She even had her first assignment, exploration of a binary system Rim ward.

As she strode to the ship, her new crew discussed what they knew about her.

"It is her first command, carries herself like she owns the world, the people on the *Challenge* reckon they would follow her to hell, sticks up for juniors," Sucos said.

"I also heard, you shouldn't try to flirt if you don't want to land on your bum, she is a martial arts champ," Ruckos returned, "Here she comes, standby."

Her new crew were waiting to welcome her on board; she had met Engineer Sucos and Ensign Ruckos before joining the ship.

"Take your stations, Engineer Sucos, Ensign Ruckos; we lift in an hour towards the rim, a system that has erratic signs of activity," Ito said as she returned their salutes and entered her new command.

The orders were to travel to the system then search for any planets and minerals after they had completed a shakedown cruise around the Forno system. Having determined that the ship was serviceable; Ito ordered Ruckos to set the course for the jump.

The Hyperjump was uneventful, and the ship arrived at a binary system with a red dwarf sun relatively close. As the ship approached the scans indicated several artificial objects, these appeared to be a derelict craft with ambiguous life signs.

Sucos reported, "Nearest vessel has one life sign which seems to be throughout through the ship, fungus perhaps? The vessel is consistent with an Imperial Scout and doesn't respond to hails."

"Ruckos bring us alongside, prepare to board and secure for salvage," Ito ordered.

All three donned their spacesuits as the *Gambler* matched airlocks, Sucos transferred to the derelict.

"No one aboard" Sucos reported, before giving a strangled cry.

"Sucos report," Ito ordered, there was no reply. However, the figure of her crewman entered the airlock.

Ruckos approached to investigate but had his suit ripped by the figure and shrieked in pain.

Roos drew her gun and flamed the grey blob before it could attack her. She ran through to the airlock and slammed it closed; then relocated the *Gambler* well clear of the hostile scout.

Using her sensors, Ito determined that there was now no life signs on the derelict vessel; so she radioed a report declaring an emergency before setting course to return to base.

Receiving no reply on the radio, Ito approached the jump point and initiated the entry to Hyperspace. Nothing happened as smoke erupted from the equipment bay; the *Gambler* remained in the system.

Having secured the ship in a stable orbit, she investigated the damage. It seemed that a stray bolt had hit the equipment and she was stranded.

"I hope that report got through. Perhaps I can salvage some parts from the derelict."

While she was organising some equipment, The sensors detected a Hyper pulse from the opposite side of the system; Ito started to reach for the radio; however, the transponder squawked the code for an Oxzen ship.

"Oh great, 'bluebags', what else could go wrong?" Ito asked herself. To maintain anonymity, Roos switched off all detectable equipment; then she settled into waiting for them to depart.

A small ship triggered an emergency beacon near the new ship, which then approached the source. A couple of hours passed, then there was more activity with two shuttles started cruising around investigating the system.

After what seemed like an eternity the Oxzen ship finished its inspection and departed to Ito's relief.

"Now perhaps I can get something done?'" Ito said as she guided her ship back to the original vessel.

Having retraced her path she cautiously approached and checked the derelict. There were no life signs; so Ito transferred over, her gun in hand to see if the ship was serviceable. All indications were that it was dead with no energy left in the systems. The modules she needed were not able to be tested. *'The parts may be useful,'* as she removed a few of the radio and Hyperdrive modules ready to transfer to her ship.

"My mother advised never to ask 'what else could go wrong'," Ito said to herself as she returned to the *Gambler* to take stock of her fortunes. as per standard fit, there were enough provisions of food, water and air, to maintain three crew for a month longer than the planned duration, if a search ship was slow, the most significant danger was boredom.

She settled into a routine of exercise then tinkering with the equipment to see if she could make repairs. It wasn't long before she realised the radio had been one of the casualties and therefore hadn't transmitted a signal.

Still being resourceful, she soon had it spread out on the deck examining each component and trying to source a replacement from the wreck's radio. She was well underway and had just reassembled the transceiver ready for a test when the sensors detected a Hyper pulse from rimward.

"Not a 'bluebag', strange ID, I will send a distress signal and see if I can get a tow," Ito said as she triggered the Distress Beacon.

The strange vessel approached tail first. "Commendable caution, though it is only a shuttle," Ito commented.

The radio crackled, "Shuttle *Little Red*, Captain Firebrand, do you require assistance?"

"*Rambling Gambler*, Hyperdrive disabled," Ito transmitted, the accent was a problem sounding like the bluebags; perhaps they learnt Galbasic from them.

"What crew do you have? I have limited resources," Firebrand sent back.

"Captain Roos, crew Sucos and Ruckos, from Goosos, Nitrogen-oxygen 75-25," Ito responded using the standard format for alien vessels, though it jarred her nerves lying.

"Perhaps I can give you a tow?" *Red* responded.

"Sigma Epsilon?" Ito asked in return.

"Grnatz would be closer," *Red* replied.

'*Damn a bluebag lover,*' She thought, then declared, "Do not send a signal or energise your drive, I have you in my sights." Leaping to those controls and aimed her cannon, but before she could zero in on the shuttle, it hit its drive and skipped to the side as she pressed the trigger; an overwhelming lassitude descended making her collapse at the weapon station.

Ito struggled awake to find two men in spacesuits standing on the bridge covering her with pistols.

The shorter one asked, "Remain calm unless you wish another nap. Why did you fire on us?"

As they looked like Corellian rather than Oxzen, Ito assumed the standard response to them, "Sorry I thought you were Oxzen."

"We are here, what can we do?" The man asked.

"My hyperdrive is down due to accidental flash damage," Ito said.

"Your crew?" He asked.

"Dead, a thing broke in and killed them; I destroyed it," Ito admitted, "The crew will be a problem to replace."

"Grey Ooze in the form of a man?" He asked.

"What I saw of it, yes," Ito answered cautiously.

"You were lucky, not many survive the Zombie beast," He said, "My friend Humph the Droman told me he cleared out an infestation here a little time ago, why didn't you hail him?"

"I had just finished repairing my radio when you turned up, I thought that he was on an Oxzen ship," Ito explained, "That is annoying because I have met him before and he would have been a great help."

"I am Steve Firebrand, show me the equipment I do have some spares," Steve said, "What is your drama with Oxzens? I have no problems dealing with them."

"They swarm a trade planet and exclude everyone else, I just avoid them," Ito took him to the equipment bay, "Over here, I will show you."

Steve examined the bay and after talking to his shuttle, asked, "Could you place the Hyperdrive on standby?"

Ito did so, while he mumbled to himself waving his hand over the modules as they gave a couple of crackles.

"Well it seems that modules A and C are Unserviceable, you're in luck I have a couple of spares. If I bring them over; will you be able to fit them?" Steve asked.

"Yes," Ito snapped, thinking, *'In my sleep.'*

Steve gave her a wry look, "Kev keep an eye on her, I will be back in a moment. Gizmo is getting the parts out of the storage cabinet."

As promised he returned with the items and handed them over, "You will be able to fit these?" Steve asked again, Ito gave a curt nod, so he said, "I will stand by until you are underway." Gesturing to Kev, they transferred back to the Red shuttle and moved it away.

With the visitors gone, Ito soon had the modules fitted and tested, powering up the insystem drive she steered the *Gambler* to jump point, without another word.

The *Gambler* arrived at the hyper jump point where she engaged the drive. Exiting into the Forno system with a less than favourable report to deliver. She had been away for longer than the department had planned for the task.

Having landed the *Gambler*, she marched over to the debriefing building to deliver her report.

Ito conveyed the news that another race was active near their borders with Corellian features. The administration received this potentially adverse news; balanced by the assessment that the AC system under investigation was likely beneficial for minerals. The loss of her crew was not received well. The scientists were interested in the news of the elimination of the attacking beast and description of its form.

After a week of investigation, Ito was recalled to the debrief department, to receive the verdict.

"Lieutenant Roos, it has been determined that you are not responsible for the loss of your crew, we analysed the report that you delivered, and the alien vessel approach protocols will be amended."

"Yes, sir," Ito said with relief though she didn't let this show.

"Crew will be assigned, and your ship will complete the survey of System AC," The Captain ordered.

"Aye, Aye sir," Ito said as she saluted and marched out.

She returned to the *Gambler* where the last of the repairs and restocking was nearing completion.

Settling in and cleaning up the last of the mess, Ito grumbled, "Can't those mechs clean up after themselves."

Before the time of liftoff, her new crewmen were Engineer Jiloos Foos and Lt Heta Hostos, who would arrive later in the afternoon.

At the advised time two women arrived with their luggage in hand, hailing the ship, "Lts j.g. Foos and Hostos reporting for duty."

The pair marched aboard and saluted their new captain.

"Welcome aboard, I am Lieutenant Roos, stow your gear away, and I will brief you on our mission," Ito said as she returned the salute.

After the girls had done this and returned to the cockpit, Ito invited, "Sit down, have you heard what happened to my last crew? I am now prepared to prevent any further incidents."

"Yes, the word is that you were lucky to escape that beast. Usually, the infected ship is blasted to avoid contamination. The board policy is to deem all hands lost," Foos said.

"So they informed me, our mission is to return to that system and complete the survey, once done we then approach a potential client system to observe," Ito said.

The *Gambler's* crew had settled into this routine, they assumed their stations and carried out systems checks before the appointed departure time.

"Ensign Foos as the engineer, please ensure that adequate repair modules are available, I was stranded until a passing shuttle provided modules to enable me to return. Since I now know the policy with the zombie infection, my luck was in that the radio was damaged; I don't believe I should rely on that sort of luck in the future," Ito said.

That settled, Foos rechecked the stores and left to arrange the extra spares, returning later with a cartload. Then stored these away securely.

As the departure time arrived, the *Gambler* lifted off and headed to the jump point. Engaging Hyperdrive the ship departed towards AC system; emerging cautiously to survey the area. Several small craft were detected, and each was examined and logged as salvage or wreck.

The planets they saw were dry and hot, Ito commented, "These are too variable to be habitable, on long-range sensors the small red sun may have a planet in close orbit."

Once Foos reported her final sweep as confirming the previous assessment, Ito ordered departure to the red sun.

As it was only a short jump, they were soon orbiting a planet covered in water and vegetation.

"Promising if you don't mind the stars whipping past," Ito said, "There is a suitable sun further rimward which is our next port of call, this one is likely where the spacers came from, so we go in quietly with all caution."

"Aye, Ma'am," Hostos said as she set the new course.

The ship emerged in the planetary plane and drifted at entry speed towards the sun, as they went noted each planet as they approached. Once through the ice cloud, they travelled past a couple of gas giants with multiple moons which while cold, were worth further investigation. As there was no artificial energy detected they probably weren't being exploited. This lack of signals meant that space exploration was in its infancy.

After the *Gambler* passed the inner gas giant, the next planet was a small, dry, red planet; this was a source of radio transmissions though sparse and primitive. So there was some activity so that the inhabitants may be looking for alien ships.

Eventually, they approached a green and blue planet with a high sea to land ratio and much more likely, as the sensors indicated a breathable atmosphere similar to Forno.

"Engage the cloaking field, avoid occlusion of the stars," Ito ordered. This technique involved reading radar frequencies and locally broadcasting an inverted wave to cancel returns. The avoidance of star blocking required being aware of the sight line between the target planet and stars.

"Heavy radio traffic on multiple bands, several thousand mobile transmissions in low orbit and airspace, there is also sea vessels," Foos reported.

"Logged," Ito acknowledged.

After several days of observation to locate a likely candidate for approach, the approved model for the contact was an isolated country with firm control of their population. While most of the radio transmissions were in unknown languages, the computer was able to translate a sample of the most likely country.

The selected country called itself the Democratic Peoples Republic of Korea, with the southern neighbour calling itself the Republic of Korea. As most of the seaborne trade was between the South and the rest of the world; the Northern state would likely welcome the business from anyone.

The radio transmissions were belligerent and warlike, especially towards the southern neighbour. The South, in turn, broadcast a description of how good the life was in South Korea which resulted in attempts to jam them by the North.

"This according to our training brief is the perfect place to start our program. They claim to be at war with most of the world except for their Northern neighbour China and a couple of others, emphasised by their protests of unjust boycotts. They would be keen to trade with us to acquire advanced weapons and goods," Ito said, "So once we have a language tape, I will descend and see if I can speak to those in control and negotiate a basis for a treaty."

After several weeks the time came when Ito was confident in the language so wearing makeup to match the inhabitants. Using a shuttle Roos descended to the surface and waited for contact with the Government.

Ito landed her shuttle at an airport. The Korean soldiers soon surrounded her vessel, dismayed that such an aircraft could penetrate their defences unchallenged.

Dressed in local style and looking like an inhabitant except for her height and hair colour, "I come in peace to the Peoples Republic of Korea. I am from a far distant nation who sympathise with your struggle," Ito stated, "I have available goods and technology to help you throw off the yoke imposed on your glorious Country."

This speech hit the right chord, and the listeners gushed in enthusiasm as they had heard that the Australians were trading with the stars. The authorities soon invited Ito to an audience with high officials, and between them commenced trade negotiations. She wasn't allowed to complete the task as she didn't have a senior enough status to meet diplomatic protocols. She promised that a full ambassador would be assigned to their country as soon as she reported the contact.

To demonstrate the technology Ito called down the ship and had her crew run rings around the local fighters. Taking a military commander to a range, she proved the power of her sidearm by destroying the target spectacularly. She had ensured that she didn't use a too powerful a weapon, only alluding to the potential.

Having set a basis for the treaty to be arranged, Ito farewelled the Koreans and lifted to return to report the good news to the Fornoon Government.

After the debrief, Ito was assigned a desk to be available for consultation at need, as this was the programme that the Government followed. An ambassador and staff were appointed, and they lifted off in a small group with two ships to land, with a third vessel in a stationary orbit to observe.

While they were gone to set up the next stage; the enforcement fleet was assembled to wait for the order to proceed.

"Lieutenant Roos you are promoted to Lt Commander and assigned to Customs Corvette *Braveheart*," Admiral Faroos ordered, "Congratulations Commander, you will join the E Fleet as an auxiliary vessel."

"Aye, aye, Sir," Ito acknowledged, saluted and marched out to locate her new ship.

Second command

FINDING THE *BRAVEHEART*, ITO WAS PLEASANTLY surprised to see Foos and Hostos wearing new Lieutenant insignia.

"Congratulations, hanging out with a hero rewards your efforts," Ito said tongue in cheek, "So, we have been assigned to the 'watch and see' role."

"Beats chasing rocks," Foos said, "We have a crew of six other ranks, and once we enter the operation area we have the job of charging the Bluebags an entry fee."

"That should be fun," Hostos said, "I love it when you can get a credit out of them."

The time arrived, and the E Fleet was ordered to lift and assemble at the red dwarf star that Ito had discovered.

After a time the order was given for the E Fleet to move to the new planet called Earth. This task force was to support the new friend Korea who with the Forno Fleet would set the Earth on the correct path to proper governance.

They entered the system once the last Oxzen merchant had cleared it, leaving Braveheart to act as Customs guard at the Grnatz entry point. This task was with the instruction to intercept and levy an entry tax on merchants.

The E Fleet soon had helped subdue the Enemies of Korea, and a signal was received with a copy of the authority to represent the Earth Government signed by Kim Jong-un President of United Earth.

The next few weeks went to plan with a few merchants reluctantly paying the tax.

This assignment proceeded until a Hyper pulse heralded the next client.

Ito ordered an intercept course and radioed the vessel, "United Earth Customs, standby for inspection,"

Back in English came, "In a pig's eye, who the hell are you?" With the sensors reading that the ship had powered up screens and weapons.

"Stand down. Or we will fire on you," Ito returned wondering what he meant. She had gestured to the weapons officer then she felt dizzy, staggering to the seat she collapsed. Lt Hostos came in, seeing that the bridge team were unconscious, she grabbed the radio at the weapons desk and repeated, "Standby for boarding party,"

Then in Galbasic came the warning from the red saucer, "Do not fire on my ship, doing so may damage your vessel. If you don't stand down and talk, I will take steps; the next dose will have you sleeping for a long time, *Big Red* over."

Hostos reached for the cannon controls and fired towards the ship; instantly the gun blew up rupturing the hull. The emergency doors slammed shut to prevent air loss; then Hostos collapsed across the controls triggering missiles.

Ito struggled back to her feet to find her wrists in shackles as was all her crew. Several men in armour were standing on guard; The leader directed several to search the ship for the other personnel. Strangely they were accompanied by a slim teenage girl dressed in flight overalls.

"Who the hell are you?" Ito demanded.

"Forgotten me already, Captain Roos? I am Captain Firebrand," The leader said as he cleared his visor.

"You," Ito said dismayed.

"On what authority do you intercept, and fire on me when I am traversing my system," Firebrand asked.

"On the authority of United Earth," Ito stated, "There is a fleet guarding the Earth."

"And you would have a document to support this?" Firebrand asked sceptically.

"Let me loose, and I will show you," Ito said confidently.

"First may I inform you that my team are wearing enhanced suits which are very effective," Firebrand stated then he released the shackles.

When he noticed Roos eyeing off the girl, so he said to the girl, "Pippin, would you be a dear and bend that rod into a pretzel?"

The girl after giving him a puzzled look, said, "Sure, Dad." She reached over to the indicated item, then quickly ripped it from the wall and tied it into a knot without apparent effort. This ability was startling, as she seemed at the most sixteen and with that voice, to be younger.

Despite being startled, Ito accessed the computer and retrieved the document. This readout was in Galbasic; it declared that the ship was a customs ship for the United Earth.

Captain Firebrand read down the page until he read the signature legend rendered in both Galbasic and Korean script.

He burst into laughter declaring, "That idiot! He barely runs his country using coercion; most think at best that he is a congenital idiot and certainly doesn't speak for the United Nations."

Then assuming a formal pose, "As the Captain of an Australian registered Ship, signatory to United Nation's conventions, you are under arrest for piracy, you have the right to remain silent. If you require legal representation, the court will provide this at an inquiry," Firebrand said.

Ito jumped to grab her pistol, but Firebrand wrenched it from her grasp and broke it in two. "Naughty girl, back into handcuffs," Firebrand said as he put them back on despite her struggles, she was a hand taller and expert in unarmed combat.

"Pippin, would you survey the ship and see if we can fly it back to Elysium?" Firebrand asked.

The girl nodded and ran off soon returning with the report, "The explosion has breached the hull. The ship is not serviceable for Hyper."

"Take these prisoners back to the *Red*, and we shall return to Elysium," Firebrand ordered.

Ito thought, *'The fleet scares him.'* She went along quietly as directed.

When a couple of the crew resisted, Pippin just pinned them both under her arms and walked out without visible effort.

After clearing the *Red's* airlock, the guard escorted the Fornoon to cabins where they were locked in separating men from women.

Once the guard had departed, Ito asked, "Is everyone fit?" then receiving the report of health, "What do think we can do?" she had considered and rejected several plans, but was willing to entertain fresh insights.

"I was watching the equipment as they brought us in; if we can get out of here, the ship itself is standard and not hard to fly," Foos advised.

"I saw several apparent civilians, these would make useful hostages," Hostos said.

"I have already surveyed the cabin; it is a discrete enclosure within the ship. If we make a fuss a little later, perhaps the guards may open the door to quieten us?" Ito asked, "I will tap code to the rest of our crew and advise them to observe the routine and suggest the timing."

As the ship was still adjacent to the jump point, it reentered Hyperspace to leave the system.

"Not keen to face our E Fleet," Ito laughed, "If they depend on the Bluebags for help they are in for a disappointment."

After exchanging messages, the men called for food and water. The guards delivered this with too much security to start anything. So the crew went back to biding their time.

It was then Ito's turn to test, having observed that the captors were gentler with females. Encouraging her companions to make a fuss, she secreted herself close the door, confident that she could deal with an unarmoured man.

The intercom sounded, "Please quieten down, ask nicely for your needs and they will be met."

Ito waved her crew to increase the noise.

Over the ruckus, the intercom stated, "Settle down, or restraints will be applied."

Ito said, "They wouldn't dare." She waved for them to carry on. She was dismayed as one by one the girls slumped to the floor before feeling sleepy herself.

Ito woke to find her crew now strapped into their bunks with the teenager saying, "Be aware I don't like being dragged away from useful work to pander to your whims. If you promise to be quiet, I will restore your freedom. We have only a few more hours before handing you over to Oxzen Navy custody."

Faced with the inevitability of helplessness, Ito said, "As you wish, I would appreciate some movement as it is rather restrictive in this cabin. My crew and I are merely following orders."

"I will confer with Captain Firebrand to see what we can arrange without compromising security," Pippin promised, looking a little absent.

It wasn't long before she advised, "I can accept your parole and allow one at a time to exercise."

She then unstrapped the crew and allowed them to move, "There will one crewman assigned to each one allowed out, and I will monitor your behaviour."

"Do you have a place of exercise? I need to work out the cramps?" Ito asked with the idea of searching more of the ship.

"Certainly we do, that is how the humans stay fit," Pippin said, "I will take you there when you wish. Please select two to accompany you; then the others can take turns."

Roos considered this a strange phrase but went along with Pippin and arrived at a large cabin where she could see equipment and a padded floor for martial arts activity.

Roos tried each machine before ending at the mat, contemplating this, she asked, "I would like a workout would you suggest a partner and can you supply me with suitable clothing?"

"Certainly, over in that room you will find an outfit, I will be waiting for your return," Pippin offered.

"A slip of a girl like you?" Ito asked sceptically.

"I may surprise you," Pippin laughed.

Shaking her head, *'well if she was silly enough, just as long as she doesn't expect me to go soft.'*

Ito returned dressed for action and was surprised to find that Pippin now matched her height and apparent weight. She had also changed into a martial arts outfit.

"How did you do that?" Ito asked.

"I am from Droma," Pippin returned, "Now run through your warm-up routines as I assess your requirements."

Ito shrugged and commenced stretching, mock throws and practice break falls. After watching this for a time, Pippin started shadowing Roos' moves.

"Any time you are ready?" Ito said as she stood in the ready position.

Pippin copied, and the pair went through the standard lifts and lowering. After several moves, Ito started to raise the pace and attempted to throw the girl. While she gave no resistance to completing the throw, Pippin returned the throw just as quick and dropped Ito to the mat without effort.

After a time Ito was becoming hot and sweaty, Pippin seemed as fresh as she started. So Ito admitted that she had sufficient exercise and called a halt.

"Thank you; I will change and return to the cabin to allow someone else to enjoy a little freedom," Ito said.

After resuming her uniform, Ito walked out and found that Pippin was as initially had escorted her, slim in flight overalls. With no fatigue evident with the girl, whereas Ito felt like she had been through the wringer and was struggling to hide this.

Rather than admitting this minor distress by asking how the girl was able to do this, Ito kept her peace. When she stepped into the cabin, she hand-signalled Foos to challenge the girl to the martial mat.

"Have a good workout they have excellent facilities, tell me how you enjoy the exercise," Ito said.

41

After a while, Foos returned looking well worn with the story that Ito had endured. It was then Hostos' turn who told the same story with Pippin looking as bright as the first time. This ability left them wondering just what was this slip of a girl.

Still, it filled in the wait until at last; the ship made a landing and soldiers arrived to escort the *Braveheart's* crew off to their new housing. It was a surprise, these weren't Bluebags but appeared to be Imperial troopers. After housing them in separate accommodation, Roos was instructed to accompany a small squad for interrogation.

Arriving at the room Ito was offered a seat in front of an officer dressed in Oxzen Navy uniform, a Corellian, so she was still puzzled.

"Good day, I am Commander Blohm, You are Lt Commander Ito Roos?" Blohm asked in Galbasic.

"I am the Captain of *Braveheart*, assigned to customs duty for the United Earth Government; I protest the treatment I have received from a mere civilian," Ito stated in Corellian.

"Noted. The document that purports to support your claim is in dispute; until further investigation, I am afraid you will remain our guest. I hope that you find your accommodation suitable. Please enjoy the stay," Blohm said, "As this is essentially a military base still in construction, please allow for a little restriction on your movements."

"May I inquire why you are in Oxzen Uniform?" Ito asked.

"My sub fleet was cut adrift by the Empire's collapse. Commodore Rham decided to align with the Oxzen sector and develop a planet," Blohm answered.

"Whatever floats your boat, Commander. I still protest and wish to contact my superiors," Ito demanded.

"We are dealing with your protest; we don't have direct contact with your principles. My Government will pass on the notification to your people in the shortest time possible," Blohm said, then signalled the escort to return her to her crew.

She had to be content with this promise and once she was with her crew briefed them on the state of play, "Well it seems we are guests of Imperial renegades who are going to inform our superiors of our plight."

"So when do you suppose we get back home?" Foos asked.

"That is in the hands of the gods. The Elysium people have to talk to someone who can pass the message. In the meantime, the authorities intend to investigate to see if we are legitimate. If the Navy prove that, they should return us to our ship, and Elysium charges Firebrand with false imprisonment," Ito related, "So for now, have a good holiday, mind what you touch as this is a military base and they won't tolerate sticky fingers."

"As that is likely to include anything mobile, not much we can do," Foos admitted.

"I will move around and see what I can learn," Hostos suggested, "And charm a little info out of someone."

While they were discussing this, a Lambda shuttle lifted off and headed out. As this was a busy base, this was not noteworthy Ito didn't pay too much attention as the Red saucer was still on its pad.

A few days passed, and there was a sudden surge in activity with vessels landing and being loaded with provisions and troopers, when the Forno crew asked, they were brushed off and told to mind their business.

Then a squad turned up and herded Ito with her crew into cells. Surprised Roos was furious at the treatment and was less than happy especially when a lieutenant arrived to pass on the news; that the government had determined that the Fornoon forces had illegally invaded the Earth. The crew were now under detention for the duration of the invasion.

When the officer had finished delivering this news, there was a mass liftoff of Imperial-class fighting ships and support freighters.

"Damn looks like the cavalry has departed," Ito said, "And we are stuck in here."

Nothing they could do about the situation, so they had to cool their heels and wait for something to happen.

After what seemed like an eternity, the troop escorted Ito to Commander Blohm's office; he said, "Good morning Commander,

I am sorry the accommodation is less than I promised. The investigations are now complete, and we have adjusted your status to prisoner of war. Under our convention, we are not allowed to question or require you to work. The Navy has lifted some restrictions, and will repatriate you as soon as practical."

"I suppose I have to accept this, hardly in a position to argue," Ito said, "I will still protest the civilian's action."

"I am sure the Government will give it the weight it deserves, Commander," Blohm said, "For now you will return to your quarters and be assigned appropriate care. Good day."

Ito saluted and marched out with the escort.

Back in the cells, Ito said, "The news is, we are prisoners of war, and as soon as possible we go home. The when is the problem."

Eventually, the fleet returned and disgorged hundreds of Fornoon soldiers and ship crew. Several Fornoon cruisers also landed to Ito's dismay. She hoped that the rest of E fleet made their escape.

An escort arrived and asked Ito to accompany them, at Blohm's office, "Good morning, Commander, the investigation is complete, and there was war action which has resolved with a peace treaty with the Fornoon Government and the United Nations of Earth. Shortly your people will be transferred to Forno," Blohm informed her, "It has been pleasant dealing with you, I look forward to a more congenial circumstance in future."

"Thank you, Commander," Ito said shaking his hand, "Any idea how long? I need to reassure my crew, who were not involved in any conflict."

"The holdup is at the other end, your government has to arrange neutral ships to do the transfer," Blohm advised, "The captured ships are reparations for the damage that your invasion caused. I have sighted evidence that at least yourself made the original approach."

"I arranged talks with a sovereign country. My government signed a trade and defence pact; my statements stand, Commander," Ito said then was marched out.

The ships eventually arrived, and the troopers loaded the Fornoon personnel aboard.

When the transport ships entered Forno space, there was no fanfare as it hadn't been a successful campaign. The Senior Captain in charge of the mission had escaped with the majority of the E Fleet, leaving only those damaged and unable to hyperjump.

As a ship captain, the Admiralty debriefed Ito separately. Having delivered her report, she had to cool her heels while they worked their way down the seniority until they eventually called her to the chamber.

"Lt Commander Roos, this ship which captured your crew, how would you explain the occurrence?" The Captain asked.

"The approach was standard protocol. I hailed this ship requesting a customs search; the captain answered unintelligibly, then I repeated the challenge. The captain asked on what authority I had for this in Galbasic," Ito said, "When I threatened to fire, I passed out, then my off-duty officer came in to find us all unconscious, at which time she repeated the challenge. The answer was a warning that firing would result in damage to my ship. My officer then fired, and when the weapon's accumulator exploded the hull was breached. We woke up to find that strangers had boarded the ship at which time a man identifying himself as Captain Firebrand, who challenged the validity of the authority and from there we were taken to Elysium."

"Interesting, apparently much the same technology was used to overturn the Government we were supporting on Earth," Captain Feados said, "I believe since you have a working knowledge of this Firebrand and his technology at least on the receiving end. The board orders you to investigate and create a defence."

"Yes Sir, I did observe that apparently, they are immune from stray hits of the stun gun," Ito said, "I believe that once we have analysed the beam, we can generate a protective field."

Scientist Engineer

THE ASSIGNMENT WAS A WORKSHOP IN THE CENTRAL industrial area; Ito would be able to call on specialist workers to fabricate equipment. It was also near the spaceport so that when something needed testing, the Ministry could assign vessels without delay.

One day, Ito marched into the laboratory to find Lt Foos looking happy.

"Ah Foos, have you discovered something?" She asked.

"Yes, I have acquired a shield and a handgun from a trader. I have tested them on lab animals and can extrapolate the effect to a ship-sized cannon," Foos reported, "The larger gun itself is probably not worth the effort to duplicate. The existing ship shields can be modified to suit. The downside, it requires extra power and time to bring up the function."

"So it is useful. I will report to the board and be assigned a ship to test it with," Ito said.

The team assembled several test fields and cobbled up a working cannon to provide a stronger beam to show the protection.

The initial trials were promising, and the ministry approved them for further experiments in the event there were more Oxzen incursions.

As a science officer cluttering up the ship, her team were as welcome as the previous day's leftovers; most of the crew were also aware that they had lost their last vessel.

The workshop tested several versions, and the best was incorporated first in those ships likely to encounter hostile Oxen ships. With a few assigned to mercenary crews, these were encouraged to act as 'pirates' near Oxen shipping routes.

Ito had a thought; if ships needed protection, the same didn't apply to Android pilots, there was a resistance to having them as pilots of human crewed ships, perhaps having a robot controlling a small vessel with a limited task, these would neutralise attacking fighters. Those swarming Imperial tie fighters had been the Oxen tactic which overwhelmed the E Fleet.

Ito made a report recommending construction of half-sized spacecraft which saved resources by eliminating the requirement for life support with the robotic brain directly connected to the sensors and controls. A skeleton ship could provide the Navigation and Hyperdrive to move a large number of these to the target; the lightened carrier could then retreat out of harm way after delivering the robots.

When queried she explained that the merchant syndicate that had been opposing the Old Republic before the Empire had used these in actions. They had to be backed up by regular ships as there were some limitations, the colossal carrier the syndicate had used became a prime target.

A prototype was constructed using at first remote control to monitor the robot brain. The team hadn't fitted armament to begin the experiment, just the targeting sensors and shields. Against Forno Fighters in simulated combat, the team determined that three or more would defeat one fighter at a time. While using the remote, the time delay allowed the Fornoon pilot to randomly out fly a single test drone. Further tests using the autonomous robot controlled fighters showed that the faster reflexes of the drone were able to defeat Fornoon pilots using two against one, and one on one successful at fifty per cent.

Fitting the robot fighters with limited weapons to use against Oxen ID-ed asteroids demonstrated that the robots would quickly attack these and ignore Fornoon transducers.

The reports were favourable to the ministry as each robot was less than half the expense of a regular fighter with none of the cost, time and training of the pilot.

The team suggested that the design for the carrier would allow Hyperdrive for a small core vessel with the transported robots released as a cloud after being given a basic course and target. Just having these circling nearby would distract an enemy and show up on sensors as a whole fleet of combatants. The now much smaller core ship could now retreat to safety. Without the life support for fifty pilots and perhaps seventy support personnel the resulting empty carrier was a minute target easily overlooked.

After several projects had started to come to fruition, the Ministry offered Ito a temporary duty in a Ship similar to the *Challenge* as the First Lt. As this was a slight demotion, Ito wasn't too keen, but space-time was better than flying a desk. She had in the meantime had established high standards in many required areas, so her overall status had improved. This appointment would score in both leadership and teamwork.

The ship was like an old home week, with the job mostly involving administration and watchkeeping in support of the Captain who had an overview rather than hands-on duty.

The appointment was for a six-month stint while the replacement First Officer was still serving on his current ship.

At the end of this placement, Ito was briefed a couple of times and assisted with updates for the equipment she had designed.

Agent Provocateur

LT COMMANDER ROOS WAS ANSWERING THE SUMMONS to headquarters; hopefully, for another assignment, the last two were just to let her know that they hadn't forgotten her and to pick her brain with the development of weapons and defences.

She was ushered into the Admiral's office and invited to sit.

"I suppose you wonder why we keep bothering you with false starts? No matter, this time I have a task for your unique talents," Admiral Hostos said, "Do you know the system Faroo, which Captain Roos explored for us? The Oxzen have colonised it as their own."

"Yes, sir, I had heard that they did," Ito answered being aware of the official status.

"The Department orders that in company with another ship to visit there and restore Forno ownership," Hostos ordered, "You are to see if that provokes a hostile reaction. A task force will be standing by to receive your 'distress call'."

"Aye, aye, Sir," She acknowledged.

"The strategic situation and likely opponents are available at Captain Huros' desk, Carry on Commander," Hostos advised.

"Sir," Ito marched out a little ambivalent and sought out Huros.

As she found his office, she was a little put off that Lt Hoos was waiting there.

"Ah, Lt Commander Roos I was expecting you, you know Lt Hoos?" Huros said.

"Seems most of my life. You have the data, Sir?" Ito asked hoping that the orders didn't include Zento.

"You are to take command of the *Arzkeen*, Lt Hoos is the captain of *Gerno Bluff*. Here are the coordinates of the system where you will visit to reclaim our territory," Huros said, "Currently intelligence describes the system as having one port with one merchant ship a week visiting, one customs shuttle and ten light fighters of obsolescent design. Any Oxzen relief is two weeks delay after dispatching a signal."

"Yes, sir," Ito said, "Unchanged from the last I read of the data,"

"The backup force is four armed merchants and two of the new robot carriers," Huros advised.

"Nice when you find that they follow suggestions, each has fifty robot fighters?" Ito asked.

"Yes, that is the design," Huros said, "Now, you prepare for liftoff at 0900 hours in two days with the backup ready three days later. The carriers are slow, so they will first regroup at our closest system and be available within two weeks. If you engage an outclassing force, you are to regroup with H Fleet to re-engage."

"Aye, aye, sir," Roos and Hoos acknowledged, saluted and marched out.

As they left the Admin Building, Ito commented dryly, "Together again?"

"Yes Ma'am," Zento replied with a grin, confident that he had leeway as a fellow captain.

"If we work together on this, we should come up smelling like roses," Ito said, "Just remember to jump when I say so, no embroidery."

"When would I do that, Ito?" Zento asked looking innocent.

"Ha. Come to my ship *Arzkeen*, and we will pull the data to bits and reassemble into something we both can follow," Ito said leading the way, "So how deep was the brown and smelly last time?"

"You know me, a cute smile rescues you from all sorts of dramas," Zento quipped receiving a raised eyebrow in response.

Arriving at the *Arzkeen*, Roos laid out the data and reviewed the system they were to visit.

"We track through these three systems to enter from this vector," Ito said as she indicated the path on the holographic chart. "We then approach the planet ignoring hails as Forno doesn't accept that anyone is there. The Admin expects that the customs shuttle will make the first intercept, then call the fighters to back it up."

"At this time we send a signal that hostile forces have invaded our territory," Ito said, "We disable as many as possible then jump back to the assembly system to join H Fleet."

"Sounds the standard format," Zento said, "Latest intelligence suggests a light freighter is due. Also, someone is trying to organise a tourist route."

"They should be no threat," Ito said, "Questions?"

"No, it should be a cakewalk," Zento said, "See you there."

"The Carriers should discourage any retaliation," Ito said confidently, "At Faroo then, you owe me a pint."

"Ma'am," Zento returned as he left for his vessel.

The time arrived, and the two ships lifted off to start their journey.

At the calculated time the pair emerged from Hyperspace and cruised in towards the planet Faroo.

The radio transmitted, "Oxzen Customs, identify ships, standby for inspection."

"Ignore them," Ito ordered, "No one lives here."

"Unidentified ships, this is Oxzen customs you violate interstellar protocols, assume stationary orbit."

"If he approaches, give him a quick zap to teach him to behave," Ito ordered, "Then standby for fighters trying to intercept."

"Shields up, here he comes," Ito said, "One shot to singe his whiskers."

Arzkeen's lighter laser hit the shuttle as it approached. It reversed course blaring an emergency call.

"Ha, there he goes, sensible of him," Ito commented.

"Several energy signatures at the spaceport, consistent with fighters," Foos reported.

"Rodger. Standby *Bluff,* see if we can catch them low and

slow. Knock out at least two; then we are out of here," Ito ordered, "Radio H Fleet that we are under attack by unknown belligerents."

"Aye ma'am," Hostos acknowledged.

The Sensor Monitor announced, "Hyper pulse inbound, light freighters ID Oxzen."

"Acknowledged, maintain a watch on them, we expected those ships," Ito said, "Let's deal with the fighters first; if they have any sense the civilian ships will reverse their course as soon as they detect the action." She then focused on the fighter group, aware that they would have limited endurance.

The Forno ships concentrated their fire on the lead fighter, disabling it, the remainder split into two groups and dodged, discharging laser fire at any opportunity.

"We can deal with them, they are burning fuel at a high rate so will have to break off soon," Ito said.

The Monitor reported, "Those Oxzen ships are running at full speed on an intercept course."

"Darn, *Bluff* fire a shot across their bows," Ito ordered, "That should settle them. Don't hit them as they are prime prizes."

"Monitor, have you ascertained their class?" Ito asked, still concentrating on the immediate threat.

"First identified as Light freighters with shields up, category unknown. Energy pattern now consistent with Corvettes," The Radar operator reported.

"Damn, Let's see," Ito said, "Red saucers, energise anti-sleep shields."

"Aye," was all the weapons controller could say before the intercepting pair arrived in range.

Ito struggled from the slumber to find that bane of her life, Firebrand standing over her.

"Not you again?" Roos groaned.

"Yes, dearie, perhaps you should take up knitting as a hobby?" Firebrand suggested sarcastically, "You should know the drill by now come along quietly, or we carry you."

Reluctantly, Ito followed directions, knowing that resistance was futile.

After being locked up again, the ship descended to the port, and they were bundled off by Oxzen police into the cells. As Ito's crew joined her with those from the Bluff, she heard the sound of the two ships as they landed with prize crews.

Having a miserable moment Ito contemplated how she could report this, but soon the H Fleet would blockade the planet, and they would have to surrender up the prisoners.

For now, all they could do is watch the activity at the port; handlers dropped cargo lifts and guided squarish shuttles from the longer ship. These glided over behind the hangers, while they unloaded freight from the smaller.

Over at the Forno ships, activity indicated that workers were preparing them for defence use, that wasn't good, if they changed the IDs it would put them in the firing line as enemy combatants. The captured ships took off to assume orbit.

After a couple of days, the action resumed, this time with first the fighters practising formations, then it seemed that they were preparing scooters for ground defence.

"I wonder what they intend to do with them?" Ito asked herself, puzzled.

After the workers had loaded dozens onto the two saucers, she was still puzzled as these lifted off and speared into orbit, returning for another load.

After the second trip, the fighters were loaded on and then sat waiting.

"I think that they have guessed that we have friends on the way, eh Zento?"

"Good idea, boosting those fighters to orbit, though our force should deal with them quickly," Zento said. "What do you think they are going to use the scooters for?"

"I don't know, perhaps decoys? They can't carry anything that would do more than bubble the paint," Ito said.

"Strange ideas this Firebrand friend of yours has, the pair

that boarded my ship were a furry chap and a Corellian," Zento said, "Koos put up a struggle, but the skinny furball just grabbed him by the scruff and carried him at arm's length to the airlock."

"That would be one of those Droman and a Terran companion. Firebrand's companion seems to be a teenage slip of a girl who dealt with two the same way," Ito said, "Had a Martial arts session with her, left me struggling for breath without her raising a sweat."

"Since you usually give me a hard time on the mat, I find that hard to believe," Zento said.

"I still don't, she said that was the first time she had done any wrestling, just watched for a minute and then matched me," Ito said ruefully, "I sent my two officers, and they came back with the same tale."

"Good topic of conversation, so where is this Droma?" Zento asked.

"Anti-spin nearby, the almanack it lists them as non-technical, planet-bound pacifists who are not interested in a trade, except for a Big Bear who traipses all over the place, I had met him years ago," Ito related, "Now it seems there are at least three."

"Sounds like a fairy tale. So anything we can do now?" Zento asked.

"Nothing except we sit tight, enjoy the scenery, either a rescue or eventually they send us home," Ito suggested, "Since the Intelligence data was stuffed up, it shouldn't hurt our careers too much."

"My signal included the data that it was Firebrand's ship. They will now have the new shields operating which will prevent snooze time I didn't prepare until too late; they caught us. I will write into ship's routine to anticipate that any approaching alien ships may use these devices, so it best to have the field running earlier. We are still working on how to fix the delay in energising."

"Seems that hindsight is accurate," Zento said.

Nothing happened until the H Fleet was due to arrive, then the fighter pilots dashed into the red saucers which lifted off into space.

"There they go, should be over soon," Zento said.

"If they received my message, they would outclass the locals," Ito said confidently, "The robots will just sweep aside the decoys, and then handle the defenders with ease."

As this was happening in the late evening, new stars started sparkling as the fleets engaged.

"Strange they seem to a long way out, flashing in pairs?" Ito commented.

"Too far to guess," Zento answered, "If the robots are firing on the decoys there should be only one flash."

The firefight stopped and restarted in different sectors as the two fleets engaged, the weapons discharges ceased, so now the prisoners held their breath waiting to see what ships would land.

Their spirits rose as Four Forno ships landed, however, the celebration was short-lived as the fighters also arrived followed by the two red saucers.

"Damnation what went wrong?" Ito asked rhetorically. Then thought, *'those damn decoys were using the energy absorbing field, how the hell did Firebrand guess we would use robots?'*

Later the next day new ships orbited, glowing in the sun. Then a Lambda shuttle landed, and Oxzen military figures marched over to the *Red*.

"That tears it, the one in the lead is Blohm, we will be soon having a chat," Ito said.

A squad of troopers approached and opened the cell door, "Lt Commander Roos, Lt Hoos you are to accompany us for an interview," The leader said.

Roos shrugged at Zento and stepped out to fall in with them.

The squad arrived at the ramp of the *Big Red*, escorted into the map room.

"Good day Commander, Lieutenant, please take a seat. For the record I am Captain Blohm," Blohm said, "Would you care to explain your actions?"

"Our government sent us here to survey our planet, and we found invaders in residence," Ito declared, "They attacked our ships, so we retaliated."

"Interesting, my report indicates that you fired first on an unarmed vessel performing their legitimate duty," Blohm said.

"Forno had historically claimed the system and the scouts had installed the correct beacons by interstellar protocols," Ito stated, "Intelligence had informed us that the Oxzens have disabled the beacons and usurped the system."

"Nice story, I am afraid it doesn't match our records, the Oxzen survey team detected no such beacons and the system lies within the sector boundary arc," Blohm said, "I am not here to debate viewpoints, the usual method will be followed to return you to your planet."

"If that is all, please return us to our crew," Ito said.

"I was hoping for a more pleasant meeting, but you follow your orders, I follow mine," Blohm advised. "There are only minor casualties so it should be straightforward."

"Manyana, Captain," Ito said saluting and was then escorted away.

"Hasta la vista, Commander," Blohm called after.

When they arrived back at the cells, Zento asked, "What was that language?"

"Earth Spanish, 'tomorrow' and then 'after the feast', means if and when we meet, the Spaniards are a bit vague and have dozens of feasts," Ito laughed, "Depending on the context, it can also mean not if I see you first."

"Oh," Zento said shaking his head still not sure of the explanation.

Time went interminably until at last, they were escorted to neutral ships and boarded the Goosos vessels for transport back to Forno.

Going through the routine of an interview at the debrief building; the administration accepted that the intelligence assessment was lacking. However as this was the second ship Ito had lost, she was not to expect a combat vessel.

After cooling her heels for a time, she noticed an ad for an opening was available on a medium merchant, so she contacted the company, and was called in for an interview.

"Good morning Commander, why would you be inquiring with us?" Manager Notos asked.

"I have a leave of absence until the story of losing my ship has blown over," Ito admitted, "They determined that it wasn't my fault and I lost no crew."

"I have read the report, your luck is variable," Notos said, "I have a recommendation from a senior merchant captain. Very impressive, he was disappointed that you hadn't followed that career."

"The Navy has a flasher uniform," Ito quipped.

"The ship is the *Golden Dream*, the position of the First Officer is vacant, and the captain is due for retirement," Notos said, "Interested?"

"Yes indeed, my feet are itchy," Ito agreed.

"The position is yours," Notos said, "Join the *Golden Dream* as soon as you are able, it is due to lift at the end of the week. Welcome aboard."

Ito shook hands and departed to seek out the Dream.

Merchant

ITO RESEARCHED THE LOCATION OF THE *DREAM* AND found that it was parked in the back blocks well away from polite company. It was a dreary corner with access for freight delivery. After a long walk there it was, hardly a shining example of an efficient vessel.

Having located the *Dream*, Ito approached the ship and hailed the *Dream*. A crewman wandered out and asked, "What do you want?"

Ito had to bite her tongue, remembering that merchants weren't subject to the same discipline as the Navy.

"I am Ito Roos; I have an appointment with Captain Mostos," Ito said.

"Okay, follow me," The crewman said turning to lead the way to the captain's cabin. Knocking on the door, he announced, "A visitor for you, Boss." then opened the door after a bellow, 'Enter'.

Ito entered to find a bewhiskered man slouching in a seat, "What do you want?"

"Ito Roos, I have been appointed to the position of the First Officer," Ito said.

"Oh yeah, I need one of those, the last one skipped," Mostos grumbled, "Reckoned I overworked him. Do you think you can handle the load, don't want a slacker."

"Work is my middle name," Ito said dryly, "I can carry my share."

"If you are still game, see the boy. He can show you your cabin," Mostos said.

"I will perform to my best ability, Sir," Roos said.

"You do that," Mostos said in farewell and slumped further into his seat.

Thinking, '*What the hell have I gotten myself into?*' then spotting the crewman who had guided her.

"Excuse me, could you show me the First Officers cabin?" Ito asked.

"You are out of luck he's gone," He said making a poor judgement.

"She is here, I won't ask so nicely next time," Ito snapped, running out of patience.

The crewman braced and pointed the way, until they reached a door, "Here you are ma'am," He said, "I am afraid it is just as he left it."

"Your name, crewman?" Ito asked.

"Crewman 1st class Bertos Hostos, ma'am," He answered.

"Shall we start again? First Officer Ito Roos, pleased to meet you. Any relation to Heta Hostos?" Ito asked.

"My sister," Hostos answered, then thought before asking, "Oh, Commander Roos? Heta talks about no one else."

"Only good things I hope, I liked working with Heta, she is very efficient," Ito said then taking a glance at the shambles, "Would you do me a favour and clean this up before I return?"

"My pleasure, Ma'am," Hostos said enthusiastically, "The crew will be glad to know we have a real officer."

Ito left the ship returning to her flat, pondering again just what she had got herself into, but the reaction of Hostos was a pointer that there was some hope.

"Time will tell," She said to herself as she packed her kit.

While she was doing this, Heta Hostos walked in and gave her a query look.

"I have a new job as the First Officer, with your brother on the *Golden Dream*," Ito answered the implied question.

"Have you lost your marbles? That mobile rat hole, I have been trying to get Bertos off that," Hostos said then sighed, "Well if anyone can fix it you can. Good luck you will need it."

"Thanks, most of the problem is the captain, the company would like to see him retire to the pasture," Ito said, "Okay I am off, you should be fine, once I am out of the picture."

"Break a leg, first officer," Hostos advised with an ironic salute.

"You too, Heta," Ito said saluting, "I will have to get out of that habit, now that I am in the real world."

Ito returned to the *Dream* and marched aboard to stow her kit, then started to tour the ship, Bertos must have passed the word around that there was a new broom to fix the merchant freighter.

Spotting Bertos, Ito said, "Crewman Hostos, would you introduce me to everyone?"

"Certainly Ma'am, Come this way," Hostos grinned as he led the way.

"Mr Botos, the Purser," Indicating a mousy man who glanced up before going back to studying his coffee.

'A real live one,' Ito thought as Bertos escorted her to the Engineering Bay.

"Engineer Moos," Adding, "First Officer Roos."

"Welcome aboard, lassie," Moos said, "Have you been on a working ship before? You have Navy printed all over you."

"Spent some time on the *Challenge*," Ito answered.

"Since you will be carrying most of the load, you took the wrong turn," Moos laughed.

"I am on the nose with the 'Powers That Be' at the moment. So I need some safe runs on the board," Ito said.

"Work hard as you like, at the moment all you will get is blisters," Moos said, "Just keep the boot banging out of engineering deck."

"I will wear my slippers," Ito promised, "See you around, Chief."

Moos waved as they left to see the next department, 'He will do the job,' noting that the equipment was bright and functional, despite being worn and dated.

Next was the freight deck where Foos and Joso had the cargo neatly stowed and securely locked down; there was no rubbish lying around to cause hazards. So the Purser wasn't incompetent just ignorant.

At last, they entered the bridge, her new place of work, it was tidy but only just finished with smears of fluid still drying on the surfaces. At the Radio, and the Navigation stations were Heros and Justos who seemed competent enough. They seemed cheerful that Roos was now in charge.

"What's the weather like where we are going?" Ito asked.

"Fair to middling, if you like eating dust," Heros said.

"So Justos, running the smooth way?" Ito asked.

"Mustn't spill the captain's brew," Justos said, "It would corrode the deck plates."

"How is the population along the way?" Ito asked, "No surprises likely?"

"No only friendlies, though a couple like us to spill a little of the load," Heros said then looked a little apprehensive about letting out a secret, relaxing when Roos didn't comment.

"We lift 0900 tomorrow, all cargo aboard ready?"

"All reports are on the computer screen, Botos is on the ball, he doesn't like surprises or problems," Justos said.

"Who does the cooking?"

"Hostos and I make some basic stuff. If you are fussy, I will show you where the pots and pans are," Heros said, "If I didn't do some I would starve."

"Or poisoned if Botos was made to do it," Justos chimed in with an ironic laugh.

"On a three-crew Scout, you learn to cook or starve; please note that I am still alive. As long as others take a turn they will stay that way; I will check the stores myself to see if we have a reasonable pantry."

Ito made her way to the kitchen and mess hall, the last aptly named with the method seeming to be to only clean when you can't find a dish. She looked around to assess the stores, she surveyed the pantry and noted that the basics were all they had.

"Time to order a better variety of victuals, herbs and spices," to herself and went to nail the Purser down.

"Mr Botos, I have looked at the pantry, I believe that if we had these," Ito said handing over the list, "We may eat a little better."

Botos just glanced at it before flipping it back, "Can't afford fripperies," Botos said in a disinterested tone.

"I have some credit left from my last ship. If you can't be bothered, I will get it myself," Ito stated.

"You do that, as long as you don't expect me to applaud," Botos grunted.

"Yeah wouldn't want to disturb your rest." She could have saved her breath.

Locating Crewman Hostos, "Come with me I am going shopping."

Not looking over-enthusiastic, He asked, "What do you need Ma'am?"

"Do you like the grub bait they serve, well how about something that has a little taste?" Ito asked.

"'I am ready, let's go, Ma'am," Bertos said now interested.

The pair marched over to the commissary and were soon loading the required stores onto a trolley they had borrowed.

"Once we take this back to the ship I will teach you how to cook food which has some taste. Don't worry that you will be stuck with all of it, Heros and I will still take turns."

"Thanks, boss, glad to help," Bertos said.

They returned to the ship and packed away their treasure, "Reckon old Botos will knock this back and still eat the slop that he is fond of?" Bertos asked.

"Time will tell, I know I will prefer something better," Ito laughed and started demonstrating scout cuisine.

"Basic but tasty, easy to knock up with limited equipment, rotating these herbs and spices adds variety," Ito said as she went through the cooking process, "The food also keeps the taste long enough for duty people to enjoy it when they come off watch."

Bertos tasted it and declared, "Great, and seemed to take no effort."

"Just don't overdo the spices," Ito said with a smile, "Remember to be a spendthrift with the herbs and a miser for the spice."

"I will learn," Bertos said, "Beats comic books on my bunk."

"Oh? I thought something a bit more challenging would be your preference?"

"I used to when I thought I had a chance to transfer to the Navy," Bertos said a bit down.

"Work hard for me, and you never know," Ito advised, "Remember that a lot of little skills add to promotion prospects."

"Sounds good, I am all ears," Bertos agreed.

"Mind you, more exciting jobs carry increased danger; I nearly bought the farm on my first command. And before that, the time playing infantry was on the dangerous side of exciting. A thrown rock can spoil your day just as easily as an Ion Cannon."

Together they cooked a meal for the crew, so it was ready when they walked in expecting the usual hash. The aroma alone surprised the people as they served themselves and sat to eat; the smiles told it all,

"Who cooked this?" Moos asked.

"Crewman Hostos," Ito said giving him a wink, "I gave him some pointers."

"Yeah? As long as he keeps this up he is on to a winner," Heros said.

'Two sections down two to go,' She thought.

Bosos only needs a little humanity and learn the joy of living; the bridge a little discipline, the skill was there just needed a little direction. At this stage, it left the captain to deal with; more data required the problem ran deep.

The lift-off was due early morning, so after an hours systems check, Ito was satisfied that essential maintenance hadn't been any shortcut in action. It was probably only time before that happened, but so far Chief Moos had kept up the task with diminishing spares.

Having assured herself that the ship wouldn't fall apart on liftoff, she settled for the night ready for a walk around well before due time.

At the appointed time, Ito announced, "Ready for liftoff, sir." to the Captain.

"Whatever," Came back the answer from the cabin.

With a raised eyebrow, "Energise gravity drive Mr Justos." The named glanced at her in surprise but actuated the device.

"Crewman Hostos steer North, liftoff." "Engaging drive, accelerate to Mach 0.5," She did the last but still said the order. When you were solo, it was okay to say it under your breath, as it acted as a mnemonic to make sure you don't miss a step.

The *Golden Dream* rose smoothly into the sky as advertised, *'so far so good'.*

The *Dream* cruised out to the jump point at a typical merchant freighter's speed using minimum fuel. This speed was torture for someone used to the military which didn't ration fuel.

The dream arrived at the jump and engaged Hyperdrive, entering the grey without drama. As Justos was the duty officer, Ito ordered, "Your watch Mr Justos."

"Aye, ma'am," He acknowledged with a cheeky grin, on a small merchant it was just, 'yours'.

Ito went aft and checked in each department. The galley was neat and clean, in the cargo section the stevedores were completing their inspections, "All secure boys?"

"Aye Ma'am," Foos answered, with a little pride that someone was interested.

"Carry on the good work," Ito said to convey a little well done.

Arriving at the engineering department, Chief Moos has just finished handing over to his hand Mech Etos.

"Chief, humming along?" Ito asked.

"Naturally, Miss Roos," Moos said, "At this pace, it rusts before it wears out."

"What can it do if a nasty is on the tail?"

"Rollover and pretend to be dead," Moos laughed, "We then open the captain's cabin, and the fumes will deter them."

"The captain? Is he much help?"

Glancing around Moos told Etos, "Go up to the bridge, the radio needs the crystals checked for cracks."

Etos nodded and hurried out.

Once he was gone, Moos said, "One of the most capable merchant captains, until he hit a few bad patches and then the bottle. You served on the *Challenge*?"

"Yes, a fine ship."

"Captain Mostos had a similar ship until he refused an assignment because he wanted to close a good trade," Moos said, "Then he was bumped down a couple of ship classes and the rot set in."

"Yes that can happen, care must be taken not to rock the boat as rewards are great, while the subtle punishments are hidden and deadly. I blotted my copybook a couple of times, while the bosses agreed that it was policy failures and not mine, here I am."

"Sounds like my career, promising then misfortune, I have been sucked down the same path as the captain," Moos grimaced, "Birds of a feather are tarred together."

"Expect me to halt the slide, in my best interest of course. When I drag myself up by my bootstraps, all those who work with me come as well."

"I depend on that, Missy," Moos grinned, "Or should I call you number One?"

"Missy will do, Chief," Ito laughed, "So the captain, light a match under him or find a cart big enough to transport him to pasture?"

"Look better on your resume if he is booted back upstairs," Moos suggested.

"Good point, any ideas?"

"When the old man did the dickering we made money, Botos just accepts what he is offered, he will never make a real merchant," Moos said, "Afraid to spend a mil to earn a credit."

"Modestly I have a few talents in that area; I doubt that me stepping into the job will upset either man."

"Botos doesn't challenge the captain; perhaps when the coin starts to roll in, the Old man could be stung into proving he still has the touch," Moos suggested.

"One can hope, Chief, my watch will be on soon enough."

"Yes, Missy," Moos said.

Ito waved as she headed for a snack and rest before she was needed next.

The routine settled in, and the *Dream* emerged from Hyper to find a backwater colony called Hern, the population was eager to receive their stores. As a recently settled planet, it was raw with dirt roads meandering into the distance. Around the port were the usual shanty towns interspersed with more substantial Warehouses and Taverns.

After landing and having the customs inspection completed at the Hern Port; Ito was waiting for Botos to emerge and approach a merchant.

Tired of waiting went looking for him and found him in his usual stance with his mug of coffee.

"Mister Botos, thinking of doing your job any time today?" She asked.

"I will get around to it," Botos grunted.

"Give me a list of what you need, what we have to swap, and I will do it for you," Ito said trying to keep her temper.

"The captain is my boss," Botos glanced at her to see if she would leave, then with a shrug slid a tablet towards her, "Here is the data, fill your boots."

Taking the tablet, Ito said, "Sorry to spoil your rest." She could have saved her breath as Botos just ignored her.

She went to the rec room and studied the data; this was a bit sparse, but with a little thought, it would do.

Locating Bertos who had just come off watch, "Crewman Hostos. Tired of lounging around?" Ito asked.

As this was normally a prelude to exercise or something interesting, Bertos looked a little ambivalent.

"Aye, Ma'am," Bertos said.

"Several things; I need a hand, you may learn some merchant techniques, and I have a friendly face to talk to," Ito said, "Sounds like fun?"

"Aye, ma'am," Bertos answered with a little more enthusiasm.

"Off we go, this time I have to visit all the warehouses to see what they have and what they need," Ito said.

Together they canvassed the warehouse offices and public bars, to see what was the atmosphere and the locality of possible customers.

As this was a rough, new colony, Merchants conducted most of their business at the latter; so going to the bar, Ito asked the barman who might be likely freight dealers.

The barman assessed the two facing him, Ito fit and well armed with Bertos a backup, "Try Festos over there he knows where they hide all the bodies, just keep a hand on your wallet," He said indicating a table towards the rear.

"Thanks, Have a drink on me," She said flipping a few credits on the bar. The barman just wiped them off into his pocket as he knew what was in the bottles.

Grabbing her drink and gesturing Bertos to a vantage spot, Ito walked over and greeted the better-dressed man at the table, "Mr Festos?" She asked.

"Depends on who's asking?" He grunted.

"First Officer Roos off the *Golden Dream*, I am searching for a merchant I can trade."

"Perhaps, what merchandise do you have?" Festos asked slightly interested, "Where is Botos?"

"Resting," Shes said, "Here is the stuff we have."

Festos did a quick survey, "So, nothing new, see Jestos over at the Crow's Head Warehouse down the street; he handles this range of goods; I will add what I have to sell." He downloaded some information on the tablet, "Get your coin from him, and we will make a deal on my goods."

"Thanks for your time," Ito said, stood and beckoned her crewman, then went to look for the named warehouse. She had entered it earlier but found no one at the counter.

"Perhaps we bang harder this time, Jestos might be having a snooze," She commented to Bertos.

Once they had located the warehouse, the pair entered and

knocked on the counter. After a few loud knocks, a grumble came from the rear, "What do you want?"

"Mr Jestos?" Ito asked, "First officer Roos from the *Dream*."

A man stumbled out scratching his belly, "That's me, you're a bit early, Botos doesn't visit me till later."

"I am taking over the job, it is too much bother for him," Ito said, "Here is what we have, give me your best offer."

Jestos gave her a look and surveyed the list, "Twenty thousand credits," Jestos stated.

"For that, I could have saved myself the trip. To make it worthwhile, I would need at least fifty thousand."

Jestos brightened up at the challenge, though he said with a sorrowful mien, "That would leave me broke, no one would pay the wholesale price; I could stretch the offer to twenty-five."

"Know anyone else who would like this invaluable cargo? If so, I won't take up any more of your valuable time."

"Now don't be hasty. Come into my office, and we can sit down while I watch my life savings disappear, and my children sent to an orphanage," Jestos invited.

Once seated, Jestos reviewed the goods, "I see some items that Botos doesn't usually offer me, perhaps we can swing a little more?"

After some chin scratching, "Let me see, throw those in, and I can scrape up Forty," Jestos said.

"Forty-two and you have a deal; I have to feed this growing boy you know." Pointing at a surprised Bertos.

"Forty-one, my best offer," Jestos said.

"Done, on the next visit what would you like me to bring?"

"It will take me ages to move this at your extravagant charges, but I suppose I can use these," Jestos smiled as he added several items, "If I can promise my customers a good price on those we will both be happy."

"These goods that Festos has, could you supply them at mates rates?"

"I could, but he wouldn't send any more marks over to be fleeced," Jestos advised, "Here are the prices which the other merchants pay which still allows him a fair profit." He had written this information on a scrap of paper.

"Thank you; I won't tell him where I found it. If my Uncle Fedo were here, he would nail his hide to the wall to get the best deal."

"Fedo Roos? I thought the name was familiar," Jestos said, "If I had known earlier I would have had more fun stringing you out, and you may have ended a couple of thousand better off."

"Now you tell me," Ito laughed, "It has been a pleasure, I will make sure that I return and entertain you a little better."

On the way, she said to Bertos, "Can you look a little starving when I throw you a line?"

Ito and Bertos now returned to the Bar where she approached Festos. After signalling for drinks, "Ah that Jestos stung me deeply, barely have beer money," Ito started morosely, "I could only get a couple of containers of these at those prices. I could help you clear some space in the shed if you were kind?'

"Well if you need the ballast, I could throw in some odd bit or so," Festos grumbled, "I would have to move in with my mother-in-law if I gave away too much."

"I am trying to make a good impression with my first trip how about another six at a group rate?" she countered.

"Three extra is the best," Festos said, "Otherwise the bar would go broke if I had to move my sign out."

"Four? And I have a case of genuine bourbon from Aaska."

"Aaska where's that?" Festos asked.

"Me to know, it will clean out your gut no dramas."

"Done," Festos said, "You are more fun than Botos. he drops an order on the table and bolts."

"Part of being a merchant."

"When's old Gedo Mostos going to visit?" Festos asked.

"He may come looking for his medicine," Ito suggested.

"Once Jestos unloads, I will send the boys out to drop this stuff off, Bourbon and credits to be waiting," Festos said standing and shaking on it, "It has been a pleasure having my lively-hood stolen."

"You drove a hard bargain; I will have trouble covering it up to the boss."

"Roos, any relation to Fedo?" Festos asked.

"Uncle, he would have skinned you," Ito grinned.

"Yes, he likely would. It won't be long before all the merchants run and hide when they hear that you are coming," Festos said.

"Good to have met you, I will sneak in and surprise you next time we are passing," Ito waved as she left.

She gathered Bertos and returned to the ship; he asked on the way, "He didn't look as upset as he made out to be?"

"What he lost in profit margin, he gained with the entertainment," She said, "I've read the past results, we are at double of the last visit and will have a full load to fill the hold."

Having surveyed her surroundings casually, Ito spotted movement behind. "Umm heads up we have company, want to bet they have friends at the next alleyway."

Bertos settled his pistol, "Why would they, not like any cash has changed hands?"

"Perhaps they think we have some," Ito said out the side of her mouth.

She swung a little wide as they neared the suspect alley. A couple of figures moved from the shadows and moved forward casually, as faster steps behind caught up.

Ito having watched this approach out of the corner of her eye then ducked a billy club which was swinging at her head and delivered a kick to the fellow's stomach doubling him up, then delivered a diaphragm punch which flattened his companion. Bertos had pinned a third against a wall after pushing him against it, face first. The shadows started to charge but thought better of it when she pointed her pistol at them. These men then backed off.

"Let that man go. Don't tie up your shooting hand while others are lurking nearby," Ito advised, and Bertos slammed his man hard enough to discourage any fight then drew his pistol.

"Good point. You handle yourself well Ma'am," Bertos said.

"Nasty Kindy I went to," Ito said straight-faced, "If no one else wants to play. Shall we return to a more civilised place?"

"Yes, there is probably some work waiting for me," Bertos said.

Once she entered the ship, she sought out Botos and handed him the bill for the new stuff which he nearly had a fit over before reading the invoice for the cargo to be unloaded. He noted that the difference was well in profit so he couldn't complain about that, only whinge how he would fit in the new cargo.

"That is your part of the ship; you can let your boss know if you need more hands," Ito said leaving pleased with herself.

Botos just grunted, easing himself up to get Foos and Jaso on the job.

Despite his protests, the cargo was exchanged and stored neatly before the Dream was due to lift.

After the jump, there was a bellow from the captain's cabin, "Roos get in here."

Ito shrugged and entered, "You bellowed?"

"Botos is complaining that you overloaded the hold, probably now we have to move the stock at a loss," Mostos said.

"Only a loss if you let Botos sell it. I think I can get a good deal from either of the next two stops. If the first doesn't buy the whole lot, we can finish with the next."

"And not have enough spare room to load what we usually pick up at Grenz?" Mostos grumbled.

"Grenz? If you warned me it would have been nice. I could have bought more and made a killing."

"I seem to be missing a case of my bourbon, know anything about that?" Mostos demanded.

"Was that yours? It had no name on it and was cluttering up the pantry, so I sweetened the deal with Festos," Ito said innocently.

"Ask next time, I suppose you struck a good deal," Mostos said, "Fedo taught you well, eh? We used to have a competition running, to see who could rip the most skin off the grounder merchants. Those were the days." The last with a sigh.

"Picked up a few hints, I can always learn more from a master."

"You do that," Mostos said, "Out."

"Aye Captain," Ito said as she marched out with a grin he couldn't see.

'Step one,' she thought, 'Now no stumbles, and we are on the way.'

The next system to be visited as Mostos told her was Grenz. By the records, they usually bought all the goods that the ship had purchased from the Hern Colony. On the earlier visits, there had been larger deliveries which had all been taken up. So she was confident that she could move the full amount.

The ship swung into a low orbit over a large green planet dotted with cities. The extensive sealed roads indicated that this was a longer settled world having established itself as a trading hub. The customs team carried out the inspection efficiently; soon they vectored into a spaceport on the outside of a city with the usual warehouses and facilities to cater to visiting travellers.

As the record also had a contact name, she had a better start as when she was on the Challenge they had visited, and Fedo bought similar goods so had a fair idea about the relative value.

Making a few notes, Ito was as ready as she could be so when with Bertos in hand headed to the first stop and located merchant Ferna who was trying to hide his desire to receive cargo.

"Good day Mr Ferna, how is your wife Heno and your daughter Fen nowadays?" Ito asked, "I am Ito Roos, I was with Fedo Roos a few years ago."

"Oh the silent girl," Ferna said, "Too much to hope that Fedo didn't teach you everything?"

"Hardly remember a thing, I have to depend on you being kind to a beginner. Here is my load, if you can't take it all, perhaps you can suggest someone who can help."

"Since I like Fedo, I can put the weights on him to reciprocate if I am too generous with you," Ferna said, after reading the data, "I believe that 30 k would be straining the friendship, but I will stretch it for the sake of old times.'

"Perhaps I do remember a little, my ship carried it all the way here and to at least cover that I need sixty," Ito said looking disappointed.

"Forty and I would almost have to give it to Fedo without covering handling," Ferna complained.

She pretended to have a memory surface, "I vaguely remember he paid seventy-five and gloated over the deal," Ito said, "Reckons he skinned you and he would have spent another couple of thousand and still made a profit. And that was Five years ago."

"Really? I didn't remember," Ferna said, "Well I can go Forty-five, which would leave me a small margin to work with when I deal with your uncle."

"Bertos, what was the name of that merchant? Berno or something," Ito asked absently, to receive a nod from him.

"Funny, he would undercut my offer and leave you worse off," Ferna groaned theatrically, "I will be losing after I pay storage and handling. Okay, I am sweating blood but will Fifty cover it?"

"That should keep the wolves from the door, just promise me that you won't tell Uncle Fedo?" Ito asked.

"You have my word on it," Ferna solemnly promised and shook hands.

"Thank you; perhaps I can get a better deal next time? I am off to Etuadean next, could you help me select the right load to buy?"

"It would be my pleasure," Ferna offered, "What I can't supply, I will put a word out to make sure you get a good deal. Perhaps suggest that Fedo wouldn't be happy if I told him that Berno shorted his tally last visit."

"We can't upset him like that. He probably thought he got the best of the deal, must be slipping in his old age. Oh, don't tell him that," Ito said looking worried.

After dickering a while, Ferna struck a deal for the new load, and Ito returned to the Dream satisfied that she was making a profit at each step.

Botos grumbled again as he had to juggle the load to fit it all in the holds.

"Don't worry I have reported that the ship is doing well and allow the boss to spread the glory to all the crew," Ito said, "If something goes pear-shaped I am sure I will get the blame."

Botos grumbled, but he sounded a little brighter if that was possible.

After Etuadean; the next run was back to Forno with the cargo hold full of rare minerals, some purchased, and other lots on consignment.

Ito had tallied the total up after unloading at the terminal, and the balance was looking promising. Another circuit like that and the *Golden Dream* would be in the black. Life was starting to turn around.

While she was settling the last of the spares and victuals, she noticed that Botos had added a better range of goods and lighter beverages than that had been in the stores before.

As she toured the bridge, she observed that the *Challenge* had set down nearby, on impulse she radioed, "*Golden Dream* to *Forno Challenge*, First Officer Roos. Who is your current Captain?"

"Me Ito, they can't get rid of me that easy, are you coming over for a chat?" Fedo Roos asked.

"Give me five, and I will be over, *Dream* out," Ito said.

Trotting over, Ito called, "Hello the *Challenge*, First Officer Roos, permission to come aboard?"

"Come in, come in, Ito," Fedo called from the top of the ramp.

When she had entered, Fedo said, "You are looking fit, is a first officer up or down the scale?"

"Down I am afraid, but I have turned the pointer towards the better," Ito said with a grin.

"What's this I hear you are stirring everyone in the sector? I got trimmed five per cent in Grenz; Ferna wouldn't tell me where he received the idea," Fedo said.

"Oh really, how could I have had anything to do with that," Ito tried to sound innocent.

"Well don't let me catch you at it, the deals have taken me years to work the best price," Fedo complained.

"I am just pushing the proverbial uphill with a fork," Ito said, "Do you remember Gedo Mostos?"

"Yes, how is old Gedo?" Fedo asked.

"Just about dragging the bottom," Ito said, "There is a slight chance I can get him motivated, but if I fail it is grounding for him."

"Hmm, I don't see if I could do anything except remind him how far he has slipped," Fedo said, "If you continue to turn the ship around as you have done, the hurdle will make or break Gedo."

"On a brighter note, how is the *Challenge* faring?" Ito asked.

"With this crew, almost perfect, with you as my Number 1, it would be perfect," Fedo laughed.

"The Powers That Be decreed that the Navy was better off without me for a while," Ito said, "I think someone set me up for the *Dream*. I don't know yet whether to track them down and do something nasty or to thank them."

"Time will tell," Fedo said with an innocent air then asked, "Want to have a wander through the Challenge?"

"Better not or I won't be able to stomach the *Dream*," Ito grimaced, "I have raised the Morale meter 10 points which only just brings it into positive figures."

"Well keep it up, and you will be back in the good books. Just stop white-anting my business," Fedo said, "I will see you off and make sure you leave all the silver spoons behind."

"Ha! It has been a pleasant visit," Ito said.

After Ito had returned to the *Dream*, while it was a bit of a letdown, she had started the long climb to make it the best ship it could be.

Reviewing the program for the next tour, it was the same. Ito had purchased those items that Jestos had wanted, plus a few that she thought may be useful as sweeteners.

Botos was a little animated and seemed almost happy to be challenged to find storage for the load. They were lifting with a full hold this time.

Emerging into the Hern system, they made planetfall and secured the ship. This time Ito went straight to Jestos to commence the negotiation. She was ushered directly into his office

"Welcome Ito Roos, what do you have for me this time?" Jestos asked, then as he surveyed the data, "Ah looks promising."

"All that you asked for, plus a couple of teasers, to test the market," Ito answered.

"Mmm. I have barely finished moving the last lot, and some of the customers are a little tardy with their bill. With this stuff, I can offer Thirty to start and catch up the next visit," Jestos started the bargaining.

"I had to fight my way through a hoard of your competitors to get here, embarrassing to have to stop them throwing money at me, the lowest offer was fifty," She said, "I ignored it as insulting."

"And you said that with a straight face?" Jestos asked, "You are learning too fast. Forty-five and I have to raid my first child's school fund."

"Didn't you say that you had more than one child, I remember hearing that you had a starving hoard?" Ito asked, "I was considering Sixty from Festos, he mentioned cutting out the middleman."

"Ha, he would want to pay with used socks, I can scrape up fifty if I lean on the slack payers." Jestos offered.

"Since you were so generous last time; I suppose I could take a small loss; Mind you I will have to make it up next time."

"Done, I promise to have a little more cash next time as long as you can deliver a bit more of your new line," Jestos said shaking on it. "My children will have no candles to blow out on their birthday cakes; I don't know how I will face them."

"I am sure that you will think of something. Convince the kids that the smoke and flames are dangerous for their health," She suggested.

"Oh, good idea, I will try that," Jestos said, "Best you see Festos before he gets too drunk and tight arse."

"Thanks, I will see you next time," Ito said.

"I will look forward to it," Jestos said, "Farewell."

Roos walked out to seek Festos and see what he had to sell.

After an hours haggling, she left a happy Festos with ten per cent more than last time. With a little more cash and some spare room she made a couple of more deals to pad out the hold.

Having transferred the loads, the *Dream* was ready for the trip to Grenz.

Botos scurried around ensuring the all was stowed snugly, this without too many grumbles.

Captain Mostos called her, "Number One, my cabin.'

Ito entered, "Sir."

"Relax we are in the real world, not too bad a deal, though I think I will come on the next visit, and show you what an expert can do," Mostos stated, "Run along I expect a nice meal to make up for the shortfall."

Hiding a smile, she left to arrange that, as most of the crew were busy securing the cargo, she started the cooking with a few additions that she had picked up from the markets.

So when everyone had completed loading they were delighted to find that dinner was ready to serve and a special treat. Ito served a meal in containers and was about to take that up to the Captain, only for him to walk into the mess hall for the first time since she boarded. Hastily putting it on a plate, she had it waiting by the time he arrived at the server.

"No need for that, I am capable of dishing out my own, sit-down and enjoy yours, Number One," Mostos said as he did so, taking a seat next to her.

After tasting, he said, "This is great, about time that someone learnt to cook around here."

"I am glad you like it, still a little short of my best, everyone else was busy, so I chipped in," Ito said.

"Well I hope that you are training someone else for this, you have a too important a job to use up your time," Mostos said.

"Crewman Hostos is coming along grandly, won't be long before he shades my efforts," Ito said with a wink at Bertos, who beamed.

"So, Grenz is next?" Mostos asked, "I should visit a couple of my old friends and see if they are still alive."

"The merchants said they missed you, said I drove too hard a bargain and that you were a soft touch," Ito said.

"They tell everyone that, complain that you are sending them to the poorhouse not like so and so," Mostos laughed, "I will soon show them that I can still drive a good bargain."

Once they had landed at Grenz spaceport, Mostos was waiting

for when Ito and Bertos started off the ship for the rounds of the merchants.

"If you are ready best we get them before they are fully awake, nice touch to ensure ship time is ahead of ground, so we are bright and bushy-tailed," Gedo said.

"I remember that Uncle Fedo used that to good effect," Ito said.

"Your boy, coming along?" Gedo said indicating Bertos.

"With some fatherly advice I am sure he will make a credible merchant one day," Ito said.

"Ha, don't push your luck," Gedo said.

Still, they arrived at Ferna's warehouse where Gedo walked in and greeted like an old friend, "Ferna, you old scoundrel, haven't they hung you yet?"

"They have to hook me first. You have put on a little condition, won't get a medal for the next run?" Ferna said.

"Muscle just slipped a little, a couple of safety pins will soon fix that. I have a good load, and Berno tells me your customers are so desperate for any product that they are kicking the doors down," Gedo said to start.

"He would lie to his grandma if she hadn't already disowned him," Ferna disclaimed, "Let me see your rubbish, I may have an odd spot on a shelf to fill out of charity."

Ferna scanned the tablet, "As a friend; I can offer 35 k for this load; it will clutter up my shelves for months," He said.

"Do I have to spend the next six months pushing my ship because I can't afford the fuel. Sixty would be giving it away," Gedo moaned.

"The exercise wouldn't hurt you, for the sake of your poor crew having to watch you sweat, I can stretch to forty," Ferna offered, "My poor children will be begging on the street."

"I thought they were already, Berno said were a Fagin," Gedo getting into the mood, "How about Fifty-Five, Bertos can go on a diet."

"Throw in this and this," Indicating some other items, "That would lighten your load to make it easier to push."

"I was saving those for a special customer, what will I tell him?" Gedo said.

"The same as you told the bar girl, that I was too smart for you," Ferna suggested.

"Now that is a fib, okay it is a deal, so what is bound for Etcadean?" Gedo shook on it.

"Oh a little of this and a little of that," Ferna said, "Now they cost me a lot, and I was waiting for Fedo Roos to come in so I could tempt him."

"Ito, would you like to have a look around the town? Bertos can keep me company as we may be a while," Gedo suggested.

"As you wish, I wouldn't like to cramp your style, Captain," Ito said, "I will tease a couple of other merchants and tell them what Ferna talked you out of."

This promise received a protest from Gedo and a smile from Ferna.

As she strolled out thinking *Yes things are looking up.*

This advance had started the mood for further involvement of Gedo in the running of the ship, even took the helm (to show Bertos) for a watch.

He was now exercising, shaving and wearing a clean uniform, visiting the sections to talk to the crew.

After a year of this routine, a call from head office brought good news instead of the usual bad.

"Number One, my office," Gedo said, "I have some news for you. I am transferring to another ship with my best officers. I am afraid you are stuck with the old girl and have to break in new people. So once we hit Forno Port, you are the Captain."

"That is mixed news. So what class are you getting?" Ito asked.

"A bit bigger and newer, the *Bren Haven*," Gedo said, "Perhaps Hostos may make a good third?"

"I would have to train up a new cook," Ito answered, "Not an armed class?"

"No, and just the right size, so that I won't be bothered with side trips," Gedo laughed.

"Those cut into the profits," Ito said, "So I will look forward to being white-anted by you, that should make life interesting."

"I think we may offer a little competition," Gedo said, "Carry on, number one."

"Aye sir," Ito acknowledged.

The Forno port arrived the cargo discharged, and Captain Roos escorted Captain Gedo Mostos off the *Dream* to assume his new command.

Then she waited while her new officers were assigned, but first to deliver the good news.

"Leading Crewman Bertos Hostos, to the bridge," Captain Roos ordered over the intercom.

"Aye Ma'am," Bertos said as he arrived, the shine still new on that rank.

"The time has come to the end of your lazing around, I think the Third Officer position should stretch you a bit more," Ito said, "It is still nearly the lowest of the low. but I expect a lot as well."

"I am overwhelmed. Thank you, Captain," Bertos said.

"You earned it, Mr Hostos, carry on," Ito ordered.

He smiled and saluted then settled into his new post as navigator.

The two new deck officers arrived and extra crewmen to fill the lower rung after Ito promoted Foos to Purser and Joso to the leading hand of the cargo wranglers, Etos became the new Chief Engineer.

Two new first and second officers, Fostos and Jaroos, engineer's mate Naroos with another two as Cargo crew.

After assigning jobs, Ito gathered the crew onto the bridge to brief them.

"Welcome Ladies and gentlemen, we have a massive task to produce, just about everyone is new to their position, and we now have high expectations to perform to the previous mark," Ito stated, "I have the fullest confidence that we will soon better it. That is all carry-on."

"Aye, Ma'am," They all responded as they went about their jobs.

When everyone confident with each task, Ito organised the next tour, the tower gave the clearance for the departure, and the *Golden Dream* took for its next round of dealing.

The first port was Hern as usual where she found Jestos waiting, "Welcome Captain, What do you tempt me with today?"

"Most of the usual, a few extras and a sharp pencil," Ito said, "News travels fast, Gedo only just received his shiny new toy."

"He beat you here, so he has filled my shelves up, and I can only squeeze a bit more in," Jestos moaned, "I suppose I had better take a look, though don't expect me to pay much."

"I have a ship full of beginners what can I tell them if I return empty-handed," Ito said looking sad.

"Out of friendship I can offer 30 k for this," Jestos offered.

"I would hate to be an enemy, it cost me Sixty to bring it here," Ito returned.

The to and fro ran on until they achieved a fair price, each called the other robbing scoundrel before shaking on it and the usual promise to do better next time.

Then on to Festos for much the same result. While not better, this made the usual mark, so Ito was satisfied. It would be strange returning to the ship and have everyone happy to see the deals she had struck. The new escort Noos was a silent spectator and just there as muscle.

Purser Foos was waiting, eager to exchange the cargo and organise the storage.

Almost like pushing the door and finding it open, it was nearly too easy, "I suppose I had better get used to it," Ito said to herself.

With the regular profits, the *Golden Dream* was starting to live up to its name, and Bertos was starting to engage in the trading side of the business and that he had learnt the ropes. When the company posted Fostos and then Jaros, Ito quietly promoted Bertos to the second and then the first officer position. Bertos was starting to pressure Ito for the Captain's position. Not that that worried her because she expected to be bumped up the roster and into a more prominent ship once the company gave Bertos the nod.

Never the less it came as a surprise that she was ordered to report to the Navy Administration for an interview.

Ambassador

LT COMMANDER ROOS MARCHED TO THE Administration building where an aide ushered her to the admiral's office. The department had called Ito using her old Navy rank which boded well for the possibility of military command.

"Commander Ito Roos to see you, sir," The secretary announced.

Ito marched in and saluted.

"Good morning Ito," Admiral Hostos said in welcome, "I suppose you would like to know what I have in store for you?"

"Many guesses have entered my mind, but please have the pleasure of surprising me, Sir," Ito replied.

"It has come to my attention that you are wasting your talents as a merchant," Hostos said, "So I have a little task to perform, it requires your considerable talents and shall we say luck."

"You have my interest, sir," Ito admitted.

"Now it may seem over the top as an honour, but it does carry a high risk. I want you to be the Ambassador to the Empire at Aurea," Hostos said, "Calm and diplomacy are necessary for the position as is strategic skills."

"A very great honour. I would expect some danger or career diplomats would be appointed?" Ito asked rhetorically.

"The hierarchy is shall we say touchy, and a couple of esteemed Ambassadors have been returned in pieces when they commented adversely on Empire policy," Hostos said, "Not ours but it makes career diplomats just a little nervous."

"Mmm, I will need to catch up on my reading. So when do I leave?"

"Next week, I have five ships assigned to convoy you, as the route is hazardous," Hostos advised, "The position carries the status of acting Commodore, as well as Ambassador Pro Tem. Good luck, Commodore Roos."

"Meaning I'll need it, Thanks, Sir," Ito said saluting before marching out to find her new fleet and Flagship. Wondering why it needed the promotion of three grades for this to be carried out, even temporary Ambassador was rarified heights.

On the way she picked up the brief on which ships and Captains, "Good, the flagship is the *Challenge*, Captain Roos, Lt Commanders Hostos, Foos great, Lt Commander Zenos, sensible man, Mmm, Commander Hoos; now I know why the luck is needed.

There was the *Challenge* waiting, "Old home week I wonder who is still in the crew?" Ito thought.

There was the required guard of honour complete with the Chief Boson's Mate ready with his pipe, how she hated this time wasting when she stood in the ranks. Still, protocol demanded that the ship's company announce to the world their new status as Flagship.

The pipe sounded the guard snapped to attention. The Captain saluted, and Ito Roos returned the salute.

Captain Roos stood waiting at the dais and repeated the salute, "Welcome aboard Ma'am," Fedo said.

"My pleasure, it is great to see the old girl again," Ito said, "You are looking well. If you have had your fun, shall we adjourn to the ready room and we can have a chat on the task."

"Sounds good to me," Fedo said, waving towards the ramp, "Chief Ghos hides it well, but he is looking forward to his favourite student returning."

"How would you know that? Uncle Fedo?"

"He almost smiled, I could hear the face cracking," Fedo said.

The arrived at the ready room and displayed the galactic map, "There is our destination; The Empire is currently reduced to the Corellian Sector. I have the job of presenting our case to the new

Emperor. Rumour has it that the top two are Adverse Adepts who have touchy trigger fingers," Ito said, "On the way, there are rogue ex-imperials. These are trying to set up their little kingdoms. Intelligence only lists one Sun Destroyer, and that one is with the Oxzens."

"So I heard, Rham is at least a reasonable man. The others are an unknown quantity," Fedo said, "With five in our convoy it seems overkill. *Challenge* by herself is a formidable force."

"Needs must when the 'powers that be' set the policy. The strategy is to show sufficient strength to set the status, just powerful enough to be noticed, and not so much that it makes them nervous," Ito said.

"We shall see, the other Captains will be joining us soon," Fedo advised, "Ah there is the first." As the pipe sounded with a little less flourish,

Another two echoed shortly after and then at the last second the fourth.

"I bet I can guess who was last," Ito grimaced.

The four captains arrived, and yes there was Zento Hoos wearing commander's rank, with Lt Commanders Hostos, Foos and Zenos.

"Welcome, excellent to see you all, ready for a boring cruise?" Ito said as she returned their salutes.

They all laughed aware that was unlikely to happen if Ito Roos was involved.

"As you see, this is the destination, the Empire. This path avoids most of the pirate dens," Ito said, "Zento, please remember that the Imperials believe they are the same. Their Government doesn't like anyone reminding that they are a remnant."

"I have had it pounded in by everyone I see, that they are regrouping and ready to expand any second," Zento said ruefully.

"Expect to have a reminder every time that I see you," Ito said then added, "Captain Roos is the tactician, and he will call the shots if he says duck do so with alacrity."

"The techs have fitted all ships with the anti-sleep shield, I found out the hard way to switch it on early," Ito said, "I don't expect to run across the Oxzens but a stitch in time. Questions?"

"Nothing useful, we have dissected the orders at our last brief,"

Zento said, "And just twiddling our thumbs have come up with the same policy."

The brief settled the Captains returned to their ships.

"Well, Uncle Fedo, what do you reckon?" Ito asked relaxing when the others had departed.

"Sounds like Hoos is still a work in progress, Foos and Hostos passed through the *Challenge* after you, and I hear they benefited from your mentoring, Zenos is a reliable officer and can handle unusual situations," Fedo considered.

"I could have picked worse, if Commander Hoos can restrain his enthusiasm, he will be useful," Ito said, "I will go for a tour, please give them the heads up for no fuss."

"I will tell them you are only a diplomat, that will do it," Fedo laughed.

Ito made her way down the familiar passageways greeting some old faces and seeing startled fresh faces as they tried to fade into the paintwork.

Entering Engineering, Roos spotted Chief Ghos and went up to him and said, "Good day Chief, have any puddles you need cleaning up?"

"No, my last victim dried it up with his bum when he put his foot in it. Welcome aboard Senior Ensign," Ghos said.

"As funny as always," Ito said, "Good to see you. How is your protege Leader Bosos?"

"Lucky lad is chief on his favourite student's ship," Ghos said, "I loved the look on his face, first the promotion then the captain, I still laugh at the memory."

"I will put a good word in with the hierarchy for him to replace you when you swallow the anchor," Ito suggested.

"Never happen, they plan to preserve me and scare newbie ensigns for generations," Ghos said.

"I thought that had already happened before I came here, they scare naughty kids at kindergarten with your image," Ito laughed.

"Get along with you," Ghos said.

"I will see you around, Chief," Ito said.

He just waved, with her ship tour completed, she adjourned to the VIP cabin, now designated the flag suite.

It promised to be frustrating, as a flag officer, she was expected to stay out of the way and let the crew get on with the job.

The lift-off time arrived, and Ito joined the bridge crew in the new Commodore's seat close enough to the action to see what was going on but enough out of the way to be not a bother.

The ship lifted off and proceeded to the jump point with the other four maintaining formation alongside. At the second system, the radar showed several blips on an intercept course; Captain Roos ordered Action stations and the five ships prepared for battle.

The ships were running empty with the cargo holds housing fighters. Captain Roos ordered these launched to group off to the side accelerating for a speed advantage. The convoy reformed into a tight formation to swing across the edge of the oncoming group while the fighters attacked the other flank before regrouping to harass the rear of the opponents. The bogies broke off in confusion. Then decided that they were outclassed and hit maximum boost, now concentrating on escape.

"Fighters return to your ship," Fedo ordered, "Reports."

The reports came in as the freight team secured the fighters in the cargo bays.

The casualties were one fighter lost, another damaged though able to return for repair. The pilot of the first was located and retrieved by a shuttle, which had been dispatched soon as the hazard level was low enough. The opposing force had lost two fighters and a Converted Freighter. These crews were picked up at the same time from their escape capsules. When informed of the destination a couple elected to return to their capsules, assuring the rescuers that once the Fornoon left the system, the rogue fleet would rescue them.

The remaining rescued crew were happy to return to Aurea as that was their home and they expected a welcome there if not warm. They weren't keen to stay in the rogue fleet.

The fleet reformed to resume the travel, reaching the jump point to the next system without further incident. All the ships settled into the routine after entering hyperspace.

Ito took the opportunity to interview the survivors.

Waiting in her day cabin a knock at the door to announce the crewman, "Petty Officer Rory Coulthard, Ma'am."

"Come in have a seat, Petty Officer," Ito invited.

"Thank you, Ma'am," Rory said, "I should thank you for the lift."

"I will accept it on behalf of the shuttle crew," Ito said, "What was the aim of your leader, you don't have to answer if that is a secret."

"I can guess that he thought you were a freighter convoy," Rory said, "Lately pickings have been slim, so he assembled a larger force to overcome the resistance."

"Sorry to spoil his day," Ito said, "What position do you fill?"

"Engineer's Mate," Rory said, "I believe that I would find a similar or better position on an Aurean Freighter once I get there."

"Okay enjoy your cruise and good luck."

"Thank you, Ma'am," Rory said then walked out to allow in the next passenger.

"Lt Ester Fairburn, Ma'am,"

'Come in and have a seat Ester," Ito invited, "Many women among your crews?"

"Few and I am the senior," Ester said, "I am the weapons officer on my ship."

"At your rank, I had my first small ship, though I shouldn't brag," Ito said, "What do you expect, a civilian ship like Rory?"

"Yes, I should be able to find a freighter which is desperate enough. I have heard that returning crew are viewed as untrustworthy while the Imperial Navy grabs all the crew they can out of the merchant fleet. All the so-called rogues end up in the civvy fleet," Ester laughed.

"Good to know, need anything?"

"No they are looking after me," Ester replied.

"Thank you, carry on unless you have a question."

"Any slots open with your fleet?" Ester asked.

"I am afraid not, we are over crewed, and the Navy's policy is strictly Fornoon," Ito said, "Sometimes it is annoying, I have run into a few who I would have loved in my crew."

"I have a date with a cherry pie so if that is all, Goodbye, Ma'am," Ester said.

"Run along tell Chef to save a slice for me," Ito said, '*I will do another interview and then claim that slice.*'

The steward announced the next interviewee, "Crewman Hermann Schroeder, Ma'am."

"Come in and have a seat, I have a few questions mostly about your home, nothing military. What is Aurea like?"

"Mostly rural as we are the food bowl for the Empire, even more essential, now the sector is smaller," Hermann said, "I expect to be snapped up in one of the factories as a mechanic."

"I hear comments like that you should keep them to yourself; If you are going towards the Mess Hall, I have my eye on some cherry pie."

"Sounds good to me, Gustaff has shared his cooking art with your chef, and if he baked it you are in for a treat," Hermann said.

She stood and in company with Hermann made their way there.

Unfortunately, the word had got around, and there was a lineup, Ito shrugged and joined the end.

However, before she could blend into the crowd, Chef spotted her and bellowed, "Hey Ambassador, don't hide back there I have your slice waiting."

Embarrassed, Ito walked forward to the crew's cheers to arrive at the head of the line and receive her slice. By the number of pies, Gustaff and Chef had been having a baking competition. So there was plenty to go around.

The two cooks insisted that Ito should taste both, and by their looks they wanted her to bless theirs, being ever the diplomat, Ito took a bite savoured it with a smile as it was delicious. Taking a swig of water, She grabbed the other slice and tasted the second sample. Mmm, excellent slightly different but she couldn't separate them. What to do?

"I declare them a draw, sorry Chef, I think you have a competitor," Ito said, "Until we get to Aurea we are in danger of becoming fat."

Fedo said from behind, "I don't think there is much danger in just four days."

"If today's effort is a guide, it still could," Ito said with a grin.

The bridge gave the warning for emergence from Hyper; this meant all strapped down in case the ship had to dodge debris. The Sensor station called all clear, and the convoy carried on to the exit jump point.

"One more system to go after this system, then we are at our destination, don't drop your guard just yet," Fedo said with a wink at Ito.

"Incidents have a habit of dropping on you just when you think your destination is in sight," Ito agreed.

The jump and passage through Hyperspace were uneventful but bearing in mind, the earlier advice 'Action stations' was declared before exit.

As they emerged and set the course for the final jump the Sensor station called no detectable emanations, Fedo was just about to stand down to space state 3, when alarms rang to show a hyper pulse had erupted on a converging course.

"Report," Ordered Fedo.

"Four ships travelling in close formation, ID Oxzen," The Sensor Officer said.

"Condition Orange, battle stations," Fedo ordered.

"Hold fire, challenge and identify, energise anti-sleep shield," Ito added to the order.

"Show images to the main screen," Fedo ordered.

Onto the screen, The screen displayed four saucers travelling in a vertical diamond formation.

"Caution Droman ships, diplomacy first, no overt action," Ito advised.

As the Fornoon ships were line abreast with the *Focus*, Hoos' vessel the closest; they were at a tactical disadvantage. The position of the *Focus* blocked weapons support from the other Four.

Over the radio, "Stand to while we carry out a customs inspection," Hoos broadcast.

Before Fedo could countermand, Focus had focussed a tractor beam on the nearest saucer.

There was a blur of movement, and the four discs spun as one and lined up with the Focus.

The sensor officer announced, "They discharged the sleep gun."

Ito smiled and thought '*a stitch in time.*'

Then an ion cannon lashed out and damaged the *Focus'* tractor mount, disabling the ship, as the next Fornoon vessel in line emerged from behind the *Focus*, was hit at the cannon mount as was subsequent.

Fedo roared over the radio, "Disengage and reverse course."

As the Fornoon ships obeyed this order, the four saucers lit up the cosmos and flashed away at Corvette pace.

"Damage reports," Fedo ordered.

"Tractor Mount damaged, hull breached, repairs underway, no casualties," *Focus* transmitted.

The other two were similar.

"May I have the radio?" Ito asked and when handed it, stated, "Commander Hoos, you were to hold fire which includes tractor beams."

"Ma'am," *Focus* replied without further addition.

"The ready room, Captain," Ito ordered.

"Yes Ma'am," Fedo acknowledged when they entered the room and closed the door. Ito let out a frustrated scream.

"Sorry sir, I had to get out before I broke protocol and told Hoos publicly what I thought of him," Ito explained, "Now we have to regroup and assess the situation."

"We have two serviceable ships, likely the other three can be prepared in a few days for hyper-drive," Fedo advised.

"We remain in orbit until the techs stabilise the repairs, then the two serviceable should proceed to Aurea to complete my mission with the others following when ready," Ito suggested.

"Sounds sensible," Fedo agreed.

"Those Droman ships weren't aggressive, not that our orders permit us to admit fault," Ito said, "The yellow saucer, we have met the captain and couldn't have been a more sociable entity. Another I had dealings with, I was but a child in her hands, she looked like a mere child."

"Yes over the years I have had contacts with them, and I agree with your assessment," Fedo said, "Where do you think they are going?"

"By the course and my luck, I would assume Aurea," Ito suggested.

"For now let's get the group back together, we leave the fighters with damaged ships, which are vulnerable while under repair," Fedo decided.

"You can pick them up on the return trip," Ito agreed, "Now that I have the steam out of my head, your convoy sir."

"Aye ma'am," Fedo laughed.

They returned to the bridge, and Captain Roos organised the repair programme, ordering the fighters and shuttles from the serviceable ships to disembark and form a cordon around the damaged vessel.

With the repairs underway; once the remaining three were declared combat ready, at least insystem. The reduced group resumed travel towards Aurea.

As they emerged from Hyperspace, they were challenged by a wing of large ships and ordered to a stationary position.

"You have entered Imperial space, state ship and the reason for entry, inspection required, stand down from all weapons and shields," The radio blared.

"Friendly welcome," Fedo said aside, then on the radio, "Forno ships *Challenge* and *Haven*, transporting Ambassador Roos to Aurea; complying with the order."

"Stop all drives, stand down from Action stations and assemble in the recreation hall," Fedo ordered over the intercom.

A heavily armed team boarded and examined all aboard, singling out the rescued Aureans and took them aside for interrogation. Protests were brushed aside with the inspection teams inspecting every article and container.

After an extended period, the team completed the inspection, and each ship was assigned escort fighters and directed to proceed. The rescued Aureans would be handed over to authorities when the ship landed.

On the way, Ito commented, "Good thing Zento wasn't here he would have popped a blood vessel."

"And I thought foreign vessels received a hard time entering our system," Fedo said, "As a friendly merchant I would avoid anything to do with this system."

"Put it down as war state preparation," Ito returned, "A situation a merchant should avoid even if the profit margin is tempting."

Maintaining as much dignity as possible the ships slowly proceeded to the planet where the fighters guided them to the spaceport.

Already parked were five saucers, two red, a yellow, blue, and blue with a yellow flash.

"I have seen the two reds and the yellow, the larger red captured my ship twice using that damn sleep cannon," Ito said, "Perhaps I can advise the Imperials to give them a little payback?"

"You would have to be very persuasive, the Imperials treat all visitors with equal contempt," Fedo advised.

"You know me, the nicest person there is, I can charm a merchant into giving me a bargain and leave them thinking they should have thrown in their best shirt as a bonus," Ito said.

Fedo just laughed.

Once landed and cleared customs Roos and her escort proceeded to an administration building to present her credentials.

Eventually, a clerk accompanied her to Der Fuehrer's department where a senior aide interviewed her and viewed her documents.

While the staff processed the credentials, Ito asked, "Those vessels parked there, they were involved in an altercation at the last System before this one? I wish to complain to your justice system."

As she was asking this, a dark figure came out of a side office and asked, "What is your interest in those ships?"

"I am Ambassador Ito Roos," Ito said and when he didn't

comment, "The four smaller ones attacked my convoy as we were travelling peacefully to here. The larger has been involved in covert activities."

"Well it seems I have an interest in the yellow one, could you confirm the identity?" The dark figure asked.

"I believe it is the *Yella Terra*, Humph is the captain, and is registered with our declared enemies the Oxzen sector," Ito reported.

"That confirms my data, I am now going to approach that one and interrogate the crew," Dark said, "I am Adept Klien."

This confirmation made Ito a little nervous as Intelligence had warned her that this adept was notorious for having a short temper.

Klien used radio and summoned a troop of soldiers; he then instructed, "Your people will remain here; you may accompany me to this vessel."

"Yes, perhaps I can deliver some information on how to deal with them," Ito said. Though Klien just swivelled his head towards her. His real mood hidden by a dark mask.

A platform carrier arrived, and the troops stepped on leaving a gap for Klien and Roos to follow. Once all were aboard the platform moved smoothly over to the *Terra*, a smaller vehicle travelled from the larger red ship and deposited four figures.

Arriving at the Terra, the soldiers stepped off and formed a cordon around the ramp. Following, Klien signalled to the captain of his guard.

The captain bellowed, "Imperial guard, all crew are to assemble at the bottom of the ramp."

"Why?" From the speaker.

"The Empire demands it," The Captain shouted.

The speaker answered, "Since you asked so nicely, we will be out as soon as we have our party togs on."

This reply didn't please the captain, and he was about to repeat himself, Klien held his hand up to refrain.

Ito raised her eyebrows, though Klien was inscrutable behind his mask.

After a short wait, a procession of figures led by a large familiar bear, the other figures were all in armour similar to the Imperial troopers.

"Which one is Captain Humph?" Klien asked, and about a dozen figures raised hands including the bear.

"Good day Adept Klien. I am, how may I help you?" Humph asked.

"I will ask the questions," Klien snapped, Humph just gestured amiably to continue.

"You aren't a Droman, I would know," Klien said then staggered as Humph did something.

"Were you involved in an attack on Imperial ships and aided a fugitive?" Klien demanded once he had recovered his poise.

"If you mean when Commodore Rham's people fired on me? I did warn them that I was using an energy absorbing screen. I regret the loss of life and property. I have since replaced his lost ships," Humph stated, "I believe the alleged fugitive you refer to is a citizen of a friendly nation."

"I care little about the renegade Rham's loss, the ships were Imperial fleet," Klien said.

"What about the attack on my ships, Adept Klien?" Ito said.

"Hello, it is my old friend Captain Roos, you are looking well," Steve Firebrand said as he stepped forward and cleared his visor.

"You! Adept Klien, do something he has attacked my ship several times," Ito said.

"Come with me," Klien ordered drawing his sabre, and his troop braced.

"Put away that, we have equipped the suits with energy-absorbing screens, and things would get messy," Firebrand suggested, "Besides your boys look like they need a rest.

Klien glanced back to see his soldiers struggling to stand.

"Perhaps you would like to come aboard and be comfortable, while we discuss this disagreement?" Humph offered.

"I will, coming Ambassador?" Klien decided.

"Dromen are ethical entities, it is safe enough," Ito advised seeing it was a stalemate.

They all moved in with the Humph troopers remaining in the

airlock area. Assembling in the map room, Humph waved to seats and said, "I can provide evidence that I was in unclaimed space. My ship was going about its legal business," Humph stated, "I have some reservations about the status of the Empire. I have heard it said that the Emperor at the time of the incident had died and the territory reverted to the governments which had governed them."

"The Imperial court on Corellia had jurisdiction at the time," Klien said, "I demand that you face investigation there."

"We have clearance to lift. I have perishable livestock loaded," Humph stated.

"I can cancel that with a call," Klien snorted.

"You would have to depart the vicinity of the ship before you could do so," Captain Cox advised.

"I have recordings of both incidents with the relevant data, both support a different interpretation and designate that both were in a neutral system," Humph said, and an avatar laid data sticks on the table before Klien.

"Mere merchants do as I tell them," Klien snarled.

"I hold the status of Ambassador, Humph is a consular representative for Droma," Captain Cox responded.

"Ha, that doesn't get you anything on our territory," Klien sneered.

"I hold a Commission of Commodore in the Oxzen Navy, and I am bound to defend these ships," Firebrand stated.

"I tell Admirals to jump," Klien replied then considered.

"It seems we are at an impasse, very well, depart, I may not be so easy to deal with the next time we meet," Klien stated and stamped out gesturing for Ito to follow.

Ito thought, '*That wasn't very satisfactory,*' however, she kept her peace and Klien offered no comments, reboarding the carrier in silence and returning to the Administration Building and Klien then strode off.

Ito found her group and asked her assistant Veoos, "Any problems?"

"No they are efficient, did your meeting bear fruit?" Veoos asked.

"No, it was very frustrating, those red saucers are the ones that have been giving me such a hard time," Ito said, "Klien allowed them to leave and ignored my complaints."

Making a decision, Ito asked the official for an interview with Der Fuhrer, who answered, "I will see what I can do."

The official walked off into an ornate office and returned shortly, "The Fuhrer will see you."

Ito was shown in and introduced to a mature man in a dark uniform heavily encrusted in medals and braid, "Welcome Ambassador Roos. How can I help you?"

"I need to return to my disabled ships and protect them from aggression from the Oxzen Convoy, who are likely to threaten them as they did on the way," Ito said.

"Would a couple of Corvettes be helpful?" Der Fuhrer asked, receiving a nod said, "Bertram would you contact Herr Grasha and have him assign two Corvettes to my charming guest."

"Thank you, Sir," Ito said, "I would be most grateful."

"Anything for our new allies, I look forward to a long association," Der Fuhrer said.

Bertram ushered her out and directed her to another office with H. Grasha on a nameplate.

Entering Ito was introduced to the occupant, "Herr Grasha. This lady is Ambassador Roos; I pass on Der Fuhrer's request for assistance."

"Good day Madam, why do you need two warships?" Grasha asked.

"I have three ships in the adjacent system, the Oxzens damaged them, and the Oxzen group may attack them while they are vulnerable," Ito said.

"Well if the leader agrees, I suppose I can humour him," Grasha said, "They are there strictly to ensure good behaviour and do not involve them in any squabbles, the captains will be ordered to avoid confrontations except in self-defence. Is that understood?"

"Perfectly, this is only a mercy mission to protect my people," Ito agreed.

"Be ready to lift in an hour, and the Corvettes will be assigned," Grasha advised, "*Dark Dream* and *Dark Dawn* will join you as your ships head towards the jump point."

"Thank you, sir," Ito said, "You have been most helpful."

"Bring them back in one piece, and you are welcome," Grasha grimaced.

"I will do my best to do so," Ito said as she left eager to arrange the liftoff.

"Veoos hold the fort and set up my office," Ito said to her staff, "I will be back in a day or so."

Ito entered her car and told the driver to run her out to the *Challenger*.

As she entered, she said, "Just for a short jolly I am not taking over. I have some escorts to run back to the other ships to convoy them back and keep them safe."

"And if certain ships happen to be between?" Fedo asked.

"If they behave themselves nothing should happen," Ito said innocently.

The time arrived, and the *Challenge* was ready. The last of the Oxzen ships had lifted off and disappeared.

Her two ships lifted off and headed the same direction; the saucers had accelerated and despite advice regrouped at the jump point.

To the side, two large blips showed Corvettes moving to rendezvous with the Fornoon ships.

"Here come our friends," Fedo said, "Very impressive and those are quite useful, it must have been a big smile you gave, Not Klien?"

"Hardly, I can only guess that he is human," Ito said, "I am under strict orders not to bend them, as long as no one shoots at them, they won't help."

The four ships reached the jump point, and they entered Hyperspace. As it was only a short move, Fedo had called Action stations ready to exit.

After they had entered the system, to one side, a hyper pulse erupted, and several blips appeared, with one disappearing almost immediately. The remaining blips were close together and emitted Oxzen signatures.

The radio blared *Focus* again, "This is Fornoon Navy, cease drives, you are under arrest."

Instead, the blips emitted flashing red shields and started firing at all the Fornoon and Imperial ships, which returned fire with explosions erupting at both targets and ship turrets except *Challenge* because Ito had yelled, "Don't fire they are decoys with Energy-absorbing shields."

"Damage reports," Fedo ordered.

"What the hell? Captain Hinz, *Dark Dream*." Hinz demanded.

"Robot decoys. Don't fire and nothing happens, the beams are harmless," Ito answered.

After the reports were in, it seemed only the *Challenge* was Hyper serviceable.

Hinz radioed, "You have the only hyper ready ship, go back and report, our ships need repair facilities."

Ito debated with herself whether to go home or to Aurea. If her luck was in, Klien might have returned to Corellia. Home would be on her record as a fail. Best to talk her way out of trouble at Aurea. She could always blame the attack on the Oxzen.

"I will do that Captain," Ito answered, having made the decision.

"That went a bit sticky, Uncle," Ito said to Fedo to indicate the next was unofficial. "We could return to Aurea, allow the blame to rest with the Oxzen ships and report an ambush."

"Needs must when the devil calls the tune, it is close enough, those decoys did attack us," Fedo said with a nod. Then aloud, "Navigator set a course to Aurea we have to report the incident."

The *Challenge* jumped into Aurea went through the cordon, landed at the port and headed to Grasha's office.

As Hinz had signalled ahead with a bare-bones report and Ito only had to add that she had ordered the ships not to fire. This report allowed Grasha to assume that Ito was not at fault, apportioning most of the blame for trigger-happy Navy personnel and automated weapons.

He dispatched the required recovery ships. Ito headed for the *Challenge* to accompany them to investigate further.

Emerging into the system, Ito contacted the *Dark Dream*, "This is Ambassador Roos have you secured the decoys?"

"Hinz here, no they were firing at the ships interrupting repairs, and we had to knock them out with missiles," Hinz said.

"No matter, I could design better ones in my sleep, the IFF transducers may have been helpful," Ito considered.

"The ships repairs are well on the way, and within the week the ships will return to Aurea for final restoration," Hinz reported.

"That is good to hear, it certainly isn't the outcome I desired to start my duty here," Ito admitted.

"Hinz out,"

"Rodger *Dream*, *Challenge* out."

"Well Uncle Fedo, has my luck saved the day or am I wearing it thin?" Ito asked.

"Time will tell, perhaps caution is the road you should follow for a while," Fedo advised.

"Perhaps you are right, these Oxzen? Should I start to mend fences?" Ito asked.

"That wouldn't hurt if you take it slow, our government is officially not interested having had their nose bloodied so many times," Fedo advised.

"I will take that on board, I will see what I can set in motion," Ito said, "Not knocking Chief Ghos but being a partner with a Droman is tempting."

"They won't permit aggression to innocents," Fedo observed.

"Ha, they are good at stopping it, though," Ito said.

Should Blue and Green be seen?

AFTER A TIME SETTLING INTO THE TASK OF RUNNING AN embassy, the *Challenge* had departed back to Forno, through the channels the administration announced that they would hold a reception for the diplomats.

Ito wasn't happy that she had an invitation to a formal banquet. Reluctantly she found her gown and poured herself into it. She wasn't pleased with the effect as she had the build of a well-muscled athlete, "Any chance I could get a seat behind a pillar so I can snatch a couple of zeds?"

"I am afraid not Madam. That is where the organisers place those out of favour or about to be declared war. The middling is best; the prime seats nearest the dignitaries are for enemies and untrustworthy friends," Veoos said.

"I suppose you are right," Ito conceded, "Wouldn't be fun if Zento Hoos had the job?"

"Very amusing Madam," Veoos said looking pained.

"Perhaps you are correct," Ito said, deciding to end the banter.

The time arrived as Ito stepped out of the car and walked gracefully down the carpet, the Major Domo announced, "Commodore Ito Roos, Ambassador for Forno,"

She was escorted to the table and seated; she had just settled when the announcement came, "Her Highness, El ali Sartz, Ambassador for Oxzen sector, Her Highness, Captain El ali Algertz of Oxzen, Captain Rosebud envoy for Droma."

The attendants escorted three women, two blue and one light brown, to seats across from Ito.

"Good day," Ito said politely.

"Good day, I thought Fornoon had fangs and ate their babies?" Sartz asked with a smile, "I am Sartz."

"I am afraid you have us confused with the Oxzens," Ito grinned, "I am Ito."

"Rosebud and Algertz," Rosebud introduced herself and companion.

"Rosebud, are you from Australia you have the accent?" Ito asked.

"Droma, my father Humph is responsible for inflicting the Aussies on the Galaxy," Rosebud said.

"I have met him first as a bird on Mike Cox shoulder, at the time he had a child's voice, the last time he was a big bear with a deep voice," Ito said.

"Algy had a word with Pippin and suggested a couple of changes," Rosebud said, "Algy is Steve Firebrand from an alternate universe."

Roos was left a little confused with that explanation, so changed the subject. "I have become unpopular in some circles. I believe the Fornoon policy of using disaffected locals to sign up as allies and then use military force to establish a trade advantage is flawed," Ito said, "Shared trade is better than exclusive after the conflict ends."

"I heartily agree, while there are some people believe it is better to send young people to do the dangerous work than using diplomacy. Unfortunately, this means soldiers and police are still needed," Sartz said.

"I would like to discuss this further but ears are flapping. Perhaps a little meeting between giggling women would be appropriate?" Ito suggested.

"Sounds fun," Sartz said, "So are you enjoying Aurea?"

"The area that I am allowed to see is pleasant," Ito replied.

"Yes indeed," Sartz said, "Here are the meals, at least the food is excellent."

The chat reduced to small talk until the VIP s had finished their speeches and Der Fuhrer departed.

"As we leave should we gnash our teeth and snarl?" Ito suggested.

"Perhaps just an evil smile?" Sartz replied with one, "Goodbye."

"Grr," Ito responded.

Once back at the Embassy and attired in official clothing, Ito commented, "That turned into an entertaining evening. Veoos, I may have an invitation to afternoon tea. Please facilitate this quietly."

"Yes Madam," Veoos said.

After a few days, Veoos had arranged the meeting, and Ito dressed in pilot's overalls then made her way to the port, she arrived at the Snapdragon and entered.

"Good afternoon, Sartz, Algertz and Rosebud, may I come aboard?" Ito asked.

"Please do," Rosebud invited, "Oh you didn't have to put on all your finery to visit."

"Comfort first," Ito laughed, "and anonymity."

Rosebud escorted her to the map room; she commented, "Tea and scones? I see that the Aussies have corrupted you?"

"I find it pleasant, nicer than blood and gnawing on bones," Sartz said.

"So I believe that we are in accord with terms of the trade?" Ito asked, "Frankly, I have yet to meet an Oxzen that I haven't liked. My first experience was meeting Roxz on Fvelsving."

"If you found my husband's uncle likeable, there is hope for you yet," Sartz said.

"He is a sweet old darling, mother," Algertz said.

"Perhaps I wouldn't go that far, as I met him as a merchant talking trade," Ito said.

"Were you a merchant in a past life? Cover your ears daughter; we mustn't allow merchant talk to corrupt you," Sartz said.

"Oh Mother, we are both merchants, I am still learning. Dad still complains about the last time you conned him," Algertz said.

"It is also part of our training, and I learnt from one of our best," Ito said, "Privately, Uncle Fedo shares my view on civilised trade."

"So what do you suggest, I believe that fair trading without force is the best way to conduct business and benefits all," Sartz stated,

"Our sector has systems regularly join because they see the benefits to themselves."

"I agree. We lose clients by revolts as quick as we acquire them. I suspect the odd voluntary one is only bowing to the inevitable," Ito related, "By the time the dust settles from the civil war, I think the trade would have been better off sharing."

"Our Government has a responsibility to protect our citizens from hostility, this in turns means that resources are diverted from economic growth to do so," Sartz said.

"So what shall we do about it? I have submitted several papers recommending change; I receive 'interesting, but'," Ito said. "With the hint that it is not favourable for advancement. Before this appointment, I was captain of a small merchant freighter and the best results were from independent systems."

"As I have found. While nominally a ruler, to maintain this I have to demonstrate my expertise as a Captain and Merchant," Sartz said, "I do have a fleet of freighters and occasionally bump Rainbow's partner to do this."

"Rainbow is my mother," Rosebud said, "My dad built the ships for her, my brother and me."

"Interesting, getting back to our point. How do you think we should approach this?" Ito asked.

"I have studied the psychology of both parties. I will draft a proposal for each, slanted to appeal to their ideas," Rosebud offered. Almost immediately another Rosebud walked out startling Ito and placed a version before each of the women.

Ito studied this, surprised that such a detailed document could appear so quickly. "This is excellent, it should appeal to my superiors," Ito said, "May I look at your version?" she asked Sartz.

When they had swapped, Ito could see the subtle difference, in the Oxzen case, the wording slanted a little more to the financial aspect rather than promoting Fornoon hegemony by being more subtle in alien dealings.

"How did you do this?" Ito asked amazed.

"Rosebud is too modest, she has twenty-one brains to entertain, this is just a minor challenge," Algertz explained.

"I am not that good, but yes I enjoy some challenges. Since I don't sleep, I have been working on the document since the dinner," Rosebud said, "I feel that conflict is a waste of energy."

"As do I, even though the two principal career pointers involve leadership and teamwork which show up well in conflict," Ito said, "Trading and captain of a ship also do as well, but it is on dry paper at the end of the year."

"Against quickly wrote in blood and drama in the dispatches?" Sartz asked.

"Precisely, I see we are of a like mind. I will review my copy and forward it to the Foreign Department for consideration," Ito said, "Now this ship, I have had a tour many years ago through Humph's vessel. I am interested in learning more about Rosebud's people."

"To acquire one as a partner, you would need to approach either Humph or Steve Firebrand, both build this model. The requirement is to be a Droma friend, and you should be aware that the ship would belong to that Droman. He or she will spend centuries living in it as their territory," Sartz advised.

"We have a treaty with Earth, however not yet the sort that would allow me to approach and purchase a ship. This proposition is especially awkward since they have taken two of them from me under hostile circumstances. Humph would be the pivot on this understanding taking effect," Ito said, "I am very interested."

"Are you familiar with education helmets? Here is mine it will teach you all about the ship," Rosebud said, "Once you have the basics I will conduct you on a tour of my ship."

Ito looked to Sartz for guidance. Sartz shrugged as she said, "It is her ship to do what she wishes."

Ito took the helmet placed it on and waited for the deluge of data to overwhelm her. After the stream had stopped after what seemed hours, Ito noted that it was minutes.

"Now if you are ready I will take you for a tour around the ship, as you see the equipment it should make sense," Rosebud invited.

They commenced the tour with Ito being impressed on the garden lined passageways, "This is your air plant, very nice, you have more flowers than I remember Humph's ship having," Ito noted.

The cargo bays sparked Ito interest, "The deck lowers to load containers, excellent, beats loading through hatches by hand, I was puzzled when I viewed Humph's vessel as I couldn't see how they managed the larger items."

Arriving at engineering bay, instead of a grumpy old chief there was another Rosebud, as the others didn't greet her, Ito waved to have both Rosebuds grin.

As they neared the end of the tour, Rosebud said, "Peek through there, and I will wave back, that is the sessile part of me."

She did so, and there was a blob of jelly with a feminine hand waving back.

"Remarkable, and the shuttle parked above is your escape capsule?" Ito asked.

"Yes, I can carry myself up to it and park in the shuttle's cargo bay," Rosebud said, "I assembled myself in the room. When mother transferred to her ship from her home, she said it was like twenty elves lifting a fat naked woman out of a slippery bath."

"Excuse me," Ito laughed, "That image will haunt me for years."

The Tour and Afternoon Tea complete Ito farewelled her hosts and returned to the Embassy. Slipping into clothes more appropriate for a diplomat, she settled into her office, first loading a copy of Rosebud's document onto her computer. Ito revised a couple of passages which rendered it into her style. After rereading and comparing the text, Ito decided that the data was unchanged and now looked consistent with something that she would submit.

"Veoos would you come in here, please," Ito called to her aide.

"Certainly Madam," Veoos said as she joined her.

"Please you read this and advise me if it is suitable for forwarding to the Foreign Office," Ito said.

Veoos took the document and read the information, "It is similar to your previous submissions, this should pass their criteria, coming from an incumbent Ambassador. Forgive me for not commenting on the content. I believe it will receive the due attention," Veoos said.

"Please contact the ship *Snapdragon*. Invite Captains Algertz and Rosebud over for an afternoon tea at their convenience?" Ito asked.

"Yes Madam," Veoos said.

At the arranged time Algertz and Rosebud arrived to find Ito waiting at the reception area to escort them to her private garden where a table was waiting.

"Please take a seat, I took the liberty of asking my chef to bake scones for the occasion, he has spent time on Earth so is familiar with the method, I can add sand if it fits the rough Merchant image," Ito offered.

"That won't be necessary, I have enjoyed tea and scones at Mike's mother's home, to match those, they will have to be good," Algertz said.

"None for me thank you, I have no need to eat," Rosebud said.

"Would you compare these files? I have changed a few lines to meet Forno protocol; I wouldn't want to lose the impact that your words delivered," Ito asked.

Rosebud compared the two and advised, "There has been no loss of content; it does add to my understanding of Forno thought process."

"Thank you I will dispatch this on the next courier," Ito said.

"Now tea? There are strawberry jam and cream to go with the scones," Ito said.

Algertz loaded her plate and tasted it, "Mmm you may inform your chef that he has equalled Mrs Cox's scones," She said.

"That will make his day. To friendship," Ito said as she raised her cup.

"Your mother's and your titles signify what?" Ito asked.

"My father is the king/president of the Oxzen sector, duly elected by being the most successful merchant fleet owner," Algertz said.

"Your people are mad, you two represent prime hostage candidates," Ito exclaimed a little taken aback.

"Oh, we have a couple of things going for us, there are dozens of princesses here, and I have a Droman as a friend," Algertz explained, "For instance could you stop a ray blast without effect?"

"Valid point, that is good for Rosebud," Ito said.

"Shall we experiment?" Rosebud asked, "I will stand over here with my back turned, you stand behind Algertz and random poke, and I will tell you where and how many times."

Ito shrugged, and the experiment was set up. Rosebud was able to identify each touch.

"Not magic just that you are poking me as well, Algertz is wearing one of my suits which double as armour if needed," Rosebud advised, "Converting to full coverage as required."

"Oh really," Ito said.

"Useful as a disguise as well, Humph had Mike look like Adept Varta one time," Algertz said, "I could do the same if necessary. The alleged fugitive that Klien referred to was me, and as part of avoiding Rham, Humph disguised me as a Yowie child."

After this, the conversation returned to gentler things like Galactic Intrigue and Policy.

After a pleasant chat, Algertz and Rosebud were escorted to the reception and farewelled.

Returning to her office, Ito called Veoos in, "Veoos would you send this file with the next courier?"

"As you wish Madam," Veoos acknowledged and picked up the file for dispatch.

Ito settled back to reading the other signals and letters that were her responsibility. Without Veoos to sort these, Ito was sure that she wouldn't be able to move.

It seemed that every merchant and manufacturer was sure that Ito would be the source of their fortunes.

While she was doing this with half a mind, she considered that if she succeeded in arranging a peace treaty with the Oxzen, next would be to arrange to be friends with Humphs and Commodore Firebrand.

That would be the way to achieve this aim, for now, it was just daydreaming.

After what seemed an eternity, a dispatch arrived from the Foreign Office.

'We have received your correspondence, please elaborate on the contact with the Oxzen representative.' it read

Ito drafted a reply, stating that negotiations are proceeding and acceptable to the Oxzen Ambassador. The official response from the Oxzens is still waiting for ratification; Ambassador Sartz has a very senior voice in their council.

While Ito was still polishing up the reply, Rosebud came over and delivered a signal confirming the Oxzen council's approval in principle with no reservations.

The draft was updated and the signal enclosed, "Veoos, please assess this document and advise me on the wording?" Ito asked.

"Certainly Madam," Veoos said, then after reading, said, "It meets the guidelines."

"Please dispatch it by the next available courier, Veoos," Ito instructed.

"Yes Madam," Veoos acknowledged and left to do so.

After the same delay, a new dispatch arrived, *'I confirm that our council has reached the same 'on principle' agreement, imperative you arrange a meeting of Foreign Secretaries of each party to continue exploring an understanding.'*

"Veoos would you contact Ambassador El ali Sartz to arrange a meeting at her convenience?" Ito asked.

"Yes Madam," Veoos said.

The meeting was before, on the *Snapdragon*, the venue set unofficially to allay any suspicions of the Imperials. As having two sectors independently signing accords may give rise to suspicion. However, where several women were having afternoon tea, would be seen as innocuous because the regime was misogynous.

"This annoys me that such a subterfuge works, yet it is useful," Ito complained.

"So I gather that both councils agree in principle?" Sartz said, "If so, what is the next step?"

"Arranging a neutral venue to fiddle with the odd word to seek a slight advantage for their council," Ito said, "Here is not suitable as the security is on a war footing and the Imperials would look unkindly at a pact between sectors which they would prefer antagonistic to each other."

"Ah the joys of diplomacy, so what would you believe would qualify as a neutral?" Sartz asked.

"Perhaps Elysium or Earth, we have peace agreements with both," Ito suggested, "The Fornoon have consulates at both places."

"We are friends with both; I shall put it to my council, that is, I will tell my husband Loxz to get off his bum and send someone," Sartz said.

"I don't have quite the same influence with my principals, I believe that we can see it happen in a reasonable time," Ito agreed, "As Captains on a ship, we say go, and it happens."

"My end is the quicker," Sartz said, "As the Queen and vice president, as long as I don't suggest anything too radical, it is usually accepted. I am unlikely to promote an adverse agreement as I am also a Merchant Fleet owner."

"Then as a start, I will recommend both venues, and the relevant consuls can be advised to explain the meeting with the governments," Ito said, "I don't believe it should upset either."

The dispatches were sent and then the wait again.

The word came through that the ministers would be meeting in Canberra.

The Government provided a venue for the meeting, and the talks commenced, after several weeks of negotiation an agreement was arrived at, practically unchanged from Rosebud's proposal.

The parties made progress and news filtered through, Ito Roos was replaced as the Ambassador to the Empire and reassigned to be Roving Ambassador to the Oxzen Sector.

Retaining Veoos as her aide, Ito was assigned a ship to transport her around the sector. Only a basic one as her status had slightly waned, but it was sufficient.

Ito organised a visit to Wellcamp Airport, then took a taxi to the Firebrand factory where she knew that Steve Firebrand was in his office.

A secretary escorted Ito to Steve's office; she attracted many stares as the last green faces had belonged to soldiers guarding the occupants. Anne was less than welcoming. Having been pre-warned, Steve came out and greeted her, "Good day, nice to see my favourite Fornoon," Steve said, "What brings you to sunny Queensland?"

"Just testing the waters,'" Ito said, "As you are one of the two builders of Droman friendly spaceships, I would need to smooth the hurts of the past to secure one and become a Friend of a Droman. I admire Pippin and the relationship."

"Considering your actions in the past, such as facilitating the invasion of my country and my factory," Steve said, "That is a hell of an ask. But since I am such a friendly chap, I will at least listen to you. I have asked Pippin to join us."

"I won't pretend that I expect you forgive the past anytime soon," Ito said, "But I believe help in this area will benefit both our nations."

Pippin walked in, "Oh you are meeting with strange women, Dad. Better not let Mum find out," Pippin said teasingly, "Good day Madam Ambassador."

"Nice to meet you again Pippin, would it be too difficult to call me Ito?" Ito asked.

"Certainly, Ito," Pippin agreed, "I suppose you have a purpose for this visit? I thought that your people had stationed you at Aurea."

"My government reassigned me to the Oxzen sector as the Roving Ambassador," Ito said, "My task is to promote peaceful trade with all systems, using the Oxzen method. I was involved in changing the Fornoon policy."

"Sounds good. I suppose you have a difficult job convincing the Powers That Be of the good intentions?" Pippin asked.

"Very tough job I admit, nearly as hard as changing my Boss's model of trade," Ito said, "My aim is to be known as a friend of Droma."

"I must say that at each of the meetings, you were hardly friendly," Pippin said, "Still my people are open to talking through problems."

"I am glad to hear that," Ito said, "Well since I will be travelling around the sector visiting each of the consuls, we may cross paths at times. My biggest help in the process of establishing the peace terms with the Oxzen sector was Rosebud."

"That is a good start, she is my partner's sister," Pippin said, "I doubt that Steve will be as quick to trust you."

"Time will tell, I understand that the process won't be quick. Please be aware that I was acting under orders which you interrupted," Ito said, "It has been a pleasure catching up with you again, Steve, Pippin." With that, she left and returned to Canberra.

Once there she briefed the consulate and prepared to travel to Elysium and then via Grnatz to the other planets of the sector.

At each port, she searched out any Droman ships and chatted with them, establishing a rapport until at last Ito crossed paths with the *Yella Terra*.

"Hello, the ship, Ito Roos, may I come aboard?" Ito asked.

"Oh it is our curious visitor from Fvelsving," Humph said, "And a few other times. How can I help you?"

"Just having a chat establishing my harmlessness," Ito said, "Of course I do have ulterior motives; I would love to be a partner with a relative of yours."

"Well don't stand out there," Humph said, "Come in and meet the family."

"Thank you," Ito said and entered the Terra.

"Mike you know, Su Lin his better half, Tom their son and Junior my son," Humph said, "May I introduce Her Excellency Commodore Ito Roos, Forno Ambassador to the Oxzen sector."

"Oh you mean me, don't inflict that on me, Please call me Ito," Ito said.

"Oki Doke, Ito. So what would you like to talk about?" Mike asked, "As long as it is not trade secrets, we don't have too many to spare."

"As far as that goes I am sure the merchants can make all the mistakes by themselves," Ito suggested, "No just conversation, like the weather in Tullerook, is it always crook?"

"Oh dear, you mean silly sayings? Well, you came to the right place, Mike has all the worst," Su Lin laughed.

"Hey you are supposed to stick up for your husband," Mike protested.

"Never mind I should protect Ito from corruption, I remember seeing you on Aurea, and perhaps I have seen happier faces. Of course, everyone else had blanked face masks except for Humph and Steve," Su Lin noted.

"It is a poor day that one doesn't learn something, even if it is your limitations," Ito said, "Bearding Klien is perhaps not a good career move. I would suggest that you maintain a suitable distance from him in the future."

"So when did you decide that playing with gentle people was better?" Mike asked.

"Oh, I had a long talk with Sartz, Algertz and best of all Rosebud who drafted the agreement. This document eventually settled most of the angst between the Oxz and Forno people," Ito said, "And it was annoying whenever I had a good trading run, the ship is diverted to help a 'new friend' take over his government."

"As neutral observers, Su is from Aurea; Humph is from Droma, and I am from Australia," Mike related, "We have viewed most of the differences between you as bad for business."

"The point I put forward to Sartz and found she was of a like mind," Ito said, "I don't believe that the Imperials would be too excited by the agreement. We did use 'divide and conquer' to achieve our aims, but we are amateurs compared with the Imperials."

"The Dark Adepts use their unique talents for the Empire; these Adepts are destructively competitive. The usual way to rise to the peak of power is by eliminating all those standing in the way. Then maintain their position by controlling lower ranks with fear and rigid discipline," Humph observed.

"All Forno are competitive. Though you can advance by helping your boss and gain points for the teamwork," Ito said, "I have achieved several steps in promotion by this method. Compared with my classmate Zento Hoos who is an excellent leader but who is lacking in teamwork, at athletics he is great as an individual, and so on."

"If I remember from Aurea, also lacking in common sense?" Mike said, "And hard of hearing?"

"I had hoped you hadn't noticed that. My hair is slowly growing back after Zento's precipitant action," Ito grimaced, "Thankfully I didn't have to send a report about him. I wasn't exactly brimming over with sisterly love."

"So I guess that you had advised him to chill it?" Humph asked, "Otherwise you would have talked."

"Yes that was my advice, I recognised your ships and wanted to avoid any confrontation. Initially, I was happy that my shield worked against the sleeper. But there had been a counter to that which hadn't been spread to all of you," Ito commented, "I would also hope it isn't spread too far so that less than savoury races acquire either technology."

"The sleep gun is useful against the Zombie Beast as it can be used through walls," Humph said, "The only people who think the defence is necessary, are yourselves."

"Sorry that was me, I was getting a little tired of waking up and staring into Steve Firebrand's face," Ito said.

"The upshot of using your shield was damage to your ships," Humph explained, "A couple of minutes snooze, and we would have disappeared."

"I had to embroider the truth to obtain assistance from the Imperials, this ended up with two of their ships damaged because they fired on the decoys," Ito said.

"You have Pippin to thank for that," Humph said, "We had already diverted and suspected that you were trying to lay a trap, so she gave you something to shoot at."

"Yes, very kind of her, I recognised the decoys for what they were and stopped my ship firing, but as the others were on automatic, too late," Ito said.

"The automatic system is useful for debris protection, not friendly if crewed vessels are involved," Mike suggested, "Humph can disable an opponent without injuring the pilot by using pinpoint targeting with a laser."

"To get back to my program, my government is socialist. Unfortunately, some so-called socialists such as North Korea are elitist and only pay lip service to equality. The Korean leader's base their place in power on family and elimination of competition," Ito said, "By the then policy and at first sight, they seemed to be suitable as they were being ostracised and at war against overwhelming odds."

"Obvious assumption for an outsider," Mike said.

"Captain Firebrand's assessment of their leader was accurate," Ito said, "Steve's handling of the incident is something that I would try to emulate. Such techniques would probably ensure my rise to the council," Ito said, "Part of the change in policy, the notion of competition has been expanded to include all races. I would entertain the idea of a Droman being THE Fornoon and lead our sector."

"That would take some talking to get them to do that. It is against our instincts to dominate others or allow the inducing of an inferiority complex," Humph said, "We tread a fine line to prevent psychological damage by taking every opportunity to emphasise that we are very evolved tools able to perform tasks beyond unaided human abilities. You don't have a problem relying on a spaceship to get from A to B, or wondering how advanced the computer and drives are?"

"True enough, I am just content to be glad I have superior equipment, though I hesitate to treat an entity as a mere tool," Ito said.

"Our origin is probably from the 'Smorghan' people, who used organic spaceships and computers, we may be the descendants of the computers which had a side job of medical and life support," Humph suggested.

"The more that I learn still leaves me with even more puzzles to solve," Ito said, "It certainly tickles my scientific spot."

"May you spend a long life doing so," Humph said.

"So your son Junior? You call him that because his name is also Humph?" Ito asked.

"No, all boys are called that, we call the girls Rosebud or Petal as they normally have a one in twenty-one chance of being the first person of a meld. At which time the adult names him or herself according to their aspirations or interests," Humph explained, "Once I was Stargazer, short for the One who gazes at the stars and so on for twenty-five hours. Then I was The Astronaut who Gazed at the Stars. After landing on Earth while I repaired my ship, I was amused by a children's program which had an actor in a bear costume. I am now Humph who flies in the *Yella Terra*. Yella being local for the colour and Terra a pun on how harmless I am as well as an old language meaning Earth. When you can think on so many sides of an idea, it helps to pass the time."

"Thanks for adding to my confusion," Ito said, "Su Lin, how did you end up with Mike?"

"The misfortune of hitching a ride from Aurea to Elysium, I fell in love with the ship, and he came as part of the package," Su said with a fond smile at Mike give a lie to the words, "He grows on you, I almost have him trained. Dad wasn't overly fussed with me hanging around with a rough merchant, but he has mellowed in his old age."

"Your father would be?" Ito asked.

"Captain Ezra Blohm, Oxzen Navy," Su Lin said.

"Yes I know him as we have met, unfortunately officially and on the wrong side," Ito said, "I found that despite the circumstances, he was charming and efficient."

The conversation dried up into small talk and Ito decided that she may be wearing out her welcome.

"Well our little chat has been informative and entertaining," Ito said as she prepared to leave, "I hope to run across you from time to time, and like Su, I love your ship, pity all the eligible partners are pink or blue." With a laugh, to indicate she wasn't serious.

"I will have you know that is Bronzed Aus Wal," Mike grinned.

"Visit anytime, you will be welcome," Humph invited.

After saying her farewells, Ito left to attend to her task to advise her consuls who were resident merchants, as their primary function.

This routine settled in until one day, as her ship landed and found the *Terra* already there, Humph and Mike ambled over, and called, "Hello the ship, may we come aboard?"

Ito surprised with their initiative, invited, "Come aboard, please excuse the size, it is a little cramped,"

Humph started, "I am aware of your intention to become crew on one of my ships and accept the responsibility of mentor. You have made a favourable impression on my family and others of my people. To this end, I believe that if I assigned one of the latest builds to you, you could invite a person from Droma to assume this as their territory."

"Wonderful news," Ito said.

"Now you should understand the conditions. An Oxzen representative will escort you to Droma and guide you in selecting a partner. The successful Droman would own the ship and have final say on operations," Humph said.

"I understand and find that acceptable. As the mentor, I advise on the safest route and encourage the person to the best path," Ito acknowledged.

"Then it is settled, it doesn't guarantee success as you still have to locate a willing participant," Humph said, "I found Mike and after several years observing him, I invited him aboard."

"Yep, I am probably the best-educated pet in the Galaxy," Mike laughed.

"In this case, minutes are all that the candidate will have to assess your suitability," Humphs said.

"I will do everything I can to be a crew on one of your ships," Ito promised.

"Keeping the interest of your charge would be your prime function," Humph said, "Having watched the stars for a long time I welcomed the chance to explore them. And as talking to myself is not very satisfactory I needed Mike, perhaps not in the role you will be required to fill for the first few years. As having a function is desirable for sanity, and also to pay for fuel to continue my quest, I required a spokesperson to arrange cargo before a change in communication and voice was suggested."

"Sometimes I look at something and feel like saying, 'isn't that beautiful', and because of the loneliness of command, unable say it to anyone," Ito observed, "Having a fresh mind to engage would also be beneficial for me."

"I will confer with Sartz to arrange to pick up the ship and provide a ferry crew to take it to Droma. The actual time and date the two of you would organise," Humph said, "In another eight years I will need to find a partner for Junior. Perhaps by then, Tom will be ready."

"That is wonderful, I look forward to doing so," Ito shook hands on the deal.

Destination Droma

AFTER SEVERAL WEEKS, IT WAS ARRANGED TO ORGANISE the trip to Droma. Sartz being the most experienced at this task and having completed her stay as Ambassador to The Empire and Republic, volunteered to do the job.

On the day Sartz and Ito entered the new Humph's saucer, then together with the ferry crew lifted off to deliver the ship to Droma, the project was to locate and employ a Droman.

The ship itself under the Humph's system was the property of the adult Droman who accepted it. Until then, it was Humph's ship on loan to Sartz. As there had been some inquiries to locate an available candidate, Sartz had selected a location with a good prospect.

Arriving over Droma, the only radio traffic was a beacon identifying this world as a protectorate of Oxzen Sector. The panorama as they descended was uncluttered with cities; each Droman lived either on a small farm visible as faint spirals or as discs floating in the sea.

The place selected was a small harbour sheltered from the worst storms, this was where several sea ships rode at anchor, the circle of low-lying land where dozens of Dromans established home ranges. The last few years had resulted in the construction of many spaceships. Before Humph activity commenced, the life expectancy of juveniles was short because of the lack of available territories with the sea ships having filled up the available niches on the coastline with dwindling materials to construct new vessels.

With the advances that Pippin had suggested, which allowed closer living by permitting face to face conversations, this provided opportunities for most juveniles.

"What do you think our chances are?" Ito asked, the diplomatic efforts that she had put in, and the sacrifices meant that a failure would undermine the work she had done in the last few years.

"I have put a lot of research into this, making several visits to canvas the market," Sartz said, "There are the required twenty-one candidates, and no adults interested in trying. The worst case scenario is that territory became vacant since I was here."

"You suggested another site if that happened. I have a feeling that my luck is in," Ito said.

"The next step is to be interviewed by a parent who has a juvenile to be provided for," Sartz said, "Once one accepts that you are a suitable mentor, the other parents should be satisfied."

The ship was currently unnamed as that was the prerogative of the new owner, who would also name him or herself. Lately, as movies and books from Earth had been all the rage, most of the names were of English origin.

So with high hopes, the ship settled into the water of the harbour, and a boat was launched to visit the nearer vessels.

Arriving at the closest, Sartz called, "Hello the ship."

A peg-legged man stumbled onto the deck clumping along on a crutch, mumbling to himself, "Silly damned idea to be Long John Silver."

"Oh I have visitors, Ahoy there me hearties, shiver my timbers, what can I do for you?" He said this in an authentic pirate voice.

"We are looking for candidates to crew a spaceship," Sartz said.

"Got no kids, try Gail over there," Long John said pointing at the next ship.

"Thanks. Why don't you try Black beard? He has two legs," Sartz suggested.

"Oh yeah, Thanks," He said and changed into a pirate with a fierce black beard then walked unimpeded back to his cabin.

The team moved their boat over to the indicated ship and called again, "Hello the ship."

This time a woman came out and asked, "Good day, how can I help you? I am Gail."

"Hello I am Sartz, and this is Ito, we have a ship if you need one for your daughter?" Sartz said.

"Come aboard, I will put a cuppa on, and we can have a chat," Gail said.

They boarded, and while they greeted Gail, mobiles set up the table and chairs for a morning tea.

"Please make yourself comfortable," Gail said, "I have been dying to try my hand at serving tea and scones. I have invited a few of my friends, so far they have been too busy with other projects and of course they don't eat."

Sartz and Ito sat down and relaxed, "Lovely ship you have, pleasant surroundings," Sartz said to open the conversation.

"I call it the Force of the Seas, this harbour is quite picturesque at this time of the year," Gail said, "Is that one of Humph's designs?'

"Yes Humph made it for a prospective adult and Ito Roos, the new owner would select a name," Sartz said.

"Ito, what qualifications do you have to nurture a Person?" Gail asked.

"I have extensive experience with all facets of a ship's crew. I have been the captain on several; I propose that our partnership would encompass freight and merchant duties which I can carry out with consular duties," Ito said and passed over a data stick with her resume.

After inserting it into a computer, Gail considered the information. "Very impressive, though it does mention military action, you are aware that doesn't agree with our ethics?" Gail asked.

"In defence of assigned personnel. I have persuaded my government that aggression is not conducive to the merchant business; this ship while it has defensive armament, it would not be placed in danger deliberately," Ito explained, "Humph in his wisdom has equipped his ships with excessive drives so that a dangerous situation can be left quickly."

"Commendable, so what makes you a kind person?" Gail asked, "Besides you saying so?"

"Amusing question, perhaps if you asked Sartz, she is a leader in this sector and is one of those who supports my candidacy," Ito suggested.

"Well, Sartz, in your wisdom do you endorse this woman to be my daughter's mentor?" Gail asked.

"Certainly otherwise we wouldn't be here, Humph as well had to be confident to loan the ship," Sartz said, "There are more candidates for ships and new owners than there are available ships. Humph had known her for many years from when she first was in a ship's crew."

"I will call Petal here to talk with you," Gail said, "It is her decision, you should be aware that we can be choosy these days. And she has nearly ninety years to select the best pairing."

"I need reminding that I am dealing with a patient people," Ito admitted.

"Ah here she is now," Gail said as a small girl ran up, "Petal, this is Ito Roos, she has a spaceship which may be suitable as your new territory. We have been talking, and I believe she will make a good mentor during your formative years."

"Hello, Ito Roos, may I view the ship?" Petal asked, "It is a Humph's design as Mother described?"

"Indeed it is I also have an education helmet to train you in the workings," Ito said.

"Just a refresher, it is now part of our education," Petal said, "Are you coming, Mother?"

"Certainly, it is nice to visit someone else's home," Gail said, "It is still a novelty to do so."

Having finished their tea, the four boarded the boat and returned to the spaceship.

Petal was provided with the helmet and assimilated the data, After the time, Petal commented, "A little slow, our helmets are much faster to match our abilities. If I may take a tour, I will assimilate the concept more readily."

"Certainly, you may, whatever you need to make a judgement," Ito said, then as Petal dashed off at speed, "Gail, would you prefer a more sedate tour?"

"Yes, that would be pleasant," Gail said.

The three women toured through the ship greeting the Ferry crew as they passed them, Gail admired the hydroponics in the passageways with the screens which showed landscapes on the outer wall.

"This is very pleasing," Gail commented.

"Yes it is, Humph has similar gardens to feel at home," Sartz said, "It has become a trend on all ships, even those without a Droman aboard."

"It is a good idea. When I am out to sea, I do get a little bored with the waves or when sheltering in a barren coastline and only have the rocks," Gail commented, "I will install those myself, the downside of a sea ship is the lack of greenery."

Petal zipped past them several times and was waiting at the bridge when the tour had returned.

"I believe it will be suitable," Petal said, "I have spoken with your crew, and they are content with your leadership."

"Thank you, are you certain?" Sartz asked.

"Yes, I believe so," Petal said, "Mother if you agree, I think this should be my home. I will visit every time the ship comes to Droma."

"It is your decision, Petal. May your journeys take you to the ends of the Galaxy," Gail said, "If you would be so kind as to return me to the Force. Then you can move your ship to the shore and trigger the signal; all will be complete."

Ito and Sartz boarded the boat and did so, "May your travels always be fruitful and the journey smooth," Gail said in farewell.

"May yours also, farewell Gail," Ito said.

Once back on the spaceship, Petal adjourned to her new nest where she may reside for a thousand years, while the crew moved the ship to the shore for the next stage.

"Petal, We are on the coast, and we have lowered the ramp," Ito announced on the intercom.

"Understood, I am triggering the call," Petal responded. There was a keening at the upper range of the human crew's hearing which was the prelude to a swarm of fast running and swimming animals as twenty juveniles raced to the ramp.

These assumed children's forms and made their way to the alcove where Petal was waiting. After a time the parade complete, "You may raise the ramp and make ready for departure," A chorus of voices said.

Sartz nodded and did as advised. "I have been through this several times, the new adult will take a couple of days to assimilate before appearing as a teenage mobile," Sartz said.

"Can we lift off?" Ito asked.

"Certainly, Petal will be okay, and before we reach Grnatz she will be whole and ready to practice controlling the ship," Sartz said.

They were approaching the hyper jump point when a young woman walked in, "Hi, here I am, Petal until I think of a new name for myself and the ship," Petal said.

"Welcome, Petal," Ito said.

"I am studying your library and will come up with something interesting," Petal said, "For now I will observe the pilot and practice what I have learnt."

She settled into the copilot's seat and watched for some time, before asking, "May I?"

After receiving permission, she made subtle adjustments to the course and speed, then without touching the controls performed the same moves. "Just testing the rear controls, I have interacted with the navigation computer and assessed that it is a little conservative. For now, I will compare my calculations with the computer."

"I am always amazed by you people, that an entity barely out of the cradle can do what an adult human would take years to master," Sartz said.

"I was nearly sixteen before I was trusted to drive a ground vehicle," Ito said.

"Thank you. Now, what should I call myself?" Petal asked rhetorically, "How would Helen sound and the ship *Troy*?"

Ito looked puzzled, so Sartz offered, "An Earth woman who was the subject of contention."

"It has a ring to it, Helen of Troy," Ito said, "But doesn't contention in Earth parlance usually mean war?"

"I will make her a symbol of peace," Helen promised.

"That is a worthy ambition. May Helen and the *Troy* prosper," Sartz said.

First stop was Grnatz to register Helen and the ship's name. Ito would be the Captain for the record. Then for the immediate future, the *Troy* would operate as a Fornoon merchant. Typically a ship this size would have ten in the crew, and there were that many cabins.

The shakedown cruise because it was a new ship, would be close to the factory, these were handy as both Earth and Grnatz had one of those. *Troy* started on the milk run for Sartz' fleet, allowing Ito to continue the duties of Roving Ambassador.

Sartz came along for the ride and introduced them to the merchants and smooth the way as the trouble with the 'Greenies' were still fresh in a lot of people's minds, despite Ito often visiting in recent years.

Helen had consulted with Humph and learnt the voice and frequency techniques to enable her to simulate a 'normal' human. She had named herself Helen, so for a model used a Caucasian of Mediterranean ethnicity.

The formalities complete, Ito suggested that following her system of doing the rounds of the sector consulates would be as good as any to introduce her to the routine of touring.

"That is good, all of this is new, it will be some time before I am bored," Helen said.

With a larger ship, Ito and Helen converted one of the holds into a reception area with kitchen and dining rooms to allow Ito to perform her function as a Roving Ambassador.

In the other holds, they were able to carry freight to cover travelling costs as the allowance was inadequate, though suitable for her previous ship.

"I can still keep my hand in and teach you the tricks of the trade while I do so," Ito had explained to Helen and then had to tell the difference between 'tricks' the skill and 'tricks' the mode of fooling another.

As the local merchant was often the consular representative, Ito said, "We can kill two birds with one stone."

"Why would you want to kill a bird let alone two?" Helen asked.

"My ancestors were hunters; now we don't have to kill to eat," Ito said patiently, "It is just a saying to mean complete two tasks with the same effort."

"Why didn't you say just that?" Helen asked still puzzled.

"Sometimes it amuses us to embroider our speech," Ito said then added with a sigh, "To embroider is to add decoration to something functional. As an example on Earth, there were two cultures; one was called the Spartan. They disliked saying five words when one would do. The Athenians, on the other hand, liked the challenge of using long sentences to inform and entertain. Eventually, Sparta became a province of Athens because speech is a part of learning."

"I have heard of those places, so they aren't just part of a story?" Helen asked.

"The places mentioned in the legend of Helen of Troy are part of recorded history; those three places were city-states, where each was the trading centre for their surrounding towns, later these formed into larger states bound together by trade," Ito said.

"Really? Amazing what you can learn with conversations," Helen said.

"There is a saying throughout the Galaxy, if you stop learning, tell them to throw the dirt into your grave," Ito said then held up her hand to forestall the next question, "Meaning while you are alive you never stop learning." This revelation raised a laugh from Helen.

Partners

THE NEW TEAM TRAVELLED AROUND THE CIRCUIT, visiting each consulate as well as visiting merchants in non-capital cities. While it isn't a function of diplomatic ships to act as freighters, the odd cargo they moved allowed them to subsidise the activity.

Several races had colonised the new planet at Centauri Proxima, gazetted as an independent world for trade. The planet Proxima, as it was now named, was added to her touring list. Regularly visited by her as the consular agent and merchant for niche items.

This stop was arranged quickly by the locals, Ito being the explorer of record, life there wasn't overly comfortable with a red sun in the sky during the day and fast-moving stars at night. It was less than a light year from the companion Alpha and Beta Centauri where miners worked, and because the workers need a close by recreation and food supply; this made the colony viable.

So when the *Troy* landed, the consular team usually had a lineup waiting to seek support in diplomacy, mail and small freight that was urgent.

Whenever there was a free week; Helen kept her promise and visited her mother, adding extra distance on the run.

Landing in Gail's favourite harbour, Helen located the Force, "There is my mother," Helen said and slipped the *Troy* down alongside.

As there was now no hindrance, she was able to move the *Troy* alongside then dropped a ramp across, securing the two with lines.

"Hi, Mother, how are you?" Helen asked.

"Fine and yourself?" Gail returned, "Are you having fun touring, perhaps you can settle down in a hundred years or so."

"It is great fun. I know Humph is still touring and enjoying the experience," Helen said, "How are your friends?"

"They occasionally visit when they have a moment," Gail said, "And yours?"

"I take most with me and meet new ones every day," Helen said then asked, "However did you get on with life when you couldn't come close to our people?"

"We had radios and could meet at the halfway point. Otherwise, you wouldn't be here to ask the question," Gail said logically.

"I can understand why Humph was so keen to build a ship and go exploring," Helen said.

"When I first started on the *Force* I travelled everywhere," Gail said, "Though I have visited all the places occasionally returning to my favourites, now I can have actual visits to people and admire their ships without much effort."

"I have been to a dozen planets each as big and complicated as Droma, with billions of people on each, all with different stories," Helen said, "Earth alone has over two thousand languages and millions of stories."

"Should keep you busy for a couple of days," Gail said, "So how are you getting on with Ito, driven her crazy yet?"

"Oh mother, of course not, perhaps a little the other way, it seems humans aren't just happy with saying a simple sentence but have to add embroidery to stretch it out and add confusion," Helen said solemnly, "Even the explanation of embroidery is complicated. Like the lovely flowers around the bottom of the dress; it does nothing functional but makes the conversation interesting."

"I spent ten years teaching you to talk sense, and now it seems it is all wasted," Gail said with a touch of irony.

"I can speak quite clearly when I need to," Helen said, "A

computer talks logical sense but is tedious. I gather the data, then discuss it with a human. Sometimes their thought process is difficult to follow. At other times the different slant opens up possibilities for further thought."

"Yes the nonsense is creeping into our language, with some people who used to be sensible, are trying to bend all the rules in the effort of emulating them," Gail said.

"Seen any new harbours, lately?" Helen asked.

"Don't be cheeky," Gail said, "Seen many boys out there?"

"Now who's cheeky?" Helen retorted, "Naturally I have, there are a few cuties out there. Though they seem to be always going the opposite way."

"Best type, there is a couple of younger boys in the next bay?" Gail suggested.

"You would inflict me on a poor sailor?" Helen asked smiling, "I always tell people that you are kind."

"Of course not, I would make sure they are rich first," Gail assured, "Tell me all about your travels; if I can't go myself, I can still enjoy the description without suffering the discomforts of space."

"So as a dutiful child, I will tell you all the interesting points," Helen said and started.

By the time that Ito was ready to go, Helen had just talked herself out.

"Lucky I don't have a voice box, or I would be hoarse," Helen said as she returned to the *Troy*, "Now I have to learn a new set of stories for the next visit."

"I have enjoyed myself having a good look around your planet, and I have a list to fill for the next visit," Ito said, "I even justified the trip not that I would deny you your visits."

"I need to recuperate before the next visit, it is rather tiring being the centre of attention whereas with you, I just listen and pretend I am not falling asleep," Helen said.

"Ha, you couldn't pretend to be asleep," Ito accused, "When I am feeling frazzled, I find you up to your elbows in a new project."

"I am just a girl busy learning everything," Helen said, "I must keep my mind active, or it would rust, which is an occupational hazard for my people."

"I sometimes run into that problem," Ito said, "But until I hit that point, I also seek everything new that I can get my mental teeth into."

"So where do we go next?" Helen asked.

"I have been called back to Forno for a brief," Ito said, "Funny thing language, brief means short and to the point. I have yet to attend one of these that took less than a day and didn't end with me carrying away half a tonne of paperwork."

"That was most of my talk with Mum, trying to explain why humans talk so much," Helen said.

"Would you like me to remain silent for a while?" Ito asked with a raised eyebrow.

"Not you, I always enjoy our conversations," Helen answered a little flustered, then realised, "Oh you are joking?"

"This time. Please be careful how you frame your comments," Ito advised, "Some people especially the talkative, don't appreciate you telling them that they are motormouths."

"I will keep that in mind," Helen promised.

"Any other subjects that you talked about except presenting a guide to the Galaxy?" Ito inquired.

"Mum asked how my love life was going. I am only a teenager, so I have heaps of time to think about that," Helen said, "It wasn't as though my mother wasn't over a hundred when she met my father."

Once the chat settled things, the subject turned to the course that they would follow to travel to Forno, and what stores they would need.

The course set they lifted off. As the women had plenty of time, on the way, *Troy* visited Proxima to reset the IFF to Forno as it wouldn't do to approach Forno and the patrol challenge *Troy* as a foreign vessel.

"Helen, do you think that you go a little green while we are here?" Ito asked, "Not being racist; it may make movement a little less awkward without the questions."

"And my ID?" Helen asked.

"As a travelling Embassy, I have all the equipment to issue you with an official one," Ito assured her.

"I have researched your databases, included on the ID are my standing in the points system," Helen laughed, "If you set it too high they may try to kick you off the ship or me if it is too low."

"I am afraid that if you were in any competition, they would soon give you the top job and which would effectively confine you to the Capitol," Ito advised, "So let's see?"

Ito consulted the computer, "Okay, this score would qualify you for a ship's Captain of this class," Ito said, "Can't have you too good or they would give you a promotion and try to give you a new bigger ship. Naturally, if it didn't fit, it would be compared with the central database."

"Politics, the more I learn, the less sense it makes," Helen said, "Leaving this ship is undesirable."

"Politics is a way of allowing life to go on and prevent random conflict," Ito said, "I agree that sometimes it seems to slow things down but that is where the benefit comes. Our system means that it is hard to manipulate, as any detected anomalies trigger a lowering in points in other areas and drop your total score below optimal."

They entered the Forno system, and the patrol challenged. The ship IFF read Forno, and the crew all had the correct IDs they were ushered through as a Diplomatic vessel. Landing at the spaceport, Ito was driven to the Administration building for the staff to brief her on the latest Foreign Policy.

"Welcome, Ambassador. How was your trip?" Admiral Hostos asked.

"Excellent, Sir," Ito said, "My companion, Helen who is the captain and owner of the *Troy*."

"I guess she is a Droman?" He asked, "You are most welcome, Helen. The data file lists you as a Fornoon?"

"Subterfuge. In my capacity of a consular official, I can issue documents under the distressed spacers protocol," Ito said, "Only needed to prevent some officious pen pusher trying to prove his authority."

"As long as sensible people know, there should be no dramas," Hostos said.

"If you were to throw all of the examinations and competitions at her, despite being only a mere child in age and experience," Ito advised, "She would attain the top score of the lot and be in line for THE position."

"I suppose you have no ambition in this area, Helen?" Hostos asked.

"None at all, Ito said it would hold me in one place," Helen answered, "I would see the Galaxy first."

"Smart thinking, I would hate to try and restrict you," Hostos said, "Now the purpose of talking to you. The Government have promoted you to the Elder Council for your work as roving Ambassador."

"I hope that doesn't mean I am stuck myself?" Ito asked ambivalent about that prospect.

"No, you will continue on your current mission, as a full Ambassador. Visiting here as the committees meet for policy decisions," Hostos said, "I am on the council. If they tried to lock me up as a full-time member, they would have a fight."

"In that area, the Oxzens run their council much the same way. Their council consists of working Merchants," Ito explained, "I wasn't aware that ours was similar, I suppose that it limits influences."

"Yes that is the intention and why the council doesn't publicise its role," Hostos said, "The council hears my voice at the same level as any other member. I have to maintain my scores to retain both positions."

"How do I fulfil my duties to Forno?" Ito asked, "My circuit covers a large area."

"Once you are inducted, you will be issued a roster of attendance," Hostos said, "If there had been any other present I would not have been able to tell you. Helen, I am afraid that you may not accompany Ito into the ceremony."

"I understand, I can make my way back to the *Troy*," Helen accepted, "It has been a pleasure meeting you Sir."

"The pleasure is all mine," Hostos answered, "I look forward to speaking with you in the future."

Once Helen had left, Hostos said, "Now come with me I will introduce you to some councillors who will conduct the ceremony. It won't take as long as we are all busy people."

She was led to an annexe of the building and entered an airy room filled with comfortable seats arranged in an arc. There were seating enough for a hundred.

At a central table, there were seated a dozen people some who were familiar, especially one, Fedo Roos, who stood and welcomed her. "Welcome, Ito Roos, about time you arrived," Fedo said, "It is my honour to introduce you to our assembly."

"Esteemed Council here is our latest member Ito Roos," Fedo said, "I believe you know some of your fellow members, I will introduce them." He then ran through a series of names, some familiar and some that she hadn't met. Somewhat overwhelming to be introduced to THE Forno who had officiated at her graduation, on the same level as the others.

"Ah young Ito, While I am no longer THE Forno, I do remember you from your graduation," Berntos Doos said, "I will now introduce you the current THE Forno." And Berntos indicated Fedo.

"My evil deeds caught up with me. I get to stand at the parades, sit at Official banquets and forgo some of the fun of being a merchant. Within this chamber, I am the moderator and only have the one vote," Fedo said, "I still have to maintain my outside activities to remain within here, of course."

"As do we all," Berntos added, "That was a masterly document that you authored, it threw our whole policy on its ear, I was quite happy to promote the idea, and as THE Forno my casting vote was not required."

"You have honoured me beyond my wildest dreams, I had help from one of Helen's compatriots," Ito said, "Of course, I was working towards this as everyone is encouraged to have this ambition, but so soon?"

"My predecessor was the youngest Councillor, youngest THE

Forno and longest serving Councillor afterwards until she retired in honour," Berntos said, "You are a little older in reaching the council."

"Come back to my office; I will issue the roster of attendance to you and answer any questions you may have," Hostos invited.

Handing over the data, Hostos warned, "It is essential that this remains confidential, your status of councillor especially. It is the council's avenue of staying in touch with the populous in general. The computer has had its bias altered to view military skills over the same period as other occupations."

"It is the only way our council can address the merchant freedom," Ito said, "How are the client states handling the new policy?"

"Puzzled, several have reverted to self-government with the supported faction having to face the voters without our help," Hostos said, "We have approached the new administrations and signed peace treaties to allow free trade to reestablish itself. Not an easy task as you are our best at doing this. We are training up your peers to perform this task."

"I am betting one of them is not Zento Hoos?" Ito asked.

Hostos asked, "Why don't you think he would be suitable?"

"Have you read his history?" Ito asked rhetorically, "Brilliant enough officer but patience and teamwork are not his strong points."

"I have viewed his file, the only thing between him and the council is patience and teamwork," Hostos said, "This is why those qualities are required, or tyrants, charismatics and demagogues would run the Sector like they do in the Empire."

"If you have spent time there you would know that only the top people and their toadies have anything resembling a pleasant life," Ito advised.

"On the subject of the Empire, in your data file you will find the current policy," Hostos said, "They have found out about our alliance and are suspicious of the strength of the two sectors."

"Is there any activity?" Ito asked.

"Covert work yes, though their appearance handicaps them in our sector and Oxzen," Hostos advised, "Earth and Elysium they blend in, and likely they will find agents matching our features given time."

"Still I will keep my eyes open and pass the data to my consulates to advise of the possibility," Ito said, "I would have thought they were too busy with the New Republic?"

"That is one thing which would prevent them from doing anything overt," Hostos admitted, "If they tried anything dramatic on this side of the Galaxy, the Republic would step in and take over behind them."

"I suppose we could have all the merchants say how good peace is for business and downplay a military alliance," Ito said.

"Better not to even mention that," Hostos advised, "They stick their nose into everything and see the worst case in every story. Perhaps it would be better to say nothing; they tend to discount anything said as cover-ups."

"A bit of damned if you do and damned if you don't, the Earth people call it a catch 22. I will lend you the book," Ito said, "Took me a while to understand the concept but it was amusing once I worked out the key. The humour is that it has elements of truth."

"I need some entertaining," Hostos said, "So please carry on with what you are doing. Good luck."

"Good luck yourself, Sir," Ito said as she left.

When she walked into the *Troy*, Helen was waiting to find out all the news.

"I suppose I can tell you all, the ceremony was simple and I found out a lot of information such as THE Forno is my Uncle Fedo at the moment. The council meets on a 'needs' only basis, and I have the roster which allows me to run my current life without much change in routine," Ito said, "I have a slight promotion to full Ambassador."

"That is good, this council?" Helen asked, "How does it run?"

"Surprisingly, very much like the Oxzen model. Professional people who are part-time lawmakers alongside their regular jobs, doing their other task under cover, except for THE Forno who is all front for his or her term. In this case, Fedo is eager to return to being a merchant," Ito said, "The biggest news Admiral Hostos told me about, was that the Empire has found out about the trade pact. They are suspicious that we are fomenting an alliance to challenge them."

"From what I have read in the trade pact, it discourages military action," Helen said.

"Indeed but as these people use the subterfuge to the maximum. They automatically think everyone else does too," Ito said, "I am to spread the warning that Imperial spies may be active, on Earth and Elysium, Corellian citizens would fit in either. So we expect them to recruit Oxen and Fornoon lookalikes to be agents."

"The administrations are prepared to seek out infiltrators," Helen said, "One thing we should watch out for is a Trojan Horse."

"Do I have to ask?" Ito said.

"Part of the Helen story, a gift which carries infiltrators into your fortress," Helen said.

"Ah yes. If I were to arrange for a refugee from Aurea to arrive in Elysium, they would spread out a welcome mat and let them have the freedom of movement," Ito considered.

"Sneaky, I am too pure and innocent to think of that," Helen said, "During my talks with Pippin, I learnt that they brought three potential adepts back from Aurea."

"How did she know?" Ito asked.

"We Droman can receive an interfering buzz when Adepts are nearby," Helen said, "There is a difference between light and dark adepts. Our old inter-mobile frequency interferes with the dark adepts."

"Good to know," Ito said, "Did Pippin mention names?"

"A family of three named Einsland, Hans, Deirdre and Helen, boarded the *Big Red* and claimed asylum as refugees, their emanations were Light Adept," Helen said, "I will chase that story up when I see her next."

"When I speak to the Governor of Elysium I will enquire while I mention the potential threat," Ito said, "Could a Dark Adept speak light?"

"I am only running off second-hand stories, so I will have to keep a figurative ear open," Helen said, "I will consult with my people as I see them."

"I believe you are my ace in the hole," Ito said, "To use one of those terrible Earth sayings."

"Each has their purpose," Helen said, "So what is our first destination?"

"Earth then Elysium, to spread the glad tidings," Ito advised, "Then through what Humph calls the milk run just to spread the good news around."

Veoos organised this route with the authorities, and the *Troy* lifted off bound for Earth. After the usual travel time, they landed at Canberra having gone through all the routine they visited the Fornoon Embassy and briefed the staff. They would pass on the information to the local authorities and other Embassies. While they were returning to the Airport, a spaceship was landing, on a whim, Ito diverted to this instead of the *Troy*.

The ship they had seen was an Elysium merchant, The *Farstar*. "Hello the *Farstar*, Commodore Roos. May I come aboard?"

"Certainly Ma'am, please do," A crewman invited when he saw who was asking. Ito was a familiar face around the ports.

Helen gave the high sign.

"May I ask your name?" Ito asked.

"Leading Crewman Hans Einsland, Ma'am," Hans said.

"Talk about serendipity, just the man, could I have a chat with you?" Ito asked.

"I suppose so, but I had better have my Captain in on this," Hans said.

"I am here to ask a few simple questions and to brief your Captain on the current situation," Ito said.

"Follow me, oh is your friend a Droman?" Hans asked.

"I am," Helen answered, "Helen of *Troy*."

"Pleased to meet you, I spent some time with Pippin," Hans said, "She gave me the same faint buzz as you do."

Hans escorted them to the captain's cabin where the Captain invited the ladies to sit and speak.

"I am Ito Roos, Ambassador for Forno, I wish to advise you of the possibility of agents from the Empire seeking to infiltrate this sector," Ito said, "As a merchant, this is an important warning from your Government."

"Understood, that should be the extent of my involvement," Captain Stein said, "Why would my crewman be involved?"

"You may not be aware, Crewman Einsland is a latent adept, with some training he could be able to detect Dark adepts trying to pass themselves off as Aureans," Ito said.

"Grim news, so what would you like to do with young Hans?" Stein asked, "He is due for a promotion."

"For now just an interview between us," Ito said, "We won't hurt him I promise."

"Up to you Hans," Stein said, "Be careful and do you want someone to listen in, the Chief perhaps?"

"I should be right, Helen is a Droman and won't do anything to harm me," Hans said.

"Well if you're happy I will call up the Chief, please use my ready room," Stein said, then on the intercom, "Chief Griener to my ready room."

An acknowledgement came through, and Chief Griener was knocking at the door.

"Chief would you stay as a friend here for young Hans, these ladies are going to have a long talk with Leading Crewman Einsland," Stein said.

"Yes sir," Griener acknowledged.

"Don't bend him," Stein said as he went back to running the ship.

"Now sit down and relax, I am going to ask you a few questions," Ito said, "You and your sisters joined Steve Firebrand's ship?"

"Yes we arranged to be smuggled onto the Red ship; where we asked for asylum," Hans said, "Pippin spotted us as potential adepts."

"I believe I can train you to be adepts," Helen said, *"Like this."* The last sent on the telepathic channel.

"Ouch, was that necessary?" Hans asked, jumping like he had been stung.

"*Sorry I will quieten it down,*" Helen said, to the puzzled looks of Ito and Chief Griener as they had heard nothing, just saw Hans' reaction.

Seeing their looks, Helen explained, "Sorry just testing the telepathic channel."

"Are you all right Hans?" Griener asked.

"Yes, it was more of a surprise," Hans said.

"I mentioned the Imperials might be active," Ito said, "If the Dark Adepts are involved; perhaps we can set up a Light Adept team which can detect the Dark without being detected themselves."

"Sounds a little hazardous. My sisters and I went to a lot of trouble to hide from them," Hans said.

"I should have a talk with your sisters and others like yourself and allow them to make up their minds," Ito said, "If Helen can train you to at least protect yourself and be able to alert your ship if there is a hazard. At the same time, if you were to assist Helen to detect them, she can enlist her people to act as a shield to help."

"I am willing, though not if it delays my merchant career," Hans said.

"If you were to join my crew it would continue, I am a qualified merchant and ship's captain, and you can progress that at the same time," Ito offered, "Dromans also have the unique ability to provide a space suit which can act as armour and a communication asset. It should also block an adept at detecting you."

"Captain Stein and this ship employ me for at least the next run which terminates in Elysium," Hans said, "I am contracted to remain, at least until then."

"What are your sisters are doing at the moment?" Ito asked.

"Both at flight school," Hans said.

"We should meet again, the alert is only a heads up at the moment based on possibility rather than any actual evidence," Ito said, "I have been caught a couple of times unprepared."

The first contact completed Ito and Helen returned to Troy to discuss the findings, Ito asked, "Your opinion on Hans?"

"He is a potential Light Adept with no detectable agenda, I am in the learning stage and haven't any skills as yet to stretch further," Helen said.

"I have rung Steve's office, and he will be there tomorrow with Pippin, I think we should give them a visit and consult with them. From what I know of Firebrand he has ideas which lead to breakthroughs," Ito said, "Which is annoying at times."

"We can use the shuttle, then land in his parking area and just walk over," Helen suggested.

They unloaded the shuttle and organised the clearance for the trip. The small craft lifted off and followed the route assigned, arriving at the Firebrand factory where they parked on the spare heliport.

Together that walked over to the Administration building and were shown up to his office. As animosity had settled down with time, the factory welcomed them.

"Good day Steve, this is Helen, my partner," Ito said.

"Ito, Helen welcome. How can I help?" Steve asked, "Something important?"

"I believe so, the Imperials are becoming interested in our sectors," Ito said, "Because we are getting close and becoming friends this arouses suspicion as that is the way they operate."

"And what can I do?" Steve asked.

"It is Pippin's advice Helen is seeking," Ito said, "The Einsland family that you brought back from Aurea?"

"Yes I remember, Hans, Deirdre and Helen. Pippin suggested that they were latent Adepts," Steve said, "So what would you like Pippin to do?"

"A few pointers in identifying Dark Adepts and those who have had contact with them," Helen said, "I have spoken with Hans, and while he is reluctant to do anything soon, his sisters are in the middle of flight training."

Pippin came in at this time and asked, "What exactly is the help required?"

"I am trying to set up a barrier to prevent infiltration of our sectors. I propose a team of Sentinel Adepts to alert us to Dark Adepts arrivals," Helen explained.

"And how would you suggest this help would take the form of?" Pippin asked.

"If you help me research the telepathic frequencies of Light and Dark Adepts," Helen said, "Then work out a strategy to form teams to detect the Dark agents."

"Sounds interesting. I have been in the presence of Klien, the little I picked up from him wasn't pleasant," Pippin said, "When Humph reverted his inter-mobile to our old mode it gave Klien the staggers. It seems it disrupts his connection with the Dark side. Years ago when Humph was on Coruscant; Varta and the Emperor avoided him like the plague. They didn't get close enough to give Humph a reading, just stayed at the fringes to watch him without interfering with cross signals."

"And now since we all cascade our signals, Klien could move close without detecting us as long as we stay off the light and dark marks. He wouldn't be able to detect us; I wonder if we can train our friends to change their frequency?" Helen mused.

"Probably not, Humph suggests that is the connection to the Light overmind," Pippin said, "Luckily for us using the inverted Dark frequency didn't connect us to the Dark overmind. Though the Zombie Beast uses the Light frequency to control those with a little ability."

"What do you think these overminds are?" Helen asked.

"Perhaps Humph may have a better idea; I would be only guessing," Pippin admitted, "I think it is something to do with a symbiotic life which dwells in people from that area. Su Lin had some but was too weak as a child to qualify as an Adept and Gunther Telon has none so is immune from the control of the Zombie Beast."

"We have shields against the Zombie beast, does that interfere with the Light Adepts?" Helen asked.

"I haven't noticed or thought to ask," Pippin said.

"I will chase down Humph he may know a little more," Helen suggested, "I will call in later, goodbye till then."

"Keep in touch," Pippin said, "I will see you around."

"Goodbye Ito, nice to see that you are on the good guy's side," Steve said as he escorted them out.

"Always was, especially now that we agree on the same policy," Ito said, "I have been annoyed by you, though an admirer of your talent in coming up with ideas on obscure things which turn out correct."

"I have funny jumps in thoughts, I sometimes amaze myself where I get them from," Steve said, "So take care, may we always remain on the same side, farewell."

"Farewell," Ito said as she boarded the shuttle to return to Canberra.

"We are off to Elysium to talk with the Governor," Ito said.

They lifted off and headed towards Elysium. Breaking out of Hyperspace Helen answered the Patrol's challenge, and the patrol ship escorted the Troy through to the spaceport.

They had radioed through, and a vehicle was waiting to take them to the Governor.

"Welcome, Ambassador Roos, how can I help you?" Governor Telon asked.

"Thank you, I need first to inform you that there is a heightened threat from the Imperial agents," Ito began, "The Empire is aware of our new understanding, and they have become interested in our sectors."

"Yes I was expecting that, paranoid regimes suspect everything," Telon said, "If it isn't one of their underlings after their job it must be someone plotting. They would suspect that if two enemies are suddenly buddies, it has only one aim."

"They have been interrogating merchants about the trade pact details," Ito said, "While they only could tell the truth, the Imperials would still think that it is a cover-up. And suppose that the merchants are well briefed or only know what their authorities told them."

"About any other people, I would say you were crazy, but that is them to a 'T'," Telon agreed, "So what do you propose to do about it?"

"I intend to consult with Humph. The Einsland family are potential adepts," Ito said, "I have an idea that with the Dromans, with a team of Light Adepts; we may forestall any action."

"Thinking as they do, if we stop them, they may think 'Aha they are hiding something deeply'?'" Telon asked.

"Ouch, that is a point, even as a Merchant and a ship's captain I am not that devious," Ito laughed, "Have you read the book Catch 22? It is amusing, roughly means either is the right one or both wrong. This opinion depends on your viewpoint."

"I have heard the Aussies refer to it," Telon said wryly, "Or they quote an ancient prophet, Murphy."

"I am sure that they just throw those into the conversation to put sensible people off their train of thought," Ito said.

"Full of it aren't they?" Telon said, "However if we prepare ourselves, we can pretend that we don't know. Unprepared it could be hard to catch up."

"So I will proceed, I may need to borrow the Einslands. Hans is due here next week and will be available for reassignment," Ito said, "He is worried that this may compromise his ambition to be a Merchant."

"I have read his file, he is overqualified now, just requires a little experience," Telon said, "The Administration can assign Hans to a third officer's post."

"It just so happens I have that spot vacant," Ito said, "Would that be convenient? My ship technically is on loan from Oxzen sector and is registered there."

"Considering that Helen can run the ship by herself, very convenient," Telon said, "I will ask him, and I suppose that there are also spots available for two graduating pilot cadets?"

"That is a helpful suggestion," Ito replied with a smile. "They would have to be volunteers."

"I wouldn't have it any other way," Telon said, "Though I will dangle an advancement as an inducement.'

"I am experienced in mentoring eager young officers," Ito said, "And Helen would love to have some young companions for a change."

"Don't worry, Ito; I will visit you at the old people's home," Helen teased and received a grin.

"Do you expect the *Yella Terra* anytime soon?" Ito asked.

"Tomorrow possibly," Telon said, "No later than the next day."

"I will do the rounds of the Merchants to inform them of the developments," Ito said, "So I have several tasks which will fill a few days."

Ito left to do this and briefed the consulate and several Merchants as to the possibility of covert activity. Different sectors kept a watching brief on Elysium as well as the other planets in the area if only for trade purposes.

As Governor Telon predicted, the *Terra* landed to discharge cargo and negotiate a new load.

Ito wandered over to the *Terra* and stopped at the ramp. "Hello, the *Terra*. May I come aboard?" Ito called.

"Welcome Ito and Helen," Humph said, "Come aboard."

"Hi Ito, Helen, What are you chasing this time?" Mike asked.

"Several things, I will inform you that your old friend Klien has his eyes looking this way," Ito said, "This new trade pact makes him suspicious that we are seeking to expand into what he considers his backyard."

"As he would," Mike commented.

"If Dark Adepts were to infiltrate our sectors, we need to be ready for covert surveillance," Ito said, "I am trying to recruit Light Adepts to detect them. Once we do that; we can decide the remedy, either watch or intervene."

"Do you remember the Einslands? I have a plan to train them to be Adepts," Helen said, "First I have to convince them that this is a good idea."

"So if these Dark Adepts move in and are detected, what then?" Su Lin asked.

"I would enlist your help as well; I have heard that you have the symbiote organism that is the basis of Adepts?" Ito asked.

"Yes, it allowed the Zombie Beast to capture me. I needed Mike to rescue me," Su Lin said ruefully, "It wasn't a pleasant experience. I have since helped in the removal of several infestations."

"Interesting, I had a little run-in with one of those, and I was lucky to escape by zapping it," Ito said.

"I was tested as a child but deemed to be too low a talent to compete with the higher ranked. The training usually starts at an early age. The school aims the training to prepare to be a Dark Adept; perhaps I was also too ethical for them," Su Lin added, "There was one kid who seemed the centre of attention, and they took him away, Tomi Kleinmann if I remember correctly?"

"Reckon it is Adept Klien we ran into at Aurea?" Mike asked, "Or just coincidence?"

"I doubt that he would be amused if asked that question," Humph said, "So have you an idea where we are headed?"

"If Elysium had a qualified Adept to do the training, perhaps a trip to Coruscant to recruit one?" Mike suggested.

"I am tied up with my consular runs, and I have a commitment to visit Forno regularly," Ito said, "This is confidential, my government has appointed me to the governing council, this is an honoury job but does set policy."

"Congratulations, I suspect being confidential means it is best no one else knows?" Humph asked, "I suppose I can have a run to Coruscant and see if I can talk one into helping. The possibility of Imperial interference may interest them."

"My thought as well," Ito said, "As it would be an official task I can swing expenses."

"Not that it is needed, but as merchants say; knock back a credit, and there goes your credibility," Humph laughed, "Once I unload the cargo at my last stop, I will take a sabbatical and run out there. Maybe there is freight just waiting for a ship."

"Pity I can't visit home, with Klien hanging around that wouldn't be a good idea," Su Lin said.

"Just visiting the Republic may raise a red flag," Mike suggested.

"I will leave it with you. We will work on at this end to identify potential recruits," Ito said, "I will now go onto Grnatz, and the rest of the 'milk run'."

They parted company, Helen and Ito lifted off to travel to their next destination. Arriving in the Grnatz system, they landed at the spaceport and sought out Loxz.

"Good day, only good news this time?" Loxz greeted them.

"Sorry, apparently our good work has been noticed in the Empire, and they are suspicious that we are forming a military alliance," Ito advised, "My Government gave me the heads up that there may be agents checking us out."

"I believe they haven't stopped," Loxz said wryly, "I am aware of their thought process so if we protest our innocence, it would only confirm their suspicions."

"I am investigating the possibility of forming a Light Adept team to detect Dark Adepts before they harm," Ito said, "As you say, too obvious a preparation would draw more vigorous attention. If we don't, and we are caught unprepared, the consequence may be worse. Our biggest asset is that the strongest enemy is on their back doorstep, and we are on the opposite side of the Galaxy."

"I suppose we should prepare for the worst and hope for the best," Loxz said, "My merchants have reported increased questioning whenever they enter nearby sectors; not enough to interfere with business but it is approaching the Old Empire's level of meddling."

"I will do the rounds, giving each stop the good news," Ito said, "Anything that you would wish conveying to my people?"

"No nothing exciting, trade is booming, and everyone I talk to is happy," Loxz reported, "Without the hassle of border restrictions, everything is running smooth. If the Imperials start interfering, that will grind at a slower pace."

"Yes, that is why I helped sort the previous mess out, it is a work in progress in my sector," Ito said, "The inertia caused by a sudden change in policy. The only ones complaining are the toads having to live in a bigger pond."

"Power corrupts," Loxz noted, "The more absolute it gets, the more that it corrupts. In the end, the powerless suffer the most."

"On that jolly note, I will be on my way, goodbye until I can think of something else to upset the apple cart," Ito promised.

"You are nearly as much fun as Humph and Mike, Goodbye," Loxz said.

As they walked towards the consulate to brief them, "He is a nice man, for a king and merchant," Helen said.

"I have always had a good report with him," Ito said, "A busy man who can always get things done, much like Uncle Fedo."

The rest of the round went smoothly, and they headed back to Elysium to check on progress.

When they had landed at the spaceport, a vehicle was waiting for them to take them to the governor.

"Welcome back, spread the glad tidings?" Telon asked.

"Everyone was delighted, if not surprised," Ito said, "Merchants by occupation need to know where the winds of strife are blowing."

"And defenders also, if there were no bad news we would soon be out of a job," Telon said.

"To quote from an Earth book. 'They will beat their swords into ploughshares and their spears into pruning hooks and study war no more'," Ito said.

"I suppose I can return to being a farmer," Telon said, "I wouldn't hold my breath just yet, though."

"My position is secure there is always someone who is on the losing side of some deal or gets drunk and then expects my office to fix it," Ito said, "Of course my valued workers handle the sticky bits and do their best to help everyone at least in their mind."

"Yes as it is here, my position is the panacea for all ailments," Telon said, "Now for the update on the progress. I have about twenty people who have shown ability in adeptness if that is a word."

"I haven't heard that said, but you can make it one," Ito said, "I spoke to Humph, and he has agreed to go to Coruscent to ask an Adept to train our candidates. It may incite the situation if it becomes known to adversaries."

"A narrow path to be walked, I have arranged the candidates, with enticements," Telon said, "So if your offer to mentor the

Einslands is still available. When we can organise the billet, they will join your ship."

"Certainly whenever is convenient, Helen is of course on the ship now as are my retinue who run the consular side," Ito said, "I will do my bit as both Ambassador and Merchant while I am here. So I am here for a few days."

"I will allow you to carry on, Goodbye," Telon stood and shook hands.

"Goodbye," Ito said, "I hope my next visit is only good news."

Ito completed her rounds, and because one aspect of Helen was with her, she heard that the new crew members had joined.

Having completed her circuit, Ito returned to the *Troy* to find the Einsland trio there.

"Please meet Hans, Dierdre and Helen Einsland your new flight deck officers," Helen said.

"Welcome aboard, I will work you as hard as I can so that you can learn as much as possible," Ito said, "Captain Helen is a Droman, who is polite enough to stand aside to permit others to make mistakes. Not that I expect that to happen. My door is always open for conversations, Chef and Chief would love extra hands to keep their departments running."

"Helen has shown me through the *Troy,* and it is even better than the *Big Red.* Which was overcrowded because of our fellow Aureans," Hans said, "Helen has allowed us to update with the education helmet, and I look forward to putting it into practice."

"The cabins are roomy, the last ship had us in one cupboard-sized cabin," Dierdre added.

"So how will we separate us two Helens?" Helen Einsland asked.

"Two ways, Captain and Ensign when Official, Petal for me when casual," Helen Petal suggested.

"Still confusing, so what happens in the longer time frame?" Hans asked.

"Off duty, practice telepathy and other paranormal abilities, on duty watch keeping, other times for exercise and relaxation," Helen

Petal suggested, "If you have any spare time I am sure I can round up something."

"I see that we won't be sitting on our hands too much," Hans commented.

"Carry on Ensigns. Though I may address you as Mister to confuse matters," Ito said, "Ma'am will do for me except informal where I am Ito."

"Yes Ma'am," A Chorus acknowledged.

Life resumed normality; Ito completed the briefing of the consulates, it was now a case of watch and wait.

Ito dropped into one of Helen's lessons which were more in the line of experiments.

Hans was concentrating on a ball rocking it back and forward; this was an improvement as he was smiling.

"Excellent work, Mister," Ito said, "Has anyone else done this?"

"Yes, Dierdre can lift it off the table without dropping it too often, and Helen rolls it about the same as Hans," Helen said, "They can also communicate from the ends of the ship without using the intercom."

"Can you form a shield?" Ito asked.

"Yes we have made progress in that area, I can't detect them if they raise one and it is also a physical one as well, I tried to ping them with a ball, and it bounces away before it reaches them," Helen said.

"I suppose we can practice focus until we have a teacher who knows more," Ito said.

These exercises went on until the *Terra* announced that it was inbound to their current port.

As soon as the *Yella Terra* landed, a party of four figures made their way from the Terra towards the *Troy*.

"Hello *Troy*, may we come aboard?" Mike called.

"Certainly please do," Helen said.

"Master Adept Hoght Boyne, his apprentice Adept Nige Cassel, and you know Humph," Mike introduced the party.

"Welcome aboard, please follow me. I will show you to the Commodore," Helen invited, "I am Captain Helen of *Troy*."

"Ah one of the fabulous People from Droma," Boyne said, "I am delighted to meet you."

"I am privileged to come from there, courtesy of Humph," Helen responded.

Cassel just nodded and followed his master onto the ship. Helen directed the visitors to the map room where Ito and the Einslands were waiting.

"Good day Ma'am, I am addressing Ambassador Ito Roos?" Boyne asked.

"Yes, you are Master Boyne?" Ito responded, "I thank you for your visit to our sectors."

"Well since I am here, best to get to work," Boyne said, "And what would you have me do with these officers?"

"I suppose Humph explained the dilemma, the Empire has its eye on our sector," Ito said, "Agents have been active, Navy Intelligence expects that the activity will be stepped up. If Dark Adepts become involved, I believe that having at least some of our Adepts in place; it may be advantageous."

"And I was asked about the possibility of training them?" Boyne asked, "If I didn't believe that there was some chance, I wouldn't have come."

"So Hans, Dierdre and Helen, why would you want anything to do with this hard work?" Boyne addressed the three Ensigns, "I am aware that you were bribed with promotions to attend this experiment."

"We escaped from Aurea to avoid contact with the Dark Ones; they have little patience with those who don't follow their beliefs, and we have heard how they treat those they do detect," Hans said, "This program may be one way to counteract their influence."

"High ambition, traditionally I would say that you are too old for the rigours I would inflict, but the lessons have been learnt to avoid detection," Boyne said, "I feel several potential souls, who at least that would be partially trainable."

"Who would they be?" Ito asked, "I thought that Helen had found them all."

"Helen of Troy, Veoos and you would benefit from my torture. As would Su Lin and her son Thomas," Boyne said complacently, "Thomas at least is the correct age for the standard induction."

"I believe that Governor Telon has facilities suitable for a training area," Ito said, "I will take you over and introduce you."

"That would be pleasant, I remember Berna Telon from before I began the climb from novice," Boyne said, "I came from Aurea myself before the Dark Ones formed their Empire."

While they were walking over to the Administration Building, Ito asked, "These Dark Ones, what is the difference and why would they follow a different path?"

"Difficult to explain," Boyne said, "We of the Light deplore seeking power for its sake, while to the Dark Adepts, it is a tool to gain position and more power. There are some aspects which are dangerous to learn and deadly in effect; the dark ones aren't selective in any destruction. Even if innocent bystanders are involved, something that rational beings avoid. But unless you are beneficial to the Dark, it is inconsequential to them."

"Ends justify the means?" Ito asked.

"Precisely," Boyne said, "I can detect more talented people. I suppose this is no accident?"

"Governor Telon has gathered as many as she could identify," Ito said.

"Once introduced, I will separate them into levels so that exercises may begin," Boyne said.

Mounting the steps, the receptionist directed the party to Telon's office where Governor Telon officially welcomed the Adepts.

"Welcome Master Boyne, I am glad that you have come," Governor Telon said.

"Thank you, Berna, it has been a long time since School," Boyne said.

"Hoght? After all this time, amazing, is that what happened to you?" Telon asked.

"Indeed, and you a Governor?" Boyne said, "Since I have come all this way to see your candidates, I should meet them and see if my trip has been fruitful."

Governor Telon escorted him to the auditorium where the group was assembled to meet him.

Once introduced by Telon, he began walking slowly across to the centre of the stage, he seemed oblivious to the gathering, meditating he started calling names silently. One by one each stepped forward into two groups one to the left and one to the right.

'*Ito Roos to my right,*' Ito heard in her mind. She did so and found herself with Helen and the three Einslands among the eight waiting.

Speaking aloud, "Those on my left, Adept Cassel will take through exercises, while I will take the other group."

Each group had about fifteen people of all stations, leaving none behind. '*Come with me*' Boyne sent and walked off into a side room where benches had been set up. '*Picture a flame before yourself, then feel the heat grow and the flame steady.*'

Ito closed her eyes and did so, building a small candle flame in her mind before her. '*I didn't say close your eyes.*'

So she opened them, and there was a tiny flame in front of each student, all of which popped out as they saw them.

'*Trust in the flame; it is your friend.*' As he said this; Ito concentrated again to see it reappear. '*Feed the flame,*' so Ito breathed mentally on the flame which slightly flickered as it grew.

She was distracted by a roar of flame beside her as Helen Troy overdid it, '*Let the flame go.*'

"Ah, Helen of Troy, a little gentler perhaps, we don't want to burn the place down," Boyne said with a smile.

"I will have someone pass out training balls, I would like you to practice passing these between pairs," Boyne said, "Helen of Troy would you be so kind as to come with me? Ito if you would join us for a moment?"

Ito and Helen followed him in, "I won't keep you too long from the beginner class," Boyne said, "Helen's talent is remarkable with yours not much behind; which would be unusual for a non-Corellian. I suspect that our ability is because of a Symbiotic lifeform. If my guess is correct; the people from Droma may be a pure form of these lifeforms. Continual close contact with her is why you have untapped talent."

"Ito if you would leave us and avail yourself of the first lesson, I will join you shortly," Boyne suggested.

"Now Helen would you form in your mind a flower," Boyne started, "A bud to start then observe it unfold into a flower before resolving to a seed." Behind her, Ito glanced and saw first the bud then flower before becoming a seed.

Ito walked in and found the class happily rolling balls back and forward between them, joining in she soon had the knack of doing this. She was amazed; the Einslands had taken days to learn to do the same. It seems that Boyne had planted the idea and technique as he spoke.

Helen and Boyne soon did as he had suggested that he would, 'Next lesson, picture a bud. Allow it to grow before you,' Flower buds of all shapes and sizes appeared in the air before the students some growing while others remained as they first appeared.

'Relax' "and attend to me," Boyne said, "That is as much as you should concentrate in the first session. I am pleased with your progress. While it may seem that it has been only a short time, you will find that fatigue will set in quickly at this early stage. Dismissed until tomorrow at seven o'clock."

"Ito and Helen of Troy would you attend me for a moment?" Boyne asked.

She came over and waited with Helen, "Come with me, and we will see how the other group have done," Boyne said. The walked to the other room where Cassel was dismissing his group.

"Adept Cassel, how are your students?" Boyne asked.

"Most of them show quick responses and the rest with a little more work will soon achieve novice status," Cassel advised.

"Meet my star pupil Helen, within days she will achieve your standing. This ability is because she has twenty-one brains to apply to the problem. Ito has absorbed our symbiotes from her and will achieve the Adept level in time," Boyne stated, "I am going to recheck

Captain Cox and see if the same is the case. He may be one who is so sceptical that he refuses to believe it is possible."

"That can happen, I wouldn't be able to help him break through unless he was determined enough," Cassel said.

"Thank you, ladies, I will see you in the morning," Boyne dismissed them.

Ito and Helen returned to the Troy; Ito said, "That took about twenty minutes maximum, and I am tired out."

"Oh is that is what you call it, I have never felt 'tired' before, the exercise has drained me of energy," Helen said.

"I haven't felt this tired since I tried Martial Arts with Pippin and was unprepared for her ability. She was at your stage of adulthood; she had never seen the techniques as far as I know and yet she wore me to a frazzle. I am aware that you match your effort to my needs," Ito related.

"I will swap mobiles as soon as I am back on the ship and allow this one to recuperate," Helen said.

"I am jealous; I can't do that. I will take a lie down on my bunk which will have to be sufficient," Ito said, "As I expect that the Einslands will, even though you have been exercising them. For now, I will come out in an hour and have a chat with the kids."

After the hour's rest, Ito walked out trying to look healthy, to find the three Einslands looking tired. "How do you feel?" Ito asked, "I feel as tired as you look."

"Such simple tasks and I feel like been through recruit training," Hans said, and the girls nodded in agreement.

"Captain Helen complained that was the first time she has felt like that, though she did some extra work for the Master," Ito said.

After a night's rest, the team was ready and waiting at the Auditorium. There was no change as they went through the same routine apparently to see if they had forgotten. It wasn't quite as tiring as the first day, so Boyne added a couple of extra exercises which soon had them drained. Helen just swapped mobiles to carry on.

After several weeks the training had reached the point where the next phase would commence.

Boyne arranged the students into pairs for this exercise, Ito and Helen were then introduced to Light Sabre use, "These sabres are used as a defence against guns," Boyne said, "By using your spatial senses you should be able to deflect blaster bolts away from yourselves."

"Here are practise swords, Adept Cassel and I will demonstrate with the standard warmup routines," Boyne said as the two raised their swords and went through blocks and attacks, choreographed to allow the movements to be seen and set moves remembered.

"I have done extensive fencing with metal sabres and foils which have similar moves," Ito said.

"Very good that should cut our time down," Boyne said, "Of course the 'live' blades will cut through anything except another blade, so there is an extra need for care."

Handing a pair of swords over Ito and Helen were told, "Start slow, I doubt that Helen has even seen a sword before today,"

"Ito has one on her cabin wall, I always wondered what it was for," Helen said, "Of course I have read Earth books which gave rather graphic details on what they can do."

The pair followed the Adepts lead, gradually speeding up to match the Adept's previous speed.

As Ito had said she was competent with foils which are lighter than the practice sabre; if still heavier than the Lightsabre. The difference being the pommel which was heavier and thicker because it contained an accumulator and field generator.

During a rest break, Helen asked, "Do you have the designs of these? I should be able to make a pair."

"That task forms part of your training," Boyne said, "Here is the design, you can take them with you when you finish the session." He handed over a data stick.

"Do you mind if I view them now? Helen asked, "Then I can start on them now,"

"If you wish, but I would prefer that you complete the session first," Boyne said a little puzzled.

"She is a Droman, she can read it here and start work back on the ship at the same time with another mobile," Ito explained.

"Proceed, I should observe her behaviour," Boyne said.

Helen inserted the stick into a computer ran the data at high speed and shut it down again. "I have done the viewing, the assembly is straightforward enough, I have noticed a couple of changes I can make to improve the design," Helen said, "If that is permissible?"

"It has traditional values which the Dark side change at a whim," Boyne said, "I will compare the designs as long as they are not too radical it should be acceptable."

"For now continue with the exercise," Boyne said and once in position again, "Begin."

After the girls went through the basics and had the measures down pat, Ito had fencing experience and Helen, a quick pupil. Boyne called a halt, "Hold for a moment and change partners, I will engage Roos, and Helen if you would pair with Cassel. We shall move onto faster styles."

These ran at a faster pace which with Ito having competed at fencing was able to assimilate quickly and start to extend Boyne; she was aware that he had actual combat experience.

"Hold, I would guess that your experience included blunt swords and adequate protection?" Boyne asked.

"Yes from the age of seven," Ito said, "I have been age champion for many years. Ranked in the top ten all-comers as an adult."

"It shows, with live swords there is no protection that a person can carry," Boyne said, "Except for the sword itself and ship-borne shields."

"A friend has personal shields of two types; one is similar to the ship deflector and the other energy absorbing which would destroy the field and battery of the light sabre. As it overloads the shield accumulator as well, it is not much safer for the shield carrier," Helen said, "Though it does give me an idea for wrist and forearm protection using the deflector shield."

"Show them to me once you have a model to demonstrate," Boyne said, "You may rest for now and if you would send in another pair."

They bowed off and went to seek another pair, seeing Veoos and Dierdre, "You pair should join the Adepts for some more fun," Ito said.

"Yes ma'am," they acknowledged and entered the side room.

"Let's go back to the ship I need a shower then I will join you in the workshop and see what you have been up to," Ito said.

When Ito came into the workshop, she found a couple of Helen's mobiles busy manufacturing and assembling components.

"How is it going?" Ito asked.

"I have just started testing the subassemblies," Helen said, pointing to a light beam in a cabinet. She passed a metal rod across this beam; the blade cut the metal into halves.

"So that works," Helen said, "Now this is the deflector shield." This time she moved a glowing metal tube; this bounced off without being cut by the sword field.

"This can be incorporated into a gauntlet and arm brace to protect the forearms and wrists. By the Star Battle movies, that is the favourite target for the bad guys," Helen explained, "A complete suit would restrict movement too much."

"The blade, how is it produced?" Ito asked.

"A narrow deflector field at whatever length you are comfortable with," Helen said, "And two visible laser pointers to delineate the edges so that you can see it. For me, that is unnecessary as I can see the field."

"I would like to see you the complete the assembly, but I had better do a check on the ship," Ito said, "Yes I know you have been doing it." This because Helen grinned.

Ito walked the ship checking into each department, finding everything was running to schedule, then accessing her council roster found that she had just enough time to arrive there for the next meeting. Ito left the ship and informed the Adepts that she was obliged to visit her home planet.

"I am due to visit my system and report," Ito said, "I will be away for about a week."

"I can excuse you, continue your drills as often as possible," Boyne advised.

Giving her farewells to the students, Ito returned to the ship to begin the journey home.

Helen was still working on the gadgets and assured Ito that two working sets would be ready for display by the time they returned.

The trip was uneventful, and Ito entered the rear of the administration building to attend her first council session.

Fedo Roos called the meeting to order; they followed the routine and voted on a couple of matters. At the end of this Fedo noted that Ito was in attendance and called on her to report, "Ito Roos, please bring us up to date what is happening in the Oxzen sector?"

"I have dispatched the report; I will add that we have Light Adepts from the Republic, who are instructing suitable candidates in their art. Currently, we haven't observed any Dark Adepts," Ito said, "I will brief Admiral Hostos in detail afterwards."

"Thank you, Ito Roos, if there are no questions I will call this meeting adjourned," Fedo said.

Fedo joined Hostos and Ito in the Admiral's office, "So what have you been up to?" Fedo asked.

"Wearing myself to a frazzle, I have the talent to become an Adept, so the Light Adepts, Master Boyne and Adept Cassel have been drilling me in the art," Ito said, "Making me work harder than Ghos did on the *Challenge*. My new status is strictly confidential, don't spread this to unfriendly ears."

"May I ask what status that would be?" Hostos asked.

"Light Adept Apprentice, back to the bottom of the heap," Ito said with a grin, "Some days it just doesn't pay to get out of bed. It seems hanging around with Helen has infected me with Symbiotes which allow strange abilities to emerge."

"May I?" Ito asked, then telelifted a couple of small ornaments from Hostos' desk and juggled them. "You wouldn't believe how tiring that is when you first do it," Ito said as she returned them to their original position.

"Telekinesis, and all the other talents that the Adepts are supposed to have?" Fedo asked.

"Yes, Helen is building Light Sabres to complete our equipment, my skills in fencing are an asset for this," Ito said.

"Interesting, so where is this going to take you?" Hostos asked, "Is it compatible with your current obligations?"

"I understand that the Republic employs its Adepts as envoys and councillors," Ito said, "They do have other tasks such as travelling magistrates. The Empire use theirs as enforcers of the Emperor's policy."

"We have been monitoring the Imperials, and it seems they are looking our way very keenly, so expect some more activity," Hostos advised, "Keep us up to date with your progress."

"Currently we have thirty students, including Veoos, Helen and me, well along the way to being functional Adepts," Ito said, "At least to the point where we can detect Dark Adepts at work. They can hide from Light Adepts, but with the Dromans teaching us as well, we have resolved this problem."

"I gather that there is a high attrition rate among the Dark, as they compete with duels to the death. This practice, in turn, means the top ones are vicious and very competent," Fedo said, "I hope the Light ones don't do that?"

"No, that can be a problem, but with Helen's breakthroughs I believe I can address this disadvantage," Ito said, "Droman can isolate Dark Adepts from their Overmind which then restricts them in their talents."

"Farewell until next time," Hostos said.

"Take care, Ito," Fedo said.

"I will; take care, Uncle," Ito said as she returned to the *Troy*.

"Well Helen, I have passed the good tidings, as well as to my bosses the news about our Adept progress with the caution to keep it to themselves," Ito said.

"If we are clear we can head back and drop into a couple of Consulates, and see what they are up to scratch," Helen said.

"Let's away; I have arranged the lift-off in an hour. We are a little shorthanded as our best people are lounging back at Elysium," Ito said with a grin.

"And jealous that we get to rest," Helen said.

The Troy lifted off to head back to Proxima and Earth, at the last Ito diverted to talk to Steve Firebrand and update him on the progress.

Entering the office, Ito said, "Hi, I am on my way back to Elysium. I am one of thirty students with a Master Adept visiting from the Republic. Some were surprised at being selected, none more than myself. Hanging around with Helen, I have caught a bug which gives me the ability to become an Adept. The jury is still out on if that is a good thing, though damn tiring you should know.'"

"Good to hear, so Helen is an Adept student, doesn't that conflict with the Droman peaceful ethic?" Steve asked.

"Like yourself, if you can neutralise your opponents without harming them, that is desirable," Ito said, "Otherwise, I wouldn't be talking to you now. May I ask Helen to give the two of you the once over for ability?"

"If it doesn't hurt?" Steve said, "Okay."

Helen looked at him and declared, "Yep he has the bug. And so does Pippin."

"So what does that mean?" Steve asked, and Pippin nodded.

"If Master Boyne were to see you, he would put you to work as an Apprentice," Helen said, "And make you sweat. I just about run out of energy, and that hasn't happened to me before."

"Sounds interesting," Pippin said, "How do you start?"

"Let me see," Helen said, "Think of a flame hovering in front of you. Without losing the image open your eyes."

A small flame appeared in front of Steve and Pippin. "Now feed it slowly, very gentle Pippin," Helen said as one flame almost roared.

"Okay let it dim and disappear," Helen finished.

"That became hot," Steve said, "How did I do that?"

"I planted the idea as Master Boyne did to me," Helen said, "Nifty eh?"

"I feel what you mean about the energy drain," Pippin said, "Would you hold my hand?"

"Sure," Helen did so as this was the way Droman passed information.

After thinking for a minute, "That is great, I can see what you learnt without the sweat," Pippin said, "I am sorry Steve, you have to do it the hard way. And if you leave the schematics for the swords and braces, Steve will put his quirky mind to it and lift it another notch."

"I have a copy here," Helen said as she handed it over, "Have a good look at it I made some improvements to the Adept's model."

"Have fun. We go to Elysium, goodbye," Ito said.

"Thanks, have a good trip," Steve said, "Will need to burn the midnight oil for a time."

The *Troy* pointed its nose to the heavens and followed it.

Landing on the Elysium Port Ito and Helen went over to the Administration building to see the state of play.

"Master Boyne, how are we progressing?" Ito asked.

"Far better than I expected, Ambassador," Boyne answered, "It is well that I had low expectations."

"How is your apprentice handling the workload?" Helen asked.

"Being a teacher focuses your abilities, while he grumbles when he thinks I am not listening, he is improving," Boyne said, "Have you been keeping up with up your exercises?"

"Of course, I wouldn't want to restart and suffer again," Ito said, "I dropped in on a Droman/human pair, and it seems it is catching. Helen transferred the techniques and Pippin will train Steve Firebrand up to Apprentice level. He is somewhat ambivalent about it as he was a technical apprentice thirty-five years ago."

"I have as many students as I can handle here at the moment," Boyne said, "I believe that Helen can continue as an instructor after a time. How was your build of the Sabres?"

Helen handed over the first model, "Would you inspect this?"

Boyne did so carefully before stepping away from everyone and energising it. Passing the sabre through the basic warm-up modes, then testing it on a spare piece of lumber, slicing through it without effort. Shutting it off and after handing it back examined the log ends.

"A masterly work," Boyne stated, "Student Ito, remember that you must assemble your own until you reach this standard."

"I was aware of that requirement, and this is my effort," Ito said, "And yes I tried several times before Helen was satisfied." Then she passed over hers for Boyne to examine; with much the same outcome.

"Well done. In this you are ahead of the others, despite being away," Boyne said, then asked, "You have something more to show me?"

"These are the arm braces which add protection from glissading blades," Helen said as she offered the items, "These have a deflector shield built in, these shouldn't interfere with movement."

Boyne examined these and tried them on under his sleeves, drawing his sabre he went through the warmup stances and said, "I do notice some restrictions, but that is because I haven't used anything similar. With my experience, I don't think I would need them."

"I have been practising with them, and I haven't noticed the weight," Ito said.

"The advances you have made are remarkable, those are the smallest shields that I have seen, and the sabre is more compact than mine," Boyne said.

"Hopefully we won't need them. It is not something to play catch up with," Ito said.

"Indeed, tomorrow you are to rejoin the advanced class, and we will continue your education to fill in the gaps that you would have learnt over several years," Boyne said in dismissal.

So the next morning it was back to basic training to lay the foundation for the more complex study.

After a few more weeks Boyne decided that he could hand the task over to the more advanced students. "Time for us to return home. Fare thee well, practice often and avoid conflict," Master Boyne said as he left to board the Terra.

"Well we are on our own, I had better return to my rounds and find what has gone pear shape," Ito said as she headed for the Troy.

As they had been away from their rounds for a time, there was a lot of catching up to do. Especially Diplomatic and merchant activities, the Einslands had rejoined and were able to fit their Adept practice in combination with their ship and merchant duties.

Arriving at Grnatz Ito started the rounds with Loxz and updated him with the state of play. "Not much has changed just yet; We have about twenty Adepts at the journeyman level, enough to start the process of sentinel," Ito said. "The only danger would be if a Dark Adept was cornered and lost his cool."

"In this case, no news is the best," Loxz said, "Need a load to take to Droma? If so I have a small one."

"If it is a help, I was going there," Ito said, "Helen would like to chat with her mother."

"Magnificent, it is on its way," Loxz said.

Ito finished the consular and merchant rounds to show their face and introduce the new crew to the figures that they would have to deal with in their career.

Adept

ON ONE LONG RUN BETWEEN SYSTEMS, HELEN approached Ito and the other students in the next training session.

"Remember the little ray shooting drone in the Starbattle movie?" Helen asked, "I am constructing a facsimile to practice blocking ray blasts."

"Why do we need those, I thought our shields did the job?" Ito asked.

"We can use the sword and braces or the full body shield, not both," Helen explained, "If attacked by multiple guns it could still overload the accumulators."

"Sounds like a challenge," Ito said, "So when are you ready to demonstrate?"

"Tomorrow, I have the frame zipping around now, just testing the autonomous aspect before I fit the lasers," Helen said.

"I will look forward to it, maybe," Ito said, "I find the regular training daunting enough."

The day arrived, and Helen had the drone flitting around zapping Hans as he was wearing the target helmet and belt. He was using his sabre and braces blocking most of the zaps. Every time that he managed to stop them all, Helen adjusted the speed up a notch.

"I am approaching the maximum speed," Helen said, "To achieve a greater speed I will need to rebuild it."

"Feel the energy build and move the blade to where it will be," Helen coached, "Be one with the sabre and feel the force."

After another five minutes, "That is enough for now, you are becoming tired," Helen said and shut the drone off.

Hans slumped as the tension slackened, "Certainly makes you work," Hans gasped.

"My turn," Dierdre said taking up the helmet and belt and stepping into the middle of the room. She was soon regretting doing so as several stinging rays got past her defence.

"Meditate, feel the energy field and sway to the rhythm," Helen advised, "I will pause the drone firing, it will still target. When the focus of the wielder or automat is targeting on your body, you will feel the point of concentration."

Dierdre soon was swaying, moving sabre and arm braces through a pattern, weaving an invisible basket around her. As she did so, Helen turned the rays on again, as the drone fired she blocked them, allowing none to hit. It wasn't long before Helen declared, "Dierdre you are at maximum speed, have a rest."

Having observed Dierdre's technique, Ito stepped up and went through the meditation, and yes she could feel the focus of the drone and anticipated the shot. By the time Helen called a halt, Ito was worn out.

"That is certainly interesting, is it similar to the sabre duels?" Ito asked.

"Yes, your opponent also focuses when on the fencing floor, doesn't your opponent's eyes look to where he intends to strike?" Helen asked.

"Certainly beginners do, the first lesson taught by the swords master is to focus on the centre of the body and detect movement with your peripheral vision," Ito said, "Doing this makes you aware of faults and intentions of your opponent."

"Yes, that is what we are training to use your mind's eye to do the same," Helen said, "I will leave this drone intact to practice with; while I am building an advanced model with some shielding around the processors to minimise the targeting generator."

"Oh great, just when I have the hang of it, you up the ante," Hans complained.

"Allow a demonstration with a small laser," Helen suggested, "Ito would you try to shoot Hans, it is only the same power as the drone's."

Ito started shooting at Hans who blocked them until Ito met the challenge and started shooting at random combined with acrobatics. As these started hitting, Hans made adjustments until again he blocked them.

"Hold, Hans did you feel the difference?" Helen asked.

"Yes it was harder to predict the focus," Hans said, "Ito's mental focus wasn't as sharp as the drone. I guess because she was thinking subconsciously about her movements as well as where she was shooting. At first, she was conscious of aiming, so the target focus was evident."

"Now to throw in a complication, when dealing with Dark Adepts, they use a different mind frequency," Helen said, "Like so."

The students looked at her," You are there but not?" Hans said, "I am only picking up vague random signals."

"In your mind's eye, look for the shadow," Helen instructed.

Ito did, and a vague shadow appeared around Helen and small tubular shadows running in several directions including Helen's nest.

"I can see shadows," Ito said.

"That is the Droman connective channel, and was why we interfered with each other," Helen said, "The Dark frequency is the inverted waveform." Helen concentrated, and the shadow became ominous before resuming her normal cascade.

"I can't stay on that frequency and mode too long because it is quite uncomfortable," Helen said, "I started to feel a thunderstorm of power building and something seeking my mind."

"That I would guess to be the dark overmind, even viewing it was unpleasant, with an overtone of power eager to be used," Ito said.

"The Light seems to be peace-seeking and openness, why one would swap, I have no idea," Dierdre said.

"If you desired power and control, which is the very thing I find most repelling with the Dark Adepts," Helen E. suggested, "Initially

I suppose, the drive would be the curiosity to find the Dark motive and get drawn into the web."

"Curiosity killed the cat," Ito said, "Can we use a different frequency ourselves? The Dark Adepts possibly having been Light at one stage and would sensitive to that."

"I will select another frequency," Helen suggested, "See if you can view this one?"

The four students meditated and saw the shadows reappear.

"Now focus on that, until the shadows become bands of light," Helen said, "You have done it."

To Ito, Helen suddenly became a glowing figure connecting each of the students in the same glow. Then returned to normal as Helen went back to her cascade mode.

"That is wonderful, yet I felt something missing," Ito said, "I suspect by changing we lost the Light Overmind."

"Yes I had the same feeling," Dierdre said, "Now if we varied it slightly?"

With their eyes closed, Diedre became the centre of a glow which flickered.

"I am close enough to feel the Overmind and yet apart," Diedre said.

"I can't see you in my inner mind," Helen said, "I still physically see you, but mentally you are invisible. I will change the new drone to have a filter which only allows only some Dark mode to escape."

They parted for rest and to resume ship routine.

At the next session, the four humans practised the phase changes until each could see the other yet Helen could not.

"If I synchronised with you I could 'see' you, but that would interfere with my mobiles," Helen said, "So I will have to get used to only using my ears and eyes again."

"Since we don't have that problem, it shouldn't be a drama. It does take concentration and energy, best to use it only when necessary," Ito said, "Lift your left index finger to let everyone know you are changing?"

There was agreement all around by copying the signal.

"Of course your motor signals still radiate, but that doesn't give any clues to intentions, sufficient body training will restrict the motor emanations to a minimum," Ito said, "So Helen, how is the new drone coming along?"

"I am bringing it now," Helen said as another Helen arrived carrying it.

"Who wants to be the first victim?" Ito asked and when no-one stepped forward did so herself picking up the helmet and belt.

She was quickly involved in protecting herself as she found it harder to predict the targeting as the emanations were fuzzy and low powered. Adjusting her focus, soon she was in the groove and followed the speed of the drone as Helen changed the pace to higher rates.

After everyone was introduced to the new drone and went through the process, they reached a point, when all were competent with the new drone. The emphasis returned to ship duty to progress the other aspect of pilot and merchant training

The *Troy* team dealt with consular and merchant tasks while they were negotiating trade at the routine stop on Proxima.

They were settling into complacency when Ito felt a strange feeling that someone was watching. As Veoos and Hans were with her, she gave the signal and varied her frequency to the special one. The feeling diminished though didn't disappear as if the centre of the disturbance had noticed the sudden fade.

"Heads up, we may have an adept on the prowl," Ito said, "Keep the conversation to voice and discrete without being obvious."

"Stay here, I will drift over and see if I can isolate our eavesdropper," Ito said. She stood up and laughing added a bit louder, "I have to see a man about a dog, does anyone need a drink?"

She wandered over at an angle towards the toilets and was pleased that the fuzzy spot remained where it had been, with the attention still centred on the other two. Using her radio, called the *Troy*, "Hi Helen, would you bring over that package on my desk?" This message was the code that Ito needed her sabre as there was likely a Dark Adept. The latest version of the arm braces blended in better with the clothes they wore. The Sabre while compact and discrete, still stood out if you knew the giveaway shape.

Ito circled to the bar, studying the fuzzy centre in the mirror and located a couple of likely looking men. Somewhat out of place in newer Aurean style clothing. Most travellers from there wore a version but gradually as those showed wear had started substituting local clothes.

Returning to the table with fresh drinks, Ito asked, "Recognise the Aureans on that table?"

"They look a little familiar, I think I remember a couple like that in uniform," Hans said, "I will drift over, act a little drunk and see if they recognise me."

"Relax until Helen arrives with my package, so I can back you up if it turns to worms. The best reading I have is that neither is Klien," Ito advised, "Ah here's Helen." Helen walked in with a small bundle. Each of the team had pistols except for Helen who had an internal sleeper.

Hans stood and staggered a little off kilter towards the pair, "Hey, is that you Frederich?" Hans asked in Corellian, "Small Galaxy eh? Who is your buddy?"

The pair stiffened and then recovered, "Sorry you must have me confused," Brown hair said in Galbasic, which gave away the understanding of what Hans had said.

"Oh sorry, you look just like my old chum from recruit school," Hans apologised. He then retraced his steps unsteadily.

Hans slumped down with his back to the pair. He said, "Yes Frederich and Johann from my intake, they were selected early for different training after only a few weeks. I remember as they were proper stuck ups and didn't want to mix with the proles."

"I guess the sort that would stand on their supposed inferiors to reach heights," Veoos said, "They have remembered and looked startled."

The pair made a decision and made their way over to stand over the table, seeing Hans with three women decided to pick a fight.

"Hey, barfly, how about sharing the birds with real men?" Brown hair asked belligerently.

"Gentle with your name calling, pilgrim," Hans drawled as he rose to his feet standing in the ready pose.

Brown's sidekick started to draw his pistol until he noticed that Ito had already pointed her gun.

Brown hair sneered drawing a light sabre and flourished it. "Don't try shooting,"

Hans gestured, and his sabre flew to his hand to be held at the ready, commenting, "I wouldn't think about that either."

The two sabres registered on the people at the nearby tables, and there was a general exodus from the area.

"How about Frederich and Johann? Closer?" Hans said, "Hans from the 553rd intake."

"Really why didn't say so," Fred said, then relaxed his guard and putting away his sabre, a smile not reaching his eyes.

Hans shut down then hooked his sabre on the belt, "Still a little touchy as I remember, so what have you been doing since those days? I am on a freighter."

"Just hitching around looking at new places, heading for Elysium where I hear that fellow Aureans are living," Fred said, "Might land a job in construction."

"They are looking for Ship crews as well," Hans said.

"Been on the ground too long," Johann said.

After taking a closer look at Hans' companions, Frederich said, 'We should move on, perhaps we will see you around.'

The pair drifted out of the bar to confer.

Once they were out of hearing, Ito asked, "Opinion, have we blown our cover?"

"Partially, but their superiority complex will make them think that there is only one low-level Light Adept and not a worry," Helen said, "I was able to overhear some of his thoughts, he has a superiority complex in spades."

"From my memory and we only crossed paths for a few weeks, he had it bad then," Hans said, "From his fringe self-talk he considered Ito and Veoos to be inferior beings, Helen didn't register."

"I have sent another mobile to watch them," Helen said, "They are standing in the shadows watching the exits."

"Do you think they will try to follow you?" Ito asked.

"Just me, it wouldn't occur to them that you were my boss," Hans said, "Which is to our advantage; if I leave by myself, they will follow, perhaps try and capture, though I gave them pause producing the sabre."

"From my senses, only Frederich is an Adept, the other is a soldier," Helen said, "They are relaxing not concerned as they would expect an odd adept to be drifting around."

"We have several choices, leave as a group, they would follow to the ship and trace it to our task, Hans by himself they would try to capture," Helen suggested, "and I can provide disguises which would cover both identity and mask any emanations."

"The last mode, that way they won't follow and find out what I do," Ito said, "Yes, that is best leave a slight puzzle as to what ship Hans is on."

"They will automatically think he is a roustabout," Helen said.

"It is better to allow misconceptions than drawing heavier flack by giving him a lesson in manners," Hans said.

"Another mobile is on the way and carrying a suit each for you to wear past them," Helen said, "By the time they realise we have departed they won't know which ship."

The mobile arrived and handed over blobs for the team to use once out of sight. After a short few minutes, the team including the two Helen mobiles, each now looking entirely different and dressed nondescript, before they drifted out in pairs. The suits had the extra advantage of covering their telepathic abilities. Helen being the suits could still keep an eye out for the Imperial duo without any heads turning to scout the surroundings.

One Helen peeled off to join the observer in case the target pair split up, "Just adding to the watcher watching the watchers." Helen said in their ears.

"Johann has just returned to the bar," Helen reported then shortly later, "Back out again looking annoyed, he guessed we had given them the slip. They are now heading towards the port hoping to spot us."

The team entered the *Troy* and removed the suits, "Now we monitor the ships and see which one they enter," Ito said.

Helen was still following, changing her appearance whenever she could do so, ensuring that she wasn't spotted. Until at last they gave up and walked to a ship parked towards the outer areas. This area was usually empty as most freighter crews didn't like the extra distance.

"Must be a new one that they don't want to be scratched?" Helen suggested, "I will give them a little while, then I will be an old drunk trying to find my ship and see if they say the name of their ship."

After observing for an hour, Helen carried out her plan; so as an old ship hand and half drunk stumbled up to the ramp and demanded, "Is this the *Tumble*?"

"No, go away, it is the *Bandersnatch*," Johann shouted.

So Helen stumbled on and approached several other ships asking the same question so that Johann wouldn't get too suspicious.

Back on the ship Helen tapped into the Port computer and found that it wasn't the Bandersnatch but the *Grande-Force* registered in Fvelsving.

"Not overly keen to let people know who they are," Ito said, "I will try to pull a few strings, can't be seen to be involved or it will ring the alarm bells. Our next port of call is Earth," Ito added, "My old friend Firebrand has a few very special gadgets."

The trip to Earth was uneventful, except that the customs ship reported that the *Grande-Force* had passed through on the way to Elysium.

"Well that clears the way for our visit," Ito said, "I expect that there are agents active here. The advantage is that they don't personally know us though I guess an Adept can pass on a mental image."

Using the shuttle to travel to Charlton and the Firebrand Factory Ito landed in the car park. Ito made her way up to Steve's office.

"Good day Steve," Ito said, "I have a problem, and you may have a remedy."

"Good day to you too," Steve said, "And just what sort of problem? I am still recovering from the last visit."

"You remember my sober friend from Aurea?" Ito asked, "He has a few friends visiting our planets."

"These friends of his, they like the shadows perhaps?" Steve asked.

"I met one on the way at Proxima," Ito said, "How is your progress with your apprenticeship? If you are getting bored, Helen will pass on a couple of new toys to fix that."

"You are paying me back for the trouble I have given you. You are mean," Steve fake groaned, "So what does he look like?"

"How is your meditating?" Ito said, "I will form the face in my mind. Would have been a little awkward to take a picture."

Steve relaxed and allowed his mind to drift with the waves. Within his mind, an image formed. "Fascinating, not someone I would take home to meet my missus."

"Did you receive the mental key?" Ito asked.

"So that is a Dark Adept, very disturbing," Steve said, "If that is a sample of them I want nothing to do with Klien or his boss."

"We may not have that choice," Ito said, "They are becoming interested in us. By Helen's analysis, they believe that they are superior and will not take us seriously."

"I have some methods of surveillance that I would rather not become public," Steve said, "Pippin can use her mind in parallel with this to find some intruders if she can isolate them to a relatively small area."

"While I love to learn more of this, the hints that I have would tell me that this is one invention best left with you," Ito said, "Having put a flea in your ear, which sounds annoying, I will leave it in your capable hands."

"Most annoying, travel far and safe, Ambassador Roos," Steve said.

"Meaning as soon as possible, Manyana, Commodore Firebrand," Ito said as she left.

Ito returned to her shuttle and rejoined the *Troy*.

"I have put the problem to Steve, much to his delight," Ito said, "While I passed the information on Frederich to him I received back a hint that he can do a lot with his special tools."

"What toys does he have?" Hans asked.

"Steve didn't like me putting a 'flea in his ear', I guess putting a small sun in the middle of a Sun Destroyer could spoil someone's birthday party," Ito suggested, "The how I do not want to know."

"So next stop is Elysium?" Dierdre asked, "Frederich said he had said that is where he was going."

"I sent a Hyperwave message with the code for a heads up and to employ an arm's length surveillance on the *Force-Grande* or a ship matching that description," Ito said, "I suppose we head for Elysium and see if we can spot something."

After making *Troy's* preparations, they lifted off and headed to Elysium; arriving in-system to encounter the customs patrol.

When the inspection team came over, Ito asked, "Hello, have you seen this ship," handing over a picture that Helen had drawn, "Possibly named *Force-Grande?*"

"The records show that we intercepted one similar, and marked it as clear, though for the life of me can't remember any details," Lt Bourne said.

"Not a good sign, the ship had at least one Dark Adept who likely interfered with your memory," Ito said then asked, "Helen can you see if you can pick up any fragments?"

"I will try, now Lt Bourne, this won't hurt, please empty your mind of thought and relax," Helen said, the pair stayed quiet for a moment before she announced, "Yes Frederich was here and tried to read his mind, this upset the memory."

"Now I remember, nasty bloke looked deep into my eyes, next

thing I was back on the shuttle," Bourne said, "Is there something I can learn to stop that?"

"Without the full treatment, it would mean that he would resort to violence," Ito said, "I am afraid that while you do have some talent, it is not enough for full protection. A Firebrand Spacesuit does provide some, but again it may provoke his reaction. Everything that you have heard about these Adepts is true."

"Slight comfort," Bourne said, "And having a friendly adept would have the same result?"

"The four of us had encountered him, but as we were trying to stay undercover, we could do nothing," Ito said, "If we pretend that we don't know they are here, the Big guns won't become involved."

"We had been alerted for that ship, and now I can pass on a report," Bourne said, "Now that I can explain what happened, I won't look an idiot if my boss examines the encounter log."

"As long as you use the code, without being too specific it shouldn't alert the agents that we are on to them," Ito said, "I should arrange a little accident for Frederich. Oh, nothing too fatal Helen." The last to reassure her.

Having settled Lt Bourne, assuring him that he hadn't failed in his duty; the *Troy* continued to land at the Elysium Spaceport.

Parked in the back lots was the *Force-Grande*, as *Troy* was a consular vessel, the Spaceport Department allotted a more appropriate site. After the team had unloaded the vehicle, they drove to the Administration building to brief Governor Telon.

"Governor Telon, are you aware that a Dark Adept is in Elysium?" Ito asked.

"Yes Ambassador, the message was received, and we have surveillance teams in action," Berna said, "As per your advice there is only standard security with our Adepts keeping tabs on the security. The patrol identified the ship as *Travelling Haven* from Tatooine."

"At Proxima and Earth, it was *Force-Grande* from Fvelsving. However, my investigations indicate the origin is Corellian and Empire," Ito reported.

"Now your companions, how are they progressing?" Berna asked.

"Very well, I recommend their promotion to Lieutenant and assign them to independent command," Ito said, "I would also confirm them as journeyman Adepts, on the quiet for now."

"Excellent progress, I will formally award the promotion and pass on the recommendations," Berna agreed and called the subjects in and awarded the promotion.

Assuming a formal mien, Berna said, "Lieutenants Hans, Dierdre and Helen Einsland, congratulations on your promotions, may you serve our nation well." Shaking their hands.

Light Vs Dark

WHILE THE *TROY* WAS ON ELYSIUM AS PART OF THE TOUR circuit; Ito and Helen visited the Adept Academy, to see the progress of the classes.

The first intake was now taking on students themselves. Remembering the catastrophe of the Dark massacre at the Coruscant Academy, the administration instituted extra security precautions.

Entering and speaking to Lt Dierdre Einsland who was one of the instructors.

"Welcome Ambassador Roos and Captain Helen," Dierdre said, "About time you visited."

"Hi Dierdre, the lessons are progressing?" Ito asked.

"Since everyone is complaining about the workload, it is going great," Dierdre said, "The Academy has expanded into selecting young children as beginners, and they seem to take to it like ducks to water not like us old hens."

"Useful metaphor," Ito said with a smile.

"Come, I will introduce you as the source of all their misery," Dierdre invited with a grin.

"We are all students; that would be entertaining. The young will eventually take the reins and run with it," Ito said.

Dierdre led the way showing the classrooms where different levels of lessons were being carried out. The Kindergarten was the most interesting as the children were performing forms that Ito hadn't attempted. Some of these consisted of more peaceful pursuits such as hovering in one place while telejungling.

Seeing this, Ito asked, "Now why didn't I think of that?"

"Because it doesn't involve the avoidance being skewered or fried?" Helen suggested.

"That is so, being a practical person I am afraid I hadn't seen the point," Ito said.

"It should promote meditation and concentration," Helen said, "Let me think."

Helen concentrated and rose into the air. "Well that is one part of me, I have to split my attention to stop the rest floating around."

Lowering back to her feet, Helen looked absent; She said, "Warning! Several Dark Adepts are approaching."

The duty instructor spoke to his class, "Attention, quietly pick up your things and move to the safe room."

The class alighted, grabbed their books and moved calmly to an area on the wall which slid back to reveal a door which opened into a room. Once the last child was inside the door closed, and the wall resumed an unmarked facade.

"It is fireproof and would take a bomb large enough to flatten the building to breach the door," The Novice Instructor said.

"Senior Adepts are to man the entrances," Dierdre said.

"Where would you like us to stand?" Ito asked.

"Follow me, I am Dehn," He said. Turning Dehn walked towards the entry drawing his light sabre as he went.

As they arrived at the hall, dark figures charged in, several had pistols while others held sabres.

Seeing the defenders, the ones armed with pistols started shooting.

The defenders deflected the blasts, directing them back at the aggressors making them duck.

Ito, Dierdre and Dehn fanned out to meet the Sabre wielders charge.

Ito quickly disarmed the first attacker before swinging between the second man attacking Dehn. He had been having difficulty defending.

Helen used her sleep gun to settle the gunmen; She then quickly tied them up to ensure they took no further part in the attack. By now Elysium troopers had entered and stood guard on the captives.

Helen moved over and smoothly intercepted the disarmed Adept, picking him up like a baby and bundled him into a cupboard.

By now Ito had fenced her opponent to a standstill blocking every move and throwing him around every time he tried to use telekinesis.

They had just secured the last enemy Adept; the doors burst open again, and a dark figure strode in.

"Hello Klien, what brings you here so far from home?" Ito asked, "The Emperor may miss his right-hand man."

"Talk is cheap, surrender my men and stand aside," Klien snarled.

"I don't remember inviting you here," Ito said.

"Why are you involved?" Klien asked as he surveyed the situation, "You are a foreign diplomat not one of these rebels."

"I helped start this school. So I have an interest in its health. What is your intention?" Ito asked watching him for the inevitable attack.

She saw Dehn starting to move into a challenge position, 'Keep out of this; he is too good for you.'

"To nip this cancer in the bud," Klien said, "Step aside, or join the rebels under my foot."

"At the moment your boys are cooling their heels," Ito reminded him, "And your ship is under guard."

Klien slid forward and swung to be blocked casually by Ito's sword, she followed with a riposte; the blades flew in a dazzling display of speed and dexterity. After several passes, Klien stepped back and tried a telekinetic throw, barely lifting Ito before she turned the tables and slammed him against the wall.

"Naughty, perhaps you didn't notice the Dark force damper we have?" Ito said, "Doesn't hinder us."

Klien didn't say anything just resumed the sword attack flashing as many attacks as he could without getting through her defence except one which hit her shield brace when she blocked instead of ducking; which would have left her open to the counter-attack. This encounter put him off his stride as he had expected the blade to either slice her arm or force a stumble. This lapse left an opening for Ito, and she cut through his sabre handle. Before she could follow up with another attack, he drew another and with a blaze of moves covered his escape through the door.

"Make sure no one tries to stop him; he would cut them down," Ito warned over the security radio, "Let him depart."

She turned back to the staff who were still trying to make sense of what happened. The total time from warning to the dust settling was five minutes.

"How is everyone?" Ito asked.

"None hurt, the Dark attackers are bound and gagged," Dehn said.

"Don't take your eyes off them, the Adepts are still dangerous," Ito said.

"I will have a chat with them when I get a chance," Helen suggested, "I have a couple of ideas of how to set them straight."

"Might be worth a try. For now turn the soldiers over to Security," Ito said, "Then isolate the Adepts in separate cells within this building. Making sure the damper is on and watched by our Adepts."

"We will do that, Ambassador," Dehn said.

"Klien has arrived outside the *Troy*," Helen said, "I am waiting for him to try something. I may give him a lesson in manners."

"Please be careful," Ito said, "It is strange talking to you about something happening a distance away. But I suggest we get together and keep an eye on this maniac."

"I have warned Veoos and the rest of the crew to stay back while I deal with this. The ramp is up and locked," Helen said, "The Dark Damper Field is on."

After a pause, "He has noticed that and backed off, " Helen reported, "Now he is headed to a scout. He has entered and taken off."

"I will be there shortly," Ito said, "We should give him an escort, so he doesn't hang around upsetting the pigeons."

Ito and Helen entered the *Troy* and strapped in for liftoff.

"Okay Helen, let us see what your toy can do, strap in everyone, 'G' cocoons deploy," Ito said as the *Troy* pointed the nose into the sky and followed the scout.

"*Troy* to patrol, don't try to intercept, the pilot is dangerous," Ito transmitted.

"Patrol to *Troy* acknowledged," the radio crackled.

"Our boy is driving at maximum for that class, we are closing," Helen said.

"Just close enough to follow," Ito said, "I don't know what his range is, but potentially he might throw an asteroid at us."

"Could make a new sport playing tennis with those," Helen said.

"Might catch on. However, letting one past would be a bit inconvenient," Ito said.

As they approached the jump point, it seemed that Klien had detected them and veered off so that his jump direction wasn't evident. The scout ship continued towards the Asteroid belt and started weaving through the rocks.

"I believe that it may not be too good an idea to pursue too close," Ito said, "Could you extrapolate his course from his potential entry?"

"I could chase a bit, but I would rather not scratch the paintwork," Helen advised, "If I were to jump in that direction, it would be the first of a line to take me towards the Correllian Sector; also to a thousand others of course."

"A vague direction will do for now. If *Troy* gives up in disgust and a shuttle with a cloaking field were to shadow him until he left for parts unknown?" Ito asked.

"If you join me in the forward shuttle we can have a little fun," Helen said, "I am warming it up now."

The shuttle launched and soon was dodging the debris slowly catching up on the scout, as the shuttle was a typical overpowered Humph's model it had no problem keeping the scout in sight. Klien, once he had determined that the *Troy* had broken off the chase, slowed to a more sedate pace.

Klien's scout drifted towards the entry point of the asteroid swarm trying to locate *Troy*. Helen had moved the *Troy* out of sensor range, supposedly attempting to guess another exit. Klien didn't find the ship, so decided that he had enough breathing space, accelerated towards the jump point.

Klien's scout approached a different point and engaged his Hyperdrive. Helen's shuttle right on his tail as it was suitably cloaked.

"I suspect that he would more likely depend on his Adept senses to monitor the surroundings rather than radar," Ito said.

"I am about to break out of Hyper," Helen said.

The shuttle did so, coordinating with Klien's scout so that there was only one Hyperpulse generated. Klien cruised for a few minutes before re-orientating and jumping again in a different vector. Helen was able to match this and followed; in the meantime, the *Troy* with the balance of Helen also followed one step behind to maintain contact with her mobile.

The ability was because Helen knew where she was going because she was already there as a guide. Caution was required because if Helen broke the link between the parts, the absent mobile reverts to an intelligent suit needing an armature to function.

On the second emergence into normal space, Ito was able to detect several large vessels which were Klien's destination. Helen immediately reversed and jumped back to the last system where Troy was waiting.

Rendezvousing with the *Troy*, Helen returned the shuttle to its hanger and with Ito returned to the map room to confer on the next step.

"I counted Five capital ships waiting," Ito said.

"And another dozen support and shuttles. One of the capital ships is a Star Destroyer," Helen added.

"Only a match for Rham's detachment so I doubt that it is intended to invade our sectors," Ito said, "Of course, reinforcements could be in the next system."

The team used the Star chart to work out the relative positions of the two Systems, concluding that the one which they were currently orbiting was just a decoy, and the Imperial sub-fleet was closer to Elysium.

"Admirals Rham and Hostos need to know about this deployment," Ito said, "We return first to Elysium and then take a message to Forno."

Troy was set to return to Elysium; after parking, Ito and Helen set off to the Administration Building to confer with Rham.

After being escorted into his office. "Good morning Admiral, I have strategic news which you should know about."

"Good morning Ambassador, I suppose it has something to do with your friend Klien?" He asked.

"Yes, He has a detachment waiting in an uninhabited system," Ito explained, handing over the data.

Rham loaded the information and assessed it, after some minutes said, "I see just a guard if a little excessive. Big enough to deter action by us yet too small to be a threat."

"I concur, enough ships to achieve a successful invasion would leave their home sector vulnerable to invasion from the Republic," Ito said, "Though the presence of this force means taking precautions with merchant ships and the installation of garrisons for the more isolated systems."

"If we were to confront at this system another detachment could infiltrate and destabilise somewhere else," Rham said, "Working this out is why I have the shiny buttons."

"I will now deliver a copy to my people and give the heads up as I go," Ito said, "I will make Firebrand's day as I pass."

"Thanks, you two seem to the bearers of bad news," Rham said.

"I always do my best to alleviate boredom," Ito said as she left.

Re-boarding *Troy*, Helen soon had the nose pointed first to Earth to visit Steve Firebrand and give him the new data.

Landing at Westbrook Airport, Ito used her shuttle to travel over to the Firebrand Factory and made her way to his office.

After exchanging greetings, Ito arrived at the reason for the visit, saying, "Heads up, Klien has a task force in this system." Handing over the data, "Not an invasion force but just sitting this close is as effective as a blockade."

"Mmm, I would have to agree. Is Klien aware that we know?" Steve asked, "I can use my toys to spy on them."

"Sounds interesting, does your equipment travel that far?" Ito asked, "Though we have to assume he at least suspects that we on to him."

"Without giving too much away, recently I have been in contact with someone who needs my help, and I have practised this technique to the point where I am confident," Steve said, "Also I am developing a method to neutralise these Sun Destroyers without harming the crew. The last because of Pippin's sensitivities."

"Being a partner with Helen, I am aware of that," Ito said, "She didn't like me humiliating Klien despite his lethal intentions."

"It does make me feel a little ambivalent," Helen admitted, "I have a theory that perhaps I can convince the Dark Adepts to mend their ways."

"Wonderful ambition. Life would be much less of a challenge if everyone were courteous and helpful," Steve said, "A bit monotonous, though."

"As I was discussing with Berna," Ito said, "This is unlikely to happen anytime soon, groups have conflicting aims in life, and with the usual misunderstandings, we end up pushing the door in opposite directions and blaming the other for not cooperating."

"Yes, that is so," Steve said, "Human nature being what it is and not discounting that aliens may think entirely differently, any conflict ends up being resolved by boring talk until both sides either achieve an understanding or give up from frustration."

"Something for philosophers to debate," Ito said, "I am off now to Forno and pass the good news."

"Thanks for filling my plate to overflowing," Steve said, "I will see if I can sneak up on Klien and find out what he is up to."

The *Troy* took off for the trip to Forno without making further stops arriving in the system without drama.

Reaching Admiral Hostos office, Ito presented the data for his assessment. After considering it, Hostos said, "It seems the Empire is becoming a little unfriendly. From this, I guess at least one Imperial knows your new status."

"I am afraid so, I managed to demonstrate my ability and some defence equipment," Ito said, "As the stakes were high. I had to put in the maximum effort to protect the Academy's students."

"This force described, while we can stalemate any move," Hostos said, "Because it is there, we have to set up garrisons at the more vulnerable points without going onto a war footing."

"We need to follow a conservative path because we need to maintain our economy. The easing of the policy on trade has seen an increase in the standard of living which will be sensitive to moving to a war footing," Ito said, "And looking too warlike could justify Imperial interference."

"I agree, do you have any ideas?" Hostos asked.

"My old nemesis, Commodore Firebrand has a few ideas and specialised equipment," Ito said, "He thinks he can spy on Klien covertly. And perhaps neutralise the capital ships, though I have no idea how he could do that."

"I will work out a defence system that is practical," Hostos said, "Once I have done that I will brief the Council."

"For now I need to return to Elysium to investigate the captives we are holding," Ito said, "Helen thinks that she may be able to talk them into being useful citizens."

"Good luck with that, from my intelligence reports, their ethos revolves around the gaining of power by whatever method to overcome any opposition," Hostos said, "Those too weak to resist are used as stepping stones to gain a higher position. Those stronger toadied to until the subordinate can backstab."

"Yes a nasty philosophy, I will leave now and give Helen her best shot," Ito said, "If she can turn even one. It would be a tremendous gain in knowledge as even the lowest level Dark Adept has the full training."

"Take care, I hope that Firebrand comes through with his plan," Hostos said in farewell.

"When I find something new I will pass it on," Ito said.

Troy lifted off for the return to Elysium via Earth.

First stop was the Firebrand factory to see if he had found out anything.

"Hi, Steve, what is the gossip?" Ito asked.

"Good day, I have some news," Steve said, "Have a look at this video. I had to use an automatic camera as Klien can sense a live observer if he is close enough. I looked first, and he almost caught me before he decided it was imagination."

The screen showed Klien talking to the ship commanders, on the speakers he was saying, "These upstarts have had a couple of lucky escapes. So there will be a maximum effort with scouts to find their weak points." After a minute Steve turned the sound down, before adding.

"He rants on for a time; the data boils down to about fifty scouts checking on all of the systems in our sectors. Since we know what to look for we can either feed false information or neutralise them," Steve said.

"Too vigorous a neutralisation would make them send heavier vessels and escalate the situation," Ito advised.

"Point taken; I will distribute the data that I have and leave it up to those whose job it is," Steve said, "If we intercept the odd scout with a regular patrol it won't ring any bells. Knowing where they are is our advantage so that we can avoid the area with important facilities."

"This technique of yours?" Ito asked, "Just how flexible?"

"I haven't found the limits yet, another reason to keep quiet for as long as possible," Steve said, "I read the Lensman Series which described the using and copying of advances until the two sides were re-balanced, then another breakthrough to give a temporary advantage to one side or the other. The escalation came to the point when the destruction of whole systems by weapons for which there was no defence."

"The bold see a mountain as an obstacle to be climbed," Ito suggested, "Like my idea for the robot fighters, countered by your drones. How did you guess?"

"Had an idea, lucky for me I was right," Steve said.

"And most annoying for me. Still, it led to us being friends eventually," Ito said, "My sector is now getting used to the new prosperity."

"The losers of our last big war were required to disarm, are now the economic leaders because economics redirected their energy to peaceful activities," Steve said.

"If you have that in hand, I will deliver Helen to the Adept captives so that she can talk with them," Ito said giving her farewells.

Having boarded the *Troy* and cruised to Elysium; Helen and Ito made their way to the Adept Academy to interrogate the captives.

After a quick interview with each of the captives, Helen selected the least uncooperative, Arne.

Directing the man and his escort to a room with no distractions, which Helen had painted pink. A Faraday cage embedded in the walls charged with the dark inverse frequency to stifle connection to the Dark Overmind. A conduit to the enclosure allowed Helen to maintain contact with the balance of herself as she supplied the blocking field.

Guards escorted Arne in; Helen said, "Take a seat, I am here to have a chat. Nothing too serious."

Arne just grunted.

"As you may have guessed, I am from Droma, and I am not an ordinary woman. I only inform you of this because I want this to be pleasant," Helen said, "So where are you from?"

"Aurea," Arne said.

"I would like to visit there someday when there is no unpleasantness," Helen remarked, "My partner Ito was the Forno Ambassador assigned to the Empire. Do you have any family who would like a message?"

"No, Orphan," Arne said.

"On this planet, there are many of your fellow Aureans," Helen said, "Perhaps you may like a visit?"

"Rebels," Arne snapped.

"Most here would prefer a peaceful life on their home planet.

However, this is now their home, so they are making the most of it," Helen said, "I should inform you that the field doesn't affect my ability to read thoughts. I believe while I haven't forced my way past your shield, that some of your answers aren't factual. I am aware of the motives of the Dark Adepts to achieve power by whatever means, including hiding feelings."

"Perhaps," Arne answered grudgingly.

"In the reverse situation, you would not have survived the capture and look upon this a sign of weakness," Helen said, "My estimation of your life expectancy if you were set free to return to your compatriots, would be mere minutes after the last bit of data was extracted."

"So?" Arne asked, "Even less if they thought I told you anything."

"So. A little cooperation may see you live a productive life among friends," Helen said, "I am curious what leads someone to seek power over other entities instead of using those abilities to help."

"Each mind has its destiny and struggle," Arne said, "Is it my role in life to help an ant to climb a mountain? When it can do nothing in return."

"I would be stuck on my planet if I had that attitude," Helen returned, "I fail to detect any difference between you and that ant, not that I am omnipotent. In my quest to learn to my capacity, travel is essential, those who seek short-term gains and hinder my quest I don't look favourably on."

"If you have the power, why not run the galaxy?" Arne asked.

"To quote an old book, 'What profits a man to possess the world and lose his soul'," Helen said, "This dark overmind, what exactly does it promise?"

"Power," Arne said.

"What does that achieve?" Helen asked, "And the payment?"

"It demands nothing except that the recipient runs the assigned people his way," Arne said.

"If this mind is so powerful, why doesn't it do the controlling?" Helen asked.

Arne shrugged having no answer.

"I have been in contact with the Light Overmind and have discussed its aims, as far as I can determine it wishes all minds to reach their ultimate potential," Helen said, "Suggesting that the best way to achieve this, is by cooperation and peace."

"Weak idea," Arne said.

"And if you fail to be strong? What is the punishment?" Helen asked.

"Death," Arne said smugly, sure it wouldn't happen to him.

"Sounds like your ethos, does the Dark overmind do this or use a catspaw?" Helen asked.

"He just withdraws his powers, and your subordinates deliver the verdict," Arne said, "If that is all your questions I would prefer to catch up on my sleep."

"I am sorry that you find my questions are so tiring. The field we use only blocks the Dark; if you wish to find peace of mind you only have to open to the Light," Helen said, actuating the call to the guards, "Pleasant dreams."

Arne was escorted back to his cell without comment. Ito, who had been observing came in to discuss progress.

"He likes to believe he is a hardboiled egg?" Ito said, "If he is the best bet it may be a hard slog to change any minds."

"They aren't going anywhere unless they do," Helen said, "I can bore them into submission, but as soon as they are out of these restraints, they would revert to Dark. The brushes I have had with the Dark Overmind required my full strength to repel. It would love to have me under its spell."

"Perhaps that is what created the Zombie beast?" Ito asked.

"Not a subject I would approach such a one to discuss," Helen said.

"Since I had a run in with one before I met you, totally agree," Ito said, "So what is your next step?"

"I have set up three rooms, so my next batch is on the way," Helen said, "The other two went about the same. I have Frederich next in here. I expect the same response as the first lot. The next step is to let them stew and perhaps try the Light contact out of boredom."

Adept Frederich was escorted in and seated, Helen then walked in and also sat, "Good morning Frederich, enjoying your stay?" Helen asked, "The secure quarters reflect the assessment of how dangerous you are. Please note, that I am a Droman, not a young woman."

"So?" Fredrich asked, "When am I going to see a lawyer?"

"As soon as they learnt your status as a Dark Adept, a line formed to get as far away as possible," Helen said, "If you provide some details as to your origin as well as an undertaking to cease hostilities we may be able to allow some relaxation."

Frederich made a decision, leapt over the dividing table to attack Helen only to find himself suspended in mid-air as she lifted him towards the ceiling.

"Comfy?" Helen asked, "If you like, you can spend the rest of the day up there."

Frederich just glared.

"From now I have substituted another video feed so we can be private," Helen said firmly, "Because you have such a strong superiority complex, I can be a little more firm with you."

"When I said that I am not a young girl to be trifled with, this was understating my abilities. Without much effort, I could spread you in a thin layer over the wall," Helen stated calmly, "I consider that you and what you represent are a parasite, carrying a vile disease. This condition requires quarantining for the safety of innocent people. Your society would have destroyed an invader such as yourself as soon as they extracted all data."

Frederich received this news with silence, so Helen paused before resuming.

"My people are busy eliminating a disease known as a Zombie beast. Normally we are peaceful and only use force when those in our care need defending," Helen said, "I can read your mind and have learnt a considerable amount about your upbringing. While I have some sympathy; I also know that to reach the position you have, dozens of your peers have died. The number I can't read as you don't bother to count."

"So?" Fred asked in response.

"I predict that as soon as you were to reach a point when the possibility of a challenge to your superiors was imminent, they would eliminate you. Being captured by us would ensure this happening sooner," Helen said, "Well it seems I am wasting my time talking, return to your cell to contemplate your destiny, the path to the light is open, and the path to the dark remains blocked."

Having said this as she slammed him back into his chair and restrained him for a moment until he settled down. "Interview over, enjoy your stay," Helen said. Frederich was escorted out, and Ito came in to learn what had happened.

"How did that go?" Ito asked, "It sounded suspiciously like the last."

"I am sorry that was necessary. I had to apply a little pressure and say some things not suitable for polite society," Helen said, "I did learn some information as to their cult, and I believe that the Zombie Beast has a more pleasant view on life."

"Since I know Droma's view on the beast, I am glad not to learn more," Ito said, "He tried to jump you, then you dropped him back into his seat. Did he like that?"

"Didn't phase him, seems that happens all the time, the training they receive includes that whenever the stronger gets a whim," Helen said, "All I managed to do was affirm that I am stronger at the moment."

"What did you learn that I can hear?" Ito asked.

"The adepts selects the students for training at seven which takes another ten years; they divert most of the unsuccessful into military forces. On the way to reaching novice, there is a high attrition rate as they jockey to enter the next level. By the time, they reach third level master the numbers are whittled down to eight. The top two levels have one each, Klien and the Emperor being second and top respectively," Helen said, "The survivors are talented in combat and covert behaviour; all those with real talent and therefore potential challengers, are eliminated before they get too powerful."

"That is both their strength and weakness," Ito said, "Since Humph is due in soon, he should know the full picture."

Yella Terra landed the next day. Helen and Ito made their way across to brief Humph on the latest developments.

"Hullo the ship," Ito called.

Mike came out and invited them in, "Ito and Helen to see us."

"Ah, ladies, what joy and good news have you for us today?" Humph asked.

"A little bit of both, Helen has started interviewing our guests," Ito said.

"I have few results. So far they haven't changed their minds or attitude," Helen said, "Because I have read trace thoughts where I am close to something that they would rather I didn't know. I have ascertained that there is a Dark Overmind which encourages the seeking of power for its sake."

"Go on," Humph said.

"My opinion as to the benefit of this is limited to a minority. Definitely against the interest of the majority," Helen said, "From what we have discussed the drive would seem to be similar to the Zombie beast. Though at the moment while you have eliminated a large proportion of this entity without apparently affecting the Dark Overmind."

"Helen suggested that the Zombie may be the result and not the cause of the Overmind," Ito said, "I would suppose that if the reverse were the case, it would explain the Dark Adept increased activity rather than being consistent with a rise in paranoia."

"How is the Light training going?" Humph asked.

"Very well, the academy is entering the next phase. The Dark attack has focussed the effort on learning," Ito said.

"So how is Klien behaving?" Humph asked.

"The task force is still there, Klien regularly visits to view the collection of the scout intelligence," Ito said, "Steven Firebrand has been observing them using a remote method which he keeps to himself. This ship is one of the few places where we can even speak about the fact that this is happening."

"I have had a little education as to the method and ability," Humph said, "While limited in range, this is overcome by flying your ship via a parallel space to the alternate system of your target, then use a peephole across the hypothetical bubble."

"Sounds like magic. If it works, good for us and best not let the wrong people know," Ito commented.

"I read an amusing SF book where the teddy bear aliens used random button pushing to capture a battleship. They redirected all sorts of fluids including sewage into the bridge and stifled them into surrender," Mike said, "They had landed their smaller ship inside and because the belligerents were expecting that only a ship as large as their battleship would attack. They had no defence against such a small vessel. The same scenario was the Achilles heel of the death star in 'Starbattles' having a lack of close range weapons able to handle small fighters."

"Poor engineering and lack of foresight, when you deal with enormous energies and masses it would be easy to overlook the tiny details," Humph said, "In one of the earliest SF stories, 'War of the Worlds' the invincible invaders were brought down by Earth's viruses. One reason why interstellar ships are well protected and screened before reaching any port."

"Still every story needs a counter for the antagonist, however unlikely," Ito said, "Otherwise this sector would be part of the Fornoon hegemony, and I wouldn't have met Helen."

"We still have the problem of dealing with Klien without escalating into a war," Humph said, "We have the means, but this would risk the lives of thousands of people who are following orders. We should inform the Republic forces perhaps they may move strategically towards the Empire and rattle their cans to redirect their attention back home."

"Indeed it is a restraint on responses to overt activities by the Empire as a too harsh response would elicit a huge attack. Back to the old catch 22."

Troubles on Forno

ITO AND THE *TROY* CREW WERE PURSUING THEIR consular duties when a Forno ship announced that it was visiting Elysium Port. Once this had landed, a party made their way over to the Troy and called for entry.

"Inspector Gros, I have documents for Ambassador Roos," The leader said.

"Come aboard, Madam will be with you shortly," Veoos said as she escorted the party to a reception room and settled them into chairs.

After a short wait, Ito joined them and asked, "How may I help you?"

"I am here to pass on the orders from THE Forno," Gros said as he handed over the documents, "I am to relieve you of the duty of Roving Ambassador. I hold a warrant for the task of consular representative to Elysium. It is now the policy to have an Ambassador assigned to each system."

Ito read the documents, and it seemed legitimate, the signatory was not Fedo Roos, just THE Forno seal.

Having considered this, Ito asked, "I notice that it doesn't include my reassignment?"

"I have no instructions on that subject," Gros said, "My instruments reported that this vessel had both Oxzen and Forno registration. I would suggest that you rectify this with Forno Authorities. For now, I will present my credentials to the local

authorities and establish the Forno Consulate. Good day, Madam."
With that, Gros stood and indicated his party to follow, leaving Ito
and her crew to work out their path.

"Helen and Veoos, would you dissect this data and give me your
opinion?" Ito asked.

After a time, Helen advised, "It complies with all protocols, and
is a bare-bones statement ending your tenure."

"I see no orders regarding employment for any of the crew."
Veoos said, "I have no precedent for this."

"Your advice?" Ito asked.

"You could approach Forno for an explanation," Veoos said.

"Via Steve Firebrand first?" Helen suggested.

"Well it would seem that the Council have cut us adrift," Ito
said, "I will call Governor Telon and ask her opinion. Gros may have
provided more information to her, as I doubt that announcing such
a sudden change would sit well with her. I don't like the arrogance
of that Inspector. Of what I don't know; I have heard of hygiene
inspectors."

Ito made her way over to the terminal and rang the administration
to arrange a meeting with Berna Telon.

"Good morning, Ito Roos speaking, I would like to meet with
Governor Telon," Ito asked.

"Certainly Madam, if you come over I will take you in," The
secretary said.

She did so as suggested and soon was seated in Berna's office,
"Good morning Berna," Ito said, "Sudden changes. Did Ambassador
Gros give you any explanation?"

"Good morning Ito," Berna said, "Didn't he explain to you the
reason? He just walked in and presented his credentials."

"Gros just turned up, gave me the orders ending my tenure.
The orders didn't include any clues, he only suggested I ask my
government," Ito said, "Hardly makes me confident that nothing
drastic has occurred."

"He left a schedule of trading changes with my secretary which

I haven't dissected as yet," Berna said, "Greta would you bring that schedule in for us?"

Greta brought this in and handed it over for Berna to read, and as it was rather extensive, Berna said, "Perhaps I should allow Helen to do a quick appraisal."

Helen took the data and scanned the information, "Just about reverses all the trade protocols that were established by the treaties."

"Something is desperately wrong," Ito said as she took a slower skim through the data, "I will have to consult with Steve Firebrand before I return home."

Berna took a turn and assuming a grim face said, "When my council reads this document, they will likely tear up the agreement. This document nearly reverts everything to the previous standing, just short of declaring war."

"Since I can't do anything official now, I will go to Earth to talk to Steve and see if his gadget can find out the change," Ito said.

"There will always be a home for you here if the worst is the case, this sector is Helen's home," Berna said.

"I certainly hope it doesn't come to that as my family, friends and career are on Forno," Ito said, "I suppose the sooner I know, the better. Thank you for your assistance."

"I hope you can sort this out, I fail to see any benefit by this reversal," Berna said, "Your work among this sector has been most helpful and by the volume of trade between Forno and Oxz sector, very prosperous for all. Farewell."

"Goodbye for now," Ito said, "As soon as I have a clue as to what happened I will let you know."

Ito and Helen soon lifted off to head towards Earth to have a chat with Steve. Luckily she caught him at his factory.

"Good day Steve," Ito said, "I have a problem, it seems my job as Ambassador has finished under strange circumstances without explanation."

"Good day Ito," Steve said, "Yes, the changes the new Ambassador from Forno has delivered has my government tearing their hair out.

It seems the government on Forno has thrown everything that you worked on into the bin."

"I just received a letter saying my tenure was over, no reassignment, no explanation, and leaves my team in limbo," Ito said, "When I was at home only last month, everything was fine, my boss was still delighted with my mission almost bubbling over with praise. I wonder if Klien is involved?"

"Something that I wouldn't put past him," Steve said, "We need to get to the bottom of this. I will have to trot over to Forno and investigate."

"With your special gadget?" Ito asked, "I wouldn't mind coming with you."

"Pity I can't take Helen as well," Steve said, "We can lift off in an hour."

"If I come over in my shuttle and swap it for yours I could," Helen suggested, "A couple of days away from the *Troy* won't hurt."

"Lovely idea, then we can have a long chat while we search the heavens together for a change," Pippin said, "Load your shuttle, mine is already sitting outside."

"I have loaded myself into the shuttle and will meet you at the *Big Red*," Helen said though she didn't leave, as her presence there was her mobile, and she had been talking about herself on the *Troy*.

"Come out to my shuttle; I will fly us over to *Red*. Once there we can get this investigation underway," Pippin said.

"I had better warn Wendy to expect us," Steve said as he picked up the phone.

"I have already spoken to her; she is looking forward to meeting Helen and Ito as she has heard so much about them," Pippin said.

"Still I need to say it myself, even if redundant," Steve said with a grin.

Arriving at the *Red* waiting to greet the visitors was Wendy, Steven's wife.

"Well it is about time I met you pair," Wendy said, "So we are off for another adventure to the wild blue yonder. Captain X in action again, at least he is on your side now. Come, I have set up a cabin for you."

"Thank you, you must be a very understanding person to put up with Steve and his ideas," Ito responded.

"Helen, Pippin tells me that you are from Droma?" Wendy asked, "I suppose like Pippin; you don't require accommodation."

"I am comfortable in my shuttle," Helen said.

Having settled the cabins and learning the history of the visitors; it wasn't long before the crew assembled on *Red's* bridge as it lifted off towards the service universe portal before travelling to an alternate uninhabited Forno planet.

"Pippin if you energise the window into our universe, let the spying begin," Steve said.

The screen lit up with a familiar planet, first viewing the orbits favoured by spaceships in holding patterns. Coming into view were several ominous warships, mostly of Imperial design.

"Not a good sign, those are the detachment that Klien had waiting in another system," Steve commented.

"The balance of the ships are Forno; these aren't usually in that orbit unless the Navy is preparing to defend against an invasion."

"Take the view down to the city; we will visit the administration buildings and seek out the lay of the land."

"Ito, You have the best knowledge of where to find everything," Steve said, "These are the controls which I have set to nonsensitive until you are used to them."

She took the controls, then after some practice took the view first down to the Admin and started working her way towards Admiral Hostos' office only to find a stranger in his seat. The travelling down the corridors to the council chamber finding it empty, dismayed she made her way to THE Forno's office to see if Fedo was there and found Zento Hoos instead. Then the explanation, there was Klien in the next office, seems to be running the show with assistants bustling in and out.

"Better switch off while we have a serious talk," Steve said, "I can reestablish from where it was when needed."

"It seems everyone you had been running the place has gone; I only recognised one, Zento Hoos sitting in THE Forno's office. The last I had heard, he was an Envoy to the Empire," Ito said, "I suggest we look first for the missing people."

"It does look grim, and if you had turned up personally to inquire, perhaps you would have found them the hard way," Steve said, "My first thought is, there has been a lightning coup which took over your world; a copycat of what happened on mine."

"Can your gadget evacuate my people, I guess there is a couple of hundred key personnel with another thousand family members held hostage."

"I would have to bring in several ships to do that, taking some planning," Steve said, "First let us find out where everyone is and their condition, Once we start the evacuation it will have to be complete or retaliation would be nasty if I know Klien." He thought for a moment before adding, "Survey first, Ito if you mark on a map where the government is likely keeping these people, we will commence the search."

"I brought street maps with me in case you needed them," Ito said loading the data into Red's computer then started pointing at points of interest, "My parents home, the city prison and several likely spots run by the Intelligence Arm."

Assigning computers to all the crew the task was soon underway locating and listing detainees. Ito's parents were apparently under house arrest as was most of the families of key officials.

"I am surprised that they can do anything with the army locking up most of the people who run the planet," Ito said, "I am particularly unhappy that they are holding my family."

It was at the prison where the coup leaders were holding the senior people, Ito found the Councillors locked up like common criminals.

The cell containing her Uncle Fedo was watched by several guards, stopping the delivery of any message or answer questions.

"We will spend some time listening to Zento's conversation to see what his role is, puppet or organiser," Steve said.

"He always was ambitious, trying to take the easy way instead of the correct way I advised," Ito said, "If I turn the tables he will be lucky to be a cargo hand.'

"We have to avoid getting too close to Klien, he can feel us watching if we stay near him too long," Steve said, "Still Zento shouldn't detect us as long as he is not paranoid and sweeps the place for bugs. There is little energy emitted by our portal."

This program was carried out thoroughly as it was better to have the maximum knowledge before committing to action.

Eventually, the location and numbers needing rescuing were determined, plans were laid out for the equipment required.

There were twelve hundred and thirty-seven prisoners and hostages in total, requiring at least twelve of Humph's and Firebrand vessels.

"Now these guards, are they following orders or are they part of the push?" Steve asked, "Likely we will have to remove them so that they can't carry tales."

"Park them somewhere then separate them when we have time," Ito said.

"We have a whole planet below," Steve said, "Give them necessary supplies on an island, will do well enough."

"My people have survival training as part of the education," Ito said.

"So let us return to Earth, we can organise the supplies and arrange the ships to be available," Steve said, he then reversed the process to return to his factory complex.

Once settled in the conference room, the crew started dissecting the data dividing the areas into sectors which could be handled by one ship. Having a Droman in each ship meant that there were twenty coordinated hands from each vessel.

"The task needs to happen at the same time, to cut to a minimum the warning to the other sites," Steve said, "Of course, another problem is that it is bound to become common knowledge that a mechanism exists to step straight into someone's back door. The only alternative is to dispose of anyone intelligent enough to report."

"Not an option if you want our help," Pippin said with Helen in agreement.

"Or mine, I put in a considerable amount of planning to avoid any casualties," Steve agreed.

Eventually, the Navy arranged the ships and supplies; the flotilla assembled for the trip through the portal before hyper jumping to the alternate Forno where they reformed to make the final plans.

With twelve ships the final conference was done using holograph projections. The flotilla allotted each captain their target and quota, each then had their conference to settle the mode. The task was calculated to take an hour, which would reduce the ability of authorities to commence counter-action.

Steve would disable the larger capital ships by inducing faults which remove the ability to take aggressive action. Rham had shown Steve a technique of bridging components in the protection circuits to trip a shutdown of the main reactor; this sent the ship crew into protection mode, these ships would then withdraw to safety.

Helen and Ito concentrated on releasing the council members first as well as their dependents.

A door opened adjacent to Fedo's cell door; Helen fired a sleep-gun at all those present before disarming his observers and transporting them to the island which had been arranged to receive them.

Helen reestablished the portal inside his cell, Ito stepped out and said, "Ito Roos reporting for duty, sir. May I suggest that your new office is a little cramped?"

"Nice to see you, Ito," Fedo returned after his initial surprise, "I propose that we leave the explanations for a little later."

"If you step through this door. I can provide somewhat better accommodation," Ito said pointing out the portal, "This is one of Steve's toys I mentioned."

Fedo followed Ito through the portal and was shown his cabin by Helen. Ito then went through the same process to extract Admiral Hostos, then the remainder of the high priority prisoners. After she had extracted these people, she turned her attention to the family members held hostage under house arrest.

With four portals in action and staff guiding their charges away as fast as they arrived, the staff soon completed the task with the guards waking up on an island to find their charges and city gone.

With the people freed, the key people were brought together to have a debrief.

"Welcome aboard the *Troy*. I will explain the how at a later time, " Ito said, "I will start by asking how this situation came about? It was fine a month ago."

"I think everyone had the same experience," Fedo said, then after receiving nods, added, "I answered a knock early one morning to find armed soldiers waiting, they took me away and locked me in a cell. No explanations or authority beyond a gun in my face. Since then there has been a total blackout of information."

"I found Zento Hoos sitting in your office with Adept Klien in the next," Ito said, "So I knew something was wrong. I had my credentials cancelled with no explanation by an arrogant Inspector Gros. I was expected to return and join you, but I was suspicious and had a peek using Firebrand's toy."

"I am glad that you did," Fedo said, "A little information did sneak through when a guard delivered my meals. The gist that I have put together is that Hoos was set up to head the coalition of disgruntled military personnel who felt they had been discriminated against by the new system which they think is biased towards the merchants."

"I believe that Klien was behind the idea and fanned the embers as well as providing the extra muscle to carry out the coup d'etat," Ito said, "Once the population was under control, I believe that it wouldn't be long before Hoos found himself just occupying the seat without any authority."

"And by then Forno Sector would be part of the Empire," Fedo said, "Any complaints would be dealt with harshly by the Adepts."

"Once the dust settles, and the task force had removed the hostages from the area. I will have a little chat with Klien and Hoos,"

Ito said, "The guards who had been keeping you incarcerated are having a nice holiday on a deserted island out of harm's way. This task has to be dealt with quickly and thoroughly to prevent knowledge of the 'toys' falling into the wrong hands."

"Very good thinking. I suppose *Troy* isn't the only ship operating?" Fedo asked.

"We have twelve with the lead being Steve Firebrand who has disabled the Imperial ships to prevent them interfering," Ito said, "Nothing too damaging, the Droman contingent would never allow that. However, we can evacuate the hostile crews on the Forno ships and replace them with our friends."

"Intriguing, is the *Challenge* one of them?" Fedo asked.

"I will ask Commodore Firebrand," Ito said as she opened a channel to Big Red, "Pippin, is the *Forno Challenge* in orbit?"

"Hi Ito, yes we have removed the bridge crew, and it is just sitting there," Pippin radioed.

"Hullo, this is Captain Roos, any chance I can be sent across?" Fedo asked.

"Certainly, Ito and Helen can do that. We have completed our tasks," Pippin radioed.

"Thank you, *Troy*, out," Ito finished the conversation, then addressing her visitors, "Well it seems that we can see what crew you need then shoot you across."

"We have a bridge crew here," Fedo said, "And if you can determine what others we need it would be good to get to my home."

Ito used the portal controls to locate and examine the *Challenge*. It was empty except for the engineering section where Chief Ghos still held court.

"I can radio him and ask how the ship is going," Ito said, then rigging a speaker connection into the Chief's cabin, added, "Good day Chief, would you like some friendly company?"

"Ito, how did you do that?" Ghos asked, "I went up to the bridge, and they have disappeared."

"My team is to blame for that," Ito said, "I have Captain Roos here, and he would like to get his ship back. Any of the bridge crew reliable?"

"Yeah a couple, the new captain was a pain, talked like a spook," Ghos said, "The Imperials have just drifted away, your people?"

"Yep, as it has let out the some of the secrets; we have to finish the job," Ito said, "I will open the portal to allow Captain Roos and myself to have a visit."

"Coming Uncle," Ito invited, "Follow me, expect some discomfort as we do. Not much as *Troy* is alongside."

"After you," Fedo said as the pair stepped through the portal and onto the deck of the Challenger.

"Good day Chief, wheels haven't fallen off?" Fedo asked.

"With no one jiggling my elbow it is easy, Sir," Ghos said, "Here is a list of those you can put back to work. Where did they go?"

"Remember me talking about Commodore Firebrand? He has grabbed them and stuck them on a planet," Ito said, "I will pass on the list and start the return as well as sorting the other Forno ships."

"Good to get the old girl back to normal," Ghos said.

"I will have a tour and organise the crew to fill missing positions until we return to normal. We lie doggo until *Challenger* is fully ready to defend itself," Fedo said, "Thank you, Commodore Roos, you return to your ship and complete the restoration."

"I should do that, Sir. Nice seeing you again Chief," Ito said as she stepped back to *Troy*.

"I left a couple of happy people," Ito said, "I will pass on a list of the trusted crew to join them, and I am sure that there are a few Captains among our refugees who are keen to do the same."

After consultations the task of exchanging crews to the remaining Forno ships so that they could return to protecting the skies of Forno.

"Hello Red, Steve what are you doing with the Imperial ships?" Ito asked, "Just those being there is a danger."

"I have cleared the Bridge and Engineering sections. The first removes the fanatics, and the other prevents the return to action or escape," Steve radioed back, "I have contacted Admiral Rham, and he is sending replacement crews to remove the ships from the area as well as bringing his flotilla to bolster the Forno cordon."

"I have transferred a few captains back to their ships, and as soon as a trusted crew can join them. They will then be able to resume their true role to protect the Forno interests and later resume trade," Ito said, "I have done some discussing, and it seems that Klien had talked Zento Hoos into heading the coup."

"Once we evacuate the civilians, we return and deal with the Imperials," Steve said, "We need to isolate the Imperial forces before they have time to guess just what we used against them. The ships have had their Hyperdrive and radio abilities disabled so they can't escape or call the Empire for assistance."

"Yes, we still have a problem. The job of neutralising the Empire is now a priority, or they will attack with their full armada as soon as they realise that we have technology which is beyond theirs," Ito said.

"In the communique that I sent Rham, I suggested that we encourage the Republic to stand by for such a move," Steve said.

"The hands that need removing from the controls, are the Dark Adepts," Ito said, "I will remove the soldiers around Klien and Hoos, then deliver the bad news personally."

"Should make his day," Steve said, "Let's fix the ships while the situation is still cloudy as to what has happened."

"I will get onto it," Ito said, "I will see you soon and work out details. Troy out."

"Red out," Steve said.

Gathering the remainder key personnel Ito brought them up to date and asked for suggestions, "I need your ideas to return Forno to normal," Ito said.

Admiral Hostos said, "We need to relocate that twit in my office. How he was selected, I don't know, the last I heard he was sitting at a supply depot letting the world pass him by."

A list of projects was assembled and removing the new heads of departments leaving the offices empty until we can neutralise the leaders. The next step was to remove all Imperial personnel until all who were left were the last key people with Klien and Hoos isolated in their offices.

At last, came the moment when the team had dealt with the last few, their escape routes were cut off with all vessels that they could access disabled or removed.

Ito and Helen stepped out of the portal and knocked on Hoos' office door, Ito said, "Good day Zento, perhaps you could explain your role in ruining Forno's peace?"

"How the hell did you get in here, I am THE Forno," Zento said.

"I was relieved of my post as Ambassador; when I asked for a reason only to be directed to ask this office," Ito said, "So here I am. Why did I get sacked?"

"I felt that you were not representing the best interests of Forno," Zento said, "So I replaced you as is my prerogative."

"I have consulted with the council, and your position as THE Forno was not authorised and therefore not valid," Ito said, "You are under arrest for endangering the sector."

"Under what authority?" Zento asked.

"I am a member of the Elder Council and by authority of the designated THE Forno," Ito said, "You may remain here until I deal with your co-conspirator."

Zento collapsed into his seat before warning, "Klien will deal with you and restore me to my rightful position."

"Perhaps he is not as powerful as you think, people of peace will prevail," Ito said.

Before they could brace Klien in his lair, they found him waiting in the corridor with his sabre at the ready.

"Well met Adept Klien," Ito greeted him, "Are you aware of how precarious your tenure is?"

"I don't know how you have done this, but I am not helpless," Klien snarled, "Stand aside while you can."

"You attacked my Acadamy and threatened children, now you attack my world and expect me to accept that," Ito said reasonably, "Helen will now isolate you from your protector while I deal with you."

Helen reverted her inter-mobile frequency to the inverted form and blanketed the area preventing contact with the Dark side.

Klien covered it by charging and swinging his sword trying to hit both women, only to be blocked by the sabres halting his motion. Zento took the opportunity to come out and try to shoot Ito with a pistol, distracting her.

"I will handle Klien, you look after Zento," Helen said, then casually fending off Klien's blows added, "Now Klien, I may seem like a child in your view, and by most calculations I am. In the last year, I have acquired the skills required to defeat you; I should inform you that as a Droman, I am faster and stronger in all facets than you will ever will, even without the advantage of the blanketing field. Should you achieve the aim of removing my appendages, I would merely pull myself back together and carry on." Helen said casually and calmly, "As it would be a little uncomfortable, I don't believe I should allow that. At the moment I am considering the possibility of healing the harm that the Dark Overmind has done to your psyche."

"I am healthier by the care of the Overmind, you would benefit also," Klien said starting to tire.

Ito disarmed Zento by first blocking the ray beams then throwing him against the wall, with little effort had handcuffed him and called the *Troy* to remove him. Standing by, she observed Helen dealing with Klien. "Do you need a hand?"

"No, I am fine," Helen said, "I will let you know if I need a rest. I think Klien may ask you first. He is looking a little puffed."

The casual chat didn't amuse Klien; he then redoubled his efforts to break through to open an escape route.

"That would be futile as all vehicles have been removed from the area so unless you intend to walk back to Correl you aren't leaving anytime soon," Helen said, "The only handicap I usually have is not to be too good and instil an inferiority complex. Ito is aware of the extent of my abilities. Your superiority complex is so strong you would likely put it down to trickery."

He tried to throw Helen against the wall, she prevented the collision and returned the favour quicker than he could react, giving him a bruising encounter with a pillar. He then used Telekinesis to breach the wall and gain an exit out of the building.

"Running to where?" Helen asked, "There is no escape."

Klien made a desperate effort and transported himself through the opening then pulled the remaining wall down behind to block the opening.

Helen glanced at Ito, "I am tracking him, he is not happy that every vehicle he finds we have broken, and separated from his friends. I have transported another me to intercept his attempt to enter a building to gather hostages. That surprised him, and he has moved off into a different direction," Helen narrated.

"He has reached the spaceport, and can't find his shuttle or anything else functional," Helen said, "And every time he turns around, he finds me watching. I cheated by using our people disguised as extra Helens." Helen was enjoying the freedom of being active in many locations at once.

"Well let's transfer to him and settle this farce," Ito said, "We can't allow him to remain loose as he is just too dangerous and if it weren't that he could work out our methods, I would prefer him away from here."

So stepping back to Troy they stepped out again in the path that Klien was going down.

"If you have finished playing?" Ito asked, "I am afraid you have used up our supply of patience. Surrender and accept defeat."

"Never, I would die first before I show such a sign of weakness," Klien said.

"Try your gun Helen, he looks tired," Ito suggested.

Helen did so, and Klien collapsed in a heap, Helen asked, "Why didn't you suggest that earlier?"

"I felt it best that we teach him a few lessons first," Ito said, "I had my gun ready if he was getting too rambunctious."

Klien was searched and all his weapons removed before he was bundled into the alternate world to his little island to keep himself company.

"One problem solved, we make sure all Imperial vessels are

captured to prevent stories getting back, and then we plan to fix the Dark Adepts," Ito said as the council gathered in the map room.

Hyperwave pulses announced the arrival of Admiral Rham's contingent. Once the ships accompanying *Big Red* achieved a matching orbit; Steve, Pippin and Bento Rham joined them in the conference.

"Welcome aboard Admiral," Ito said, "Much better now that we are now on the same side."

"Thank you, what have you achieved?" Bento asked.

"The Imperial ships have been disabled using the technique described to Commodore Firebrand," Ito said, "With Bridge and engineering staff sitting on the planet below awaiting vetting."

"I picked up as many trained crew from our sector as I could, my staff can interview the captives to locate sufficient to run them," Rham said, "I gather that Firebrand is the best to organise this?"

"Yes he would be as he has been the one dealing with those and has the large gateway to transfer your ships to our normal universe," Ito said.

"Thank you; I will consult with him and get these ships organised," Rham said.

"You will be able to sit alongside each vessel transfer crews via the gates without setting off alarms until you step onto them and at the moment, they don't have a clue as to how it is happening," Ito said.

"I will have to consult with Firebrand and invent protection," Rham said with a frown, "All very good when we are the only force that knows the secret, but it won't take long before it is at least suspected and others start working on it."

"One reason that we need to nip this local problem in the bud," Ito said, "Even the puzzle will have the eyes of the Imperium looking this way. We have intercepted and isolated all hyperdrive accessible vessels and radios."

"Best I start," Rham said as he returned to his shuttle.

As the transfers were done without external signs, the process seemed interminable until the swapping of Elysium and Imperial ships took place with the latter being ferried back to Elysium for refurbishing and assignment to different fleets.

Visitors from Corellia

ITO ROOS WAS READING THE LATEST DISPATCHES FROM Forno which reported the progress of three suspected dark adepts. A transcript of the first contact was as follows.

The duty officer on the patrol vessel challenged their ship; Borg answered, "Booni Freighter *New Dawn*, Captain Borg commanding, data on the way."

"Proceed to the Customs Station," The Patrol ordered.

Borg shrugged and pointed to the vector required.

The customs and immigration inspectors came aboard with the customs officer inspecting the hold for contraband and health. The immigration official made a thorough inspection of their documents before setting up a separate interview for each of the three.

"Pilot Bern? I am Lt Doos. Booni a pleasant planet? I hear that the rainbow aurora are particularly spectacular?" Lt Doos asked."

"I believe that you are thinking of another planet, the auroras are green and blue," Bern said, "Booni is renowned for the blue crystal sands of Narnia Beach."

"Ah I stand corrected," Doos said pretending to read his notes, "Take note of the limits to your sightseeing, enjoy your stay. If you send Thum in please."

"Certainly,'" Bern said as he passed Thum in the passageway, he gave the high sign to expect test questions.

"You are next." This little advice was necessary as a guard was observing.

"Engineer Thum?"' The officer asked while Thum seated himself.

"Yes sir," Thum answered.

"You are Military trained?" Lt Doos asked

"I did a stint but decided that a merchant's life was safer,"' Thum said, "The discipline was strict as well."

"Bern tells me that the Purple sands are worth seeing on Nadia Shores?" Lt Doos asked.

"I doubt he said that. Pilots aren't usually colour blind; the Narnia Beach has Blue sand," Thum said with a raised eyebrow.

"It is my job to ask silly questions and see what responses I get," Doos said, "We have had a little disturbance, and I had fun catching one of those adepts out when he got all uptight."

"Those bastards are only there to make life miserable for us working stiffs. I admire your bravery and suspect your sanity," Thum said with a head shake.

"I agree with the first, I do have some gadgets to protect myself so was safe enough," Doos said, "Send in Shau, and I will finish this. Mind you obey the guidelines when you wander around."

Shau came in and sat. "Welcome to Forno. Do you intend to sightsee while you are here?" Lt Doos asked, "Because of the incident last year, the government restricts visitors to conducted tours."

"Just want to shake the stardust from my boots and get some dirt time," Shau said, "As this is my first tour outside of the Booni system, I will do a little acclimatising."

"When you hit the terminal there will be pamphlets showing you where you can go," Doos said.

"No funny questions?" Shau asked, "By the faces of my mates you asked a couple."

"Only so as not to disappoint you. Why do you look like a Corellian?" Doos asked.

"My people migrated from there when the Adepts took over and made life miserable," Shau said, "Before they cracked down on travel. Not a good idea to visit the old home."

"Yes if half of what I heard is true, they are nasty fellows," Doos said subtly watching for a reaction and when he didn't receive any waved Shau away, "Carry on enjoy your stay."

"Yeah, wouldn't want to meet a darkie in an alley. So see you around," Shau said as he left.

A covert operative followed as the three left the ship and toured the port precincts. First, they set out on a cover tour setting the local bars on a low burner rather than on fire. The trio spent just enough cash and limited their drinking to blend in without affecting their health. After a short time in the hotel, they made their way to the Booni Church to perform a ritual as a cover for a clandestine meeting with the local Imperial agent. When they arrived at the building with the Ankh sign; entering, the trio exchanged signs with the acolyte.

"Have you offered penance for your sins, brothers?" The priest asked, "I am Brother Simms. If you need to pray, follow me into the rectory."

The three nodded and followed their man, to behind the screen; there hadn't been any surveillance equipment available to monitor the interior. This procedure was to avoid giving away the fact that Forno was aware of the purpose of the church.

After a time the suspects left and rejoined their ship which lifted off on schedule.

The *New Dawn* was located slowly approaching Elysium; the team were aware of the increasing surveillance the closer they travelled. Going through the cycle of a challenge by patrolling ships and then on to the orbiting Custom's satellite. By then they expected a closer inspection and now fully conversant with the procedure.

The Customs agent escorted Thum into the interview room; he became aware that the interviewer was an adept. Though there was no overt attempt to read Thum's mind; it was evident that this agent was watchful.

"Welcome to Elysium, I am Lt Einsland," Helen said, "Your ID reads that you are from Booni and have cousins from Auria?"

"Yes, my people are refugees from there," Thum said, "I have heard that I have relatives living in Elysium."

"Could you give me the names?" Helen asked telepathically.

"Ouch, what was that?" Thom complained.

"I didn't mean to hurt," Helen said, "I asked could you give me their names."

Thum had covered his ability reacting the taught way. "My cousins Otto Griener and his family,'" Thum said, looking worried about meeting one of the adepts that he professed to fear.

"I will send a message. Hopefully, your cousins can be located when you land," Helen said, "Send Bern in, and I will speed up your meeting."

"Thanks, I will see you around perhaps?" Thum said.

As he left Thum gave Bern the sign to be aware of an adept, Thum said, "Cute girl, a lieutenant even," as he waved Bern in.

Bern entered and sat on the seat indicated and reacted like he had been jabbed with a pin when Helen used telepathy.

"Sorry I am not used to non-telepaths coming through, I should be more careful," Helen said, "Could you send Shau in and I am finished?"

This interview went the same way, and Dawn descended to land at the port.

Back on the Custom's Ship Helen transmitted the code for three suspected adepts were in the crew of the *New Dawn*. In her report, Helen indicated that they had covered up their abilities just a little too well, overreacting when telepathed, a non-telepath usually looking puzzled and doesn't make a fuss.

As a figure now identified as Bern left the *Dawn* and headed into town after spending a small time in a hotel, he left and headed towards the Hall with the Ankh sign. Walking in and seating himself towards the rear while keeping an eye out for possible security agents. After a while, the resident Brother made himself known and made the inquiry before leading Bern into the back for deeper meditation.

After spending a relatively short time in the chapel, Bern left and made his way back to his compatriots and passed on the information.

The three made their way to an innocuous hotel where they could blend in without being hassled by drunks. The girls settled in with a few light refreshments as they just chatted about the rigours of merchant life swapping tall stories with any who would listen.

Intelligence had advised Ito, Veoos, Helen of Troy and Dierdre where the trio was drinking they wandered in and settled in to attempt a meeting with them.

After a time Shau noticed a group of women becoming interested in what they were talking about, Two were remarkable as they were a little older than the average clients of the place and had the Forno green features, the other two were Corellian featured and younger.

The girls gravitated to their table and continued the tall tale telling. From the stories, Ito described herself as a merchant captain who had visited Aurea in her travels.

Eventually, the conversation descended into small talk, and the women introduced themselves.

"I am Ito; this is Veoos, Dierdre and Helen. We are off the *Troy*," Ito said, "Where do you call home?"

"Booni, our ship *New Dawn*, we are the crew of a merchant making a run through the sector," Bern said, "I am Bern, my friends are Thum and Shau."

"I am now from the Talent School, I escaped from the *Troy*," Dierdre said, "I am also a scout for likely students. Perhaps you may like to visit and be assessed as I know Aurea settled Booni where they have a potential for adept training."

"Our parents escaped from there when the adepts took over," Bern said, "Adepts are nasty people and best to avoid them like the plague." Bern looked worried that these may be the nasty types.

"The light adepts are pretty harmless," Dierdre said, "I haven't heard any reports that they bite. Just nibble a little." delivered with a challenging grin.

"Really? Do you have a sister in the Elysium Patrol? You look like family," Bern said after giving the code sign that he would take the bait.

"Yes, Helen Einsland is my sister," Dierdre said, "If you are still game, visit my office at this address." Scribbling a quick note and passing it over.

"I may take you up on that, but I can't stay too long as my ship leaves in a couple of days," Bern said, "I had better get back now to secure the cargo."

"I will be on the job at eight hundred hours, perhaps I will see you then," Dierdre said as the boys said their farewells and departed.

When they had left Ito, and the others also departed to have a private conference.

"What do you reckon, Dark or Light?" Ito asked.

"If dark they hide it well, light why bother?" Helen said, "They don't have that nasty superiority complex I see in Dark Adepts. I will be there with Dierdre and see if I can get him to open up."

"Veoos and I would look a little suspicious if we were there. I will listen in via you back at the *Troy*," Ito said. The girls then split up to their respective homes; while the visitors returned to their ship.

At the appointed time Bern made his way to the Academy and asked after Dierdre. The receptionist rang a number and when answered sent him through to Dierdre's office. Bern felt sure that he wasn't walking into a trap with students of all ages walking past to their classrooms with only passing curiosity for a strange face.

Arriving at the described door he knocked and Dierdre opened it and invited him in, "Good morning Bern, Come in and take a seat," Dierdre said, "You remember Helen?"

"Yes good morning, so when does the inquisition start," Bern said with a smile, "I have been hiding from Adepts for a long time."

"Nothing too nasty, I have already assessed you as a latent, and that didn't hurt a bit, did it?" Dierdre asked, 'Could I ask you to try a few tasks."

"What happens if I chicken out and want to leave?" Bern asked looking nervous.

"On your way in, did you see any security? If not, I suppose you can walk back out the way you came in. If you were a Dark Adept, there might have been wall to wall guards."

"Sure of yourself aren't you? I have heard that some Darkies are sneaky and hide their talent," Bern said, "One reason I am walking on eggs around here. If there had been the guards, I wouldn't have come close."

"Can you form a small flame in front of you?" Helen asked.

"That would confirm my status, it is the test that the nasty guys use to test the school kids," Bern said, "My parents advised me not to when a child."

"Go on be a sport," Dierdre said.

"Okay if you go to put a nose ring in, I am out of here," Bern said and made a small, weak flame, "Dad taught me that much, says I am not to do it in front of the wrong people. I guessed that you are not the nasty ones as they discourage females from joining."

"Some of our strongest are women, two fenced with Klien and fought him to a standstill," Dierdre said.

'Bull, I heard that no one has got the better of him, last I heard he was still alive, so obviously he didn't lose," Bern said.

"He was let off with a warning," Dierdre laughed, "Not that he appreciated the honour."

"Pull the other leg it's got bells on it," Bern said sceptically.

"He is in safe hands where he can't hurt peaceful people," Dierdre said ignoring Helen's head shake.

"Hypothetically, if I were a dark pretending to be nice," Bern asked, "Just what would prevent me from throwing my weight around?"

"First I would inform you that I was one of those women mentioned," Helen advised, "I am aware that you are a Dark Adept and if we cornered you could make a lot of noise. I explain this and allow you a great deal of freedom in an attempt to educate you as to where you would be better off."

Bern asked, "You did say that I could leave anytime?"

"Indeed I did. But wouldn't you like a tour first?" Helen said.

"If as you said that you know what I am, would you still let me walk out of here?" Bern asked.

"I believe that we can allow what you choose," Helen said.

"I have to trust you, so lead the way I promise to behave," Bern said.

"For your information, I am a Droman, and yes I allowed Klien to live without raising a sweat," Helen said, "I was in no danger then or now. You shouldn't test my ability."

Bern shrugged suspecting that just out of sight there were

overwhelming forces ready to pounce on him if he played up. So he stood and waved the girls forward to show him around.

"Just what is a Droman that I should be wary? I have heard stories, some of which are unbelievable, mainly about a big Teddy bear named Humph," Bern said conversationally.

"Yes he was the first of my people into space, and we can look like anything we wish," Helen said changing her face to look like a teddy bear.

Startled Bern gasped, "I prefer the cute girl," He said regretting the diminutive reference, Helen just laughed.

"I do have to be a little circumspect with my abilities, I have limitations, and I am not invulnerable," Helen said, "I only say this to assure you that I am not a monster, just a cute girl with extra talents."

Bern gave a wry smile, "Shall we?"

Helen led the way pointing out the lessons and what the teachers were showing the students.

"Now I will take a risk and show you how your compatriots are faring," Helen said, "If you recognise the men I will know, and it will confirm your quest. I have consulted with several of my people, and they suggest that if you know the truth, you may turn away from the Dark, and embrace the Light; I talk on in this hope. Are aware that you can't contact the Dark Overmind inside this building?"

"I wouldn't know," Bern said, "I have avoided any telepathic contacts for so long it is second nature."

The path led to a viewing window where a man was sitting reading a book, Bern recognised Frederich but covered it as best he could. "Why is he locked in?" Bern asked, "On what charge?"

"He was in a party that broke in with intent to do murder," Helen said, "Ito disarmed him easily, and we secured him inside a cell where he can't cause any harm to himself or others."

"Really? No longer any point denying that I am an adept, that man is the most deadly man after the Emperor and Klien," Bern said soberly, "He was lining me up for his next target after he identified me as a potential challenger."

"I have interviewed him several times; I would agree that he is formidable and has an arrogant superiority complex. I haven't detected the same mental attitude in you or your two friends, which is why I have allowed you so much latitude," Helen said, "The last pair tried to muscle their way through the sector, and they thought they were invincible. They are in the next rooms resting."

"So what do you intend to do with me, now that I know what I was sent to find out?" Bern asked, "I doubt that you would like me to deliver the data."

"I could use mental force to revise your memory, as this would be against my ethics I would prefer to avoid doing it," Helen said, "There are others who wouldn't be bothered by this restriction."

"How much time do I have to think about it?" Bern asked caught between a rock and a hard place.

"Until you leave the planet, Ito will be waiting to have a chat and give you a final chance," Helen said, "As her other title is Commodore, you understand she will be a little reluctant to allow you to remember what you have learned."

"So what would happen if I accessed the Light Overmind?" Bern asked.

Helen passed the necessary frequency to Bern, "There you are, open yourself to the Light, who doesn't think of herself as an overmind, rather a mentor," Helen said.

Bern opened himself carefully to the suggested frequency and entered into a mental rapport with an overall peaceful feeling. Nearby he could feel Helen's benign presence.

"Welcome my son I have been missing your presence. I am available for your peace of mind," The Mind intoned, "Listen to my daughter Helen who will help you find peace. If you desire you have the ability to close yourself from me."

The Overmind faded to the background leaving a close rapport with Helen. Her presence was nearly as potent yet peaceful with a hint of an immense reserve of power, which was daunting yet supportive; dissolving the contact left Bern feeling empty.

"Man, that was something. Would you be the strange intellect that the bosses are so worried about?" Bern asked.

"Part of it I suppose, I am not the only one," Helen said, "I feel that you are wavering in your resolve so that I won't test your patience. Feel free to leave and brief your partners who I feel are of a like mind and receptive as you. We will keep a gentle watch on you until your decision. This surveillance may be pressure on you, but my partner needs to control the situation, believing that the information that you have could threaten the peace of millions of planets."

"I have my duty, as you have yours," Bern said, "We aren't at war, I haven't broken any laws or threatened violence. I suppose that if I hung a sign around my neck suggesting something nasty you may find an issue. I will suggest that my Government wouldn't allow the same latitude. So I thank you for such information that you have provided; I would advise my superiors to stay friendly and cease any belligerence."

"Reasonable statement, if you wish there is a refuge here," Helen said, "You may leave, and I would prefer to see you as a friend."

"Thank you, I am unable to say anything further at this point," Bern said, "May the force be with you."

"And with you," Helen said and then watched as Bern left.

Bern made his way to the meeting point to relay what he had found.

Exchanging shrugs, the three left and headed towards the church where they spotted their man wearing the red scarf.

"Otto Griener? I am Thum Dern, your cousin from Booni," Thum said, "Your father asked to pass on his best wishes and see how you are going."

"Everything is fine; Mari and the kids are fit and healthy, I have a job fixing land speeders," Otto said, "How are Mum and Dad?"

"They are well and enjoying retirement," Thum said, "Would you like to come to the tavern, we can have a few drinks and catch up on old times."

"Sounds good, I have permission from Mari as long as I walk home," Otto said, "But first I should give my confession. I will have to think up some new stuff for Brother Nicholas to entertain him.'" Otto said giving Thum a conspiratorial nudge.

They made their way to the church and then into the back room. The quick visit to the tavern done, Otto led the way to his house and introduced them to his family.

"These are my cousin Thum and his friends Bern and Shau; my darling wife Mari, children Greg and Susie," Otto said, "They eager to meet you and wanted to know all about Booni."

The trio settled down for the domestic conference the visitors were regaled with questions; the Children gave news about their studies.

"What school do you go to?" Bern asked being polite.

"To the Academy for Talents, it is great fun," Greg answered.

At a query glance from Thum, Otto said, "Authorities interviewed the children at their old school, I couldn't refuse obviously."

"I understand," Thum said, "Well we have imposed enough on your hospitality and should return to our ship, bound to have some work waiting."

Otto shook hands with the trio and walked them out.

"See you next time we travel through," Thum said, the three then travelled back to the *Dream*.

Ito decided that the time was right to finish the task of either recruiting or rendering the adepts harmless; gathering Helen and Deirdre, they arrived to board the New Dawn and arranged a meeting.

Captain Borg called them to the bridge, where they found Dierdre, Ito and Helen waiting.

"These ladies want to interview you before you leave," Borg said, "Just what did you get up to?" Not expecting an answer he left the six together.

"Just sightseeing. On what authority are you asking?" Thum asked.

"Semi-official at the moment, Lt Einsland is Elysium Navy, I am the Ambassador for Forno, and your passage through my sector is of concern to my Government," Ito said, "Voluntary for now unless Lt Einsland has to call the heavies for noncooperation."

"If it stays friendly I suppose we can help. We are subjects of a friendly sector and can produce documents to support," Bern said, "Under the Elysium law this ship is a sovereign territory."

"And suspected of covert surveillance and not from the sector that it is registered," Dierdre said.

"Okay, ask away," Bern said, "The ship lifts in the morning, and Captain Borg has a program to complete."

"I will start, Bern, have you obtained information covertly?" Ito asked.

"No, any data I have was freely offered by Lt Einsland and Captain Helen, all else is public knowledge," Bern replied, "When I deliver the information, it would be with the advice to leave your sectors in peace."

"Your opinion where to find Adept Klien?" Ito asked.

"A guess would be in another dimension, the how gives me a headache," Bern said, "My party only has the task of gaining intelligence without causing any fuss."

"Well, it seems that you have learnt nothing new," Ito said, "I apologise for having deleted a couple of critical memories. Now I will ask whether you wish to remain as refugees?"

"We would need to consider that for more than a few minutes, the repercussions of accepting would be fatal if our superiors found out," Thum said, "If you have removed memories I didn't notice and hardly gives me confidence with your ethics."

"Klien or a like mind would have just eliminated you as a threat after learning all that you knew," Helen said.

"True, so can we give you our answer on the way back?" Bern asked.

"Yes, the information you now have is already known to the Emperor," Ito said.

"Helen, the *Troy* is yours? The records show that it is registered in the Oxzen Sector, it operates as both a consular ship for Forno and merchant for Oxz?" Bern asked, "Strange combination."

"That is the way a Droman can live off the planet, and except for a few with the Elysium Navy, that is the way all of us live away from Droma," Helen said, "Interested?"

"I blush to admit yes," Bern said with a grin.

"Depart in peace, Captain Borg is due to return in two weeks, perhaps we can discuss this further," Ito said.

"We will have an answer then, otherwise we have to return to our base," Thum said.

The women left to allow the team to assess their future.

"Can we access this Light Mind?" Thum said.

"Should we risk that?" After a nod, "Here is the frequency," Bern said.

They merged into the presence of Light, "Welcome my sons, what would you like to know?" The warm presence asked.

"Can we be shielded from the Dark Overmind?" Bern asked.

"You do have that ability if you wish, the contact with my brother or myself is entirely voluntary. It takes a strength of mind to allow contact to happen," Light said, "In asking that question you have grown beyond servitude to either of us."

"I don't suppose the Emperor would appreciate such a change?" Thum said.

"This is the frequency that you should avoid," Light said passing the data.

"Thanks, we have to discuss the implications," Bern said together they changed their contact to resume their usual rapport.

"Amazing, so now what do we do?" Thum asked.

"I think we have burnt our bridges and Corellia is the last place we should show any part of ourselves," Shau said, "Arriving home with gaps in our memory probably means our life expectancy is short."

"So we throw our chips in with these Adepts?" Thum said, "Even if all was rosy with the boss, we now have targets on our backs for all comers."

"Or we can find a hole and drag it back on top, His Nibbs isn't about to come anywhere near here," Bern said, "I suppose we can ask and hold out for the best deal we can get. While strong those girls could learn a lot from us."

"So do you think we should catch up with them and give them the good news?" Thum asked.

"What can we lose?" Bern said, "On the way out we can let Borg know that he doesn't have to put up with us any longer."

They gathered their gear and on the way past the bridge located Borg, "Sorry to break it to you. From now you don't have to put up with us. It seems that it is safer for all if we split our company," Thum said, "I am sure that you are heartbroken by this news."

"Why are you still here? I thought all my passengers had left earlier," Borg said puzzled.

"We just forgot some gear, lucky we remembered before you lifted," Thum said.

"Okay buzz off, I am busy," Borg grumbled.

The three glanced at each other and then walked off.

"The girls are so sure of themselves aren't they, so likely we won't have far to go to meet them?" Bern said.

As he suspected there was a vehicle standing nearby with the women inside.

"Took you long enough, climb in," Helen said.

"As long as that is the last time you fiddle with our minds," Shau said, "It is not polite."

"If you are with us and can be trusted, I will show you how to avoid that happening," Helen said.

"What are Ito and your connections?" Bern asked.

"I am the owner and Captain of the *Troy*. Ito is my partner and mentor," Helen said, "And my best friend."

"Fine and Dierdre, you were crew?" Bern asked.

"My family stowed away on another Droman ship and arrived at Elysium, Helen identified us as latent, and together we formed the Academy, for a time we were supernumerary crew under Ito's training before resuming our place in the Navy," Dierdre said.

"I feel it is best to have you stay on the *Troy* where Helen can keep tabs on you," Ito said, "If that is not suitable, there are spare cells at the Academy."

"The *Troy* sounds better, as long as it doesn't inconvenience you," Bern said, "It would allow us to learn what we are getting ourselves into."

"There is accommodation for casual passengers so that we won't be crowded," Helen said, "So get in, and we will take you there after we take Dierdre home."

The men loaded the gear and themselves into the car; Helen drove to the two destinations. Arriving at first the Academy then the *Troy* where the luggage was transferred to the cabins assigned.

Gathering in the map room which doubled as a crew dining area, Ito introduced the new crew to the rest. "Bern, Thum and Shau please meet my secretary Veoos, Lt Hans Eisland, and last but not least Chef Gustaff, who we all depend on for excellent cuisine."

"These three are here to educate us on dealing with the empire and help train us in advanced techniques."

The new crew settled in with little problem as the three adepts were familiar with shipboard protocols and working ethics.

Taking turns in the Gymnasium, they showed the novice adepts some of the finer points of sparring and while Ito showed the latest light methods of avoiding harm.

"It is certainly a novelty being able to converse rationally with someone and learn new techniques as most of what I have learnt was by dodging lethal attacks by my opponents. The tricks shown were more to demonstrate how little I knew without giving me ammunition to harm my instructor," Bern said, "Once out of college it was a dog eat dog, and the devil take the hindmost. The few friends except these two seemed to die quickly until the message trickled through not to trust anyone."

"So how did you stay friends with Thum and Shau?" Hans asked.

"Good luck, we made a pact to watch each other's back is how we survived. Keeping a low profile so that we didn't attract attention. Warning each other when a move was afoot so that we were able to divert the potential adversary into taking on someone else either successfully or fatally," Bern said, "Thum especially was good at seeming to help the winner and ensuring that our boss didn't view us three as foes."

"If the Elysium Government asked you to be part of the action against your erstwhile brethren?" Hans asked.

"Apart from these two, they were all out to kill me," Bern said.

After a few months of drilling *Troy's* crew, the new light Adepts were transferred to the Academy to act as Adept master instructors.

War Clouds Gather

ON HER NORMAL ROUTINE, ITO HAD CALLED INTO Hostos' office to be updated with the military situation. With the reversal of the coup, she had been working full time restoring the trade and diplomatic services to normal.

"Good day sir, anything I should know about?" Ito asked.

"Yes, the closer merchants to Imperial space have reported a buildup of military exercises," Hostos said, "By the charts here, the activity seems to be towards restoring hegemony of the rebel systems. These other exercises are closer to us."

"Any idea as to their aim?" Ito asked.

"The setbacks they have encountered with the failed coup attempt here has alerted them to our sector's military ability, sometimes it doesn't pay to be too good," Hostos said, "Naturally we couldn't allow the incursion to succeed and Forno appreciates your efforts to restore our government."

"Only carrying out my duty. So what is the plan?"

"A scouting mission, publicly we are still friends, though I doubt any from this sector would be overly welcome."

"With Helen providing disguises I can circulate and see if I can assess the mood."

"That is the best way; the merchants are keeping their eyes and ears open. However, most contacts keep to business in case there are agents."

"I will talk to a few and see what to avoid."

"It is your task, farewell."

With that Ito joined Helen on the *Troy* to plan the mission.

Having laid out the background with Helen, Ito decided to visit Uncle Fedo to ask for the best people to have a chat.

Eventually, she tracked the *Challenge* down and went over to talk to him.

"Hullo, *Challenge* may I come aboard?" Ito hailed.

"You are always welcome, Ambassador. The Captain is waiting on the bridge," Lt Fostos replied.

"Thanks, I know the way," Ito said, then made her way down the familiar passageways to find Fedo holding court with his crew.

"Welcome aboard, ma'am," Fedo said, "May I introduce Commodore her Excellency the Ambassador to Oxen Sector, informally my niece, Ito Roos." Fedo exclaimed with a grin at Ito's embarrassment.

"I will call you Sir Uncle if you keep that up," Ito said.

"So Ito, what brings you here to my humble ship?" Fedo asked, "More sabre-rattling?"

"I need to pick your brain, to find out what the Impies are doing and the best people to ask.'

"Most of the merchants keep their eyes and ears open for any political news, places to avoid or to gain sweet pickings. Keeping your mouth shut is advised unless you only talk to who you know."

"I can smell a spy at fifty paces, and that was before I received my new training."

"The *Challenge* is doing a cargo run which takes us along the frontier, want to catch a lift?"

"My ship is a little conspicuous due to my official duties, so if you have a couple of cabins for Helen and me or a spot for my shuttle."

"Always room for an extra friend, are you going tourist or taking up the First officer's post?"

"The number one post would give me a cover, and sharpen my merchant claws. Going Tourist would bore me to tears."

"The berth is yours, and Helen is happy to help out in

Engineering? The hanger deck is vacant for the shuttle as we aren't carrying fighters."

"I will have Helen fly our kit over and load up. Helen can then set up camp in the shuttle for the tour.'

The *Challenge* ready for departure left Forno and headed towards the first port of call Hern, Ito took a turn at escort for Fedo as he visited the warehouse of Klienan. She stood by the door and let her mind drift assessing the political ether; there were no overt moods just the usual guarded thoughts more to do with commercial level intrigue. Normally she avoided doing this as it offended her ethics being able to eavesdrop.

Once the trade talk had finished, Fedo asked. "What is the mood of the Impies?"

"The usual agents are sticking their nose where it doesn't belong," Klienan said, "They stand out a little as not being interested in trade or drinking. From their questions, they are after ship movements as that is sensitive data for merchants, they don't get much gossip."

"A loose-lipped merchant would be soon broke if he allowed the competition to know too much, let alone nosey strangers who you can't trust. I tell you a few things because I know you aren't going to pass it on," Fedo said, "Besides I know you don't tell me things I could use against my competition."

"Who is your silent companion?" Klienan asked, "Seems familiar."

"Your memory is slipping, you knew me as captain Roos," Ito said.

"Oh, so what happened with the *Golden Dream*?" Klienan asked, "I had Hostos doing the merchant gig, entertaining as he seemed to learn all of your tricks."

"The Powers that be kicked me upstairs. I am with Fedo doing a little sabbatical and getting in touch with my old gang as a merchant," Ito said.

"As long as you aren't bringing another ship to overload my warehouse," Klienan said.

"You are safe; my normal run is in the next quadrant," Ito said.

The next port on *Challenge's* circuit was Herm where they met Jestos who told much the same tale as Klienan; and then calling in at Grenz to speak to Fera and Berno where they gave more detail.

At last, they *Challenge* reached the closest port to the Empire on the planet Fvelsving the two Roos made their way to Roxz' warehouse, to be greeted by him at the door.

"Welcome, Fedo you have a new companion, no an old one,' Roxz said, "A long time Ito."

"Indeed I am adding a little extra on this trip; I am having a sabbatical with my uncle," Ito said, "Also how are our old friends next door?"

"Oh much the same, sticking their nose where it doesn't belong," Roxz said, "And what is your interest?"

"There are hints that they may wish to expand their borders again," Ito said, "So some data before it hits the fan is helpful. It seems we rocked the boat by giving Adept Klien a black eye with the help of your relatives."

"By relatives you mean the Dromans and friends?" Roxz said, "I had heard some rumours. There has been a dark one roaming around so keep an eye out for him. There have been corpses turning up where he has visited."

"They tend to be a little untidy, I should keep away from him as I don't wish to spoil my holiday," Ito said, "Fedo is here to work, I will go for a wander and keep my ears open."

"You do that, So Roxz what do you have to tempt me with this time?" Fedo asked.

The men settled in for the bargaining, while Ito drifted out and casually cruised around. Finding a quiet bar, she ordered a drink and sat covertly observing the clientele. Helen found her there and sat down to keep Ito company.

While they sat and watched the world go by, a disturbance erupted over in a corner. A menacing aura was emanating from a dark clothed man who was having a heated argument with a couple of *Challenger's* crew. As push came to shove, the two crewmen started to draw pistols; the dark man drew a sabre and threatened with it while pinning them in a corner, "Tell me what I want to know, or you won't have legs to leave here," Darky snarled.

There was a sudden exodus for the door from the surrounding tables as the patrons made good their escape leaving the victims to their fate.

Helen wasn't happy with the treatment, so said, "Can't a person have a quiet drink in peace?"

"Stay out of this, or you will be sorry," Darky snarled, "This is empire business."

"And since when is this an Empire planet?" Helen said, rising to her feet, *"I will wrap this fellow up in a trice Ito."*

"I will cover you with the sleep gun," Ito telepathed back, *"my experience is as long as I didn't target an Adept, it doesn't register as a threat, and the sabre can't deflect the ray".*

Darky used telekinesis to slam the crewmen into the corner and turned to face Helen, to him she looked a young female an easy mark to terrorise. Deciding to make an example of her; he tried to throw her back into her seat without success, Helen responded by pushing him to one side. This enraged Darky who swung his sabre to trim her hair. Helen's sabre blocked this attack, and he was suddenly defending rather than attacking. The victims had used the moment to scramble out of the bar. Now frustrated, Darky attacked Helen who had little effort evading or blocking the blows, making him scramble to cover himself from the potential return cuts. He had telepathed for help and through the door came several Imperial troopers. Ito had spotted them and put them to sleep as fast as they entered. The clatter of falling bodies distracted Darky, and he had his sabre cut in half by Helen. Darky started to run but didn't get far before Ito had shot him and he also performed a faceplant.

"I suppose that means our cover is blown?" Ito said, "Grab Darky, and we had better return to the *Challenge*."

"I was just starting to have fun, he wasn't a match for Klien, and I needed the exercise," Helen said while she hefted Darky over her shoulder and made her way out the door.

Making their way over to the *Challenge* where they placed Darky into a back cabin which had an isolation screen for the dark adept frequencies. Once they had done the job, Ito went back to Roxz' warehouse to brief Fedo on the developments.

"I hope I haven't endangered your ship, but I have that troublemaker locked up, and I am afraid some Impies have observed our activities," Ito said.

"I suppose we had better load up and move on," Fedo said, "I suppose you had a good reason?"

"He was corralling a couple of our crew, and Helen was compelled to step in before they were injured," Ito said.

"They are alright? I suppose that was best," Fedo said, "So Roxz what is the likely move of the Impies?"

"As soon as the message rises high enough they will send as many ships as possible," Roxz said, "When Humph had his little trouble, Adept Varta brought a Sun Destroyer and had Rham's squadron to help to turn the planet upside down. I have heard the rumour that your sector has half the top adepts in the lockup."

"Officially no, and none on my Planet," Fedo said, "Once I load up we are out of here and heading back home."

"We can swap the loads this afternoon, and it had better be a while before I see you again," Roxz said.

"In that case, I will return to the ship and make preparations to depart," Fedo said, "When this fuss is over I will be back to make a bargain with your best product."

Fedo and Ito returned to the ship where preparations were well under way as Helen had started the process, taking the liberty of giving orders as 'Ito'.

Helen met Ito in the entry resuming her normal appearance before the crew tumbled to the subterfuge.

"Good trick, Helen, just don't let me catch you," Ito said, as Helen had been her suit she already knew that Helen had started the work.

Loading complete and all crew on board, the *Challenge* lifted off and headed out to the jump point. As Fedo initiated the jump, hyper pulses announced the arrival of heavy ships.

"Our luck is in, better not push it," Ito said.

"So we have a guest? Just what are you doing with him?" Fedo asked.

"Had to bring him he saw too much, the troopers went to sleep before making any observations," Ito said, "He can join his friends once I know what he has been doing."

"Your part of the ship, as long as my crew are safe," Fedo said.

Helen had set up a safe room to interview and started the process.

"Good day, I am Helen. May I ask your name?"

"Adept Arnold, you will regret this action my friends will hunt you down and eliminate you."

"Good trick if they catch us, I didn't realise that your sect had any friends. So are you going to cooperate or do I have to extract your information, such as what did you hope to learn by terrorising my friends?"

"I will tell you nothing."

"Have you heard of the mental task of not thinking of a camel? It seems that you aren't very good at it and I have learnt that your orders are to find Klien. So have a rest, you are going to find him shortly."

Leaving Arnold to stew in his juices, Helen made her way to find Ito to convey the information.

"Adept Arnold believes he is a tough nut to crack, he was trying to find Klien, so I offered to deliver him there."

"That didn't take you long; I don't suppose he was cooperative?"

"Like taking candy from a baby, which is a strange saying."

"You just have to put up with the crying, your target having no other defence."

With the cargo loaded, the *Challenge* was on its return voyage to Forno. Once there Ito expected that the new prisoner would be parked on the alternative world to be cut off from any help.

Adept Arnold had been quiet, not offering any conversation when receiving his meals which he ate in silence and seemed to have accepted his fate.

At Forno spaceport, Ito handed Arnold over to the local justice and rejoined the *Troy*.

"I suppose the next stage is to visit Coruscent to brief the republic and see if they are interested in the situation," Ito said.

"I will look forward to that, I have become too cramped doing the same rounds of the Milk Run," Helen said.

"I am sorry to have limited your journey; I haven't seen that side of the Galaxy either. The council has suggested that I should be the best diplomat for this task."

After loading up on all stores, the *Troy* lifted off to start the journey and on the way visiting all potential planets to gather further intelligence.

At the jail, in the main city, it was arranged for the next supply shuttle to transfer Arnold to the alternate universe.

The contingent of escorts arrived at the reception and presented their orders.

"I am Lt Gros to pick up the prisoner Arnold," Gros said, presenting the documents.

"Sign here, and he is yours. You are aware that he is dangerous?"

"The boss has armed us with sleepers; he will be secured and gagged."

Once Gros had finished the paperwork, the party with the prisoner made the way to the port and boarded the shuttle.

With the inter-dimension portal open it made the short hop through to land in the same position it left an hour before now in the alternate Forno planet. Contrary to normal procedure Gros released the prisoner and made the way to a hut where the stores were to be left.

Waiting was Zento Hoos and Adept Klien; as the escort entered the building, the guards were disarmed and tied up along the wall assisted by their erstwhile commander.

"Welcome Gros, did you have a pleasant trip?" Zento asked, "It has been a difficult wait over these last few visits."

"Necessary to calm suspicion and arrange a hyper-capable shuttle." Gros said, "Adept Arnold was the key for this to happen."

"Welcome Master, they have treated you well?" Klien asked, "These Light adherents are a pushover with their trusting behaviour."

"Yes they thought that they extracted the information covertly while they only learnt what I wanted to be known," Arnold said, "On Corellia, I would have been hung from my fingernails until they extracted every last iota of my memory."

"Still time we made our way back to our native dimension, I have to make plans to counter some of the tricks they used to thwart our efforts," Klien said.

Reboarding the shuttle with Klien and the other adepts replacing the guards, the crew strapped in and returned to Forno orbit via the Dimensional portal, but instead of descending to land at the port, the shuttle hit the maximum drive and streaked towards the hyper jump point before other craft could pursue. The vessel jumped several times to throw off pursuit before rendezvousing with an Imperial Corvette.

Admiral Hostos was furious when Huros delivered the message to his desk. "What the hell happened?"

"Lt Gros organised a substitute shuttle and disguised the fact it was Hyper able. Because he had completed the task without drama several times the supervisors were complacent," Captain Huros said, "I have disciplined those responsible, there are fighters now assigned to guard the portal. Gros slipped under the radar by using a cover identity provided by the security section."

"As the Terrans say, lock the gate after the horse has bolted, well the most dangerous have fled so now we are guarding an empty jail," Hostos said, "Call the defence board we will have to act quickly before the data is acted on by the Impies."

"I will get the action beginning," Huros said, "When intelligence is in, I will present it to the board."

"Do that," Hostos said, "Signal Commodore Roos that the rooster has flown the coop."

The signal was transmitted, and Helen found it puzzling. Helen said, "Signal from Headquarters. 'Rooster has flown coop', does that mean something?"

"I would assume that Klien has left the alternate world and returned to normal space; he is likely home and hosed," Ito said,

"This means we have to speed up everything as Klien likely has his scientists hard at work to remedy the disadvantage."

While they could plan it would depend on the HQ to implement most of the preparations at the Forno end and relay the news and warning to the sectors involved, while *Troy* continued onto Coruscent.

After several way-jumps, the ship entered the Coruscent System to be escorted to the Adept Academy to begin negotiations with Republic government.

To meet them was Master Adept Hoght Boyne, "Welcome sisters, grave news proceeds you."

"Yes, we received a message that Dark Adept Klien had escaped from his incarceration. We have to presume that he has secured several of our weapons and has clues to the workings of other critical methods," Ito said, "I have confidence that our sectors will accelerate preparations to forestall Dark action."

"What does your Government intend for the Republic to support this?"

"If you prepare to invade the Corellian systems it will divide their forces. No actual movement has to be made; the obvious posture should be enough to give them thought."

"And your strategy?"

"We have a technique to board and render their Capital Ships ineffectual by triggering safety protocols. Then by using sleep rays to remove the engineering crew to prevent them from restoring the systems. They don't usually fortify Engineering as they have little respect for technology."

"The Imperials have over a hundred Sun Destroyers and five hundred Corvettes which are manned by at least one Dark Adept who acts as a Political Officer. It is that entities task to maintain the aggressive stance of the ship."

"It would also be intended to target the bridge crew, effectively removing the head with the legs so to speak. The fighters which are the real protection, by using a myriad of robot and decoy buoys to nullify them which would then distract the focus away from the manned craft."

"Do you have the data for these last?"

"Helen will download the designs and deployment strategy. The other task that you could provide is to deploy these as a cloud from your sector while we do the same from other vectors. We would approach the capital ships from another dimension, undetectable at the moment."

"I would assume that all who know or suspect this tactic would be working on the detection and protection from that form of attack?"

"We can stop the sleep rays with a modified shield, and I would presume something similar for the dimensional access."

"The key to success would be the nullifying of the Dark adepts."

"We have had some success with that, three adepts have converted to the Light and several others nullified by sealing them in shielded quarters. The shields prevent contact with Dark Mind while allowing contact with the Light if they so desire."

"The key Dark members are the Emperor and Klien, who would intervene against any further conversion."

"This Emperor, what do you know about him?"

"What little we have before he assassinated his predecessor is that he was known as Adept Arnold and very good at acting harmless until he was ready to strike."

"That was the name of our last capture, perhaps why he seemed to walk into our trap. He didn't display any exceptional talent; I would have rated him no higher than Journeyman." Helen said, "It was during his delivery to join Klien that the escape happened."

"That is consistent with what we know about him."

"To return to strategy, if as many as can be built of the robot fighters and drones, and you fanned these across the entry points to create the semblance of thousands of invading light vessels. I have recommended the same tactic to my superiors."

"On paper, we are equal in tonnage to the Empire, though because we have a larger territory the units are somewhat thinner in the sectors. However, once they are distracted by another front, we can consolidate on the borders without being concerned with being outflanked."

"It is an overwhelming superiority complex engendered by civilised races being seen as weak because they don't eliminate all opposition before they can challenge. This behaviour is because most sensible people are more interested in trade; you can't sell the latest gadget to a slave or a corpse."

"Pragmatic capitalism I believe describes this mindset. The Dark philosophy is that the victor gets the power; the end justifies the means. Still, it is in the Republic's best interest to avoid a confrontation by the Empire when the balance is so close. Neither side can win a war of attrition, the victory last time was by poor judgement and being caught in a trap of their own making."

"So I can leave the nuts and bolts to your administration while I see if I can turn the rebel squadrons to our side or at least neutralise them."

"Quaint terms, the isolated groups are eking a living by stealing from Merchants, short-lived as soon as they become active the ships avoid traversing the systems. The contacts we have initiated are tenuous as most of these trust the Dark only slightly less than the Republic."

"The last contact I have had with one of these was to give them a bloody-nose; the rescued crew were happy enough to be separated from their boss even though it meant returning to Imperial control. Putting forward an alternative such as joining a civilised planet such as Elysium should be a useful carrot. The government would employ them as crew on warships with the Oxzen Navy or on merchant ships earning a living without having to dodge ray blasts."

"Good luck Adepts Ito and Helen, may your endeavours be fruitful."

"It has been an honour, Adept Boyne."

With the republic on the side, the *Troy* headed towards the first system which had an isolated fleet which had set up a base. Locating was difficult as besides hiding from Imperial and Republic attention they were also covertly waiting for passing merchants and other vulnerable vessels. Having a Humph's design arrive meant they were cautious in approaching as the reputation was formidable. So when Helen announced that a small vessel was hailing them to establish identity, Ito saw this as an invitation to talk.

"Ship is the *Troy*, Helen commanding, do you need assistance?"

"*Haven Kin*, Gerber commanding, Are you aware that hostile vessels are nearby?"

"Copy *Haven*, I wish to speak with your authorities regarding these."

"Follow me, and I will take you to my boss. You may retain shields but don't power up weapons."

"Thank you, may I ask from where you come, your accent is Aurean?"

"Yes caught by my tongue, do you have news from there?"

"From the area and we are in contact with a colony from there, Elysium run by Berna Telon."

"I have heard rumours about that planet, way on the other side of the Galaxy."

"We can talk more once we meet your people."

The two ships moved towards an Earth-size planet further in where an orbit was assigned while a shuttle crossed the gap to the *Troy* and after docking alongside the airlock a figure disembarked and entered. Removing the space helmet to reveal a feminine face, "Hi I am Janice Gerber, I came over because you identified as a girl and now I find two."

"Hi, This is Ito from Forno, Hans Einsland from Aurea and I am Helen from Droma. You indicated that you are from Aurea?"

"Yes, it has been several years, Hans how is the home planet?"

"Under the Fuhrer's thumb still, I am based on Elysium as are my sisters," Hans said.

"Berna Telon, would she be Admiral Telon?"

"Retired from the Navy and now the Governor, Elysium is a new planet and still a bit rough."

"Sounds lovely I heard rumours that Commodore Rham is there."

"Yes, he is now an admiral in the Oxzen Spaceforce, his squadron protects the sector."

"Now to business, are you a merchant? My colony needs replenishment."

"Yes but we aren't carrying much as I am on a diplomatic mission," Ito said, "I can arrange another ship to come once I declare it safe. In this area, there has been pirate activity."

"I am afraid that would describe my old Captain, he died when he took on the wrong traveller and while the rest of the detachment rescued most of the crew, we are a remnant of smaller supply ships. We can't return to the Corellian sector, and this system is barren. If you speak to our current Captain, I am sure he would appreciate a ticket to Elysium."

"I can arrange that after we talk, I am the Forno Ambassador to Oxzen sector which has Elysium as an associated system," Ito said.

"Captain Bernard Gerber will be interested as life is a bit hard, and I believe that he would entertain joining Admiral Rham and become useful again. I will radio the news if I may, and you can arrange further talks."

"Relative?" Hans asked, hoping that the answer was not a boyfriend.

"My father, I was attached to another ship when the old Empire broke up, and they stranded us in Limbo."

"Rham had much the same happen, while he was on the other side of the wheel, he was able to locate an empty planet and volunteer to become part of the Oxzen sector. Is Limbo the name of your planet?"

Janice laughed and said, "Yes, It was the old Captain's idea of a joke as his detachment was posted here because of suspicions that his loyalties weren't one hundred per cent for the Empire. Not enough to be relieved but turning up now would mean grounding for the crews."

Janice accessed the radio and selected the channel. 'Lt Gerber calling from the *Troy*, Is Captain Gerber available?"

"Yes, Lt Gerber, go ahead, is the ship friendly?"

"Yes, Captains Helen Troy and Ito Roos, Ito is envoy to Oxzen sector where Elysium is a system. Commodore Ito has a proposition for our detachment to join the Aurean colony there. Lt Einsland is from Aurea."

"Instruct them to land, and I can have a chat. Resume your patrol Lt.; Commodore Roos, please lock onto this beacon and land at our port."

"Will comply, *Troy* out. Thank you, Janice," Ito said.

Janice saluted and returned to her ship to follow orders.

"Nice girl, eh Hans?" Ito teased.

"Um yes, is she a potential Adept?" Hans asked.

"Yes, I noticed some telepathy, another reason that Aurea would not be a suitable home," Helen said.

The *Troy* entered the atmosphere and descended towards the ground where a rough clearing where several small ships were parked.

Selecting a spot clear of potential cover, Helen set the *Troy* down and waited for an approach. Within a short time, a small party walked over to wait for the crew to open a door. As they weren't heavily armed, Helen dropped the ramp and joined Ito to wait for for the party's entry.

"Hail the ship; I am Captain Gerber, May I come aboard?" A tall Middle aged man asked.

Ito stepped out and offered her hand, "Good day, I am Ito Roos. Please come in."

"What would you like to discuss?"

"I am surveying ex-Imperial groups to find out if they wish to join the Aurean Colony on Elysium," Ito said.

"Lt Gerber radioed more details after she resumed patrol. You are a Forno Envoy, so what is your part?"

"Captain Helen Troy is a citizen of that sector, while I am interested as one of the founders of an adept Academy based there. We have determined that Lt Gerber is a latent adept and would benefit from instruction. The academy can train adults in the art. Myself, Helen and one of your countrymen, Lt Einsland, have benefitted as would several of your party."

"I was passed over by the Corellian Academy as not suitable, so why would you expect that I would be interested or eligible?"

"We follow the Light Path; I have experience in detecting those people who would accept the training. The other situation is that Lt Gerber mentioned is that you are trapped in your present situation."

"Perhaps she exaggerated a little, but the idea of joining our compatriots has merit. She said that Berna Telon and Bento Rham lead the colony?"

"Yes, I would consider both my friends and have had many diplomatic discussions. I can provide coordinates to allow your ships to travel safely and Helen can provide those codes for passage."

"I attended the pilot's course with Rham and had served with Telon. So I would expect that you know Bento's wife?"

"I found Narn a charming woman," Ito said.

"As a fellow captain I would challenge that claim, and I suppose Blohm is still with him?"

"Yes, he is a captain in the Elysium detachment of the Oxzen Navy, as is his daughter Su Lin."

"Well, either you are well briefed or telling the truth, as you can tell I have some talent with empathy, and I believe that you are truthful. So the actual movement, you can guide and form an escort? We lost our capital ship when Boris took on the wrong ship, and it was crippled. Your ship is similar to the opponent."

"The *Troy* was built by the entity who may have been the pilot involved, Humph, Helen's fellow Droman."

"I have heard that Droman have a reputation for frustrating freebooters," Gerber said.

The discussions proceeded after transferring the data; Captain Gerber presented the prospect to his council, deciding that affiliating with Elysium was in their best interests.

"It was almost unanimous, so if you wish to lay out the plans for making this happen, we can make it happen," Gerber said.

"I can provide coordinates and best route to follow, I have completed this several times," Helen said, "Perhaps it would be best if the *Troy* arrived first so that the government is preparing your new home. Also, I need to relay the codes so that you show up as friendly. Pausing at the last system jump point would also facilitate the arrival."

"I would expect that Rham would be a little cautious if the Imperials are becoming active."

"Once I explain the circumstances he will welcome you with open arms, he recently acquired several ships and had a problem crewing them," Ito said, "A Sun destroyer and three corvettes as well as support vessels."

"How did that happen, they don't usually lie around waiting to be salvaged?"

"Adept Klien had them in orbit around my home planet, we evacuated the crews, and Admiral Rham took possession. He interviewed the crew, and about eighty per cent jumped at the chance to become Elysium subjects. Except for Klien and a couple of others the imperial loyalists are still safely imprisoned."

"You mentioned Klien escaping? By reputation he would be a difficult opponent, so how was he captured?"

"He took a little sleep and woke up on a deserted planet. I captured one man who I thought was a novice adept. He, unfortunately, turned out to be the Emperor disguising his abilities, and he took over a resupply shuttle to return Klien, and a couple of other adapts back to Corellia."

"Just how do you put an Adept to sleep? Nothing I know can do that."

"An ally invented it, the ray has caught me several times, so I am glad he is on my side now," Ito said ruefully, "By the time that you join Rham, his ships will have both the projectors and protective shields fitted."

"I will prepare the ships and load up what we can fit. Any chance of taking some of our crew we would be strained to carry everyone," Bernard said, "We would like you to transport thirty women and children."

"Certainly we have extra accommodation which would handle that many," Helen said, "I dare say they would be more comfortable and be suitable envoys to smooth the way into Elysium."

"And suitable hostages for our good behaviour, Though I do trust your motives," Bernard said.

"They will be safe; I even have a top chef to prepare their meals. Would you like a tour?" Ito asked.

"Certainly I will assemble a party, my wife would appreciate a change to her routine," Bernard said, "Her name is Hesta, as we don't have enough ships, she has been planet bound."

After an hour Berard returned with four women, "My wife, Hesta, with Gabriel, Martha and Tashe. They are all pilots, so are naturally curious about a new ship."

"Guten Arben Kapitans, New ship?" Hesta asked.

"Guten tag mien Damen, Yes only a few years old, we use it for diplomatic visits and small freight," Helen said, "For myself, it is home and a way of seeing the Galaxy."

As they entered the bridge, Hesta commented, "That is just like one of ours, I would feel at home conning this."

"It is based on that design as we are similar in the statue, that is a practical consideration."

The small party made the way around the *Troy* and were impressed by the layout and accommodation.

"I especially like the gardens, an excellent idea."

"Essential for my wellbeing, my people have only recently left my planet, and we live in a park-like environment surrounded by open space and vegetation, except for some who enjoy the open sea. I grew up on a vessel, though mostly within sight of land and forest."

"It seems to be idyllic. Is Elysium nice?"

"Very, it has only been settled for a few years, once out of the settlement it is pristine."

"Do you think we will be welcome?"

"Certainly they are still growing and have depended on foreign workers to fill the employment gaps. Most of these are from a new planet called Earth who could pass for Aureans and have a similar language. I base my form on them."

"Interesting, to practical matters, I would expect to be ready for departure within a couple of weeks. Would that be a problem?"

"I have calculated that this would be suitable, the *Troy* is designed as a fast turn around freighter. We have no pressing need to be elsewhere. Though be aware that trouble from the Dark Adepts is looming and the government is preparing our sectors for a likely conflict."

"Bernard told me. Here we live under the constant threat of the Empire returning us to their compass. As labelled renegades, we would expect poor treatment if we survived."

"Elysium is based on the old Aurean democratic system, with a Light associated Adept Academy similar to Coruscent. Ito and I helped establish the academy."

"Sounds good, we joined the Spaceforce to be away from the corruption and conflict. This action sounds a little counterintuitive, but we find that ship life is stable due to discipline."

"I can follow that reasoning, so how does your family end up together? I heard the Imperials usually split them up as passive hostages."

"They also like to keep the potential problems in one basket to keep an eye on them. We were isolated when our resident Adept returned to Corellia to contend for position when the old Emperor died. As he failed to survive or return, no one knew about us, and we were isolated."

"We have intelligence that lower echelon Adepts are used as political officers to keep the crews in line. I believe that it is not conducive to teamwork."

"Yes, it is hard to run a ship in a crisis if you have to second guess a person who is looking over your shoulder, concerned that if you say the wrong thing it will get back to the adept who has the authority to countermand, replace or even execute anyone."

"Not a good situation and I hear that the adepts are misogynistic and don't trust women?" Ito asked.

"Never met one who considered me as anything but a subhuman. I made captain on a supply ship, which didn't require an observer."

"Light Adepts don't interfere, being the resident adept myself; I am still the boss with Ito a partner. I own the *Troy* and expect many years of enjoyment and perhaps partners," Helen said, "If you are content, we can start planning the loading and arrange the route to your new home."

"I can't see any impediment to this happening. I will set up my side and begin to program the tasks," Hesta said.

With that, she gave farewells and departed to set the wheels in motion. With intensive effort all by everyone, the day arrived when they had loaded the last bit of luggage, filled the tanks, and the convoy was set to depart with *Troy* leading headed out to traverse the light years to Elysium.

The group consisted of twenty small military and support vessels which as they were slower than the *Troy* restricted the speed. Despite this, the convoy arrived at the last system jump point to regroup while *Troy* proceeded on to Elysium to prepare a welcome.

"Good Morning Governor Telon, I have a few guests to introduce to you," Ito said.

"Good morning Ambassador, since we are formal I suppose this is an official function?" Berna asked.

"May I introduce Commander Hesta Gerber, spokeswoman for the Limbo detachment, they are ex-Imperial detachment eking out an existence towards Coruscent," Ito said.

"Good day Commander, how would you like me to help?"

"Guten tag Admiral, My group wishes to join your colony. My husband Captain Bernard Gerber has the command of twenty vessels, with three hundred crew aboard," Hesta said.

"I remember him, if you have Commodore Roos' blessing, you would be most welcome, and Admiral Rham will be delighted to find employment for your crews."

"I have spent some time with them on the way back from coruscent, and they have several candidates for the academy among them. The ship completed the mission, and on the return, I could collect these worthy additions to Elysium," Ito said.

"Well, Hesta would introduce the rest of your party and inform me of the whereabouts of the detachment. Captain Gerber has served with me, and I would be delighted to be reacquainted."

"He is at the last jump point before entering Oxzen Sector. Ito thought having twenty military vessels arriving without invitation may cause a little angst with the patrol."

"I dare say so, I will notify Bento of the expected arrival so he can make the appropriate arrangements," Berna said.

With the advice provided to the people involved who tabulated the events, and the new ships and crew enrolled as Elysium subjects with the families settled into accommodation and school for the children.

Battle Preparations

WITH THE NEW ARRIVALS SETTLED, ITO MADE HER WAY to Bento Rham's office to brief him on the developments.

"Good day admiral. My mission was successful; the republic has seen the necessity of being prepared for conflict with the Empire. The proposal to form a front from our sector would allow them to concentrate their forces and act as a deterrent against military action."

"Good day and good news, both on preparation and the bringing of Gerber's ships into the fold. The trained crew are at a premium, the training of recruits is in full swing, but older heads are useful," Bento said, "We have had several of these groups arrive because the rumour had circulated about the possibility of Imperials going on the offensive. The isolated bands would be the first to suffer, and there would be little sympathy from either side for uncommitted ships."

"Forno is working at capacity, constructing robot fighters and the required carriers to transport. Capital ships are a premium as the building lead time is long. Of course, our adversaries have the same problem. The battle plan is to neutralise the capital ships by non-lethal means so that they are ineffective. When the alarms go off the ship withdraws with all its fighters until the crew rectifies the problem. With our adepts in control, and both the bridge and engineering crews removed it would be difficult to bring it back into service."

"My Chief engineer gave Commodore Firebrand the key.

You seem to know the inside workings of your government as an Ambassador?"

"I have inside access as besides a military rank I have a link to the governing council, on the quiet."

"You seem to wear even more hats than I do, so we prepare and wait? Situation normal in our business."

"I will now put my adept hat on as there are several of your new citizens who show abilities to become new adepts, I will need all my diplomacy to convince them that this is a good idea as the process is tortuous."

"We should put our minds to the task and prepare for something we hope doesn't happen."

"Unprepared it would be a disaster, the Imperials can say go, and everyone jumps. This process works in our favour as while they are moving they still need final orders, and initiative is discouraged by the suspicion of independent thought."

"And the resident adept is standing behind you to enforce the Emperor's orders, very stultifying; mine was absent when I made a move to Oxzen Sector. Which is what he is there to prevent."

"Our intelligence officers would have loved that power, but any attempt to implement was stamped on. It was the motive behind helping Klien invade Forno and one spook who helped him escape from where he was held. Those in merchant and navy distrust these mindsets and doubt their ability in actually commanding a ship when initiative is required."

"My experience, except for Blohm who was acting while the adept was absent. Now with his ship, he is back in his element."

"My next stop after settling the potential adepts is home to brief my people on the preparations at this end."

"We have the drone production in full mode at several factories, as there are human-crewed fighters that they will confront, the Droman insist that the standard deflector shields are used to reduce the loss of life."

"Yes, I am well aware of their sensibilities, as we depend on their abilities to carry this out."

"I will keep in touch, have fun talking the victims into it. I have observed the torture sessions, and frankly, you couldn't tempt me to undergo the test."

"Hanging around Droman seems to be the key for non Aurean people, your resident earflea Firebrand is undergoing training because of the years spent with Pippin, and myself with Helen. I have the preparation of martial arts training so seemed to have slipped through the worst without too much stress."

"I feel that Steve deserves every hassle he gets from someone else for what he has served out to all."

"Concur, I am off to the Academy to introduce the new apprentices, Goodbye for now."

Ito arrived at the Hall to be greeted by Dierdre Einsland acting as the head instructor, "Good day Ito, here to see your handiwork? Everyone is busy with the new intake."

"Any finding the program daunting? I dumped them into the mix without too much preparation, though I encouraged them on the way." Ito said.

"The children are having great fun. The rest of the families are arriving soon? The message I received is to expect another fifty or so potential adepts?"

"They had been bunched together to remove them from the Corellian Sector, just short of locking them up as potential troublemakers as nearly happened to you."

"I wondered how they ended up together; they called their last home Limbo?"

"Yes, they were waiting for the axe to fall when the old Emperor fell, which left them with no one knowing where they were."

"I was still caught up in the military on Aurea. Steven Firebrand and Pippin helped my family escape," Dierdre said, "Under the nose of Klien, as did quite a few of my peers who you dragged into the Academy. Not that I am complaining as it is far better than being under the gaze of the Dark Adepts."

"Some of the next batches are older than you and will need some serious persuasion to begin the adept study. If it weren't for the strategy of neutralising the Imperial Capital ships, I would allow them to remain ignorant and untormented."

"So what is that plan?"

"The Dromans short out several relays in Engineering while a party of our adepts clear the Bridge and Engineering crew using sleep rays when they are distracted with the alarms going crazy, the relays send a message that the fusion reactor is about to blow, which in turn shuts down the drive and main weapons. Without the Bridge and engineering crews to organise repairs the ship is out of action. This action is done from an alternate universe using Firebrand's portals. The Droman can reach through a small portal behind the panel and do this without anyone seeing it happen. Of course, once our side has used this trick; everyone will be working on shields to prevent reoccurrence."

"I suppose a bomb could be delivered easier, no doubt that is why the Dromans don't like the idea of the Dark side knowing?"

"First thing that came to my mind and why the space force needs to complete the preparations as quickly as possible; the devious minds of the Imperials will work on both the attack and shields once they are aware of the implications. Klien has experience of both facets so will be keen to develop a defence."

"The dark adept on the bridge would have to be neutralised first?"

"Essential and requires using caution when gathering intelligence as they can detect minds close-by. Admiral Rham is delighted that he is getting hundreds of trained ships crew to man his ships. The force can quickly train the Terrans and Oxzen in piloting, but these sectors lack the experience in fighting a space battle. My sector has experience in small level actions against inferior armed ships as they avoided clashing with better-equipped systems."

"Here we are at the lecture room for the older students; it would be beneficial that you can demonstrate that it is possible for the elderly to assimilate the training."

"Thank you for that gem; I will give a brief lecture then field questions."

Kevin Colbran

"Students please welcome Commodore Ito Roos, ambassador to the Oxzen Sector for Forno."

"Ladies and gentlemen, I stand before you as one who has been through the training and shows that it is possible to survive and reach the Master Adept at an advanced age. While some of you may doubt the benefits of joining the Light as adepts, it is a wonderful experience. My friend and I have faced the strongest of the Dark Adepts and survived. The training is as arduous as explained and usually begins at a young age where youthful resilience is helpful. The main reason is that training is needed over time to prepare the apprentice in philosophy to avoid the Dark Mind. I acknowledge that you have experience in the adverse mindset of the Dark Adherents so perhaps this is unnecessary. My introduction is due to living with my partner Helen of Troy. She is from Droma without these entities help our sectors would have fallen to the Dark Adept attacks. I thoroughly recommend the training however far that you progress and I look forward to serving with you."

"Any questions?" Dierdre asked.

There were only a few regarding the program which Ito soon answered, and after taking her farewell, returned to the *Troy*. The ship made its way to Earth to bring Steve Firebrand up to speed as well as brief the United Nations with the latest developments.

Entering Steve's office she greeted him, "Good day Steve, how are the Earth's preparations?"

"Going gangbusters, my factories are flat out building everything needed to wage war with the Imperials. Even just replacing that which was lost in the Korean fiasco as well introducing spacecraft to the economy has turned everything upside down. My desk is flooded demanding delivery of years of production by yesterday."

It took a few minutes to assimilate the local jargon before Ito was able to work a reply, "Um yes, well here is more data to crowd your desk. Think of it as payback for the hassles that you visited on my people.

"You are mean, life has certainly been interesting since we met, I am much stronger for the stress. Pippin is insisting on progressing my training and tells me I am almost at the journeyman adept stage. I have been assisting a counterpart of mine in the process have talked to your alternate and talked her into not starting anything with Alternate Earth, in the process, I assisted another Rham in detaching from his Empire by neutralising an adept. An invigorating experience."

"So I have found, so my counterpart didn't go through the wringer like me?"

"Humph wasn't around to assist; his alter ego Gazes at the Sky is now loose in that continuum. The help to the dissidents by your people wasn't implemented, Just an attempted imposition on Terraus, my country's alternate, together with my Steve we invited Loxz to commence trading first and 'you' saw the benefits of co-trading as you now do here. This agreement forestalled any conflict and set up our current situation there."

"Sounds good, I may see if I can visit when we calm this situation. In the other sectors as well as the Republic are preparing for the task of neutralising the Dark adepts."

"Any plans to fix them after success?"

"That will be a task and a half; it may take years before the Galaxy is safe from their actions. I watched the 'Starwars®' series, and possible outcome is not too promising with isolated pockets resurging activities. Any complaisance would unleash the threat again."

"As we have found on our planet, the First world war led to the second and many smaller conflicts as one group thought they were hard done by; or the victors were arbitrary in assigning boundaries putting ancient enemies in the same basket or a new philosophy tried to establish their way by conflict. In one of my alternates, religion is in the process of starting one."

"Peaceful trade is preferable, as I have often heard from the Oxzens you can't sell anything to a slave or a dead person."

"More to do with being the biggest frog in the pond, the winner ends up in a smaller mudhole when the fighting stops, with the poor worse off if they survive."

"With that jolly note, I will deliver my intelligence to the authorities and collect their updates to pass on to my government. I hope to see you in peaceful times."

"May the light pave your way. I have been in contact with Light Mind, a wonderful experience."

"As I have found, see ya round like a rissole, whatever that is."

Ito carried out her mission and then left to return home to Forno. On the way doing a whistle stop at Proxima. Reaching Forno, she made her way to Admiral Hostos' office to pass on the updates.

"Good day sir, things are on the boil, any news from the front?" Ito asked.

"Good day Commodore, you have been busy with the data we have received. News from on the border is there have been incursions. They deny any involvement by trying to blame "pirates", they do this to test our resolve and preparations. Our envoy is constantly being watched, and only fed snippets meant to reassure him that nothing is happening."

"Situation normal, no change as yet. Our groups are flat out and detecting spies at every facility, too much surveillance on our part draws the attention. The official stand is that the sectors are merely restoring lost vessels and upgrading older ships in a normal course of events. A bit of a catch 22 as being too vocal about not hiding anything sets the alarms going that we are covering up a deeper secret."

"It seems that all preparations are flowing smoothly, with the Republic starting to crowd their border it may be enough for Klien to pull his horns in and talk sense."

"An adventure towards our sectors leaves there own boundaries exposed to counter-attack from the rear. Following their normal tactics, they would invest in a knock them down technology and forget the small stuff by relying on superior numbers of small craft. Our proposed tactic of flooding their sector with decoys and robots simulating an overwhelming force while neutralising their bigger ships during the chaos. The Republic has typically used large numbers of small fighters acting independently which is a problem for the Imperials because they don't trust independent thought."

"That is to our advantage. So far no suspicion of the imperials building another planetoid battleship is planned, but as it fits their mindset, my office is studying a plan to combat one. Perhaps they have learnt from their previous failures and will avoid that course of action," Hostos said.

"At the moment we have a quick fix for one of those until the adepts spot the possibility and invent a shield to prevent placing a bomb via the parallel world portal. I expect that our scientists are working against them using it on us?"

"Yes, progress has been made for that with patrols guarding against using Parallel Forno to bypass. Keeps me awake at night thinking about it, we are constrained by our ethics to use that scenario against a civilian planet."

"Whereas they are not, their ethics dictate whatever eliminates the opponent is justified."

"Is Steve Firebrand able to infiltrate the Corellian sector?" Hostos asked.

"On the next trip I will ask, perhaps I can go and obtain a fresh eye on the layout. Firebrand is capable of doing this undetected, but he doesn't have the military training to gain the maximum intelligence. It seems he carried out some espionage in an alternate universe where our counterpart was trying to infiltrate Earth; he had success in walking into her office and leaving data to convince the Forno and Imperial forces that trading was a better option. There was only one low level adept involved in the Imperial detachment."

"Sounds like a versatile set of gadgets, I will have to speed up our defence in case the Imperials come up with the same idea."

"And once we both have the defence we are back to even abilities. Ever a dog chasing its tail."

"My next call is back to Firebrand and see what we can do. Helen and I are racking up the parsecs. Still, it beats flying a desk, sorry sir," Ito said, "I will leave you to carry the load for Forno."

"Forgiven, for now, Godspeed, Commodore," Hostos said.

The return trip to Earth was uneventful, and Ito was soon

talking to Steve, "What is the chance of looking over the Emperor's shoulder?"

"Maybe not that close, he would be watching and listening for any eavesdropping but I can seek out and view the overall strategy of the system, and I believe eavesdropping on individual scientists would be safe enough, maybe if a few key personnel were given a holiday from their hard work it could put a spanner in the works. Or make them waste resources increasing security. They probably have guessed by now that we have the expertise so it won't be a surprise if strange things occurred."

"The longer we can keep them guessing the better, I don't wish to push them into action before we are ready."

Having decided that a clandestine venture was desirable, Helen and Ito joined the crew of *Big Red* and set out via the alternate Galaxy to the unpopulated version of the Corellian sector. This universe was one where intelligence hadn't evolved.

"After only a short time communing with the Light Mind is strange when the touch is not there, though it does help that Helen and Pippin fill that missing ambience," Ito commented as the absence asserted.

"Yes just like a missing tooth filling you only notice that it is not there," Steve said, "Still it won't be long, and the light will fill the niche. Pippin has alerted us to the approach of the Corellian sector, and we should use the mental phasing to prevent the Dark Adepts detecting our presence."

"Better to practice the skill before it becomes necessary, though we are cut off from the Droman while we do this. They can't join us when there are two on the same ship."

"Breaking out of hyperspace now, I will monitor the radio to detect if any vessel is nearby before opening a portal," Pippin said.

After a few minutes scanning with all detectors, Pippin said, "No evidence, so opening a portal to scan the Normal Galaxy, good no ships nearby, rotating scan and mapping coordinates. My sensors are only passive and receiving transmissions and where they block the sun and stars. I will throw up a model of what I saw enhanced to position the detected vessels about our ship."

A ring of lights appeared in the map holo projection in the navigation room. Each point had a series of writing associated with it.

"If you wish to inspect a particular ship, think on it, and the image will expand and so will the identification symbols. I am shutting off the portal so that you can use your usual thought frequency."

"Good, that is hard work, I suppose you have a record?"

"That is what I used to recreate the system. There is eighty Sun class destroyer accompanied by three corvettes each, with fifty fighters patrolling the volume within a thousand kilometres of each. It would be reasonable to decide that this was a usual deployment of assets. This area being the Corellian system it is as expected most heavily defended. This leaves another twenty groups spread among the other five systems they consider home territory."

"That was quick, we have gathered most of the intelligence we need, and we have only arrived. I suppose we should do some reconnoitring to see how fixed the ships are in orbit or if they move around in case someone does eavesdrop."

"I will move closer to the planet. We can see if laboratories are working on the shields and rays."

The *Red* circulated through the system occasionally pausing and surveying. As the shield and ray emanations were familiar, Pippin was soon able to locate a few centres of activity.

"It seems that the Impies are working on the defence, can we get a little closer and observe how they are conducting the work and if they have adepts involved?"

"Getting closer with active scanners increases the likelihood of detection, there is a small one well away from vessel activity, so perhaps this would be easier to sneak up. Using a robot controlled camera will reduce the possibility of an adept detecting prying eyes. Once established that adepts are absent we can use stronger and more direct vision."

The *Red* moved to an adjacent position and opened a portal, recorded video of the areas within the workshop and then settled in to review the recording.

"It seems this isn't a favourite home for an adept, so we can use live video to access the activity."

Setting the camera for direct view, and then moved around the workshops recording all frequencies as they went. At one computer station, a light flashed, and the operator smiled and reset his view before turning and looking directly at the camera, "Welcome, I am pleased that my theory is correct, please feel free to communicate."

"Audio on, good day, what would you like to know?" Ito said taking note of his reactions.

"What would be the chance of my friends and me catching a lift to Elysium?"

"Every chance, willing or not, I will open a portal, and we can talk face to face."

"Do you think that wise? With a flick of a finger, he could set off alarms." Steve asked.

"I have felt his mind, and there is no subterfuge, it is your technique to grasp the nettle firmly and follow your instincts. I will step across and have a talk you can stand by to snatch the crew."

Opening a larger portal, Ito stepped through and greeted the man, "I am Ito Roos, and you are?"

"Bryan Murton, I am pleased to meet you, would you like to meet the others?"

"In a moment, first to satisfy my curiosity. Why are there no adepts present?"

"He insisted on stepping through a field against warnings and had to be evacuated suffering memory loss. For some strange reason, they haven't replaced him."

"That confirms your travel plans; I don't suppose you have personal shields for the sleep ray?"

"I am working on it; the question implies it is feasible."

"I should talk with the rest of the crew and ensure that they are happy with the prospect of evacuation."

"Once that adept was gone we have had long talks after ensuring we had neutralised all listening devices. Fortuitous that Adept Zed had a lapse of memory as he was suspicious of us."

Bryan then called the other seven members to the room and introduced them to Ito, "This is our ticket out of here, Ito Roos is here to find out our progress."

"And where does it leave us, I don't believe that you will leave the workshop in one piece." Su An said.

"I think that after we take you aboard our ship, that there would be a small accident with the power generator," Ito said, "So if you would give me a guided tour while you assemble what you wish to take with you."

"Certainly, it is a pleasant change to be asked. Come this way, and we will soon show everything you wish to know."

The tour completed, this was redundant as Helen and Pippin had already recorded all the pertinent data. Ito invited the lab crew to step through with their belongings while Helen helped contrive an accident with the generator. The alarms were blaring as Ito and Helen stepped through the portal and shut it off. Withdrawing a distance the camera showed a small disturbance as the fusion plie melted with sufficient power to mean that an investigation would be inconclusive as to a cause.

"I hope that you don't miss your home? I believe that you should be happier on this ship. Commodore Steve Firebrand, Captain Pippin are the pilots of the *Big Red*, I am Commodore Roos, Captain Helen Troy and we are supernumeraries. These are Bryan, Su, Hert, Greta, Jean, and Kris late of the Imperial Laboratory. We are happy to deliver you and your data to Elysium."

"So Bryan, why the desire to move?" Steve asked.

"It would be normal procedure to close the lab the same way as you did once the data was delivered with us still inside. Best way to ensure our boss received all the credit."

"That would be a disincentive to complete the task quickly?"

"That also makes it hard to recruit volunteers; it is the same with the other facilities, a poor reward for hard work. While the adept was watching, there was little chance of covering up progress."

"I am the source of most of what you are working on to duplicate. I will be most interested in viewing your efforts. At the moment I have the raw data to view."

'We would be delighted to compare notes, the dream of working and living free was only a hope."

"I am from a planet called Earth, Pippin and Helen are from Droma and Ito is from Forno, we have visited Elysium many times and have found it a pleasant if rough place being only recently settled from Aurea."

"My people are from Aurea if you would take us to any of these places I would be delighted to further your work."

"I am sure that you will be provided with the best facilities once settled, I would welcome you to my factory workshops where we are well versed in the techniques. The memory field piques my interest; it could be used to bring the dark adepts into the Light."

"It would be our pleasure, as it could facilitate returning to our homes without the oppression from the Dark side."

Having settled their new passengers, the *Red* turned towards Earth and after clearing the Corellian sector returned to normal space to complete the jumps required. The first destination was Elysium to debrief with Admiral Rham and deliver the data concerning the Corellian layout and possible strategy they may employ.

"While we have nipped one research workshop, it illustrates the danger of delaying any move on our part," Ito said, "Our ethics handicap us by needing to wait for the potential enemy to make the first move and declare war. Though Klien did invade and then escape legal custody, Forno could use this to justify further action. However, it leaves our allies uncommitted."

"Our envoy from Oxzen sector has assurances that there is no action contemplated and that they are investigating the hostile actions of renegade groups. Forces approaching the system would identify these as a large garrison."

"These new immigrants have information that the Empire is actively pursuing technology which can only be used to nullify our advantage. If forced to admit the existence it can be explained that it is necessary to defend against aggression."

"Officially that is what the Government is paid to decide. Naturally, they do so on our advice. If we neutralise their fleet without harming anyone we could argue that our forces are merely rendering obsolete vessels less of a navigation hazard."

"So our headquarters plan for an action, then wait for a trigger. Overt preparation could justify the Imperial reaction, not that the darkies need an excuse, breathing without the Dark control would be enough." Ito said.

"Since we have argued ourselves in a circle, what is your sector's plans for the nest move?" Rham asked.

"Steady as it goes, for myself carrying data from one authority to another fills my time. I intend to brief Loxz and see what his thoughts are before heading back to Forno again."

"Travel well," Rham said.

At the spaceport, Ito found that the *Yellow Terra* had just landed so made her way over to talk. "Hail the *Terra*, Ito here may I come aboard?"

"Please do, for what do we have the pleasure?" Humph asked.

"Just touching base and see what your opinions of the building angst from the Imperials are," Ito said.

"The same as always, you either stay out of their way or pay tribute," Humph said, "What have you been up to?"

"Returned from Corellia with a few passengers, who were working on counters to the possible use of sleep rays and portals. They would prefer to work in a peaceful environment. The downside is that there are other more secure factories working on the same task."

"How far advanced?"

"Enough to set off an alarm to tell that I was watching with Steve Firebrand," Ito said.

"Official policy?"

"Still friends with the Empire. The Imperials are conducting investigations of renegade groups who have been agitating near the borders. The rebels get the blame for incursions such as the frustrated coup on Forno. If we challenge any Imperial ships on the wrong side of the line, they are chasing renegades, and if they accidentally fire on our ships, sorry it was a mistake."

"The Impies are notorious for poor navigation, though very accurate if you wander into their turf. What have you been up to lately?"

"As a Diplomat and Navy officer it is hard balancing the peace, apart from uniting renegade ships with Elysium and rescuing scientists from oppression, I try to complete my rounds to help Forno merchants remain profitable. Steve is entertaining the scientists at his factory developing counters to the counters ad nauseam."

"Just like the Oozlum bird, which flies in ever decreasing circles until it disappears up its cloaca," Mike suggested.

After a few puzzled looks, he received laughs or groans depending on how often that they had heard this saying.

"On that note, I am off to Loxz and pass on the good tidings," Ito said as she returned to the *Troy*.

The Troy continued the diplomatic rounds until she returned to Forno, where the fleet was assembling.

"Admiral, all well here?" Ito asked.

"There has been an incursion into the Garbin System, one of our new colonies, suspect Imperial; initial reports suggest as many as fifteen capital ships involved," Hostos said, "Is the *Troy* fitted with Firebrand's portal?"

"Yes, would you like to have a peek?"

"That would be helpful, do you need another eye?" Hostos asked hopefully.

"Certainly an extra eye and strategy insight would be useful. We can be on our way in an hour."

"The office won't need me for a couple of days, and I would like an opportunity to get a closeup evaluation."

The *Troy* lifted off and entered the alternate Universe before jumping to the coordinates of the threatened Garbins system. As the ship moved to the planet with a small portal open to scan the orbit, hundreds of indications showed that the estimated numbers were accurate. Helen downloaded the data and projected the system as a hologram in the map room.

"This display confirms our greatest dilemma, our total Navy, just matches these which would be a war of attrition that neither fleet would win. Even using our new tactics would be difficult so I will have to confer with the Oxzen to arrange help. Another concern is this a bait to see how advanced we are and allow them to advance their tactics."

The survey went on for a time, and it was apparent that this was a baited trap. If Forno were to ignore this, the Imperials would invade the next system until either Forno reacted or risk the defence forces being trapped in the home system. A ring of scout ships with companion fighters was set to carry gathered data back to Imperial headquarters. At Forno, this hadn't happened, and it wasn't until Klien had returned that the Imperials found out about the technology.

"To nip this trap in the bud, we need a hundred per cent clean up with no Hypercapable ships escaping. If we eliminate these, the Empire has the resources to replace them and double down until we collapse."

"With twenty capital and another fifty smaller we need at least that number to neutralise them, and we don't have that many fitted with the necessary equipment."

"Earth and Elysium would love to help on the prospect of keeping a share of the ships. The other problem is about three hundred thousand potential prisoners to deal with even if eighty per cent come over to our side. And we can expect at least twenty adepts as well which would require at least that number of Light Adepts to handle."

"We have the information, back to Forno, I will assign scouts to the nearby systems to warn of further incursions. I can't weaken the Forno Garrison in case they jump in one move." Hostos said.

"We can use the decoy buoys and robot fighters as system garrison to keep the scouts company. A quick survey would detect a larger presence then the intelligence would suggest. The IFF transponders would need to be set to non-aggressive mode so a casual transit won't start any action. The scout can monitor and reprogramme if attacked."

The *Troy* headed back to organise a strategy to combat the incursion. With the data available the council began deliberating the options.

"I will brief Firebrand and Rham on the developments and ask them to convene here for their input," Ito said.

Arriving on Earth, Ito made her way to Steve's office and delivered the news.

"It seems that the Impies are on the move, testing the water before we are ready. Your assessment of a catch 22 situation is valid. At the same time Forno cannot allow further advancement of the task force," Steve said, "Can we encourage the Republic to rattle their cans from that sector?"

"While the Imperials have adequate forces in reserve, though having a large force unavailable would make them reconsider the position," Ito said, "It seems that I should contact them after I see Admiral Rham."

"I will brief my people and arrange some help for your sector. The Earth Defence Force is eager to test the ships and training. They would see this as a suitable exercise," Steve said.

Ito visited Rham, he concurred with the assessment and promised to address the Forno Council.

Setting the nose of the *Troy* towards the Republic, the ship proceeded at maximum speed. While there was hyper-wave radio, it wasn't secure. The possibility of Imperial interception was likely; physical data had to be delivered.

Master Adept Hoght Boyne was waiting and greeted her, "Good day Adept, you bring worrying news? We would expect this event as spending resources is the Dark way."

"To solve this problem using the technique planned for the main attack would reveal these tactics and allow them time to develop a defence. Steve Firebrand suggested approaching the Republic with an incursion to distract them from pursuing this baited trap. If the

Forno sector uses existing strategy it will result in attrition that they can ill afford," Ito said.

"I believe that a naval exercise close to the border of a size which should attract their attention and would suffice," Hoght said. "I believe that one is due shortly, a rapid deployment exercise would test the readiness of the ships and crew."

"If you would time this for action in two weeks of my return it would create the necessary incentive to withdraw. We can then muster sufficient traditional assets to confront the occupation without inviting massive retaliation."

"I will approach the High Command and put forward your proposal, expansion into undeveloped areas would provide resources and could result in the enveloping of our borders from another direction." Hoght said, "I should provide an answer within a short time as an exercise in mobilisation is overdue."

Hoght departed, and Ito spent time exploring the Coruscent Academy, observing the training of the apprentice adepts. These were younger than Elysium's classes as this academy inducted at a younger age.

After a time, a runner called Ito to Hoght's office for the decision.

"The Commanders have decided to bring forward an intended mobilisation a little closer to the border than usual. Every time the Republic has done so, the Imperials mobilise within striking distance assembling a fleet of larger firepower to preempt an invasion. Then the Republic Fleet forms another standby group set to stalemate a preemptive strike. After several moves and countermoves setting up a stalemate, the Republic forces commence a graduated stand down. When the Republic Fleet stands down and resumes normal patrols, so does the Imperials."

"The Imperial Navy tends to be reactive, while they wait for decisions from the Emperor. Each commander has a set response to intelligence and initiative is covertly discouraged."

"This is to our advantage as Imperial buildups can be discouraged by small raids in a different system, sending forces scrambling to meet the perceived threat and disrupting formations. Republic fighters are Hyper capable, unlike the Imperial types."

"I have suggested garrisoning nearby systems with scouts and decoy buoys to suggest a greater force than otherwise possible. If the Imperials scout closely they would be unprepared for an actual full garrisoned colony," Ito said, "The scouts then pass on intelligence with the buoys guarding their retreat, the skirmishing fighters can then enter the system before the incursion can set up a defence perimeter. The support vessels are vulnerable at this time."

"By the time you have returned and arranged your counterattack, the exercise will be underway and having a major buildup by Forno would leave the Imperial taskforce without reinforcements. Travel well, a ready code transmitted by us will signify the start."

"Thank you may we meet in happier times."

The *Troy* made the long journey back to Forno. As the ship entered the system, she found an array of ships ready for the move to the invaded colony. Among them were several Earth ships with the only missing ships Rham's larger capital vessels.

Walking into Admiral Hostos' Office, Ito asked, "Good day sir, Rham and Firebrand busy elsewhere?"

"They are standing by in the alternate Universe, as a reserve if plans go wrong. Naturally once the action starts plans are out the window with all common sense and each captain has to use initiative for actions afterwards," Hostos said.

"I should join them using Helen to the best advantage. The *Troy* is also a little too conspicuous to be a part of the fleet."

"Yes, I would have suggested that. The Republic is on board?"

"In a day, they will transmit a weather report saying storms are likely on Coruscent. This announcement is the code to announce the deployment of several exercises to practice mobilisation."

"And Forno's move to regain Garbin System," Hostos said.

Ito spent the next day, arranging for the ship's stores with Helen.

"An old Chinese curse 'May you live in interesting times' it seems this is now," Ito said.

"The hardest task is to minimise innocent casualties, the Imperials are not under the same constraints," Helen answered.

"Now we listen for a general transmission from the Republic

over the Hyperwave band, amongst the weather report, there may be a storm warning. This announcement is our cue to move into the Alternate Universe and rendezvous with Rham And Firebrand at Garbin System."

"I am monitoring the broadcast, it has just started, and the forecast is on shortly," Helen said, "Ah, there is our cue, storms over Coruscent. The tower has cleared us for takeoff, and we are on the way."

As the Troy cleared the atmosphere, the Forno Fleet was underway towards the jump points heading to the Garbin System. The *Troy* used the large Firebrand portal to transit first to the alternate Forno then jumped towards the alternate Garbin.

As the *Troy* entered the system, several ships were detected, Rham's detachment of six capital vessels and Firebrand's saucers and shuttles.

"Hail *Troy*, nice of you to join us," Steven radioed, "There is a movement in the targets, they are regrouping to leave."

"That would be as a result of the Republic holding maneuvers and the Forno Fleet scrambling here," Ito said, "How are the ground forces?"

"Still on the world, once the Imperial ships are clear we can start the mop up. I would guess that the commander feels it is safe enough to do so. The first step is to neutralise the observers and then the support vessels and then deliver a surprise to the ground troops." Rham said.

The Imperial ships jumped into hyper and disappeared. As the scouts and support ships were surplus to the home system mobilisation, the Imperial commander seems to think that these could look after themselves.

When the last trace of the major ships had dissipated, Rham ordered, "Capture the scouts, then the support ships before they can escape."

As the *Troy* had the capability, Helen moved the ship's orbit to adjacent to the first scout and when Rham said, "Commence operation." Helen acknowledged and fired a sleep cannon via the portal to knock out the crew and after opening a larger portal, removed them into her ship before treating the next three in turn. Rham and Steven's ships also carried out the same task, and soon the first phase was completed.

Next moving towards the planet to intercept the supply and carriers before the captains realised the turn of events. The fleet completed this extra task quickly, and the task force had secured all remaining vessels without transmitting alarms.

By now the Forno Fleet had entered the system and arrayed themselves in defensive formations ready for a possible return of the Imperial Capital ships.

With the Forno defence force in charge of the ground operations, Rham and Firebrand ships remained in their orbits in case of a return of the Imperials.

Once the fleet had cleared the planet of troops, and the Forno fleet had set a garrison to prevent the Imperials retaking the colony; the fleets were stood down to yellow status, watching and restoring order.

At the debrief on Rham's ship, "We have captured thirty scouts, fifty fighters and twenty support vessels along with forty thousand ground troops. If we repeat our experience, we will have fifty thousand recruits for Elysium. With the experience of the Forno incursion, we will soon complete this task."

"On behalf of the Council, I wish to convey Forno's deepest gratitude for the timely assistance," Ito said.

With the last details completed the main fleet withdrew to Forno System while Rham's ships transited to Garbin planet to remove the prisoners and salvage the Imperial equipment including the scouts and other vessels. Being Earth's representative, Steve took charge of a dozen scouts and a couple of support ships. Forno's fleet gathered up the balance for their share as Rham didn't have enough trained crews for them.

Balance the Force

WITH THIS CRISIS HANDLED WITHOUT IMMEDIATE repercussions, the defence councils met to plan the next phase.

"Ladies and gentlemen, the defence forces have been successful for now, opinions please," Admiral Hostos said to open the debate.

"I believe that the Imperials will mount a major attack to demonstrate their power, this supposing that they assume that the exercise by the Republic was a coincidence and we took advantage to push out the rearguard. I would now recommend an all-out assault by our sectors and the Republic as soon as possible," Rham said, "If they assume the Republic is unready to mount an attack, the force sent to punish Forno will be bigger than the last."

"If we contain this possible move, first we disable as many capital ships as possible before moving straight onto Corellia in tandem with the Republic Fleet," Steve said, "The longer the situation continues, the more likely our advantage will be nullified. My new workers have developed a defence and variations of attack bolstering our advantage for now."

"To fully justify this action, the Imperials would have to mount a second attack, and our defence forces are then to ensure that no further attack from the Empire is possible. If a defence for small portals is successful it would require cataclysmic force to be deployed," Humph said, "Unfortunately this outcome would result in many deaths. I regret that the only way to handle the Zombie Beast is to vaporise each part as we find it. This policy is necessary to remove the threat to the Galaxy, the ethics of the leaders of the Dark adepts almost falls into the same category; the difference being that the majority of the Imperial Forces are innocent of evil intent."

"Would it be possible to neutralise the Emperor, cut the head off so to speak?" Steve asked, "I suppose being increasingly paranoid the higher up the pyramid the adepts are, that would be the first defence upgrade."

"We had him in our hands before, as Adept Arnold, so possibly a standin could be sitting on his throne at any time," Ito said, "A capture of a decoy would set alarms off without affecting the status quo. Perhaps Helen would be able to identify him."

"Yes, I have his mental signature now, I am still a little irritated that he fooled me," Helen said, "Ito and I should do a reconnoitre to see if the Emporer and Klien are vulnerable."

"Since we are in the parallel universe we can jump over and take a peek," Ito said.

Receiving a nod from Bento and Steve, the two women returned to the *Troy* to begin the journey. Without delay as Helen had prepared the ship for the trip before the shuttle left Rham's ship.

Settling into the command seat, Ito commented, "Beats starting from scratch with you on the job before I finished moving."

"No need to waste seconds while I sit in both places twiddling my thumbs; and time is of an essence."

The *Troy* headed towards the jump point and started the voyage to the Correlian system emerging into the alternate System from where they had made their last venture. Helen set the orbit as close as possible to the main planet and positioned the *Troy* ready to view the surface via a small portal which was sent exploring the main citadel. At first, there was no resistence until the viewpoint approached the centre; as it did so, the reception started to break up and became difficult to stabilise. At the last transmission approaching a security console, a red light flashed. Helen terminated the portal, "It seems we are detected, without pushing the power we can't determine to what extent. I would deem it at the same level as the laboratory we raided. No point in stirring any more flack."

"Well there is no point in hanging around here and risk detection," Ito said, "We can nip over to Coruscent and brief the Republic on the current status of tactics and offer data to upgrade their ships."

Helen soon completed the short hop over to the Corescent system in the Alternate Universe, and the *Troy* located a suitable orbit clear of potential danger. Remaining in the Alternate Universe, the *Troy* made the short hop over to Corescent before signalling to the Republic a warning that the ship would be appearing out of nothing.

Opening a portal, Helen telepathed and radioed, "Forno ship *Troy* inbound, Captain Helen, request safe passage."

The patrol acknowledged, "Patrol to *Troy*, assume orbit kilo alpha."

"Roger Patrol, kilo alpha," Helen responded, and the *Troy* emerged from the portal.

When the ship had assumed the stated orbit a shuttle matched course and a party boarded, The officer in charge was anxious to find out how they evaded all the security sensors.

"Please state nature of the visit and for me just how did you get here?" Lt Forsey asked, "My captain just about had kittens when you radioed."

"I will brief your superiors as soon as it is safe to do so but to satisfy your curiosity. The ship wasn't here when I radioed, too technical to explain but it is the remedy for the Impies," Helen said.

"Loose lips lose ships," Forsey said, "We have orders to expedite your visit, I am here to guide your way and smooth any difficulties."

With their escort on board, the Troy descended to the port that Forsey directed. Landing Ito dropped the ramp and with Helen debarked to be greeted by Adept Boyne.

"Back again Adepts Ito and Helen? Has the Empire withdrawn from your sector?" Boyne asked.

"Forno has neutralised the rearguard; advice is that they will return in force to punish our sectors," Ito said, "We have just passed through the Correlian Sector and may have set off an alarm. Have you installed the Firebrand gear?"

"Yes, the installation is proceeding to schedule, estimate another ten days and we will be ready," Boyne said, "Our Admirals are ambivalent with the technology, and can see the repercussions if this advance is known to our enemies."

"Steve Firebrand is ready to deliver the defence, this will return the situation to a stalemate," Helen said, "If we deliver the Correlia's freedom and install some safeguards, the further defence may not be required."

"So our forces will now be on standby for your signal to orbit in a parallel Corellia and neutralise the Imperial ships," Boyne said, "I expect that the majority of the Dark Adepts will be in the capital ships."

"It is their protocol as it removes subordinates jockeying to elevate themselves and paranoid superiors trying to stop this occurring," Ito said, "We have gained a considerable intelligence from the three adepts who have come over to the light."

"We have never succeeded in doing that," Boyne said, "What is your next move?"

"Return to Earth and see what updates Steve has," Ito said, "Then we wait for the Empire to respond. You never know they may have seen the light and consolidate their Sector instead of fomenting further strife."

"I won't hold my breath. Revenge is always in the forefront of the Dark mind when someone has the temerity to stand up to them," Boyne said, "So much energy wasted, not to mention the economic and social strife. Only 'self' matters without regard for innocent lives."

"If you have all the data, time is critical so we will depart without further talk," Helen said.

"Farewell. I will be waiting for a signal," Boyne said.

"May the Light be with you," Ito said, and the two women returned to the ship to cruise towards Earth.

Arriving at the Airport, the women transferred to the shuttle to join Steve for a visit.

Finding him at work with the rescued scientists, Helen asked, "G'day, Steve, what is the state of play?"

"Good day, Helen and Ito, taking some time off touring?" Steve asked, "We have most of it wrapped up, and have some toys for your ship to cover most of the vulnerable areas."

"We took a peek at Arnold, and they have a detector, I didn't hang around to see if they had a defence," Helen said, "If someone peeks at you what can your boffins do about it?"

"We can pull the covers over and hide," Steve said, "Downside it blinds us, I think we are a few steps ahead of the Imperial scientists because we have their best and the Impies have a high attrition rate for scientists."

"The Imperial mindset is you perform or die, one slip and it is the chop, so the scientists spend extra time making sure that the team makes progress without any mistakes. This caution adds up to slow and steady," Ito said.

"Our boys are happy to try, fail and try again, knowing that failure leads to success," Steve said, "Couldn't find a happier mob, anxious to please and love bouncing ideas off each other."

"If you show me the mods, I will start the work," Helen said.

"Yes, I am familiar having Pippin as an associate," Steve said, "The data is on this computer," Pointing at a screen.

Helen moved over and viewed the information at high speed. In seconds she had the whole batch and announced, "Easy, it will be ready by the time we take off."

With the crew aboard the *Troy* lifted off to rendezvous with the Forno fleet.

As the *Troy* arrived the radio call came in, "Hostos here, the Imperials have formed up a large fleet at Gerno system, I have notified the Oxzen Fleet, and they will be waiting in the Alternate Gerno."

"The Republic Fleet will be ready within seven days to standby in Alternate Correlia. If we can coordinate the push it will be all over bar the shouting," Ito replied.

"We will commence the ambush once the Imperials have become complacent, we have evacuated as many non-combatants as possible," Hostos replied.

With that, the Allies formed a covering pattern in the Alternate Gerno system and began operations. The *Troy* was assigned one sun destroyer, Helen sent a small avatar over behind the solenoid panel and applied the required jumpers, as soon as the last jumper lead was attached, all hell broke loose as in both engineering and on the Bridge flashing lights went off with sirens adding to the confusion. As orders started flying to contain the imminent annihilation, Helen opened small portals to allow sleep rays to send all the bridge and the engineering personnel to sleep.

"Let's go, team," Ito ordered as larger portals opened and with Ito leading stepped out onto the bridge, removing weapons and securing the main doors. "Helen set the security locks, then pick up the bodies and back to the Troy." Throwing a switch locked the hatches, a feature due to the paranoia of the Imperials.

With the bridge secured, Ito turned her attention to the Engineering, catching the repair teams concentrating on locating the fault, catching them from behind then evacuating them.

"My ship secured, the ship's course is locked away from harm, ready for my next task," Ito reported.

The Troy only had enough capacity to deal with two sun destroyers before the cabins were full. So after they had nullified the other Destroyer, Helen signalled a cargo ship to offload the captives.

The third ship they tackled had been alerted, but the ship was neutralised as quickly and without casualties on either side. This ship was a Corvette with less personnel to deal with, so Ito and Helen's team were able to deal with several before halting for a break.

A cloud of the smaller vessels had disabled the scouts and support ships with the crews removed, the small fry were just navigation hazards to be retrieved at leisure.

Once the task force had dealt with the major threats, Rham called a debrief meeting on his ship.

"Well, that went smoothly. The Forno fleet will tidy up and have the route as recorded as their victory. My ships will start separating the friends from diehards and repatriate the latter to an alternate planet away from harm," Rham said to start the meeting, "Any difficulties?"

"Just the large numbers of captives to process," Hostos said, "All the freighters are busy shuttling them to a holding area."

The effort went on, and eventually, the allies rendered all the Hyper capable vessels neutral, capturing the short-range shuttles and fighters on return to their mother ships.

The interviews of the captured crews by the light adepts progressed smoothly, recruiting half the number required to crew the capital ships with a training program on Earth and Oxzen to find serving military personnel to bridge the numbers ready for the next effort. On Earth especially it wasn't a problem finding volunteers as thousands were eager to be part of the adventure, despite the description of the danger; perhaps it was a result of the many science fiction TV and Movie series which depict the 'good guys' winning against overwhelming odds.

All this took time, and necessary as there was no constraint on the opponents as their fleet was still stronger than the allies. The biggest advantage of the allies was the lack of intelligence available to the Imperials. All they knew was that two expeditions to Forno Space had few returns. The latter was unlikely to make the Imperials too nervous; their arrogance was the allies asset.

Reporting back to Hostos, Ito said, "It seems that the Impies can detect our spying, and posses some fields which interfere with our viewing. We had best not give them time to upgrade their ships."

With the danger building on the horizon, time dragged as the task force completed the preparations. Eventually, the forces were ready, despite the lack of experience and unable to practice. The Australian military is trained to handle changing conditions and use their initiative for unusual circumstances.

By entering the alternate galaxy for the move to the Correlian System, at each way stop to regroup, exercises were conducted to hone the training. The strategy for the initial move was at several points robot carriers were to momentarily drop out, deposit their load of fifty robot fighters each carrying two decoy bouys and four kinetic missiles. For this exercise, they were using deflector shields rather than cause casualties among the fighters. This tactic was for the Droman help. The sudden appearance of clouds of traces all over the system would strain the Imperial headquarters with each group requiring a heavy response, as each Imperial battle group moved into position to counter the invasion, The allied ships would neutralise the capital ships from the alternate universe. With the ships being distracted by the outside menace, they would be too busy to anticipate an internal attack.

Arriving at the alternate Correlian system, the allies now with the Rebel contingent, deployed awaiting the word to send the carriers through to start the push. Of course, as everyone knows the first thing that happens is that all plans turn into the proverbial as soon as the attackers fire the first shot.

The moment arrived all of the allied fleets was in the position assigned; the flagships sent the deploy signal, the robot carriers transferred into the Corellian system and dropped their charges before returning to the alternate universe. The robots were programmed to deploy in a cloud formation before releasing the drone bouys.

Monitoring the Imperials via a small portal, Helen announced, "The Imperials have detected the robots, and are moving into the anticipated formations to counter the forces painted on their detectors."

"So far, so good," Ito acknowledged, "Is our target moving into position."

"Yes, preparing the portals to carry out operations, as is our squad for the smaller ships."

Helen opened the portal and disabled the reactor safety solenoids, this triggered alarms sending the engineering team into action to diagnose the fault.

"Seems a bit like shooting fish in a barrel, but putting the engineers to sleep is the safest thing," Helen said as she fired the sleep rays from behind sending the distracted teams falling at their posts.

Sending the view into the bridge, Helen caught the bridge crew intent on the outside and engineering developments rendering them 'hors de combat.' Stepping out onto the bridge, she used the vacated consoles to seal the bridge doors so that the backup crew couldn't help. She then set the course to the desired vector so that the ship was safe.

The next phase was for the sleeping crews to be evacuated first to the *Troy* before transshipping to a freighter for confining away from harm.

With the program underway, reports flooded in outlining the progress. The transport ships were flat out transferring the captured crews to the alternate planets, shuttling as the capital ships filled their holding bays. The sheer numbers had a slowing effect, but with confusion reigning among the Imperials, the individual squadrons had no communication with the events as one by one their companions dropped out of combat and ceased reporting. The robots were useful in keeping the Imperial thoughts on the external battle without involving too high a casualty price among the pilots. They were programmed to use evasive tactics for the fighters. The invading fighters avoid dogfighting as the target is the capital ships and the support vessels which the defenders are trying to protect.

As the attrition wore on, the surviving Imperials started to withdraw to closer orbits over Corellia as the headquarters began to realise that something had gone wrong with their perfect defence. This tactic backfired as this concentrated the ships and the final few were neutralised bringing this phase to an end. When the allies had completed the evacuation of the crews and the ships heading towards stable orbits; the ally leaders then assembled in Rham's ship to discuss the next move.

"I have probed the surface, and there are shields to prevent the use of the small portals within the Imperial Headquarters," Helen reported, "The heavy weapons aren't protected as yet so we can proceed to fix them to allow a ground offensive."

"There have been a few objections to the use of the stun guns firing from a safe position as the aggressive warriors feel it isn't sporting," Rham said, "I have passed the word that I don't wish to hand out posthumous medals to grieving families."

With all the ships concentrating on the ground emplacements rendering the heavy weapons harmless it wasn't long before the Allies planned the next step. Helen surveyed the Imperial Citadel and reported, "They have anti portal shields in place as well as heavy deflectors, they have locked the door and pulled in the welcome mat. There is a siege in place; they can't come out and hope we can't come in."

"Next step?" Ito asked, "Given time the leaders can sneak out to reform elsewhere."

"A small team can walk through both shields, working blind to surprises," Helen said, "Since we have demonstrated that a telepathic blocking field cuts off contact with the Dark Mind, we can expect the Imperials to use a blocking field. If I am cut off, my avatar reverts to a blob."

"So we use your spacesuits, keeping contact till that happens, best not take a full avatar," Ito said, "How many adepts can we expect?"

"With the previous captures and finding one adept on each of the captured capital ships, we have three of the third, most of the fourth and fifth level Dark Adepts, and according to our friends that leaves about five third level, Klien and Arnold," Veoos said, "A party of Light Adepts should do the job."

"If we land a task force and have these stage a diversion while the insurgent team enters quietly," Ito said.

So a small task force was assembled, Boyne and Cassel from the Republic, the three Einslands from Elysium, Ito and Veoos from Forno and lastly Steve, Mike and Su Lin from Earth. The allies selected this group as having the most experience dealing with the dark adepts.

"I have a message from the three ex-Dark Adepts; they would like to join the team," Helen said, "They are familiar with the layout and know all the defence points."

"If James Cox joins us that will make fourteen, we can then split into two teams and avoid the dreaded thirteen which seems to get me in all sorts of trouble," Steve advised with a grin.

"Logical, though I don't know why humans dislike a number," Ito said.

"Some take numeracy to ridiculous levels, the Asians feel four is also unlucky, so it is rare to find a multistory building with either floor levels, appending "a" or only using them for machinery," Steve said.

When everyone nodded in agreement to invite the ex-Dark Adepts, Helen organised the three to join them on the *Troy*.

Once the team had assembled, Helen projected a 3D model of the Imperial Citadel, "Bern, Thum and Shan, if you think about the model it will update if there is anything I haven't displayed," Helen said.

"It is as I remember, the best access is via the Garrison barracks," Bern said, the model expanded and rotated the entrance. "In peacetime, you would have to make your way past hundreds of adepts and soldiers. With all at their posts, it should be nearly empty. There are several checkpoints on the way inwards to the control centre where the Emporer and Klien would be monitoring the situation."

As he spoke, transparent corridors opened, and a pathway was evident towards a larger space. There was little detail of this room.

"This is a closely guarded area and out of bounds for our strata," Thum said when Ito looked in question.

"Are you aware of the sleep rays?" Steve asked.

"Yes, though the hierarchy dismisses them as too soft to be useful," Shan replied, "The bosses are content to allow shields around buildings and vessels if suspected the attackers may use them."

"I invented a variable ray to get around that," Steve said.

"Defence and counter, another reason for an expedient resolution for this conflict," Ito said, "Likely the Imperials will be prepared for a basic attack, and we will use the variable settings."

"I have organised with Rham and Hostos to use a ground attack to occupy the surrounding defence points and distract the defence and the command," Ito said, "Our teams will then infiltrate the citadel and proceed towards the command centre neutralising defenders as we go. We plan as much as possible, but once we initiate the first move, everything will change."

"I have probed the citadel as far as I can reach, about halfway in the telepathic fields start to appear. I will implement the anti-Dark field, so we are on an even footing," Helen said, "Klien and Arnold will think that they have the advantage without the Dromans."

"If you use my spacesuits and fearnought suits, both of which enhance strength and carry shields, this will give us an advantage if met with the standard Imperial or Adept responses," Steve said, "The standard Droman suits would allow us to communicate with outside until we hit the telepathic shields. At which time they will become ordinary suits with radio communication supplemented by using the cascade telepathy developed by Ito and Helen."

The signal came that the Allied ground forces were engaged in the attack on the main Correllian base surrounding the Citadel. The task force landed the troop carriers on the alternate Corellia, and the troops invaded the fortresses via portals before the garrison could mount a counter to the internal threat. Other troops began simulating an external ground attack to maintain a visible threat. This activity, in turn, attracted the attention of the reinforcement forces; as these columns approached the troops dealt with from the alternate planet via portals into the vehicle cabins.

While the diversion was noisily in play, the *Troy* and *Big Red* landed adjacent to the citadel then using portals assembled the two teams within the walls intending to follow separate corridors leading towards the Command centre.

Ito led team A which consisted of Bern, Veoos, Helen, Dierdre and Hans Einsland and Hoght Boyne. The two Coruscent Adepts maintained contact between the teams. As they started the move inwards, they encountered soldiers at each of the checkpoints, detecting them and disarming them before any alarms were triggered.

"You are approaching the first telepathic field," Helen sent, "As soon as you pass that you are on your own."

"If I spot the generators I will shut them off," Ito said. Then as she stepped past a doorway, the contact with the Light Mind and

Helen disappeared from the conscience as did the team members. The team contacts then reestablished as each passed the same point. Hoght radioed, "Team B out of contact, reestablished. They passed a similar field as we did."

"Move forward carefully; we are approaching the Command Centre where the Dark Adepts are likely to be watching the external conflict," Bern said, "there is another checkpoint around the corner which commands the entry door, usually has an Adept in control."

"I can't detect his aura, and I think Helen has just turned the anti-dark field on which will mentally blind them," Ito said, "It also rings the doorbell for Klien."

"The B team has arrived at the other entry and have encountered that Adept successfully," Hoght said, "I have asked them to wait until we are ready at our door."

Ito stepped out into the view of the guard and fired her sleep pistol; the adept started to reach for his weapons until the rays penetrated the cabinet and put him to sleep.

"The variable frequency worked," Ito said, "Signal B to start the entry on my count, three, two go."

With that, all the team fired their rays through the door, Hoght and Ito swinging their sabres, cut through the doors to collapse the panels inwards; stepping through the opening, they reformed inside the Centre in a defensive formation ready to face the inhabitants.

Klien had anticipated the sleep rays and was ready for action as were Arnold and another two Adepts. All four fired ion guns at the gathered invaders with the beams glancing off their deflector screens and sabres harmlessly. Seeing that this did not affect the invaders, the defenders abandoned the guns, drew their sabres and used telekinesis to throw the invaders against the wall. While it caught a couple of the team members, it was ineffective because the Dark Mind wasn't helping.

"We have you outnumbered, surrender while you can," Ito said.

"Never," Arnold responded, attacking the nearest team member, Su and Hans engaged him before he could follow up with a disabling blow.

Klien had engaged Ito while Hoght and Veoos took on the other two Adepts.

After a few checks and thrusts, Klien and Arnold lept backwards while the two junior adepts frantically attacked. Arnold made his way to a bench and threw a switch; two solid shields met at the centre with a bang.

Once the team had disarmed the two rearguard adepts, Steve and Ito attacked the shutters without success.

"Seems they braced the shutters with deflector shields," Ito said, "That is a control panel, perhaps it is the telepathic field controls."

Taking a survey of the panel, Ito threw several into the off position, on the fifth switch operation the fuzziness left her mind as Helen, and the Light mind returned to her sub-conscience.

"Ah you have found the field control, welcome back," Helen said, "Developments, the Dark Academy students have surged out and are heading towards the spaceport. There are several hundred."

"Arnold and Klien escaped behind a screen," Ito said, "Bern doesn't know what is behind, I would expect an escape tunnel."

"I have detected him underground also headed towards the port," Helen said, "We have no assets to stop them."

"I am leaving the control centre, my team will pursue," Ito said, "Steve can you mop up here I will try to catch up with Klien and Arnold."

"Okay, Running is not my favourite job," Steve said, "As I have a suspicious mind, I won't stay long in case they have set a self-destruct."

With the cleanup in progress, Ito's team made the way outside then skirted the citadel to head towards the spaceport. On the way, they encountered several groups of Imperial combatants which they had to spend the time to subdue. This delay meant that they arrived at the port in time to see a Virgil class Corvette clear the field and head towards space.

"The fox has fled the coop, and we don't have assets ready to chase," Ito said, "No point in pursuit."

"I estimate that there are about two hundred novice adepts with

Klien," Helen said, "Without an industrial base I believe that the Republic has the means to curtail the Dark Adepts behaviour."

"Next step assemble the allied council, and we will deliberate on the outcomes and plan the next move," Ito said.

In the debrief Hostos reported that the Imperials hadn't destroyed the citadel, there were booby traps along the escape route of course but clearing these weren't a priority.

"I expect that it didn't occur to Arnold that the invasion would succeed, so he didn't set a self-destruct," Hostos said, "Pity he is on the run."

"My order will deal with curtailing the reemergence of the Dark side," Boyne said, "The last time they were defeated, it took a hundred years to become a formidable threat. This return commenced by infiltrating into peaceful democracies when these societies forgot history."

"I will make it a foundation of our schools to retell these stories to delay forgetful behaviour," Hostos said. This undertaking was greeted by all present with affirmation.

"Can we leave the mopping up to the Republic?" Ito asked.

"Once the fighting has ceased, I believe so," Boyne said, "The Republic has plans to reestablish peace in this Sector. By our reckoning, the population will be eager to have peace barring a minority who gained benefits of collaboration."

"When we changed our Government's policy there was a short rebellion incited by Klien and the Empire," Hostos said.

The meeting broke up, and the Allies proceeded to the other systems within the sector quelling resistence as they found it. There was little fighting as the dark Adepts had abandoned their posts once the news of the route became known. Without the adepts maintaining discipline the few remaining capital ships surrendered rather than fleeing, declaring allegiance to the Republic. Once the invasion had commenced in the Corellian system, all the major ships had joined the defence fleet.

With the main battle resolved the Oxzen and Forno allies returned home.

After the battle.

ON THE WAY BACK TO FORNO SECTOR, ITO'S TEAM gathered to sort out their thoughts.

"It seems that we have done half the job," Ito said, "We have contained the Imperials for now, but with Arnold and Klien on the loose, with a large number of adepts we have merely put off for now."

"I suggest we consult with the Light Mind for advice," Helen said.

With everyone in agreeance that entered rapport with the Light mind, as they did the warmth embraced their minds, "Welcome children, congratulations in rebalancing the force, you have questions?"

"Do you know where Arnold and Klien have fled to?" Helen asked, "We need to tidy them up?"

"No to both questions, and if I did it would not be in your interest to remove them from the Galaxy as it would imbalance the force."

"Why?" Ito asked, "They will fester in the dark and seek revenge."

"While that is likely; the peace lover needs a counterforce for growth, the conflict was necessary to repair the damage that their ascendance was inflicting on innocent people. The remaining Dark adepts are a focal point for the Dark Overmind attracting those who see the short path to power. If your forces were successful in eliminating the last, pockets of dark would appear in every culture."

"Like one year's seed, seven years weed?" Helen asked.

"If you meditate you would observe that the driving force behind the allies is to restore peace. If you were successful in eliminating all vestige of the Empire, you could fall victim to the need to fight the small outbreaks and install a regime using Dark Techniques to maintain power, becoming the Dark Empire in effect."

"Power corrupts, absolute power corrupts absolutely," Ito said, "I see your point, having achieved peace it is time to enjoy the fruits of the conflict. Though in my lifetime it is likely that the pollution will be hard to erase from civilisation. Helen and her people will remain our guardians teaching our successors the true path to peace."

"You are truly growing in knowledge, go in peace," The Light Mind faded from their minds.

Returning to normal speech, Ito said, "Answers and more questions. Back to our homes to restore normal trade."

Arriving back on Forno, Ito made her way to the Council chambers to deliver the news of the victory.

"My fellow Councillors, our allies have been successful in quelling the threat from the Empire. Our peoples can now return to peaceful behaviour." Admiral Hostos said after delivering the data to all present.

"Please accept Forno's thanks to the valiant defence teams, while this stems the threat, we require eternal vigilance for peace," Fedo Roos responded as THE Forno.

As time restored the sector to normal, Ito resumed her usual task of roving Ambassador for the Oxzen sector a call came in from the Forno Headquarters advising of the next Council meeting.

Taking her place among her fellow Councillors, Ito listened to the business reports until Fedo reached the last item.

"I have fulfilled my responsibilities to Forno; it is time for my successor to assume the position. It is my pleasure to call Ambassador Ito Roos to step forward and accept the role of THE Forno," Fedo said to the sound of applause, it seemed that all except Ito were privy to the news.

Ito and Fedo made their way to her new office to find Helen and Veoos waiting patiently.

"Good morning Ladies, I suppose you may wish to know the reason for this invitation?" Fedo asked rhetorically, "I won't keep you long, please meet the new THE Forno."

"That is a surprise, congratulations," Helen and Veoos said.

"As my parting order, Veoos, I offer the position of Ambassador for the Earth, Elysium and Oxzen sectors, and Helen would you like to continue as the official Consular transport?" Fedo offered.

"I will be required to remain on Forno for a time, so Helen, this would provide the freedom to explore?" Ito said.

***

The parade was called to attention as THE Forno stepped up to the dais to address the graduating students.

"Ladies and gentlemen, today is the start of your careers. From here you will join your new ships to promote peace and trade among peoples of the Galaxy. It seems such a short time ago that I stood in the ranks awaiting this moment, may you serve Forno in honour,' THE Forno Ito Roos said.

Printed in the United States
By Bookmasters